A CHRISTMAS WISH FOR THE LAND GIRLS

Jenny Holmes

CORGI BOOKS

TRANSWORLD PUBLISHERS
61–63 Uxbridge Road, London W5 5SA
www.transworldbooks.co.uk

Transworld is part of the Penguin Random House group of companies whose addresses can be found at global.penguinrandomhouse.com

First published in Great Britain in 2018 by Corgi Books
an imprint of Transworld Publishers

A CIP catalogue record for this book
is available from the British Library.

ISBN
9780552175814

Typeset in 11.5/14 pt New Baskerville ITC by Jouve (UK), Milton Keynes
Printed and bound in Great Britain by Clays Ltd, Elcograf S.p.A.

Penguin Random House is committed to a sustainable future for our business, our readers and our planet. This book is made from Forest Stewardship Council® certified paper.

1 3 5 7 9 10 8 6 4 2

For my dear friend and collaborator,
Caroline Sheldon

CAST OF CHARACTERS

LAND GIRLS

Brenda Appleby – worked at Maynard's butchers before she became a Land Girl

Hilda Craven – warden at Fieldhead House hostel

Joyce Cutler – farmer's daughter from Warwickshire

Kathleen Hirst – former hairdresser from Millwood

Pat Holden – a recent arrival at Fieldhead hostel

Grace Mostyn – daughter of Burnside's pub landlord and blacksmith, married to Bill

Joan Quinn – a recent arrival at Fieldhead hostel

Una Sharpe – former worker at Kingsley's Mill in Millwood

Elsie Walker – former groom from the Wolds

BURNSIDE VILLAGERS

Cliff Kershaw – landlord of the Blacksmith's Arms

Edgar Kershaw – his son, an RAF gunner recently shot down over France

Edith Mostyn – Land Girls representative, widow of Vince

Bill Mostyn – her son, owns and runs the family tractor repair company, currently serving in the Royal Armoured Corps

BURNSIDE FARMERS

Judith Evans – an evacuee staying at Dale End Farm

Joe Kellett – farmer at Home Farm

Emily Kellett – his wife

Peggy Russell – widow

Roland Thomson – farmer at Brigg Farm

Horace Turnbull – farmer at Winsill Edge

Arnold White – owner of Dale End Farm, Attercliffe

Hettie White – Arnold's daughter

Donald White – Arnold's elder son

Les White – Arnold's younger son

SHAWCROSS VILLAGERS

Geoffrey Dawson – Shawcross's vet

Alan Evans – an evacuee staying with Reverend Rigg

Evelyn Newbold – member of the Women's Timber Corps

Giles Pickering – Vet friend of Geoffrey Dawson

Reverend Walter Rigg – Shawcross's vicar

Gillian Vernon – Colonel Weatherall's niece

Emma Waterhouse – housekeeper to Reverend Rigg

Colonel Samuel Weatherall – owner of the Acklam Castle estate

Fred Williams – landlord of the Cross Keys

SHAWCROSS FARMERS

Laurence Bradley – farmer at Black Crag Farm

Alma Bradley – inhabitant of Black Crag Farm

Muriel Woodthorpe – Alma's aunt

Bernard Huby – farmer at Garthside Farm

Cliff Huby – his son, gamekeeper on the Acklam Castle estate

Dorothy Huby – his daughter

CHAPTER ONE

'Are you sure we should go ahead?' Una Sharpe glanced at the circle of candlelit faces gathered around the table in the common room of Fieldhead Women's Land Army hostel. A low fire settled in the grate, while outside in the dark night a strong wind gusted through the elm trees.

Brenda Appleby set the Ouija board down on the table. 'Yes, come along, Una; it's only a bit of fun.'

'Fun; that's all it is.'

'Where's the thingumajig – the planchette?'

Several high-spirited voices let an uneasy Una know that she was in a minority of one.

Brenda produced a heart-shaped piece of wood from the box then placed it in the centre of the board. 'Here it is. Now, do we all know what to do?'

'We ask it a question.' It turned out that, of all people, fun-loving, modern go-getter Kathleen Hirst was adept at contacting the dead. 'Starting with an easy one, such as: "How many people are in this room?" Then we wait for it to give us an answer.'

In the flickering candlelight Una studied the letters and numbers on the board. She ought not to be so silly, she told herself. What harm could there possibly be in joining in? And yet . . .

'Ready?' Brenda asked.

'And willing!' Kathleen was the first to place her finger on the planchette. 'My Grandma Hirst was a dab hand at this lark. She could conjure up the spirit of her dead brother at the drop of a hat.'

Five other fingers joined hers, delicately poised and ready to begin. Only Una hesitated. And yet . . . death was already far too present in this, the third year of the Second World War. Allied soldiers perished daily in the blazing deserts of North Africa. Naval men went down with their ships in the Atlantic. Not to mention the brave RAF boys brought down by ack-ack guns or blown to smithereens by their German counterparts. Following her gut feeling, Una scraped back her chair and stood up.

'I'm sorry, girls; I have a letter to write,' she said by way of an excuse as she made her way to the door.

'To lover-boy Angelo, no doubt!' Kathleen raised a critical eyebrow over Una's affair with the Italian POW. '*Mi amore*, la-la-la!'

Una ignored the cascade of light laughter from inside the room. In the cold, tiled hallway she bumped into Joyce Cutler who was descending the wide stairs in her thick Land Army coat and porkpie hat. She was on her way to help an elderly widowed neighbour who had telephoned the hostel to tell the warden that two of her pigs had escaped into the field behind the farmhouse.

'Hello, Una. What are they up to in there?'

'Nothing much. Some spiritualist nonsense, that's all.'

'Aha, not the old Ouija board? Who's the ring-leader? No, let me guess: Kathleen.'

Una shook her head. 'Brenda this time. I didn't fancy joining in, though.'

'I don't blame you.' Joyce picked up on her room-mate's uneasiness. She too had her doubts about this fashionable dabbling with the spirits of the dead. Not that she believed in it exactly – she just thought it might lead to no good. 'Listen, Una, I know Sunday is our day off and it's already pitch black outside, but Peggy Russell has mislaid two of her prime porkers. I don't suppose you fancy helping me to recapture the ungrateful blighters?'

Una gave a quick nod then sprinted up the stairs. 'Hang on a second while I fetch my coat.'

'Bring a torch,' Joyce called after her. 'And we'll need gumboots for that boggy field. I'll meet you outside the back door.'

In the dimly lit common room, Kathleen volunteered to ask the first question of the ghostly presence. 'What year is this?'

The girls leaned forward to concentrate on the heart-shaped planchette. Their pupils were dilated, their chapped, work-worn fingers trembled with anticipation. Slowly the counter started to move jerkily towards the number one. Sitting to Brenda's left, Elsie Walker felt a small flutter of excitement. Number one, then nine, then four; the planchette gathered speed until it came to rest against the number two.

'Well I never!' Elsie laughed. She ran her free hand through her boyish, cropped hair. 'Nineteen forty-two. It's got that right, at least. Ask it something else.'

'Here's my next question,' Kathleen began.

'Hold your horses; it's time to give someone else a turn.' Brenda stepped in eagerly. 'Right then, whoever you are, what is the first letter of your Christian name?'

For a few seconds there was no movement. Each girl held her breath, caught between the urge to giggle and a sense that mighty, unknown forces could be at work. Elsie bit her bottom lip and cast a nervous glance at Kathleen. Suddenly the carved piece of wood slid smoothly towards the letter F.

'"F",' Kathleen whispered as she looked around the table. 'Who do we know from our pasts whose name began with an F? Could it be a Fred? Does anyone have a poor old Uncle Fred who came to a sticky end in the mud of a Flanders field?'

The wide-eyed girls shook their heads.

'Perhaps it's a Frank.' Elsie nudged Brenda with her elbow.

'Is your name Frank?' Even as Brenda asked the question, the memory of Frank Kellett flew into her head. It was coming up to a year since poor, lovelorn Frank had been found frozen to death on Swinsty Edge – curled on his side in the snow, his icy hand still clutching one of Una's embroidered handkerchiefs.

'Yes.' The planchette shot towards the word printed in the top left-hand corner. At the same moment, the glowing cinders in the grate collapsed unnoticed and sent a hot ember and a shower of red sparks on to the hearth rug.

As the disc moved, Elsie let out a squeal.

Kathleen was unruffled. 'Hello, Frank. We're glad you could join us. Do you have a message for someone?'

'Yes,' the board told them.

'You've come to talk to Una, haven't you? Is there something special that you want to say to her?'

Though Brenda had instigated the game and she kept her finger pressed lightly on the planchette, doubt wormed its way into her head. Perhaps this hadn't been such a good idea after all. *Thank heavens Una decided to make a quick exit,* she thought.

'Yes,' the board answered promptly before the planchette moved back to the centre of the board.

In for a penny, in for a pound; Kathleen pressed ahead. 'Is it that you'll always love her?'

No one breathed. The wooden heart slid slowly towards the bottom of the board then shot swiftly up towards the 'yes'.

'Goodness gracious, can anyone smell burning?' With a careless shove of the board across the table Elsie broke the mood. She jumped up and rushed to the other side of the room where the fallen ember had singed the rug. 'Quick, someone; fetch a jug of water,' she cried.

Brenda turned on the overhead electric light then ran to join her. She seized some handy coal tongs and whisked the glowing cinder back into the grate. Then she stamped on the singed patch. 'Panic over,' she reported as Elsie returned with the jug. 'But you'd better pour water over it, just in case.'

Kathleen was the only one still at the table, putting the Ouija board back to rights and eager to continue their communion with the spirit world. 'Someone turn off the light pronto. Let's hope we haven't lost Frank in all the kerfuffle.'

'Let's hope we have,' Brenda countered. 'The poor

soul deserves to be left in peace after what he went through.' Driven out in the middle of winter by his hard-hearted father, doted on by his mother who had nevertheless been unable to protect her simple-minded son, Frank Kellett had been an outcast and a victim all his life. 'What do you say we play a nice game of whist and listen to the wireless instead?'

'You two took your time.' Peggy Russell's poker-faced greeting was par for the course. The farmer's widow stood in her doorway in her brown dressing-gown and carpet slippers, straight grey hair parted down the middle and tucked behind her ears, casting a doubtful gaze over Joyce and Una.

'Yes, but we're here now.' Joyce waited for instructions while Una stamped her feet against the biting cold. Why did the wind always blow in so strongly from the west? she wondered. It must be to do with the steep valley sides of the Yorkshire Dales creating a funnel through which it gusted.

'Pigs are loose in the back field.' Peggy jerked her head towards the side of her stone-built farmhouse. 'Two of them.'

Joyce shone her torch across the farmyard. 'And you want them back in their sty?'

'No, I want them on a plate with a couple of fried eggs. Where do you think I want them?'

Peggy's sarcasm didn't dent Joyce's good humour. 'Rightio, Mrs Russell – we'll get on with it. Come along, Una.'

As the two young women clomped across the flagged yard in their gumboots, they heard the distant drone of aeroplane engines, gradually growing louder. Quickly turning off their torches, they instructed Peggy to close her door.

'Just in case it's Jerry and he spots our lights,' Joyce explained.

Una listened carefully then offered her opinion. 'They sound more like Lancasters to me. Probably RAF boys heading out of Rixley for an overnight raid on Munich or Saarbrücken.'

Joyce paused by the gate leading into Peggy's field. Every night the sound of planes flying overhead made her quake and go weak at the knees, knowing that her fiancé, Edgar Kershaw, might be one of the pilots setting out on what could well be his final mission. Best not to think about it. Best to get on with the task in hand. She opened the gate and stepped ankle deep into mud. 'Here, piggies!' she called into the darkness. 'Here, nice little piggy-piggies!'

'Spoilsport,' Kathleen grumbled as Brenda turned on the wireless. 'Who wants to listen to boring speeches on our night off?'

'I do.' Elsie sat down and put her feet up on a low stool, her neat, small figure dwarfed by the worn leather upholstery of the old-fashioned chesterfield. The other girls shrugged then wandered off to their rooms to write letters and darn socks.

There was a whine of valves as the wireless warmed up. 'It's our duty as Land Girls to listen to what our prime minister has to say,' Brenda opined. She found the station on the dial then plonked herself on the sofa beside Elsie while Kathleen stood with her back to the fire. 'And let's hope he gives us more good news from North Africa.'

They'd tuned in just in time for the political broadcast and soon Mr Churchill's lugubrious tones filled the stuffy, book-lined room. He spoke once more of Allied gains in Morocco and Algeria and of an American naval victory over Japan at Koli Point. General Montgomery was soon to launch a new offensive in Libya.

'About time too,' Kathleen remarked through a cloud of blue cigarette smoke. 'We've been hanging on by the skin of our teeth up till now.'

'Hush!' Elsie and Brenda said together.

Churchill's voice growled on then built to a climax. He told the nation that the Desert army had forced Rommel into a humiliating retreat. 'Now this is not the end,' he warned them gravely. 'It is not even the beginning of the end.'

'You can say that again,' Kathleen muttered.

'Ssh!' Brenda reached out to turn up the volume knob.

'But it is, perhaps, the end of the beginning.'

'Hurrah!' As Brenda clicked off the wireless, Elsie was genuinely heartened by the good news. 'Things are changing in our favour at last.'

Kathleen bent to stub out her cigarette on the grate then flicked the butt into the fire. 'They're certainly changing; any idiot can see that. But not always for the better.' Her youngest brother, Vernon, a boy of eighteen, was the latest member of her family to have been conscripted into the army. Clothing coupons had been reduced again, forcing some of the girls at Fieldhead into desperate measures, including cutting up their old jumpers and turning them into socks.

'Oh, Kathleen; since when did you turn into such a moaning Minnie?' Elsie jumped up to put a disc on the turntable of the gramophone standing in all its mahogany majesty in the bay window. She chose a recent favourite then flicked a switch and carefully lowered the needle. There was a hiss of static before a jaunty baritone began with the words, 'She'll be coming round the mountain when she comes.'

'When she comes!' Brenda and Elsie chimed in, tapping their feet in time to the music. They smiled and got ready to insert their own cheeky words into the next verse. *She'll be kissing six tall sergeants when she comes . . .* 'Coming round the mountain, coming round the mountain, coming round the mountain when she comes!'

There was nothing nice about the little piggies that had escaped into Peggy's back field. The two fully grown sows snorted and bolted, squealed when cornered then barged between Una's legs, upskittling her and landing her in the mud.

Joyce hauled her friend on to her feet as the runaway pigs galloped off into the darkness. 'Are you all right?'

'Yes, ta. Nothing hurt apart from my dignity.' Una adjusted her hat then thought ahead. 'We need a weapon to herd them with – a pitchfork or a rake.'

'Or something to tempt them back into the yard.' Joyce knew that Peggy kept a store of turnips in the stone barn at the far edge of the field. 'Wait here,' she told her bedraggled companion. She was gone for five minutes then returned with two choice-looking vegetables. 'These should do the trick.'

She was mistaken; turnips were not, it seemed, to Ivy and Ruby's taste. Though Joyce and Una cornered and cajoled, made tweeting noises and offered what they thought was a mouth-watering treat, the recalcitrant pigs turned up their snouts and scarpered.

'Try this!' a voice called from the gate after a full hour of fruitless tempting. Peggy held up a bucket of pigswill that she kept at her kitchen door for just such emergencies.

Una aimed her torch beam at the stern figure standing by the gate. Joyce trudged across the field and took the bucket. Within seconds, Ivy and Ruby smelt its sloppy contents and came running full tilt. At the last moment, Joyce hoisted the bucket high in the air and Una opened the gate. The pigs skidded through then came to a halt on the stone flags of the yard. Joyce and Una nipped in after them and slammed the gate shut. Now all that remained was for Joyce to rattle a stick against the side of the bucket as she guided the runaways back into their sty.

When Joyce finally lowered the bucket to let the pigs feed, Una let out a long sigh of relief.

An unsmiling Peggy looked on with arms folded. 'About time too,' she commented before shuffling back into the house and closing the door.

Una and Joyce looked at each other in astonishment as they set off for home.

'I'm saying nothing!' Joyce broke into a loud laugh. Her round face was still wreathed in smiles when they came to the tall stone gateposts at the entrance to Fieldhead. 'So, Una, what are you planning for the rest of your evening, now that we've accomplished our mission?'

'I'll write a letter to Angelo. He's finally on the mend so they've moved him to a convalescent home near the seaside. I want to ask him about his new billet.'

'And he's definitely over the worst?' Joyce was heartened by the news, knowing how much Una had fretted through the summer months and well into autumn.

'Yes – for now.' Una knew that, as yet, tuberculosis had no cure but if patients were well cared for and treated with modern medicines, the disease could be held at bay. Though unable to visit her beloved in the isolation hospital, she still dreamed of being with Angelo after the war ended – sitting with him amongst lemon trees and olive groves on the sunny slopes outside Pisa. She wore his gold cross around her neck, convinced that if she took it off, even for a single moment, it would bring bad luck.

'That's champion,' Joyce murmured as they went round the side of the hostel and kicked off their gumboots outside the back door. 'Actually, I have something of my own to tell you,' she confided.

'About Edgar?'

'No, Edgar's fine, touch wood.' Joyce tapped her forehead. 'But I've decided to move out of Fieldhead.'

Una gasped at this bombshell news. 'Oh, Joyce – you're not leaving the Land Army?'

'No, just the hostel. It feels like time for me to make a change.'

'Where will you go, for goodness' sake?'

'To a new billet, somewhere further up the dale.'

'But why?' Una couldn't understand why Joyce

would wish to move from the relative comfort of Fieldhead and forsake the company of the girls she worked alongside.

Unbuttoning her coat, Joyce stepped over the threshold. 'I want to be of more use,' she explained. 'I intend to ask Mrs Mostyn to send me somewhere where they really need me.'

'But we need you here.' Una guessed rightly that her protests would fall on deaf ears. 'You're the one who knows most about tractors and ploughing, threshing and milking. You've been farming all your life. What will we do without you?'

'You'll manage,' Joyce said with a smile. 'But don't say anything until I've told Mrs Mostyn after work tomorrow. Promise?'

'Hand on heart.' Una padded down the corridor in stockinged feet. Fieldhead without Joyce would be hard to bear. Who would save her a place at the rowdy breakfast table? Who would dish out advice about matters of the heart?

'It goes without saying that I'll miss you,' Joyce whispered as she entered the kitchen and went to the stove to warm her hands.

'Likewise.' Una was overwhelmed by a feeling of helplessness. Change was afoot. Events near and far ran out of control.

'Before we know it, it'll be time to start sprout-picking for the Christmas market.' Grace Mostyn stood behind the bar in the Blacksmith's Arms. She was well into the third month of her pregnancy and had reluctantly taken her doctor's advice to pull out of farm work due to severe morning sickness.

'The Land Army will have to get by without you,' Dr Hood had told her firmly across his wide, leather-topped desk. The sun had been reflected in the lenses of his heavy glasses but there was no denying the directness of his gaze. 'Baby must come first.'

Grace had suffered similar pressure from her mother-in-law, Edith Mostyn, who happened to be the local Land Army rep. 'Bill agrees with me; he told me so in his last letter. We simply can't have you digging ditches and mending walls in your condition.'

'I could transfer to lighter duties,' Grace had suggested without conviction.

'Such as?' Edith had run through the litany of winter jobs: sprout-picking, potato-lifting, hen- and goose-plucking and the dreaded mechanical threshing of this year's wheat crop. 'No, Grace; it's too risky. I'll telephone county office first thing in the morning and ask for your release.'

Which is why Joyce found Grace serving in her father's pub in the village of Burnside on the Monday evening after work. She took a slow sip of shandy from a half-pint glass. 'Standing out in a frozen field picking sprouts will bring on the chilblains, no doubt.' There was nothing like it to cause one of the most troublesome complaints of the winter. 'Not to mention the frostbitten fingers and the backache and what have you.'

Grace wiped down the already spotless bar then paused to take a long, hard look at her brother's fiancée. Joyce's shoulder-length brown hair was hidden beneath a green headscarf tied like a turban around her head and she sat on the stool in muddy brown dungarees, elbows on the bar, evidently exhausted after a long day digging ditches at the Kelletts' place. Still, she managed to give off a pleasant, friendly air.

'You're not here just to pass the time of day with me, are you?' Grace remarked at last.

Joyce shook her head. 'Well spotted, Sherlock.'

'I know you, Joyce. There's a reason why you didn't go straight home after work.' Grace slipped away to serve two Canadian airmen from the base on Penny Lane and when she came back she resumed the conversation. 'Well?'

'I called in to see your mother-in-law and ask for a change of billet.' There; she'd said it! It was really happening.

Grace's oval face registered surprise. 'Whatever for?'

'That's exactly what Mrs Mostyn said.' *Whatever for? Has Hilda Craven upset you? Has one of the other girls? If so, I'm sure this is something we can easily sort out.*

'And what did you tell her?'

'That I liked living at Fieldhead but I was ready for a change.'

'A different challenge?'

'Exactly. I thought perhaps I could retrain as a lumberjill.'

'For the Women's Timber Corps?'

'Yes. Or I could study for a certificate as a mechanized operative then I could train other girls to drive and maintain tractors.'

'What did she say?'

'That she would enquire at head office on my behalf, but that meanwhile, if I was serious about wanting a move, I'd better be prepared to be sent wherever they need me the most.'

'It could be in the back of beyond,' Grace pointed out when she'd had time to digest Joyce's news. 'Would you mind being billeted in a farm miles from anywhere, surrounded by nothing but bare hillsides and sheep?'

Joyce thought she would not. 'I'd have plenty of time in the evening to read my library books and write letters.' *To Edgar,* she thought but didn't need to say out loud. 'I'll miss Una and Brenda, of course.' But not the hurly-burly of meals at the long dining-room tables, the scramble for the bathrooms and some of the silliness that resulted from a gaggle of young women from Yorkshire mill towns and factories all being thrown together in a run-down manor house that had been converted into a Land Army hostel to aid the war effort. 'And you, Grace; I'll miss you too.'

'"For a healthy, happy job, join the Women's Land Army!"' Brenda wielded a pitchfork like a lance and charged at the tattered poster pasted on the door of one of the stables in the weed-strewn yard behind the hostel.

She and Kathleen had spent the whole of Wednesday lifting potatoes from clamps in the top field at Brigg Farm. Each clamp was twenty-five feet long, made up of nine-inch layers of straw alternating with harvested potatoes. The girls' job was to transfer the spuds into hessian sacks then sling the full sacks on to the back of a horse and cart before driving back to the farmyard. It was back-breaking, bone-chilling work, carried out in temperatures well below freezing, and now that the day was over, Brenda took out her frustrations on the familiar call to arms. 'Join the flipping Land Army!' She thrust the prongs of the pitchfork deep into the wooden planks. 'Take that!' she cried.

Kathleen laughed as she wheeled her bike into the nearest stable. 'Never mind, things are looking up. I took delivery of a Peek Freans Christmas cake this morning; one and nine from Stannings grocery shop in Northgate.'

'Sent by?'

'My ma, bless her. She thinks I'm starving to death out here.'

'That adds up to a lot of coupons,' Brenda remarked. 'She must have been saving them up for weeks.'

'Yes and I've got strict instructions not to open the cake until the week running up to Christmas – that means more than a month before we can break into it.'

Their easy conversation took Kathleen and Brenda indoors and down the long, dark corridor into Ma Craven's kitchen where they found the warden preparing to load the evening meal of boiled beef, potatoes and carrots on to a rickety trolley. While her back was turned, Brenda lifted the lid of the stew pot and picked out a steaming piece of carrot.

'I saw that!' Hilda warned.

'Blimey, it's true what they say – you really have got eyes in the back of your head.' Brenda retreated with a wink. She was fond of the unflappable older woman whose job was to run every angle of household affairs at Fieldhead, including cooking, cleaning and generally keeping the girls in line. 'Is there anything we can do to help?'

Hilda huffed and puffed as she lifted the heavy iron pot. 'Yes, you can carry those water jugs into the dining room, then you can set out the knives and forks.'

'Trust you, Brenda. I was looking forward to hopping into a hot bath and having a good soak before dinner,' Kathleen complained as they carried out their tasks. The two girls were well matched in personality and appearance. Both were tall with long legs, graceful figures and slender waists, though Kathleen's hair was fair and wavy (thanks to a bottle of bleach and some perm solution, she cheerfully admitted) while Brenda's was dark and fashionably short, giving her a cheeky, vivacious air that reflected her independent spirit. They were town girls born and bred, strong-minded and strikingly attractive, and on a Friday night out at the Blacksmith's Arms, they had to fend off the attentions of Canadian pilots, POWs and local farmers alike.

'What is it about you two?' Joyce had asked them when they were setting off for work one foggy morning at the start of November. 'Even togged out in dungarees and wellington boots, you manage to look as if you've just stepped off a Paris catwalk.'

Ah yes, Joyce. Brenda rapped knives and forks down on to the bare trestle table while Kathleen lined up the glasses. *Joyce will leave a bloody big hole when she's no longer at Fieldhead. There'll be no one with enough common sense and know-how to step into her shoes.*

'I'm moving on from Fieldhead,' Joyce had announced the night before as she queued behind Brenda for the bathroom. 'I'm waiting to hear where they'll send me.'

Brenda had flashed her a startled look but for once had held her tongue. It was Joyce's business, after all.

'Will you miss me?' Joyce had asked over a late-night cup of cocoa.

'Not a whit!' Brenda had assured her with a wink.

Oh, but I will! She finished laying out the cutlery and heard Ma Craven trundle her trolley down the uneven flagged corridor. *I'll miss Joyce Cutler more than I can say!*

CHAPTER TWO

Friday came and there was still no word of where Joyce would be sent.

'She'll land on her feet, you watch,' Brenda predicted on the bike ride back to Fieldhead with Una and Elsie. Worn out after a day-long stint of wringing chicken's necks at Horace Turnbull's farm, they rode into a biting wind, through Burnside then out along the single-track lane leading to the hostel. 'What's the betting the jammy beggar is sent to a manor house complete with live-in servants and a teeny-weeny veg plot for her to tend?'

'I bet you a shilling that she won't be!' Elsie went on to swear that any girl would give her eye teeth for a soft billet on a lowland estate. 'Feather pillows, clean sheets every week – the lot.'

Una rode on in troubled silence.

'What's up?' Brenda asked as they approached Peggy's farm, with the first sight of Fieldhead in the distance. 'Are you still thinking about those headless chickens running around in circles in Horace's yard?'

Una shuddered at the grisly memory but shook her head.

'Wait, don't tell me. Angelo hasn't written back yet. Is that it?'

Una didn't reply. Instead, she cycled ahead.

'Bullseye.' It was clear to Elsie that Brenda had hit the mark. 'Poor lamb, life is a waiting game when you fall for a POW – when you fall for anyone, for that matter.'

'In this day and age,' Brenda agreed. 'Take me. I swore I would never be the type of girl who hangs out of the window waiting for the morning post to arrive. I would never count the kisses at the bottom of my fiancé's letter and wonder if he still loves me as much as he did last week or the week before.'

'And look what happened.' Elsie watched Una turn off the lane into the hostel driveway. 'You got yourself engaged to Les White and that was that.'

'Yes.' Brenda patted the engagement ring that she wore as usual on a ribbon around her neck. 'For better or for worse.'

Instead of carrying on as the free spirit of old, she now spent her days worrying about which convoy Les's Royal Navy ship would be part of. Would it enter the Med under a barrage of enemy fire and sail safely through the Strait of Gibraltar only to be blown sky-high by an unseen U-boat or perhaps join the American fleet in the Pacific or else stay closer to home to guard their own British submarines off the west coast of Scotland? She spent her nights dreaming about Les, picturing his serious face and trusting blue eyes, his slightly furrowed brow and thatch of neatly parted fair hair. She had become that type of girl.

'Any news about your move?' Elsie called to Joyce as she and Brenda followed Una up the drive.

Joyce was raking leaves off the front lawn, ready to make a bonfire at the back of the house. 'Not yet. Only that for the time being the Land Army can't spare me for retraining so Mrs Mostyn is looking for a fresh billet for me as soon as possible.'

'Don't go, Joyce!' Brenda cried melodramatically as she screeched to a halt then dismounted. 'Don't leave us. We'll be lost without you!'

Joyce grinned and went on loading leaves into her wheelbarrow. 'Anyone fancy roasting a few spuds in the bonfire later on?' she called after them.

'Yes, please; count me in,' Elsie replied.

'No, ta,' Brenda yelled. 'Tonight I'm taking Old Sloper on a spin over to Dale End. Les's sister Hettie is poorly. I promised I'd pay her a visit.'

If there was one thing in this world that Brenda would never give up it was her beloved motor bike. They could take away her entire clothes ration for all she cared and she wouldn't mind if she never stirred another spoonful of sugar into her tea ever again, but to be parted from Old Sloper would mean the end of the world had arrived.

And now, as she rode along Swinsty Edge towards Attercliffe, she was reminded of the freedom it gave her, even though the blackout demanded that her headlight was dimmed and the country road was full of unexpected twists and turns. Along she sailed, her leather airman's jacket zipped to her chin, with goggles to protect her eyes from the wintry wind – past the spot where Grace and Bill had found Frank Kellett frozen to death, on towards the tiny hamlet of Hawkshead, on again, over the ridge for a first glimpse of the gentler neighbouring dale where the hills were less steep and the valley more open. Brenda applied her brakes then snaked down the hill towards Dale End Farm. She turned into the drive and came to a halt outside the impressive entrance to the Georgian house that Arnold White and his family called home.

Arnold himself came to the door at the sound of her engine. The widowed, well-to-do farmer greeted her without a smile, simply holding the door open and gesturing for her to enter.

Brenda unzipped her jacket. 'Hello, Mr White. How's Hettie?'

'Go in and see for yourself.' He nodded towards the sitting room before turning away with a click of his heels and disappearing into his study.

Brenda crossed the hallway and knocked on the door.

'Come in, Brenda; do!' Hettie called sharply. 'There's no need to stand on ceremony.'

'Aye, aye, captain.' Brenda opened the door to find Les's thirty-three-year-old sister sitting on a couch facing the French windows. There was a fire in the grate of the Adam fireplace but only one dim table lamp illuminating the spacious room.

Hettie didn't stand to greet her. She wore a paisley patterned shawl around her shoulders and her dark hair was swept back from her high forehead, giving her the air of a school governess from a bygone age. 'Come in,' she said again. 'And close that door.'

The firelight cast flickering shadows over Hettie's face, making it difficult for Brenda to judge how ill she might be. 'How are you feeling?'

'I've felt better, I admit.'

'What is it? What's wrong?'

Hettie gave a dismissive sniff. 'Dr Hood isn't saying. He's ordered some tests.'

'But what are the symptoms?' Brenda wasn't surprised that Hettie was unforthcoming. She was the indomitable sort who viewed illness as a weakness that must be resisted without fuss. 'Do you have a temperature?'

'Not really. I can't keep any food down. That's the problem.'

A closer inspection told Brenda that Hettie had lost weight, which she could ill afford to do. Always tall and angular, there were now hollows in her cheeks and her wrists and ankles were thin and bony. 'That sounds nasty,' she commiserated. 'My mother developed a bad case of indigestion when she was my age. It turned out to be a hiatus hernia.'

Hettie acknowledged the information with a faint nod. 'Christmas will be here before we know it.'

'It will.'

'I'm knitting Les and Donald a jumper each. Father will have to make do with pipe tobacco this year. Rationing makes the festive season difficult, don't you think?'

'It does.' Brenda frowned at the small talk. This wasn't like Hettie at all. Normally she would be firing questions, quick as a machine gun – had Brenda heard from Les? What did Brenda think of Mr Churchill's speech last Sunday? Had she heard about the Land Girl recently employed at a farm near Hawkshead who had arrived with a bad reputation? It turned out that the girl was indeed a bit fast so the farmer wouldn't keep her. This sort of thing was often intended as a side swipe at Brenda. Today, however, Hettie was more subdued and talking inconsequentially about knitting.

'Let's not forget that Les has three days' leave coming up.' Brenda steered the talk in a new direction. 'Next weekend, as a matter of fact.'

'Has he?' Hettie raised her eyebrows.

Brenda patted the letter in the pocket of her slacks. 'He says so here, fingers crossed. Of course, this was written a few weeks ago and things can change at the last minute.'

'Yes, who knows what may happen?' Hettie pulled the shawl more tightly around her shoulders. 'Would you put some more coal on the fire, Brenda?'

The door opened as Brenda crouched low to tend to the fire and Donald White sauntered into the room. 'Look what the wind blew in!' he declared, hands in pockets, openly admiring his brother's fiancée's back view.

The sound of his voice, ebullient and mocking, stayed Brenda's hand and she felt her face glow. *Drat,* she thought, *just who I didn't want to bump into!*

She and Donald had never seen eye to eye and the better she'd got to know him, the more blinkered and arrogant she found him. Donald White was the centre of his own little world, unable to understand that not all girls swooned under his handsome gaze, despite his thick dark hair, wide straight mouth and the pale grey eyes that he'd apparently inherited from his Irish mother. He had an easy, flattering gift of the gab that almost always got him what he wanted. Not with Brenda, however.

'Hello, Donald.' She straightened up and turned to face him, taking in his open-necked white shirt and yellow silk cravat, teamed with wide navy blue trousers. 'I called in to see how Hettie was.'

'I was in the bath when you arrived. Now I'm in my best bib and tucker, ready to nip down to the local for a swift half before I drive my brand-new Rover into town. Do you fancy joining me?'

She met his taunting gaze. 'No, thanks. I'll stay here with Hettie.'

'Please yourself.' His shrug made it clear that it was her loss and that at the same time he wouldn't readily take no for an answer. Ignoring Hettie, he moved in on Brenda, so close that she could smell the Brylcreem in his hair. 'Are you sure I can't persuade you?'

'Quite sure, ta.' She bristled and took a step back. *It was one thing to borrow Les's MG sports car whenever it suited you, but I'm his fiancée – I'm not some flighty good-time girl for you to pick up and throw away again.*

Donald grunted then winked at Hettie. 'It was worth a try, eh?' he said as he backed out of the room.

'Ignore him,' Hettie said sternly, her drawn face poker-straight.

'I do,' Brenda assured her. 'Believe me, I do.'

'There's nothing like riding Old Sloper over the moors in the dead of night to set you thinking.' Brenda stared into the embers of the dying bonfire, aware that only she and Joyce remained outside. All the other girls had gone inside to fill their hot-water bottles and take to their beds.

'Don't you love the smell of a wood fire?' Joyce's

face was flushed from tending the fire and her eyes smarted from the smoke. 'So, Miss Appleby, you say you've been thinking?'

'Yes. Don't sound so surprised.' The ride back from Attercliffe had given Brenda the space and time to let a new idea crystallize but she'd waited for the others to disperse before she shared it with Joyce. 'As a matter of fact, I'm planning to follow in your footsteps.'

Joyce picked up a rake to heap soil over the remains of the bonfire. 'How do you mean?'

'I want to leave Fieldhead and try somewhere new; that's how.'

'You don't say.'

It was too dark to see Joyce's expression. 'You don't sound surprised.'

'I'm not. You've never been one to let the grass grow under your feet. But why now? Has something happened?'

'Besides you deserting us?' Brenda did her best to keep the mood light as she unzipped her jacket and took off her gauntlets. Then she let her guard drop. 'If you really want to know, it's partly because I want to find a way of steering clear of Donald.'

'He still won't leave you alone, eh?' Joyce turned towards the house and slid her arm through Brenda's.

Brenda sighed. 'This is Donald White we're talking about.'

'What's he done now?'

'The usual. Every time I cross his path he tries it on with me – would I care for a spin in his new Rover? Would I like to go out for a drink with him? You know the routine.'

Joyce stopped outside the back door and squeezed Brenda's hand. 'I wouldn't let him drive me away if I were you.'

'But you're not me.' Lovely, even-tempered Joyce – her very name was a byword for steady and reliable; whereas she, Brenda, had acquired a reputation as a flirt and a tease, thanks to an incident she would rather forget with a Canadian pilot named John Mackenzie. 'People don't respect me the way they do you. They only have to see me exchange a single word with Donald to jump to the wrong conclusion. Sooner or later Les is bound to pick up on the nasty rumours.'

'Which is most likely what Donald intends.' Joyce would still be sorry if this were the only reason for Brenda to move away. 'It's a pity that his dragon sister can't keep him in line.'

'Hettie's poorly. She's having to take a back seat for a while.' Brenda led the way into the house. 'In any case, Joyce, I was sailing along on Old Sloper under a starry sky, feeling the world was my oyster, and that's when it flashed into my mind – what's to stop me from moving on like you?'

'That's more like it.' More like the free-spirited, daring girl that Joyce admired. They walked into the kitchen together and she warmed up a pan of milk to make two mugs of cocoa.

'Now all I have to do is pin down Ma Craven and Mrs Mostyn and pray that one of them doesn't have a heart attack when I give them the news.'

'The Ministry of Food wants farmers to grow more flax next year.' Edith Mostyn was sitting with Hilda

Craven in the warden's office. She'd driven out to Fieldhead early on Saturday afternoon after a nice lunch at Bill and Grace's house before leaving the happy couple to themselves, as she put it.

Bill was home on a brief leave, fussing over Grace and avoiding all talk of the war and life in the Royal Armoured Corps.

'You look well, son,' she'd told him on the doorstep of the young married couple's terraced home, preparing to say goodbye. His sportsman's physique was enhanced by the epaulettes of his uniform and he'd recently grown a neat moustache. 'The army must suit you.'

'I am well,' he'd assured her. 'And all the better for knowing that you take good care of Grace while I'm away.'

'Your wife is well on the road to bearing you a healthy, happy baby, touch wood. It's you we both worry about.'

Bill had smiled stiffly. 'We all have to do our bit.'

'I know we do.' Edith had turned up the collar of her fur coat and put on her plum-coloured leather gloves. 'But not in the Far East, touch wood.' Burma, the Philippines, Papua – they would be the very worst postings as far as Edith was concerned. And yet she knew that many in her son's regiment, 'The Old and the Bold', were already slugging it out there against the Japanese.

Bill had shrugged then muttered an answer: 'We go where we're needed.'

In an unusual show of motherly love, she'd embraced him.

'Careful; you'll choke the life out of me,' he'd joked.

Her son, the person she loved best in the world. They'd said their goodbyes and now here she was sitting opposite Hilda, discussing which fields in the area might be set aside for flax growing and which Ministry of Information film they would next put on in the Village Institute. Eventually the talk came around to the real reason behind Edith's visit.

'We're losing one of our best workers in Joyce Cutler,' Hilda pointed out as Edith took some neatly folded sheets of foolscap paper from her handbag. She laid her broad hands palms down on her leather-topped desk, the black telephone to one side and a folder containing the following week's work rota close by. 'She'll be a hard gap to fill.'

'Yes, but what can I do? Joyce put in a request to be moved, which is within her rights.' The local rep's trim, upright figure and clipped voice was in marked contrast to the more homely, relaxed air given off by the hostel warden. Yet the two middle-aged widows had known each other all their lives and rubbed along well enough.

'I'm only saying – that's all.'

Edith slid the paperwork across the desk. 'This needs your signature to vouch for Joyce being suitable for a transfer. You can add a remark if you wish.'

A capable, cheery girl. Hilda wrote carefully in the space provided then pushed the papers back with a sigh.

'Is Joyce back yet?' Edith looked at her watch. Saturday was a half-day for the girls, leaving them with a free afternoon to do their washing and ironing.

A glance out of the office window told Hilda that the Land Girl in question was at that moment cycling up the drive with Una, Elsie, Kathleen and Brenda. All were smiling, with hats and scarves firmly in place, their cheeks ruddy from the cold ride home.

Edith decided to intercept Joyce before she disappeared round the side of the building so she hurried across the hallway and down the front steps, flapping the transfer papers at Joyce as she cycled by.

'Hey-up; that must be the information about your new billet,' Kathleen remarked before riding on.

Una and Elsie followed her but Brenda hung back with Joyce, who leaned her bike against the wall then went to talk to Mrs Mostyn.

'I'm sending you to Black Crag Farm at Shawcross,' Edith informed Joyce. 'A sheep farm. The farmer there is Laurence Bradley. His son was called up during the summer. As a result he finds he'll need extra help with feeding as winter sets in.'

With Brenda looking over her shoulder, Joyce read the papers that the rep had handed to her. 'Whereabouts is Shawcross?' she asked.

'Out beyond Kelsey Crag, in the dale north of here. It's only a tiny village – a hamlet with a dozen or so houses. There won't be many creature comforts, I can guarantee that.'

'I don't mind.' Joyce reread the name and address – Laurence Bradley of Black Crag Farm, Shawcross. Once again the move felt very real.

'You're to start there on Monday.' Keeping the regret that she felt out of her voice, Edith avoided looking at Joyce and stuck to practicalities. 'You can catch a bus from Burnside at nine o'clock in the morning. It'll get you to Shawcross by half past ten.'

'Then I'd better start packing,' Joyce said with a smile, standing aside to let Brenda speak.

Brenda cleared her throat. 'I was wondering, Mrs Mostyn . . . is there another vacancy out in that neck of the woods?' *Why waste time beating about the bush?*

Edith gave her a startled look and for once let an unguarded remark drop from her lips. 'Oh no; not you too!'

'Yes, me too.' Brenda's heart began to race but she stood her ground. 'I'm sorry if it's a bit sudden, but it feels right for me and I'm sure it won't be hard to fill my shoes. After all, if I can learn to wring chickens' necks and drive a horse and cart, anyone can!'

Edith paused to draw breath. Despite her surprise, she quickly realized that there was little she could do to change Brenda's mind. Besides, if Edith was honest, she'd always found the unpredictable, fun-loving former shop girl a bit of a handful. 'As a matter of fact . . .' she began.

'See!' Brenda nudged Joyce with her elbow. 'I knew I wouldn't be missed.'

The rep pulled another batch of papers out of her bag. 'I did consider an alternative to Black Crag Farm when I was looking for a new billet for Joyce. Both cases are rather urgent.'

Excitement rose in Brenda, like a flurry of butterflies rising from her stomach into her throat. 'Tell me more.'

Edith read from the top sheet. 'Bernard Huby at Garthside Farm. Mr Huby has a daughter, Dorothy, but the girl is delicate. Mr Huby himself is not as young as he used to be.'

'Perfect!' Brenda's eyes gleamed. 'Where do I sign?'

'Once again, I'm afraid there will be very little by way of home comforts,' Edith warned. 'Garthside and Black Crag Farm are two of the most remote in the area.'

'Why not take some time to think it over?' Joyce suggested, with no hope whatsoever that Brenda would follow her advice.

'No need!' Brenda declared as she took the papers and signed her name with a flourish. 'Mr Bernard Huby of Garthside Farm, here I come!'

CHAPTER THREE

The nine o'clock bus from Burnside was one of only two a week that went out as far as Shawcross village. It was half full when Brenda and Joyce caught it outside the Blacksmith's Arms, having said their fond farewells to Kathleen, Elsie, Una and the others over breakfast.

'Write to me as often as you can,' Una had pleaded before she set off for Brigg Farm, muffled in a thick woollen scarf, with canvas gaiters tightly buckled around her legs to guard against the rats that would no doubt scuttle from Roland Thomson's field clamps as she spent the day lifting potatoes.

'We faithfully promise to keep in touch.' Joyce's assurance had come with a Girl Guide salute.

'At least one letter a week,' Brenda had promised, standing in the hostel hallway with her suitcase at her feet. 'And if Angelo doesn't write to you by the middle of the week, tell him he'll have Joyce and me hammering on his door!'

Una had reddened as she'd produced an envelope from her coat pocket. 'It came in this morning's post.'

'Hurrah!' Joyce had hugged her. 'I knew Angelo wouldn't let you down.'

'Unlike someone else I could mention.' Brenda's grumble was about the thin trickle of letters she had received from Les recently. 'It'll be even worse from now on: the postman only visits Shawcross one day a week – a Saturday, by all accounts.'

'Rather you than me.' Kathleen had hurried Una away to start their day. 'You two must be round the bend!' she'd called over her shoulder.

Now, as Brenda and Joyce boarded the bus on a chilly, rain-soaked Monday morning, they feared that Kathleen might have been right. The inside of the rickety old charabanc was misted up, the driver an elderly woman in a man's overcoat, her hair plaited and laid flat over the crown of her head. There was a damp, fusty smell from the worn cloth seats and dirty puddles on the floor where passengers had shaken out their umbrellas.

'Nice day for ducks!' Brenda trilled as she made her way down the aisle.

There was no response from a thin-lipped young woman sitting on the back seat or from the two old men smelling of damp tweed, smoking their pipes and hawking up phlegm as the girls hoisted their suitcases on to the overhead rack. Other passengers kept their heads buried in newspapers or else wiped condensation from the windows and stared out at the grey hills as the bus set off once more.

Inhibited by the gloomy silence that had greeted her cheery remark, Brenda settled next to Joyce for a long, dreary journey. For a while they exchanged whispered remarks, wondering what lay ahead.

Eventually, after half an hour of jolting over potholes and grinding to a halt to offload passengers,

Brenda cut through the low rumble of the bus's engine and spoke in her normal, lively way. 'Kathleen told me a yarn about a Land Girl who was billeted on a farm in the Lake District – back of beyond, and so on. No running water, no electricity. But the worst thing was this poor girl was expected to share a bed with the farmer's mother!'

'Trust Kathleen to come up with a tale like that to put us off,' Joyce murmured. Her attention had been caught by a solitary schoolboy sitting near the front of the bus, his navy blue school mac neatly belted, a gas mask slung diagonally across his chest. The boy stared at the condensation trickling down the window, making no effort to clear it away.

'She mentioned another situation where the farmer was eighty if he was a day, living all on his ownio. The girl arrived to find a heap of bloated sheep's carcasses piled up in the yard and only the old man's pet parrot for company.'

'Ugh! How long did she stick it out, I wonder?' The bus swerved to avoid two stray sheep, almost flinging Joyce and Brenda into the aisle.

'Kathleen didn't say. It does make you wonder, though.'

'Fingers crossed there'll be no dead sheep where we're going.'

'And no Pretty Polly either.' Brenda had a phobia about parrots, developed when, as a small child, she'd been forced to visit a great-aunt who lived nearby. The bird had been a vindictive sod that had flown from its perch to land on Brenda's shoulder and peck at her bare neck whenever her back was turned. 'Nasty, vicious things.'

'Think of it another way,' Joyce said after the bus had pulled up at a crossroads to disgorge the two pipe-smoking farmers and the unhappy young woman. 'This is a big adventure. We have no idea where we're headed or what it will be like when we get there. Everything will be new.'

'You're right, of course.' Brenda took a deep breath. 'We have to look on the bright side.' She fell silent for a while, swaying against Joyce whenever the bus negotiated a sharp bend. Then she began on a new tack. 'What do you most hope to find at Black Crag Farm?'

'I'm not fussy. As long as I can keep warm and have a bit of peace and quiet in the evenings. What about you? What would you wish for?'

Brenda was more ambitious. 'Hmm, hot water on tap would be nice. A room to myself with a cosy fire. A shed to park Old Sloper in.'

'Yes, I forgot about your precious motor bike. What's going to happen there?'

'I'll get used to the lie of the land first then see if Mr Huby will let me bring the old girl out here. If he agrees, I'll catch the bus back to Fieldhead on my day off or else cadge a lift. I'll get Sloper out to Garthside Farm somehow.'

Again the sway of the bus and the chug of the engine silenced them until they were roused out of their daydreams by a curt cry from the driver. 'Shawcross; everybody off!'

Brenda wiped the steamed-up window to discover that they'd arrived at a small village green with a weather-worn Celtic cross in the middle. There was a row of low cottages facing on to the green, with an old coaching inn opposite and on the third side a church with a square tower. The church was surrounded on three sides by a graveyard and next to that there was a detached house with steep gables and arched windows and then a low, green-painted wooden building with a noticeboard indicating that it was used for village meetings, jumble sales, and whatever passed for entertainment in this remote community.

Joyce stood up and passed Brenda's suitcase to her. She was about to lower her own when she saw the schoolboy stand on his seat to reach for a bulging shopping bag.

'Nay, take your mucky boots off my upholstery!' The driver had caught sight of him in her overhead mirror.

The boy jumped down in alarm then stood bewildered in the aisle.

'Here; let me.' Joyce lifted his bag down from the rack. Inside she spied a neatly folded jumper, a pair of socks and some clean underwear. She smiled at the boy. 'Go on; you get off the bus first.'

Too scared to smile back, he shuffled towards the door.

Joyce descended the steps after him and took a quick look around the empty green. 'Is someone meant to meet you?'

The boy nodded. He couldn't be more than eight or nine years old, wearing a navy blue cap to match his mac, with short grey flannel trousers and long woollen socks. Joyce noticed that his black shoes were polished to perfection.

'Who?'

'The vicar,' he managed to reply through a stammer brought on by the bus driver's barked command.

'Don't worry; I'm sure he'll turn up soon.' Joyce could only hope that this was true. The rain was as bad as ever and the hill behind the inn rose steeply to meet dark grey clouds. 'What's your name?' she asked. 'No, let me guess; you're an Alfred or an Alan. Yes, I'd say you're an Alan.'

His eyes widened. 'How did you know?'

She grinned. 'I cheated. I read your name and address on your gas mask case. Alan Evans, 15 Station Street, Millwood.'

With rain dripping from the peak of his cap, the little boy mustered a nervous smile while Joyce called to the bus driver. 'Do you know the vicar here, by any chance?'

'That'd be the Reverend Walter Rigg.' The sour-faced woman sounded as if she would charge Joyce for the information if she could. 'And this'll be the third evacuee he's taken in this year. The other two lasted less than a month. Work that one out.'

'I see.' Joyce thought it best to ignore this last remark and smiled again at the boy. 'Well, Alan, we're all in the same boat, standing here in the rain. I wonder who'll be met first.'

The answer came in the shape of a young woman in the regulation green beret and brown double-breasted coat of the Women's Timber Corps. She hurried from a lane leading down the side of the churchyard, coat flapping, towards the small group. 'Alan Evans?' she checked with the boy.

He nodded.

'Pleased to meet you. I'm Evelyn Newbold. The vicar sent me. You're to come with me to the vicarage.'

Joyce and Brenda both nodded encouragingly before introducing themselves to the new arrival.

'Brenda Appleby.'

'Joyce Cutler.'

The three women shook hands. Joyce and Brenda took straightaway to their lively comrade in arms, whose smile seemed genuine and whose handshake was firm.

'Where are your billets?' Evelyn asked.

'Garthside Farm.'

'Black Crag Farm.'

'Phew, rather you than me,' Evelyn said to both names. There were glimpses of rich, copper-coloured hair beneath her beret. Her face, dampened by the rain, was covered in faint freckles, her eyes flecked with green and grey. 'Come along, Alan; best not to keep the vicar waiting.'

Joyce and Brenda watched Evelyn hurry away with the boy, quick march.

'It's nice to know that at least one other girl has answered the call to work out here,' Brenda commented wryly. Her first impression of Evelyn was that she was a whirlwind of non-stop energy; friendly enough but with a strong will to match Brenda's own.

'She didn't mention where she was billeted,' Joyce pointed out. 'Still, I expect we'll run into her again before too long.'

By this time, Evelyn and Alan had disappeared up the path leading to the gabled vicarage, leaving Joyce and Brenda standing in the wind and rain. A net curtain in one of the cottages twitched, while a stout man in shirtsleeves and waistcoat came to the doorway of the inn and knocked out the contents of his pipe against the stone jamb.

Then, just as Joyce and Brenda were starting to lose heart, a tractor rumbled into view. It emerged from the low clouds cloaking the hillside, trundling down a green lane then through an open, five-bar gate on to the flat village green, its thick tyres shedding clods of mud on to the tarmac road.

Both Joyce and Brenda looked expectantly at the driver dressed in a black oilskin coat and flat cap.

The man halted the tractor then jumped down from the cab. He was shorter than average, with a closed expression and a seeming reluctance to meet their gaze. 'Brenda Appleby?' he asked in a flat voice, eyes directed not at the two Land Girls but squinting towards the stone cross.

Brenda stepped forward. 'That's me.'

The farmer jerked his head back so that his chin retreated into folds of skin on his neck. It was a look that suggested that he would have preferred the stronger-looking Joyce.

'Bernard Huby's my name. Come with me,' he said.

Brenda grimaced at Joyce. 'Wish me luck,' she whispered.

'Yes. Good luck.'

As Brenda rushed after Mr Huby and climbed up into the tractor cab, Joyce felt her heart sink on behalf of her friend. *Not exactly the life and soul of the party,* was her snap verdict on Brenda's new employer. Still, first impressions didn't always stick.

She waited for a further ten or fifteen minutes.

The rain eased and the clouds lifted slowly to reveal a rocky, barren hillside intersected by a patchwork of low stone walls that were a feature of the Yorkshire landscape, so different to the lush, lowland pastures of Joyce's native Warwickshire. She shivered and shook droplets from the rim of her hat, looking up to see Evelyn Newbold reappear on a bike.

'That's young Alan settled in at the vicarage,' she informed Joyce as she rode towards her. 'Still no sign of Mr Bradley?'

'Not yet.'

'Don't worry, he won't have forgotten about you,' Joyce's new acquaintance promised. 'He called in at the Cross Keys last night and happened to mention you were arriving today. I work behind the bar there during my time off,' she explained in response to Joyce's questioning look. 'There's not much else to do round here. Oh, and by the way, you won't find Laurence Bradley easy at first. He takes some getting to know.'

'Ta, I'll remember that.'

'Like most farmers around here,' Evelyn added before she cycled on.

Joyce frowned and stamped her feet to ward off the cold. She looked at her watch. Dead leaves from horse chestnut trees behind the cottages blew across the green.

At last another vehicle drove into view: a grey Land-Rover towing an open trailer loaded with sheep. A bare-headed, grey-haired man lowered the driver's window and beckoned for Joyce to join him.

She picked up her suitcase and ran to do as she was bidden. 'Joyce Cutler.' She introduced herself breathlessly above a cacophony of bleating sheep. 'You must be Mr Bradley?'

'Get in.' The question hung in the air and the two-word command wasn't softened by a smile, though the man's face had regular, straight features and Joyce judged that he would have been regarded as handsome in his youth. Her new employer hardly waited for her to shut the door before he set off.

Joyce balanced her suitcase on her knees as he picked up speed, only risking an occasional glance at his clean, strong profile as they left Shawcross behind. She put his age at around forty-five. He was tall and straight-backed – a physique well suited to outdoor work. During the first ten minutes of the drive out to Black Crag Farm not another word was uttered.

The silence didn't bother Joyce; it gave her time to take in her surroundings, which had a raw, rough beauty. The dark millstone grit that had characterized the landscape around Burnside gave way here to lighter, fissured limestone that was criss-crossed by fast-running streams sometimes spilling over cliff edges in spectacular waterfalls that splashed on to rocks then ran on to join a slow, brown river snaking through the valley. As the Land-Rover and trailer climbed the hillside, she gained a bird's-eye view of the hamlet that they'd left behind. Higher still, occasional silver birch trees found footing in the thin soil of the windswept expanse and provided shelter for small groups of hardy sheep with thick, matted coats, black faces and heavy, curled horns. Each was marked on their rump with a vivid patch of blue dye.

Mr Bradley eyed the huddles, seemingly to check their condition and pick out any that limped. At last and still without speaking, he angled the trailer at a diagonal across the narrow lane, put on the handbrake then stepped down from the Land-Rover and swung open a nearby gate. Then he strode to the back of the trailer where he lowered a ramp and waited.

The sheep emerged, bleating, blundering and jostling each other away from the gateway.

Oh no, you don't! Spotting the lead ewe's proposed escape route, Joyce jumped out and blocked the way, spreading her arms wide and ushering the errant sheep back towards the gate. Working as a team, she and the farmer soon succeeded in herding them into the field.

'You've done this before,' Laurence observed as he raised the ramp and bolted it shut.

'Yes; I've worked with sheep all my life. I grew up on a sheep farm just outside Stratford. We bred Suffolks, mostly for meat.'

He nodded a faint approval. 'It's Swaledales up here. Thick coats – they stand up to the weather better than most.'

Joyce nodded back.

'House is in the next dip,' he informed her in his usual curt fashion as he ground up through the gears.

Sure enough, as they reached the crest of the hill and passed a large outcrop of dark rock, Black Crag Farm came into view. The small, squat house nestled in a hollow, protected from the prevailing westerly wind by trees on one side but with a clear, open view of the sweep of the valley on the other. The sky above was still grey and stormy, the green hillside broken up into small fields by walls made from the local stone. There were two well-kept field barns in the valley bottom.

Joyce sat forward in her seat. If this was to be her home, she wanted to take in as much information as possible. She noted the layout of the fields and their connecting stiles, a clear stream that sprang up to one side of the crag then made its wandering way down the hillside, a kestrel hovering close to the road. At the approach of the Land-Rover the sharp-eyed bird wheeled away on a current of air. Then two dogs ran out of the yard, yapping loudly. The Border collies charged so close to the wheels of the Land-Rover that Joyce closed her eyes and prayed.

Laurence disregarded the dogs. He drove into a yard bordered by low outbuildings and backed the trailer into one of them. Then he got out of the car and walked on towards the house.

Joyce followed with her suitcase, through a small front porch and into the kitchen. Then she waited for instructions.

None came. The farmer sat by the fire to unlace his boots. He kicked them off then padded across the stone flags to hang his coat from a hook on the back of the door. Next he filled a kettle at a tap over the brown sink. He set it on an iron grid over the well-stoked fire. Finally he took a tea caddy from a shelf and spooned leaves into a teapot.

Everything was shipshape, Joyce noticed. The floor was scrubbed, the furniture gleaming and there were no cobwebs hanging from the low beamed ceiling.

The walls were freshly limewashed, the coal scuttle filled to the brim.

'Tea,' Laurence said.

She took the monosyllable as an invitation to sit at the table and take the proffered cup. At close quarters she noticed that her employer's eyes were slate grey and his brow lined. She remembered that he had a son who had recently joined the army and wondered if she would be allocated the young man's bedroom. Meanwhile, she sipped her tea and went on observing.

Green and cream tin canisters on the shelf were labelled 'Tea', 'Sugar', 'Salt', and so on. There was a dresser with blue and white willow-pattern crockery. A shotgun rested against the wall close to the door.

Was there a Mrs Bradley? She supposed not. The house lacked a woman's touch – there were no curtains, cushions or tablecloth, only one photograph on the mantelpiece of a severe-looking patriarch with a handlebar moustache. Yet somebody kept the floor clean and took out a tin of beeswax to polish the pine dresser. Perhaps the farmer was a widower who employed a daily help, or else there was a daughter or a sister who lived nearby.

'Come this way.' Laurence rattled his empty cup into its saucer then stood up.

Joyce followed again, out of the kitchen and up some narrow stairs, along a short landing with two bedroom doors to one side then, unexpectedly, up some roughly fashioned steps into the attic where there was a skylight in the ceiling, an iron bedstead, a washstand with jug and ewer and a metal rail across an alcove, presumably to hang her clothes.

There was no fireplace or electric light. Indeed, there was no light of any sort.

So much for writing letters in my spare time, Joyce thought with a twinge of regret. But at least she had a room to herself.

'Toilet's outside in the yard,' Laurence said as he descended the ladder. 'Earth closet. You'll fetch water to get washed from the kitchen sink. Unpack your things. Come down when you're ready.'

Brenda's drive to Garthside was over almost before she knew it. Bernard Huby drove his tractor across fields, zigzagging up the steep fell side, and they were soon enveloped by the low-lying cloud, making it impossible for her to make out her surroundings. She plied him with questions: had he been farming here for many years? Did he employ other Land Girls? What were the worst and the best aspects of living this far out?

The replies were short and plain: All my life. No; you're the first. I never think about it.

Like getting blood out a stone, she thought. Still, his answers, though brief, weren't hostile. *Maybe he's shy,* Brenda concluded.

She risked a quick sideways glance at her wiry, middle-aged companion. Though swamped by the oilskin coat, he nevertheless gave off an air of unflappability. She guessed that the sharp, ruddy features beneath the peak of his grey cap rarely changed expression and that he seldom gave voice to what he was thinking. It seemed he would deal with whatever life threw at him without comment or complaint.

'Is there a Mrs Huby?' she blurted out.

Bernard's voice remained steady. 'No. Not any more.'

'I'm sorry. I hope you don't mind my asking.'

He shrugged. 'You'll meet my daughter, Dorothy. You two are around the same age. I hope you'll get along.'

'I'm sure we will.' She felt the tractor veer to the right and peered through the thick mist to see that they had entered a farmyard. A dog barked, chickens clucked, light from an open door filtered through the fog.

'Hop out,' Bernard instructed. 'Follow me.'

In her attic room at Black Crag Farm Joyce opened her suitcase and took out her clothes, hairbrush, washbag and writing set. She decided she must ask Mr Bradley for a paraffin lamp or at least a candlestick, and perhaps an extra blanket for the bed.

She tried not to let her spirits sink too low as she looked around her bare, cold billet. After all, it was the work that mattered. She thought of the Swaledales that they'd released into the field – many of the ewes were heavily pregnant and would start lambing soon after Christmas. She wondered whether they would be brought into the field barns to give birth or if they would stay out and it would be a case of her and Mr Bradley battling through snowdrifts to assist. In any case, she was glad that there were two dogs on the farm to help sniff out the sheep.

'Come down when you're ready,' he'd told her.

She realized there was still plenty for her to learn about the farm routine before it grew dark, though dusk would come early on a day like today; in fact, it was truer to say that it had never really got light. So Joyce descended the stairs to find the farmer in the kitchen, boots back on and waiting impatiently for her to reappear.

He took her outside into the drizzling rain and pointed out where he kept the two dogs in the kennel by the gate. 'Not chained,' he noted. 'Strangers don't pass by as a rule. Dogs are free to roam.'

'Do they have names?'

'Grey one's Flint. Black and white one's Patch. Over there's the earth closet.' He pointed to a small, ramshackle shed with a tin roof.

Joyce could have guessed this without being told. Even with the door closed, the place reeked – of sour, wet earth mixed with human waste. There was a water tap across the yard, a zinc barrel to collect rain water from the roof, an old stone mounting block for when horses had been the mode of transport.

'Winter feed is in the first barn, tools, machinery and so on in the one nearest the house. Does the Land Army issue you with gumboots?'

She nodded.

'Oilskins?'

'No, just an overcoat.'

'You'll find Gordon's oilskin hanging in the porch.'

'Gordon is your son?'

Laurence narrowed his eyes and nodded before moving on to show her the barn containing winter feed. 'Turnips for sheep are in that far corner. Silage for cows in the corrugated-iron container.'

'You keep cows?'

'Three Friesians for milking; that'll be your job from now on. And half a dozen chickens. No pigs.'

As Laurence explained and Joyce listened, the two dogs came sniffing. They were sleek creatures, lean to the point of being undernourished, but friendly enough when she bent to stroke them. Flint, the grey one, was the bolder of the two; Patch more suspicious of the newcomer.

'Leave off,' Laurence chastised her. 'They're working dogs, not pets.'

She frowned at the reprimand and wondered whether he would apply the same standards to her – giving her minimum feed and expecting maximum work – preparing herself in advance. 'There's no light in my room,' she reminded him as he concluded the guided tour and walked back towards the house. 'Is there a candle or a paraffin lamp I could have?'

'Well, Alma?' Laurence Bradley strode ahead and flung the question at a figure standing at the sink with her back towards them. 'Do we have a spare candle?'

The woman nodded without turning round.

Joyce stood in the doorway trying to work this out. The presence of a female explained certain things, such as how the housework got done at Black Crag Farm, but raised more questions than it answered. The back view suggested she was young, perhaps no more than twenty years old. She wore a grey cable-knit sweater over a blue pleated skirt that came down to her calves. Her fair hair hung loose around her shoulders.

'She'll bring you one up,' Laurence told Joyce.

Was this his daughter? Joyce hadn't heard anything about a daughter, though. And was it simple, straightforward shyness that kept the young woman's back turned, or something more complicated?

'Alma.' His voice hardened a little. 'This is Joyce Cutler, the Land Girl I told you about.'

There was another nod as Alma put teacups into the washing-up bowl.

'Come and say hello,' Laurence insisted.

Slowly and deliberately the girl dried her hands on the calico apron that protected her skirt.

The strange delay made Joyce feel more uncomfortable. She looked from Alma to Laurence then back again. Why was she so reluctant to turn around? What exactly was going on?

'Alma,' he repeated in the same harsh tone.

The girl turned at last, hands clasped and head hanging so that her hair partly hid her face.

The awkward pause went on for a long time. Joyce cleared her throat then stepped forward. 'I hope I'm not putting you to any trouble – the candle, I mean.'

The girl raised her head and one hand flew up to her cheek.

'Alma!' A softer warning emerged through a long, exasperated sigh.

Reluctantly she lowered the hand and met Joyce's gaze.

Joyce held out her hand. 'I don't want to be a nuisance.'

The girl nodded. She bit her lip and glanced at Laurence.

Joyce caught sight of disfiguring marks on the side of her cheek and neck. They were old, pale scars that had healed unevenly, probably the result of bad burns, extending from her neck, over her jawline and up to her right ear. Only just managing to conceal her surprise, she kept her outstretched hand steady. Alma took it and shook it lightly before fleeing from the room.

'Alma is my wife,' Laurence explained at last. 'Just ask her; she'll fetch you anything you need.'

CHAPTER FOUR

The indistinct figure at the door of Garthside Farm didn't venture out into the rain as Brenda and Bernard Huby crossed the yard. The woman waited, her outline blurred by heavy mist, arms folded, leaning casually against the door jamb.

'This is my Dorothy.' Bernard made a quick introduction. 'Dorothy, this is our Land Girl.'

'Brenda Appleby,' she said eagerly.

'Pleased to meet you.' Dorothy shifted to one side to let Brenda and her father into the kitchen.

'Likewise.' *So far, so good.* Brenda's first impressions of her new situation were mostly favourable. Admittedly, the farmhouse kitchen was poky and rather shabby, but this put her at her ease because it meant she wouldn't have to bother too much about treading mud into the house or letting her wet coat drip on the floor. Dorothy was something of a surprise – round and plump with a rosy face and soft, wavy brown hair – not the delicate-looking girl Brenda had been expecting. She'd looked the newcomer in the eye and smiled enthusiastically.

'Put the kettle on, there's a good lass,' Bernard said to his daughter as he took off his cap and oilskin cape to reveal oversized corduroy trousers held up by a thick leather belt and a grey sweater with holes in the elbows, worn over a collarless white shirt. 'Brenda's had a long trek to get here. She'll be ready for a cuppa.'

'That's right, I am.' Brenda watched Dorothy fill the kettle then place it on top of an Aga cooker that heated the whole kitchen. Where the father was sharp-featured and skinny, the daughter was rounded and dimpled, fashionably dressed in a rose-pink twin set and pearls, with a grey, fitted skirt that showed off shapely legs. She'd made the most of her thick brown hair by sweeping some of it high on to the top of her head, leaving the back section to curl down on to her shoulders.

Definitely not what I expected, Brenda thought again.

Bernard pulled back a chair then shifted a pile of newspapers to let her sit down. 'Here, take the weight off your feet. There'll be plenty of time later to show you around.'

'Dad, the goat got out again,' Dorothy mentioned as she prepared the tea. 'It made a beeline for the village.'

He gave a resigned shake of his head. 'Did you go after it?'

'Dressed like this?' She twirled to face him. 'I should cocoa!'

'So where is it now?'

'Don't worry; it's safe. Emma Waterhouse has got it locked in her coal shed. She telephoned from the vicarage to say she caught it munching its way through her Brussels sprouts – made a right mess of the whole veg patch, apparently.'

If Bernard was irritated, he didn't show it. 'I'd better go down and fetch it,' he said as he took his oilskin from the back of the door and headed out again.

'Blinking goat,' Dorothy commented. Tea slopped from the cups into their saucers as she carried them to the table. 'Still, that means we can sit down and have a nice long chat. So, Brenda, here was me thinking you'd be a strapping, outdoors sort of girl and, lo and behold, you're not like that at all.'

Brenda grinned. 'There may not be much meat on these bones but I can dig a ditch and muck out a stable along with the best of them.' She held up her work-roughened hands to prove her point.

'Rather you than me.' Dorothy stirred two spoons of sugar into her tea. 'I know; I shouldn't. What with rationing and all. What do you like to do in your spare time, by the way?'

'I read.'

'Magazines?' Dorothy's hazel eyes lit up. 'Ooh, did you bring some with you?'

Brenda shook her head. 'I read books mostly. Detective novels and romances; Agatha Christie, Daphne du Maurier. I enjoy going to the flicks, listening to music and dancing as well. How about you?'

'Dancing if I get half a chance. Dad's nickname for me when I was little was Twinkletoes. I'm better at the foxtrot than digging ditches, I don't mind admitting.'

Giving Dorothy free rein to enthuse about American dance bands, Brenda found herself gazing around the cluttered kitchen and wondering where this chatty, well-groomed girl fitted in to the harsh world of hill farming. Did she ever lift a finger to help her hard-pressed father, for instance?

As if she read this last thought, Dorothy flew off in a fresh direction. 'Of course, there's a limit to what I can do, dancing-wise. I don't have enough energy to go out every weekend. Sometimes it's too much for me.'

'You're a long way from civilization,' Brenda agreed.

Dorothy ran blithely on. 'Oh, it's not that. I can get myself into town easily enough, provided Cliff gives me a lift. Cliff's my brother. He's the gamekeeper on the Acklam Castle estate. And I have somewhere to stay in Northgate. But I'm not very strong – never have been. They say it's because I insisted on putting in an early appearance: born six weeks before my time. It was the death of my poor mother, as it turned out. Afterwards, I was a sickly baby, not expected to live.'

'I'm very sorry to hear it.'

'But live I did!' The cheery exclamation brought Dorothy's tale of woe to a sudden conclusion and she reached across to pat Brenda's hand. 'That's enough about me. Now, tell me all about you and yours!'

As dusk fell on the first day at Joyce's new billet, Laurence Bradley threw her in at the deep end.

'Cows need milking,' he told her as he set off up the fell on foot, accompanied by his two dogs. 'In the shed behind the house; you'll find everything you need.'

Determined to prove herself, Joyce undertook her first task without asking unnecessary questions and quickly found the three black-and-white Friesian cows feeding in their wooden stalls inside the old-fashioned cowshed. They barely raised their heads as, by the light of one dim electric bulb, she found pails, metal churns and a milking stool amongst other paraphernalia such as yard brushes, pitchforks and rakes.

The muggy atmosphere and the sound of contented chewing helped calm Joyce's nerves. 'Easy does it,' she murmured to the cow in the first stall. She went in and set down her stool and bucket. Then, leaning her shoulder and head against the cow's bulging flank, she reached for the udder and squeezed. 'Stand still, there's a good girl. Nice and easy does it.'

The cow stood patiently while the milk flowed. It was only when her udder ran dry that Joyce thought to ask herself where she should take the full pail. Was there a dairy room next door, perhaps? She lifted the bucket and carried it out of the straw-lined stall towards a connecting door, laid her hand on the latch and was surprised when it seemed to open of its own accord.

Alma stood in her long skirt and calico apron, offering to take the bucket.

'Right you are.' Joyce recovered and handed it over. 'I was hoping this door led to the dairy.'

A glance over Alma's shoulder revealed a small, clean room with a concrete floor and scrubbed stone tables. There was machinery for bottling the milk and for scalding churns and pails – seemingly the only up-to-date concessions to an age-old routine.

Alma turned away. She carried the bucket to the table, obviously expecting Joyce to go straight back to the second cow, which she did. It wasn't long before all three were milked and mucked out – still without a word from Laurence's young wife.

Joyce grew more and more puzzled. Yes, she could see that Alma had suffered a bad accident in the past and the resulting scars would cast a shadow over anyone's life. She understood her self-consciousness and her reluctance to meet the eye of a stranger. But there was a good deal of anger in these silences; Joyce judged this by the set of Alma's mouth and the quick way she turned her head – an impatient toss that propelled her about her resentful business.

How old might she be? Joyce wondered after she delivered the last pail into the dairy and stood watching Alma scour out an empty churn. *Twenty-five at the most. More likely twenty-two. A good twenty years younger than her husband, at any rate. When did they marry? And why? What happened to Laurence's first wife, the mother of the absent Gordon?*

Alma came to the end of her bottling and scouring.

'That didn't take long,' Joyce said as pleasantly as she could. 'What happens now? Do we drive the milk into Shawcross to be picked up?'

The reply came in the shape of tightly pressed lips and a quick shake of the head.

Maybe she can't speak because of the accident. Is that it?

Alma could hear well enough, though; she picked up the sound of footsteps crossing the yard before Joyce did and hurried to the door of the dairy.

Laurence hove into view. 'Have you finished?' he asked Alma, who nodded. He turned his attention to Joyce. 'I want us to bring a ewe down off the crag,' he informed her. 'There's just time before it gets dark.'

She followed obediently, almost running to keep up. The rain hammered down hard again as they left the dogs in their kennel then bent their heads against the wind and climbed rapidly, soon reaching the outcrop that gave the farm its name. Close to, it was a forbidding sight; some fifty feet high with a sheer face and deep fissures running from top to bottom. Rain gusted against the cliff and spattered in puddles at its base. From there, fast-running trickles formed a stream that made its way down the steep hillside. There was a bleating cry for help from above so Joyce looked up to make out a single sheep tightly wedged between two rocks.

'Do we have to climb up there?' she asked in alarm. If so, there was a high risk of one of them losing their footing on the slippery rock and crashing down.

Laurence shook his head. 'I know an easier way round the back. Follow me.'

So they crossed the stream, then skirted the crag to find a sloping route across which they could scramble. From there, they looked down on the ewe and worked out their descent. Meanwhile, what was left of the daylight faded until they could scarcely see where to put their feet.

'Five minutes should do it,' Laurence reckoned.

He went first, picking his way in the gloom and sending showers of loose stones down the cliff. When he reached the sheep he turned to wait for Joyce.

'Now what?' she asked when she arrived.

'You see this loose boulder? Wait for me to shift it a few inches to one side then grab her front legs and heave as hard as you can.' He squatted and rested his shoulder against the rock that trapped the back end of the ewe. He grunted as he pushed.

Joyce squeezed on to the ledge beside him. She had to kneel to reach the sheep, afraid that if she leaned too far forward she would lose her balance and go toppling down.

Laurence pushed with all his might.

Joyce managed to hook her arms under the sheep's front legs and take her weight. The stench of wet fleece and excrement caught in her throat but with one almighty tug the ewe was free.

Laurence exhaled loudly as he eased the boulder down. The freed sheep kicked out with her back legs. She twisted in Joyce's grasp and broke away, bounding up the slope without a backward glance and obviously none the worse for wear.

Standing close to Joyce on the narrow ledge, Laurence watched his sheep run. 'Daft sod,' was all he said as they made their way back down to the farm.

'Just listen to that racket!' Dorothy's complaint about their goat's deafening bray brought her conversation with Brenda to an end. 'Lord knows why we keep the blinking thing, except that we get a pound or two of cheese from it on the sly. Keep that under your hat, by the way.'

The clattering of hooves across the yard drew Brenda towards the door. 'Maybe I should go out and lend a hand?'

'Don't bother; Dad can manage.'

Dorothy's lack of concern put Brenda in a tricky position; on the one hand she felt it was her role to help Bernard with the runaway goat, on the other it didn't seem tactful to override Dorothy.

'I mean it,' she insisted in a light, firm voice. 'Honestly, if I had a shilling for every time Dad has had to fetch the silly thing back, I'd be rich.'

So Brenda hovered at the threshold, listening to the shed door bang shut after Bernard had led the

Houdini goat inside, followed by the kerfuffle of chickens clucking and flapping.

'He's not the only one who gets lumbered,' Dorothy went on. 'Evelyn has done her fair share of bringing Nancy home after she's wandered off.'

'Nancy?'

'The goat. Black as night, British Alpine; eats us out of house and home. Evelyn's been a big help, though. She's a Land Girl like you. Or at least she cuts down trees.'

'A lumberjill with the Women's Timber Corps? We met her in the village.' Brenda got a word in edgeways before Dorothy cantered gaily on.

'Of course I'm not much use – that goes without saying. Not like Evelyn. She steps in here whenever she can, depending on whether or not she's needed at the castle. She'll feed the hens and turn her hand to anything really. But then Dad decided it wasn't fair on her, working here after doing a full day for old man Weatherall. We'd be better off with full-time help. That's when he applied to the Land Army county office – and lo and behold!' She whisked the tea towel towards Brenda, like a magician producing a rabbit out of a top hat.

Exhausted by Dorothy's babble, Brenda made her excuses. 'I'm a bit tired, to tell you the truth. If you don't mind, I'd like to see my room.'

'Right you are.' Instead of showing Brenda upstairs as expected, Dorothy flung the towel over the back of the chair and went to call her father. 'Dad, Brenda wants to see where she'll be staying.'

'Rightio.' Bernard clomped in muddy boots across the yard to the kitchen door. 'It's not much,' he warned. 'No electric out there and only a paraffin stove for warmth, but at least it doesn't let the rain in. Put your coat on; bring your things.'

Brenda gathered that her billet wasn't in the main house; even so, she wasn't prepared for what she found when she followed Bernard around the side of the house and he flung open the door to a decommissioned railway goods wagon, miles from the nearest line, minus its wheels and raised eighteen inches above ground on piles of bricks.

'I said it was a bit rough and ready,' he reminded her. 'But Dorothy thought you'd be better off with a room of your own, rather than having to share with her.'

Brenda climbed two wooden steps into the wagon to see a simple, narrow bed next to a pine washstand, with a paraffin stove near the door. The stove reeked and there was a worn rug on the floor but no windows to let in daylight.

'It's where we put the lads who came spud-picking every winter until the war put a stop to it,' he explained.

Good Lord above; I'm to live in a railway wagon! Words failed Brenda and her heart sank as she stood, suitcase in hand. Nancy the goat brayed and kicked from inside her barn, sheep bleated high on the hill and rain fell furiously as if Noah's flood was come at last.

CHAPTER FIVE

'Oh Joyce, what have we let ourselves in for?' Brenda's wailing cry when she and Joyce met at the Cross Keys next evening was heartfelt. 'Come back, Ma Craven and Mrs Mostyn! Come back, Fieldhead – all is forgiven!'

Ensconced in a quiet corner of the plainly furnished Snug, within a few feet of a blazing coal fire, Joyce sipped her glass of shandy. 'As bad as that, is it?'

'Worse. I'm living in an old goods wagon with a goat for a neighbour. The blasted cockerel woke me up at half five and my first job of the day was to go out and shoot a rabbit then skin it for tonight's supper. It was downhill from there. I mean it: what have we done?'

'We've branched out, that's what.' Joyce was glad she'd made an effort to tidy herself up and put on her decent, caramel-coloured woollen dress and a pair of brown court shoes before she'd come out to meet Brenda. It made her feel better in herself and hopefully made a good impression on her neighbours gathered around the bar where Evelyn served drinks.

'Branched out into what?' Brenda too had dressed to impress in a pair of high-waisted black slacks and a white rayon blouse with a wide collar and a frill down the front. The smart outfits had done the trick, to judge by the number of heads that had turned as the two new girls entered the pub.

'Who knows?' Joyce sympathized with Brenda's gripes. 'But if Garthside turns out not to be up to spec, you could always apply to Mrs Mostyn for another transfer.'

'Or I could stick it out.' The idea of giving in so soon went against the grain. 'Mr Huby is a decent sort and I'm sure I can make the place more homely with a few cushions and an ornament or two.' Tapping her fingers determinedly against the table, Brenda saw Dorothy enter the smoky bar with a tall, casually dressed man wearing a tweed jacket and pale green open-necked shirt. The clean-cut, dark-haired companion guided her to a seat in the corner then went to the bar.

'Likewise,' Joyce agreed. 'A few pictures and ornaments will work wonders.' She kept to herself any doubts about Laurence Bradley's uncompromising manner and her predicament with his silent, resentful young wife. Instead, she told Brenda about the letter she'd begun to write to Edgar. 'I tried to describe my little attic room to him – my nest in the rafters, as I call it. He likes to hear about everyday things.'

'I'll bet he hangs on every word.' Brenda acknowledged Edgar Kershaw's unswerving devotion to Joyce. She was sure it carried him through nightly air raids over Germany and sustained him in the thick of ack-ack fire and Messerschmitt attacks. She also recognized how terribly hard it was for Joyce to stay calm whilst knowing the danger he faced. 'I wish I could say the same about Les.'

'Come off it; Les is head over heels.'

'So you say.' Brenda wasn't so sure.

'He is. He went against his family to get engaged to you. He gave you his mother's precious engagement ring.'

Brenda stared wistfully at the diamond ring presently adorning the third finger of her left hand. 'Then why doesn't he write?' It had been more than three weeks since she'd received a letter.

'Perhaps he can't; we've no idea what top-secret missions the Navy sends him on, or if he's free to write and receive letters from loved ones back home. Does he even know that Hettie is poorly, for instance?'

Brenda shook her head. 'But he'll find out when and if he comes home on leave this weekend. And hopefully I'll see him on Saturday, if I can get Mr Huby to give me the morning off.'

'Get Mr Huby to do what?' Dorothy had spotted Brenda and floated across with her young man in tow. She barged in on the tail end of the conversation between Brenda and Joyce.

Brenda blushed and quickly made the introductions. 'I'm hoping to get back to Burnside on Saturday,' she explained evasively. 'There are a few things I'd like to pick up.'

'Including her trusty motor bike,' Joyce added.

'You don't say?' Dorothy's good-looking friend pricked up his ears. 'What type of bike is it?'

'It's a Sloper; nothing fancy but it gets me around.' Brenda would have been happy to embark on a discussion about engine sizes and top speeds but Dorothy was having none of it.

'But have you thought how you'll get down there?' she interrupted, one eyebrow cocked in the direction of her mechanically minded companion. 'There's no bus on Saturday. And it's too far for Shanks's pony.'

'I don't mind dropping you off,' the young man volunteered, hands in jacket pockets and looking with interest from Brenda to Joyce then back again. 'I have to drive Dot into town anyway.'

For a second the offer took Brenda aback. She glanced at Dorothy to check that she had no objection.

'Oh, no!' Dorothy instantly interpreted the puzzled look then giggled. 'You don't think . . . ?' She pointed at the volunteer driver then poked herself in the chest. 'Him and me? Oh dear, no!'

He took his hands out of his pockets and stepped forward. 'Come on, Dot; do the honours.'

'Brenda, Joyce, meet my brother Cliff. He often gives me a lift into Northgate at the weekend. It wouldn't be putting him out at all.'

The ice was broken and soon it was all arranged – Cliff Huby would call at Garthside on Saturday morning. Dorothy and Brenda had better be ready – Cliff knew what Dorothy was like, always faffing about and having to go back for things. They were both sure that their dad wouldn't mind if Brenda stayed away overnight and rode her bike back to Garthside on Sunday. That would give Brenda plenty of time to catch up with old friends.

'I'll see you at eight o'clock sharp,' Cliff said before he strolled away.

Dorothy sat down at Joyce and Brenda's table. 'That was a stroke of luck, eh?'

Brenda nodded in agreement. 'It means I can write to Les later tonight and make a proper arrangement to see him.'

Dorothy caught sight of a portly man in a dog collar and quickly lost interest in Brenda's arrangements. 'What's that God-botherer doing in here?' she asked in a peevish voice.

'He's handing out leaflets, by the look of it.' Joyce too was interested in the arrival of the vicar. After offering to buy Dorothy and Brenda a drink, she went to the bar and listened in.

'I'd be obliged if you'd pin one of these on your noticeboard.' The clergyman slid a leaflet across the bar top and Evelyn took it. 'It gives a list of times for my Christmas services. I'm letting people know well in advance this year.'

'I can certainly ask Fred,' Evelyn replied in a rather offhand way before turning to Joyce. 'What can I get you?'

'Three shandies, please.'

'I'm sure Fred will have no objection.' The stout vicar took up a lot of space at the crowded bar. His smile was broad, his face plump and shiny. 'The landlord here is most obliging when it comes to church notices.'

Evelyn raised her eyebrows at Joyce who squeezed forward to collect her drinks. 'How's the new lad, Mr Rigg?' she asked as she slid the drinks across the bar.

'He's settling in a treat, thank you, Evelyn. Unfortunately his mother forgot to pack a spare pair of pyjamas but he has everything else he needs.'

'That's good. It's a pity he's the only evacuee in the village, though. He could have done with a pal to keep him company.'

Walter Rigg's smile didn't waver. 'Nothing is perfect during these difficult days but we must all count our blessings. Alan is ten times safer here than he was in Millwood; that's why his mother sent him and his sister to live in the country.'

'A sister, you say?'

'Five years older than Alan, apparently. She's gone to live with a family in Attercliffe. I would have had them both at the vicarage, except that it might not have seemed – shall we say – proper for a single gentleman to take in a girl of her age.'

'Fair enough.' Evelyn turned away to serve another customer.

Joyce frowned to herself. It wasn't what the vicar said so much as his self-satisfied, holier-than-thou air that bothered her. She took her drinks and returned to her table where she found Dorothy alone and twiddling her thumbs. 'Where's Brenda got to?' she asked.

'Cliff came back and collared her. He took her outside to show her his pride and joy. His jalopy,' she explained. 'Lord knows why he thinks Brenda would be interested.'

'You don't know Brenda. Anything mechanical is bound to grab her attention.' Needing a break from the smoky atmosphere, Joyce nipped outside to tell Brenda that her drink was waiting. She heard

Cliff's voice drift across the unlit green then spotted a small figure sitting alone on the worn steps surrounding the village cross. 'Alan?' she said as she walked towards him.

The boy jumped up and backed away.

'It's all right, you haven't done anything wrong. Do you remember me from our bus ride? My name's Joyce. I was wondering why you were sitting outside in the cold.'

'Waiting for the vicar.' Wrapped up as before in mackintosh, school cap and long socks, with his bare, bony knees on view, his pale face looked pinched and miserable. 'He's delivering leaflets.'

'Yes, I've seen him. But couldn't you have stayed in the vicarage where it's nice and warm?'

'I didn't want to be there by myself.'

'Why not?'

'I just didn't.'

'Does Mr Rigg know that you're waiting here?'

Alan shook his head.

'What is it about the house?' Joyce's heart went out to the lonely boy.

Struggling to hold back tears, he tried to explain. 'I can see the graveyard from my bedroom.'

'Ah, so that's it.'

'There's a white angel on one of the graves.'

'The angel won't harm you, Alan. It's carved out of stone.'

'I saw it move – last night in the dark.'

Joyce resisted the impulse to smile. 'I don't think so. I think you must have imagined that. But couldn't you ask Mr Rigg to put you in a different room? It's a big house – I'm sure there are plenty to choose from.'

'I daren't.'

'Why not?'

'He might tell me off.' The weight of the world rested on the boy's shoulders and he gave way to tears.

Joyce offered him her hankie. 'I could put in a word for you. Would you like that?'

'No.' He was adamant through his sniffles. 'I'll just keep the curtains closed so I don't have to look out of the window.'

'All right. But listen to me, you'll catch your death of cold if you stay out here much longer. Why not come and sit with me in the porch outside the pub? Let me buy you a bag of crisps. I'll keep you company for a little while.'

The crisps did it. Slowly Alan nodded and they walked together across the wet grass, bumping into Brenda and Cliff as they finished admiring his Morris Minor.

'It's what they call chummy,' Cliff was explaining. 'In other words, a tight squeeze for four people. There's only a three-speed gearbox. It cost me thirty-two pounds ten shillings second hand – I had to save my pennies for a whole year to scrape that together. Mind you, it's coming up to thirteen years old so I might have to start saving all over again.'

Brenda was interested in every detail, particularly the cost of keeping the car on the road. 'Most working men can't afford to,' she pointed out.

'Living in at the castle helps because there's no rent for me to find. But I don't get paid any overtime, no matter how many extra hours I put in. Old Weatherall is a tight-fisted bugger – excuse my French.'

'What about getting the engine serviced?'

'I do that myself. I learned how to fettle a tractor engine off my dad. It's not such a big jump from that to looking after a car. There's still tyres to buy, though. And petrol and oil.'

Joyce saw that Cliff and Brenda had instantly hit it off. The usual alarm bell rang inside her head; Brenda tended to sail through life with a kind of breezy innocence that could and sometimes did give the wrong impression.

Cliff held the door open for Brenda while Joyce settled Alan on a bench inside the porch. 'I won't be long,' she told him before following Brenda inside. She quickly linked arms with her and whisked her away from Cliff towards their table. 'Madam, your shandy awaits,' she told her. 'Drink up while I go and buy Alan a bag of crisps.'

Two shandies later, with the boy still safely ensconced in the porch, both Joyce and Brenda had started to let their hair down. They sat back in their chairs and their faces were wreathed in smiles as Dorothy came up with racy questions about their lives as Land Girls.

'How is it, living in a girls-only set-up?' she wanted to know. 'I'll bet you there are cat fights every now and then.'

'Sometimes, if a lipstick goes missing, or a pair of socks,' Joyce admitted.

'Most of the rows are over who's used all the hot water,' Brenda added. 'Then all hell is let loose.'

'Miaow!' Dorothy said with an eager grin as she turned to include Evelyn who was winding down after her stint at the bar. 'Come and sit with us,' she ordered. 'Now, Brenda, what about men? Are they allowed into the hostels?'

'Not officially. But there's such a thing as a fire escape, if you know what I'm getting at. Or else you can ask for a late pass and have a high old time at dances put on by the RAF boys. That's what me and my pals used to do when I was doing my training at a new hostel outside Rixley.'

Dorothy's eyes widened in her round, rosy face. 'So it's not all tractor driving and ditch digging?'

'Far from it.' Brenda shook her head. 'This past year I managed to get engaged in amongst the muck and the drudgery. How about you, Evelyn? Did you snag a good-looking soldier or sailor before you joined the Timber Corps?'

Evelyn gave a stiff smile. 'Do me a favour! I'm only just turned twenty. Why would I want to tie myself down at my age?'

Joyce sensed some unease behind the bravado. 'So how did you end up here?' she asked.

Evelyn adjusted the green silk scarf that she wore round her neck. It set off her copper-coloured hair and made a striking contrast to the grey tailored jacket that she wore over dark slacks. 'The same as you, I suppose. I wanted to learn new things so I enrolled on a forestry course. I expected them to send me to Scotland after I got my certificate in July, but instead they kept me closer to home. I've been based at the Acklam Castle estate for four months now.'

'Isn't that where your brother works?' Brenda asked Dorothy, who nodded between sips of shandy.

Evelyn barely paused. 'Acklam suits me down to

the ground. Weatherall's last forestry man was called up into the Merchant Navy earlier in the year, which means that I manage the woodland without anyone breathing down my neck.'

'It's a wonder how you girls do it,' Dorothy said with a self-deprecating sigh. She smoothed out the wrinkles in her pale blue skirt then tweaked the collar of her white satin blouse. 'I'd never have believed a woman could have the strength to cut down trees – or drive tractors, for that matter. Then there's the scything in summer and ploughing in winter. It's a blooming miracle, if you ask me.'

Evelyn shrugged. 'Just because we've never been allowed to do it before now doesn't mean we weren't always capable.'

'The test will be whether or not we're allowed to keep on doing it when the men come back after the war.' Brenda hit the nail on the head as usual. 'What do you think, Joyce? Will girls be treated as equal now that we've proved we can do anything a man can do?'

'Let's hope so.' Joyce held back from predicting the future. 'If there's any fairness in the world, we will.'

'We'll have to get out the old Ouija board and see if we can find out.' Brenda turned the conversation in a more light-hearted direction.

'Ooh, yes please!' Dorothy gave a delighted squeal at the prospect.

'Or, better still, go on a day trip to Blackpool and ask Gypsy Rose Lee,' Evelyn suggested.

Joyce took a deep swallow of her shandy then quizzed Evelyn. 'This Weatherall chap that you mentioned; tell me more.' As ever, she was keen to learn all she could about her new surroundings.

'What is there to say? If you can call a man a fossil, that just about sums up Colonel Weatherall. Crusty, dusty, dried up, ancient . . .'

'We get the picture,' Brenda said with a laugh. 'And what about the estate? Is there an actual castle?'

'Yes, what's left of one; more like a heap of old stones, really.' Evelyn drank swiftly to catch up with the others. 'The colonel moulders away in the only part of the building that still has a roof while the rest falls down around his ears. One of these days I expect to find him buried under a heap of rubble.'

'And wouldn't that be a blessing?' Dorothy giggled.

'You two will have to come over to Acklam one Sunday,' Evelyn suggested to Joyce and Brenda. 'It's a mile and a half as the crow flies, a bit further by road.'

'We will,' Brenda agreed. 'After this weekend I'll have the use of my motor bike, touch wood.'

It was agreed; there would be a visit early in December, before the weather got too grim. They made the arrangement as the landlord called last orders.

'That's too bad.' Brenda shivered as she pictured the chilly goods wagon that she now called home. Then she glanced around the cosy, crowded Snug, at the assembled company of farmers old and young, all in flat caps and tweed jackets, nursing the cloudy remains of their pints of bitter. Walter Rigg was still there, brandy glass in hand, chatting with the landlord, Fred Williams, who was in shirtsleeves and braces, methodically wiping glasses as he waited for the place to empty.

'Before we go out into the cold, let's have one last drink.' Evelyn stood up to go to the bar.

'And while we're waiting, why not play a little game?' Dorothy suggested.

Happy to comply, Joyce and Brenda looked around for a set of dominoes or a pack of playing cards.

'No, not that kind of game; I mean a wishing game.'

'Rightio.' Joyce's reaction to Dorothy's whimsical idea was cautious.

'It goes like this . . .' Dorothy rose tipsily to her feet. The bottom of her blouse had come untucked from the waistband of her skirt, her lipstick was smudged and an unruly curl of brown hair fell over her forehead. 'Pretend I'm a magician. I can wave my magic wand and grant you any wish you want. Now you have to tell me what that wish would be.'

'Any wish at all?' Brenda was thrown. Half a dozen ideas came to mind – *I wish I had a room with a fire and an easy chair. I wish the weather wasn't so blooming cold. I wish Les would write to me more often.*

'Yes – a proper Christmas wish,' Dorothy insisted. 'Do you hear that, Evelyn? We're all going to share a special wish to end the evening.'

'That's easy.' Evelyn's answer came in an instant as she handed out the drinks. 'I wish they would pay me a man's wage for the man's work I do.'

'Hear, hear!' Brenda and Joyce cried.

'What's that got to do with Christmas?' Dorothy popped her lips then went on to share her festive dream. 'On Christmas Day I wish Dad, Cliff and I could sit down to a big fat turkey with all the trimmings. I wish we girls could all go on an outing to Millwood to watch *Aladdin*. I wish—'

'Hold your horses; you said one each.' Joyce leaned across the table to put a steadying hand on Dorothy's arm. 'Would you like to hear mine?'

'Yes!' Dorothy joined in with Evelyn and Brenda's raucous cries.

'Then here it is. I wish that all our loved ones, our nearest and dearest whoever they are and wherever they may be, can stay out of harm's way until the war is finally won and they come safely back home. There; how's that?'

'Perfect,' Brenda said as she raised her glass and looked from Joyce to Evelyn and then to Dorothy. 'All four of us will drink to that!'

CHAPTER SIX

'Get Dawson to take a look at Flint's back leg while you're at it,' Laurence told Joyce when his two collies jumped eagerly into the back of the Land-Rover, expecting to be put to work as usual.

In fact, Joyce was about to drive to the vet's surgery in Shawcross to pick up a bottle of disinfectant that they needed for a cow's infected teat.

'Right you are,' she replied as she turned on the engine.

She'd worked for four days at Black Crag Farm without a single please or thank-you, penning dozens of Swaledales to check the feet of ones that were lame, milking cows and mucking out the cowshed. She'd bottled and sterilized, dug a ditch and hacked away at a hawthorn hedge. She'd taken the work in her stride, but at the end of each day she'd climbed the wooden steps to her attic quarters and fallen into bed exhausted. She'd slept soundly and woken in the morning to the sound of a door opening then clicking shut on the landing below, followed by Laurence's brisk footfall and the more distant sound of tap water running into the kitchen sink.

Even though it was still dark, this was Joyce's signal

to get up and dressed. Then she would descend the stairs and pass the two doorways on the landing, down more stairs, across the kitchen and straight out into the unlit farmyard without so much as a hello from Laurence. There were the three cows to be milked, and only after that a cup of tea and a bite to eat. By this time Alma would be up, making porridge and setting out the breakfast things. She would nod at Joyce but not speak, turning away her damaged face to pay attention to Laurence's orders for the day: sweep the floors, clean out the fire grates, wash and iron, polish, bake. Alma would nod then quietly set about her tasks.

Joyce had observed the ill-matched couple without comment, though sometimes her hackles would rise at the control Laurence held over his wife's routine.

'You're not to bake scones this week,' he had told Alma on Friday morning. 'We're out of dried eggs and raisins.'

Alma had frowned, as if about to argue. Then she'd glanced at Joyce and remained silent, her face reddening as she retied her apron strings into a tighter bow before clattering dirty dishes into the sink.

If that's marriage, give me the single life any day, Joyce concluded. In any case, she was sure she would never agree to marry a man like Laurence Bradley, who was the opposite of her own fiancé. Edgar never dished out orders; he was a sensitive, devoted and kindly soul.

Glad that she'd posted a letter to him in time for the end-of-week collection, she now looked forward to receiving his reply.

'On second thoughts, leave Patch here with me.'

Laurence changed his mind just as Joyce was about to pull out of the yard. He whistled the black-and-white dog, which leaped down from the Land-Rover and went to sit quietly at his master's feet. 'Afterwards, you and Flint can join us at Mary's Fall.'

Glad of a short respite away from the farm, Joyce set off with the grey speckled Border collie. Last night and again this morning she'd noticed a reduced yield in one of the cows and discovered that her teat was swollen. Laurence had given her the name and address of the local vet: Geoffrey Dawson, New Hall, Riverside, Shawcross. 'Tell him we won't waste his time by fetching him out. We just need the disinfectant. Be as quick as you can.'

So Joyce drove down into the valley under a blue sky, glad that this was Saturday and a half day off but remembering that Brenda had already made plans for the weekend so she would have to entertain herself, unless she walked the mile and a half to the Acklam Castle estate to see if Evelyn was at a loose end. Joyce didn't think that their new acquaintance would object to an unannounced visit but she would wait and see if the good weather held before she finally decided.

Soon the village came into view; first the square church tower and then the vicarage and church hall facing on to the green. Joyce negotiated a sharp bend then came to a narrow packhorse bridge over a stream before levelling out for the final approach into Shawcross. As she arrived, she noticed Walter Rigg emerge from his house with Alan trailing forlornly behind. The vicar said something to the boy who ran back into the house and emerged on to the driveway carrying his coat, which he put on as the vicar started his car. Alan pulled his cap from his pocket then got in. As he did so, a piece of white paper fell to the ground. A gust of wind caught it and blew it on to the green.

The vicar's black Ford had already disappeared along the Burnside road before Joyce had time to stop the Land-Rover and jump out to retrieve what turned out to be a letter beginning, *Dear Mummy and Daddy*.

Making a mental note to keep the paper safe, she put it in her pocket then drove on slowly past the row of cottages, looking out for a narrow turn that ought to take her to New Hall. Sure enough, a rutted track ran down the side of the cottages towards the river where there was another bridge and on the far bank a substantial Queen Anne house with long windows to either side of an impressive doorway overlooking wide lawns and backed by mature oak trees.

As the Land-Rover slowed for the bridge, Flint crept forward to join Joyce. He slunk on to the passenger seat and peered through the windscreen, pink tongue lolling and ears pricked.

'You recognize where we are and why we've come, is that it?' she said with a laugh. 'Stay!' she told him. 'I'll come and fetch you in a minute.'

She went straight to the front door then glanced down at her muddy boots and hesitated; perhaps there was a tradesmen's entrance she should use? So she tramped along the front of the house and was about to disappear round the side when the front door opened and a man appeared. He was about thirty; tall and rangy, casually dressed in slacks and checked shirt with rolled-back sleeves. His hair was almost black and he had dark, deep-set eyes.

'Can I help you?' he called to Joyce.

She strode back. 'I'm looking for Mr Dawson.'

'Well, you've found him.' He came down the steps with his hand outstretched, taking in her uniform. 'You're in the Land Army, I presume?'

'Yes. I'm Joyce Cutler. I work for Mr Bradley at Black Crag Farm.'

'Lucky you,' he said with a slight rise of his eyebrows before glancing towards the Land-Rover. 'Well, Miss Cutler, who have you got in there with you?'

'That's Flint. He's gone lame.'

'Has he, now?'

'Yes, but the main reason I'm here is to ask you for some disinfectant for one of our cows' teats. We've run out.'

'I take it she has a touch of mastitis?' Geoffrey Dawson walked with Joyce around the side of the house. 'I run the surgery from an extension round the back. Are you sure you don't want me to come out to Black Crag and take a look?'

Joyce shook her head. 'Mr Bradley gave me strict instructions to ask for the disinfectant, nothing else.'

There was no comment from the young vet as he led her into a single-storey building constructed much more recently than the original house. Inside there was a spotlessly clean reception area leading to a treatment room and a smaller side room containing shelves stacked with medicines and surgical paraphernalia.

Geoffrey picked out a ridged brown bottle and

handed it to Joyce. 'Use this on all the teats and on the other cows in the shed as well. Do it thoroughly after every milking. I don't need to tell you that mastitis is highly infectious and it can be tricky to clear up.'

Joyce promised to follow his instructions. 'I'm better with sheep than cows,' she confessed. 'I grew up with them on my father's farm. As far as cows are concerned, I'm learning on the job.'

Geoffrey listened attentively with his head to one side, a wayward lick of dark hair sticking upright on his crown. He liked the look of the new Land Girl with the cheerful, open expression and clear grey eyes set off by the forward tilt of her brimmed hat. 'Have you got time for a cup of tea before I examine the dog?'

'Yes, if you can make it a quick one.'

She followed him through a door that linked the surgery to the main house and they entered a spacious, well-equipped kitchen with a large window overlooking a garden where there was an apple orchard that had been pruned back in readiness for winter. Joyce admired the view while Geoffrey made the tea.

'How are you getting along with our friend, Laurence Bradley?' he asked as he handed her a steaming mug.

'Well enough, thank you.' Discreet as always, she took her first sip.

'He doesn't work you too hard?'

'No. I can get by, ta.'

'Good for you.' Geoffrey stood beside her at the window.

'Who looks after your garden?' Joyce admired some neat rows of cabbages and Brussels sprouts.

'I do most of it myself. Evelyn Newbold lends a hand with the orchard when she has time. She belongs to the Timber Corps. You've met her, I suppose?'

'Yes, twice.' Aware of the time slipping by, Joyce cut the conversation short. 'Shall we look at the dog while the tea cools?'

So they went outside to the Land-Rover and Geoffrey cast an expert eye over Flint. He spoke quietly as he felt the joints of the affected leg for any swelling then examined the soft pads of the foot. 'Take it easy, old chap. I'm not going to hurt you. Aha, here we are!' He showed Joyce an ulcerated area oozing with pus partly concealed by fur. 'It most likely started with a small cut that became infected. The best thing to do is to soak the foot in hot water then poultice it. I'll give you some antiseptic ointment to apply before you bandage it. The poor chap will have to be kept off work for a few days.'

Joyce nodded. 'I'll let Mr Bradley know.'

'Tea?' he reminded her after he'd given Joyce the disinfectant and the antiseptic ointment and she'd returned Flint to the front seat of the Land-Rover.

'If I'm really quick.'

Back in the kitchen, the probing continued. 'How's Alma Bradley? Have you had much to do with her?'

'Not really.'

'But she's hale and hearty?'

'She seems to be.'

'I'm glad.'

'Why do you ask?'

'You mean, why don't I mind my own business?'

Geoffrey turned to the sink with an apologetic shrug. 'I'm sorry for putting you on the spot; it's just that no one in the village has seen hide nor hair of Alma since the wedding back in August. We're all a little bit worried about her.'

'I see.'

'I'm sorry; it's not like me to encourage gossip.' He seemed genuinely embarrassed as he took Joyce's empty cup. 'The thing is, Alma doesn't have family in the village. She'd lived away from Shawcross for a long time so the marriage to Laurence took everyone by surprise.'

'How old is she?' Joyce asked in spite of her earlier reticence.

'Twenty-two. Has she told you what happened to her face?'

Joyce opened her eyes wide. 'You mean Alma can speak?'

Geoffrey nodded. 'If she wants to, she can. She stood in front of the vicar and said "I do" as clear as a bell.'

'Her face?' Curiosity again got the better of Joyce and she returned to the mystery of Alma's scars. 'Was it a fire?'

'Yes, when she was eight years old. She lived with her family on a smallholding half a mile downriver from here. The whole house burned to the ground. I was home from veterinary college for the Christmas holidays when it happened so I remember it well. Alma was the only one who came out alive.'

'But she can talk.' Alma's choice to remain silent was a conundrum that Joyce couldn't solve. 'Thanks, Mr Dawson. I appreciate you telling me.'

He nodded and accompanied her through the surgery out into the yard. 'Let's do away with the formalities,' he said as they shook hands again. 'Call me Geoff and, if you don't mind, I'll drop the Miss Cutler.'

'Thanks, Geoff,' she said with a smile. 'And by all means, call me Joyce.'

He returned the smile and tapped the bottle of disinfectant tucked under her arm. 'Twice a day, morning and evening. If it doesn't do the trick, tell Laurence he'll have to stump up for a visit from me, like it or not.'

Joyce began the drive back to Black Crag Farm by sifting through the facts she'd learned about Laurence and Alma's unusual situation. She was preoccupied as she crossed the river but when she emerged on to the village green and saw Walter Rigg's Ford car parked outside the vicarage, she suddenly remembered Alan's letter. She would drop it off with its owner, she decided. But she fumbled as she put on the handbrake and the letter fluttered from her pocket down on to the muddy floor.

Oh dear; Alan will have to write it out again on a clean sheet of paper, Joyce thought as she retrieved it and smoothed it flat.

Dear Mummy and Daddy

The blue ink was smudged, the crumpled paper smeared with mud.

I am settling quite well here in Shawcross. I miss you a lot.

The next part was illegible so Joyce had to pick up the thread two lines further down.

> How are you both? Well, I hope you are getting on all right without me and Judith. My foster father is Mr Rigg. He is very cheerful.

More smudges marred the next short section. Then Joyce read:

> It is really quiet here. I will have to go to school in the next village, which is called Thwaite. The house that I live in is called The Vicarage. It has four master bedrooms. There is a graveyard with a white angel outside my window. It is quite lonely here. I really miss you and I wish you were here.
>
> Love from your best son,
>
> Alan

Perfectly punctuated, written in laborious, joined-up handwriting, the letter touched Joyce deeply. *Poor little lamb, trying to be brave yet obviously longing to be at home with his family.*

Home was Millwood, where the bombs dropped with fierce regularity on the mills manufacturing cloth for army uniforms, where sensible, self-sacrificing parents chose to ship their children off to the countryside with gas masks strapped around their slight shoulders, their belongings clearly labelled. Sent off to be with strangers and to cry bitter, homesick tears, and in Alan's case to look out over a graveyard stacked with dead bodies, guarded by a stone angel.

'Poor little lamb,' Joyce said out loud.

She walked up the vicarage path and knocked on the door. The vicar appeared minus his dog collar and in shirtsleeves, his belly barely restrained by belt and braces. He beamed at Joyce as he took Alan's letter and she caught a glimpse of the boy hovering nervously at the bottom of the stairs.

'That's most kind, most thoughtful.' Walter scanned the contents. 'Oh, it says here that I'm very cheerful, eh? That's nice to know.' The smile faded as he reached the end. 'Lonely? Yes, I suppose it must be. But never mind, Alan; we all have our crosses to bear.'

The door closed with a firm click and Joyce felt uncomfortable as she returned to the Land-Rover. 'Now then, Flint, I hope Mr Rigg doesn't blame Alan over the loneliness remark,' she said to the dog by her side. 'After all, that wouldn't be fair, would it?'

'You can drop me outside the Blacksmith's Arms,' Brenda told Cliff Huby from the back seat of his Morris Minor as he drove her and Dorothy into Burnside that Saturday morning. 'Mr Kershaw gave me permission to leave Old Sloper in a shed behind the forge. He said I could pick her up any time. Yes, just here is champion. Ta very much!'

Everything had gone to plan: Cliff had arrived at Garthside Farm at the appointed time. Dorothy had been almost ready. Cliff had chatted with his father while Brenda had helped Dorothy to choose between two dresses that she might wear for a night out at the flicks. The crimson one with wide shoulder pads or the slim-fitting navy blue one with the kick-pleat at the back? Crimson or navy blue? Dorothy had made Brenda decide. Then, on the journey down the dale, she'd chatted non-stop, galloping off at tangents that included the hardships imposed by clothes rationing, the relief of Malta ('At last!'), Mr Churchill's fat cigar ('Smelly and disgusting!') and the unflattering uniforms that Land Girls were forced to wear.

'I don't know how you put up with those dungaree thingummies,' she'd commiserated with Brenda from the front seat. 'I wouldn't be seen dead in them.'

'Oh, I don't know,' Cliff had chipped in with a quick glance over his shoulder. 'I reckon Brenda might be able to pull them off.'

Dorothy had picked up her brother's sly innuendo and embarrassed Brenda. '"Pull them off!" Oh, I say!'

Cliff had jokily protested his innocence and Brenda had let it go.

'Right here,' she said again as he pulled up in the pub yard. 'Champion, thanks.'

Making an ungainly exit from the cramped vehicle, she said cheerio then waved Cliff and Dorothy on their way. Then, before she had time to gather her wits, Una ran across the road.

'Brenda!' Una flung her arms around her. 'I saw you from Grace's house. Who was that in the car with you? What are you doing here? Have you come back to the hostel? Please say you have.'

'Steady on.' Brenda freed herself and saw Grace standing in her doorway, hands clasped high over her stomach in expectant-mother pose.

Brenda let Una drag her by the hand to say hello. 'I'm here on a flying visit,' she explained. 'Oh, but it is good to see you both. Una, how's Fieldhead?'

'Quiet without you, that's for sure.'

'And Grace, are you looking after yourself properly?'

'Yes, under the orders of you-know-who.'

'Your fire-eating mother-in-law,' Brenda said, quick as a flash.

'Yes,' Grace sighed. '"You must eat, you must rest, don't listen to the News; it will only upset you."'

'She's right about that,' Una pointed out as the happily reunited trio went inside. 'The last I heard, the French navy has had to scuttle its own fleet to keep it out of German hands.'

'Una!' Brenda pretended to put her hands around her neck to throttle her.

Grace laughed. 'I may be expecting a baby but I haven't gone soft in the head. I'm glued to the wireless regardless. How long are you here for, Brenda? Do you have time for a cup of tea?'

'No, I can't stop. I only came to pick up Old Sloper. But quickly, before I go I want to hear the latest about Angelo and Bill.'

'Bill's regiment is being sent to Burma.' Grace's stoical expression disguised her inner turmoil. 'We've been expecting it.'

'I've had a long letter from Angelo.' Una beamed. 'He likes being at the seaside but he misses me.'

'Quite right too!'

'And what about Les?' Grace asked Brenda.

She frowned and looked down at her feet. 'I still

haven't heard from him. But I do know that he's expected home this weekend.'

'That's wonderful,' Una cried.

Grace immediately whisked Brenda towards the door. 'Whatever are you hanging around here for?'

They shooed her out of the house then hurried her across the road. 'Go!' they ordered. 'Get on your bike and ride like the wind!'

Brenda rode the familiar road from Burnside along Swinsty Edge, past Hawkshead then over the grouse moor towards Attercliffe. Speed and the open road thrilled her as much as ever, so that by the time she slowed down for the hairpin bends on her final descent towards Dale End, her spirits were higher than they'd been for a long time.

This is just the job, she thought. *Blue skies, a touch of hoar frost on the hedgerows, not another soul in sight; what could be better?*

The road twisted and narrowed as at last the Whites' grand farmhouse came into view. She braked and felt her heart beat faster. 'Les!' she murmured as she turned into the driveway leading to the house. It was four months since she'd seen her fiancé and almost as many weeks since she'd received a letter. Now the silence would be broken. He would be waiting at a window. He would hear the bike then rush out of the door and wrap his arms around her. She would sink her head against his shoulder and lose herself in his embrace.

Oddly, though, there was no face at any of the windows. The only sign of life was Arnold White's two springer spaniels racing through the open door and circling Brenda's bike as she set it on its stand. They jumped up at her and harried her as she took off her goggles and gauntlets then approached the steps.

'Hello?' she called through the door. The hall was empty, the door into the sitting room closed. 'Is anyone there?'

Arnold came out of his study and called his dogs. There was a whiff of tobacco smoke and a closed look on his face that told Brenda that she wasn't expected or indeed welcome.

She stood on the step, enduring an awkward silence and waiting for Les's father to invite her in. Arnold cleared his throat. He was upright as ever; shoulders back, jaw clenched, immaculate in tweeds with a neatly knotted tie, gleaming gold cufflinks and watch chain. 'Hmm,' he said, before gesturing towards the sitting room then retreating with his dogs into his book-lined room.

Brenda swallowed her disappointment and tapped on the sitting-room door. It was opened by a girl with a thin, serious face. Her brown hair hung in two long plaits tied with tartan ribbons and she wore a hand-knitted fawn jumper under a plain grey pinafore skirt. Her air was shy and apprehensive.

'Hello.' Brenda spoke quietly. Events were not unfolding the way she'd anticipated.

'Is that you, Brenda?' From inside the room Hettie sounded irritated.

Brenda stepped past the girl. 'Yes, here I am, tra-la!'

A fire blazed in the Adam fireplace, making the

room uncomfortably hot. Hettie sat on the sofa with her paisley shawl around her shoulders, her dark hair combed straight back from her handsome face.

'That will do for now, Judith,' she told the girl, who backed out of the room then closed the door. 'Now, Brenda, put your things down over there, out of the way. What do make of our new resident?'

Brenda sat in a chair near the French windows, the coolest spot in the room. She looked around for signs of Les's presence: records taken out of their paper sleeves, ready to be played on the gramophone, or else one of his jackets slung across the back of a chair. 'She seems shy,' she said in answer to Hettie's brusque question. 'Who is she?'

'She's an evacuee. Judith Evans, aged thirteen and three-quarters. The three-quarters are important, apparently. Dad decided on the spur of the moment we should take in a child from Millwood. I know, I know; spontaneous acts of generosity aren't his style. But it's the war. We all have to . . .'

'Do our bit.' Brenda finished the sentence. Hettie seemed weary and had obviously not yet got over her recent illness. 'I have an idea that Joyce and I sat on the bus out to Shawcross with Judith's brother, Alan. He seems a nice little lad – shy like his sister.'

'Judith has good manners, thank goodness.' Hettie frowned then addressed the elephant in the room. 'I suppose you were expecting to see Les?'

Brenda felt her stomach muscles tighten. This was not going to be good news, she realized.

'But as you can see, he's not here. Unfortunately his leave was cancelled at the last minute. Didn't Donald telephone you?'

The knot in Brenda's stomach tightened. 'No, he didn't.'

'Oh dear. I specifically asked him to call, to save you an unnecessary journey. We all feel let down, of course.'

Brenda bit her lip. 'I suppose it can't be helped.' There was to be no Les, no embrace, no outpouring of the complicated emotions pent up inside her. How on earth was she to go on hoping and wishing, dreaming and loving her fiancé without hearing his voice or feeling his lips on hers?

As Brenda tried to bring her emotions under control, Hettie picked up a small bell from the low table in front of her. Its tinkling sound brought Judith back into the room. 'Could you ask Donald to join us, please?' Hettie asked in a prim, precise voice.

Judith disappeared and Brenda endured another tricky silence before Donald put in an appearance. 'Heigh-ho,' he said when he saw a stony-faced Brenda. 'I take it my telephone message didn't reach you?'

'That's right, it didn't.'

'But I did make the call on Thursday morning,' he insisted as he leaned on the back of Hettie's sofa and gave the distinct impression of not altogether regretting his brother's absence. 'As a matter of fact, Brenda, I went to a good deal of trouble on your behalf. First off, I spoke to the warden at Fieldhead who gave me the telephone number for . . . now, what was it? Oh yes, the number for Garthside Farm in Shawcross.'

Brenda did her best not to feel irritated by Donald's teasing manner and to look him steadily in the eye.

'Actually, I was surprised they had a telephone line out there. I called the exchange and the operator put me through to a person answering to the name of Miss Dorothy Huby.'

'You told Dorothy that Les's leave was cancelled?' A flash of anger ran through Brenda.

'Uh-oh, and she didn't pass on the message? That was very naughty of her. Not that we're not glad to see you – isn't that right, Hettie?' Giving his sister a peck on the cheek, he strolled over to lean his elbow on the back of Brenda's chair. His face came to within six inches of hers. 'And now that you're here, what can I get you to drink? Is it too early for your favourite tipple? Dubonnet, isn't it?'

Brenda gave him a withering look. 'No ta, Donald. I won't stop long – I can see that Hettie's tired.'

He turned to look out of the window while Hettie shifted position and rearranged her shawl.

'Why don't you tell Brenda your news, Hettie?' His voice was quiet, his air suddenly distracted. 'She's bound to find out sooner or later.'

His sister's frown deepened and she clutched at the neck of her shawl. 'Very well, if Brenda promises not to make a fuss.'

'Of course.' Brenda nodded then waited anxiously.

'It's the real reason behind Father offering to take in Judith,' Hettie confessed. 'He made it clear that he wanted a girl who was old enough to do some of the housework and run around after me, knowing that I wasn't going to get better.'

'Not straight away, at any rate.' Donald continued to stare at the rooks perched in the treetops in the copse beyond the barns.

'Not ever,' Hettie contradicted firmly. 'I'm afraid the doctor has given me some bad news, Brenda. I have a tumour.'

'Whereabouts?'

'Here.' She placed her hand over her stomach. 'Apparently I've left it far too late for the hospital doctors to take it away.'

'Are they sure?' Brenda's heart fluttered and she had to resist the urge to fly across the room to comfort Hettie; an action that she had the sense to know would be met with a rebuff.

'Quite certain. But please don't mention it to Les when you write. He has enough to cope with.'

Brenda nodded slowly.

'You give me your word?'

'I promise.' She stood up, turned to the window and saw five or six rooks rise from the trees and fly high into the cloudless sky. Donald kept his back to her. Hettie sighed and adjusted her shawl.

'I'm so very sorry,' Brenda murmured, crossing the room and briefly resting a hand on the sick woman's shoulder. 'I'll leave you in peace but is there anything you need from me before I go?'

Hettie flinched at her touch. 'Nothing else, thank you. Only that you keep your promise.'

The pathos of Hettie's request pierced Brenda's heart. It didn't add up. Why would a sister not want to tell her brother that she had only a short time to live? Surely Les would want the chance to say goodbye, but Hettie had demanded a vow of silence and Brenda couldn't refuse. 'Trust me, I won't mention it,' she whispered.

The coals in the grate shifted. One of Arnold's

dogs crept in through the half-open door and settled on the hearth rug. The rooks whirled then flew low over the house as Brenda left the building. She put on her goggles and gloves then kick-started her bike, carrying Hettie's sad news with her along the quiet road to Burnside and beyond.

CHAPTER SEVEN

Left to herself on her afternoon off, Joyce donned a thick jumper, a pair of slacks and her sturdy shoes before setting off on the cross-country hike to Acklam Castle.

'Straight on past Mary's Fall,' Laurence told her when he learned of her plan. 'Follow the public footpath. Make sure you're back in time for milking.'

Assuring him that she would, she left him to tinker with the engine of his Land-Rover then strode on up the hill. She took in deep breaths of cold, fresh air and endured strong, whirling blasts of wind. Clumps of brown heather and stretches of boggy ground hindered her progress as she approached Black Crag. Once there, she crossed the stream then skirted around the back of the outcrop and went on picking her way across open moorland until she reached a secluded, horseshoe-shaped cove where a stream tumbled over a ledge and splashed into a deep, crystal-clear pool. She stopped by the waterfall to enjoy the spectacle of water cascading twenty feet on to mossy rocks, feeling its cold spray on her skin. Mary's Fall. Who was the original Mary? she wondered. A local girl, no doubt, whose story had been lost in the mists of time.

Walking on, Joyce imagined long-ago trysts in this leafy, hidden place.

Her idle speculation brought a smile to her lips as she left the waterfall behind and a new vista opened out before her. The land rolled away towards a sizeable expanse of woodland and beyond that were the ruins of Acklam Castle standing on a bare knoll overlooking the river – a vantage point that would have provided plenty of advance warning of would-be invaders.

So Joyce struck out across country, glad when she eventually reached the wood and found shelter from the wind. The trees were bare, fallen leaves wet and thick underfoot, and she had to pick her way through tangled undergrowth. There was a smell of damp and decay as the sycamores, ash and beech trees eased their way towards their long winter slumber.

After half a mile of silent forest she felt a world away from war and strife. It seemed impossible to believe that the solitary plane flying high overhead – a mere glint of metal in the clear sky, glimpsed between dark branches – might carry bombs that would kill and maim. She stood a while in a small clearing and watched its thin white vapour trail dissolve. British or German? Canadian or Italian? There was no way of knowing.

'Halt. Who goes there?' Evelyn came across Joyce staring up into the cloudless sky. She rode a sturdy, dark bay cob with a thick black mane and tail.

Joyce was amused by the jaunty greeting. 'Hello, Evelyn. It's me – Joyce.'

'Yes, I see it is.' She sat quietly in the saddle, dressed in dungarees and a thick winter coat, bare-headed with her copper hair glinting in the sunlight, a hazel switch in her hand. 'Have you walked from Black Crag?'

'Yes, to see you. I hope you don't mind.'

'Of course I don't mind. We don't have much on this afternoon, do we, Captain?' Patting the elderly horse's neck before dismounting, she joined Joyce in the clearing and gestured all around. 'You see what I have to contend with? Decades of neglect; that's what this is.'

Joyce took in the tangle of brambles and unruly saplings. 'Yes. It'll take a lot of forestry work to put this right.'

Evelyn swished her hazel stick at a nearby ash sapling. 'Coppicing mainly. Youngsters like this have to be cut back in order to give the old-timers like the oak over there room to breathe.'

'How old would you say this is?' Joyce walked across to lay her hand on the oak's gnarled trunk and gaze up at its twisted branches.

'It takes a tree six or seven hundred years to grow to that size. Nelson's navy was built from good old English oak and that was Lord knows how many years ago.' Evelyn spoke fondly as she and Joyce studied the network of branches overhead. 'I sometimes think that I like these strong old oaks more than anything else in this world.'

Evelyn's talent for exaggeration reminded Joyce of Brenda. 'More than people?' she asked with a wry smile.

'Oh, ten times more.'

'Seriously?'

'All right then; twice as much.' The dark brown horse trailed his reins along the ground as he wandered over to nuzzle Evelyn's shoulder. 'Trees don't die on you, for a start; not if you look after them.'

This hit a nerve with Joyce, who frowned and dipped her head to stare at the ground.

'You too?' Evelyn asked quietly.

Joyce nodded. 'My first fiancé, Walter, was in the Royal Navy. His ship went down off Gibraltar. All hands lost.'

The horse gave Evelyn a harder shove. She pushed his head away. 'As it happens, my Jim wasn't anywhere near the front line. It was before the war started: an accident at work.'

'You must have been very young.'

'Sixteen when he was killed. Young and daft, according to my mother. You say Walter was your first fiancé. Does that mean you've bagged yourself a new one to fill his shoes?'

Joyce didn't take offence; in fact, she found Evelyn's bluntness refreshing. 'Yes. His name's Edgar Kershaw. He's a pilot in the RAF.'

'Crikey O'Reilly, you don't do things by halves!' Evelyn shook her head as she picked up the horse's reins then walked him slowly out of the wood. 'You must live your life on tenterhooks.'

'That's true. It's why I like to stay busy.'

'Black Crag Farm is the right place for you, then.'

'Geoff Dawson said the same thing earlier today. I don't mind, though.' Joyce walked quietly beside Evelyn and her horse, happy to let her new friend steer the conversation.

'So you've met Geoff?' Evelyn enquired. 'What did you make of him?'

'I liked him. He seems a decent sort.'

'He is – very decent.' Evelyn swished at a young larch tree with her stick.

'And available, I take it?' Joyce put in a sly dig.

Evelyn's face gave nothing away as she changed the subject. 'Oaks don't die on you until they're a thousand years old – and they don't make you keep secrets either,' she added as an afterthought.

'I suppose I'm meant to ask why you said that,' Joyce remarked as they emerged from the trees and had their first close-up view of the castle.

'And if I gave you an answer, then it wouldn't be a secret.' Evelyn's mood had dropped suddenly. When Captain lowered his head to snatch at a nearby clump of grass, she jerked at the reins. 'I'm sorry, Joyce, take no notice. My tongue has a habit of running away with me.'

No more was said and Joyce's interest in the ruins filled the gap. She took in the crumbling round tower on top of the knoll and nearby the remains of a large, medieval house with a wide arched entrance and narrow, Gothic windows. The walls were intact but the roof had partly collapsed. Mossy stones and decaying beams were strewn over the sloping ground. 'How is it possible for anyone to live here?' she asked.

'Not in the main house, silly.' Seemingly back on cheerful form, Evelyn kept a tight hold of Captain's reins as she led him and Joyce around the back of the tower to reveal a sixteenth-century extension, complete with stable block and servants' quarters. 'Watch out, Colonel Weatherall has his beady eye on us,' she warned as she walked Captain into the nearest stable.

'Top right-hand window. Don't let on that you've spotted him. My quarters are next door to the stables. Cliff Huby has the gamekeeper's cottage across the yard. Wait here while I unsaddle my trusty steed then we'll nip in for a cuppa and a nice long chat.'

*

My dearest Les,

Brenda wrote from her bleak billet.

I hope with all my heart that you're keeping well and that my letters are getting through to you. It's been a long time since I received one from you. Still, I do my best to keep my chin up, knowing that you will write as soon as you can. I had built up such hopes for today, picturing us together at least for a short time. Sadly, my love, it was not to be.

I long to know how you are and to hear it from your own lips. I will only believe that you're safe and well when I see you with my own eyes. In the meantime, I hope that they feed you properly on board ship and that you're sleeping well in your narrow bunk bed. There, I begin to sound like a mother instead of a fiancée!

As for my news; I have made a big change by moving out of my hostel to live at Garthside Farm, high in the dale. The new telephone number is Shawcross 636. In future you should call the operator and ask to speak to me in person, rather than relying on Donald to pass on a message. As we know, he is not the most reliable in that way.

Listen to this, my dear; I'm living in an old railway goods wagon surrounded by hens with Nancy the noisy goat as my nearest neighbour! There, what do you think of that? I'm still in the Land Army, of course, with Joyce living close by. My farmer is called Bernard Huby; happily, not a bad sort.

She paused to warm her mittened hands at a flickering lamp, filling her dreary room with loud sighs of regret and longing. It was impossible to write down the ins and outs of what she was feeling. The ongoing doubts and fears about her own wavering emotions must be carefully hidden away, along with her sharp pangs of loneliness. She must do her best to sound cheerful for Les's sake.

And so, dear Les, I'm glad to be still doing my very small bit to help the war effort. I have managed to bring Sloper up to Shawcross and intend to explore this neck of the woods tomorrow on my day off. They say there's an interesting ruined castle nearby.

I write this, my dear, wearing the ring you gave me on a ribbon around my neck and longing to see you again. But for now, I close this letter with not one but with many loving kisses.

Your very own Brenda xxxxxx

She pressed blotting paper over the wet ink, folded the paper and put it into an envelope.

Brenda had kept her promise and made no mention of Hettie's illness. Somehow, in spite of the thought she'd put into writing her letter, as she flung on her coat and ran down to the village to post it the gap between her and Les had never felt wider or more impossible to bridge.

Collections: Friday, 2 p.m. Before posting the letter, Brenda read the small enamel notice on the front of the red postbox.

'Drat, I thought collection was on a Saturday,' she said out loud. It began to seem that the whole world was conspiring against her.

An elderly woman shaking out her mat at the front door of her cottage overheard her and bustled across. 'Sorry, love; the postman comes on a Friday, two o'clock on the dot. But why not give it to the vicar?'

'Why, what has the vicar got to do with it?' Brenda muttered ungraciously.

The woman folded her arms. She made up for her small stature with an unusually loud voice. 'I happen to know that he's driving all the way to Northgate this afternoon for a meeting with the bishop. He can post your letter for you while he's in town.'

'I see.' Unsure whether or not to entrust her precious missive to a stranger, Brenda hesitated.

'Vicar won't mind,' the woman insisted. 'I'm Mrs Emma Waterhouse from number four.' She pointed towards the open door in the row of cottages. 'I clean and cook for the vicar, Mondays and Fridays. You're the Hubys' new farm worker.'

'Yes – Brenda Appleby. Nancy the goat made inroads into your veg patch.'

'That's right, she did. Your letter's important, by the look of it.'

'It is,' Brenda admitted. Mrs Waterhouse was thin as a rake, dressed in a wrap-over cotton overall, with a hairnet holding her grey bun in place. She had a determined glint in her brown eyes.

'Then hand it over. I'll give it to the vicar myself. I have to see him about the New Year bring-and-buy sale. By the way, have you got any spare knitting wool?'

Brenda shook her head.

'No, come to think of it, you don't look like the knitting type. Never mind, you still have time to embroider a couple of hankies or weave a little basket for the sale. It's on the first Saturday in January – all the money goes towards the church tower restoration fund.'

'I'll do my best,' Brenda promised meekly, though neither embroidery nor basket weaving were her cup of tea either.

Mrs Waterhouse held out a skinny hand. 'Letter,' she prompted. 'Vicar's already promised to pop one in the post for his new evacuee. An extra one won't be any trouble.'

There was no point in arguing; Brenda was obliged to hand over the letter. 'How's the boy settling in?'

'Talk of the devil,' Mrs Waterhouse said out of the corner of her mouth as the vicarage door opened and Alan shuffled down the path. He held a football under one arm and wore his customary mac and cap. 'Hey-up, has the vicar sent you out to play?' she called in her foghorn voice.

The boy put down the ball to open and close the

heavy wrought-iron gate. He picked it up again then trudged towards the green, feet dragging. 'I've to get some fresh air,' he reported joylessly from under the peak of his cap.

'All on your ownio?' Brenda quickly realized the tactlessness of her query and thought of a way to remedy things. 'I don't mind having a kick-about with you for a few minutes. How does that sound?'

Alan shrugged and dropped the ball. It landed with a dull thud. When Brenda picked it up and tested it, she found that it was practically flat. 'What we need is a bicycle pump,' she decided, tucking the ball under her arm. 'What's the betting they have one at the pub?'

Alan shrugged again and turned his head away.

Brenda winked at Mrs Waterhouse, who was a woman on a mission as far as Brenda's letter was concerned. She set off, quick march, towards the vicarage, while Brenda held out a hand to the reluctant boy. 'Come on, Alan; let's find out. And while we're at it, how about a nice glass of lemonade and a bag of crisps?'

That evening Brenda and Joyce escaped from their spartan lodgings and took refuge once more in the Cross Keys. They sat by the fire, warming their hands and feet, cheered by the hum of voices and the clink of glasses surrounding them. With no piano tucked away in a corner and only two types of beer on tap, the pub wasn't up to the standard of Burnside's Blacksmith's Arms but it was cosy nevertheless.

'You went all the way to Attercliffe for nothing?' Joyce commiserated with Brenda over the reason for her reappearance in Shawcross sooner than expected. 'Someone should have let you know that Les's leave was cancelled before you went all that way.'

'Yes, someone should have.' Having written her letter, Brenda had already moved on from wanting to blame Dorothy. In her head she was weighing up the pros and cons of telling Joyce about Hettie's illness then decided against it. 'I wrote Les a long letter to make up for not seeing him in the flesh but I can't help wondering why he didn't get home this weekend as planned. The fact is, he's probably stuck in the Med, surrounded by U-boats.'

'Try not to worry too much.' Joyce instantly regretted the platitude. Of course Brenda was worried; who wouldn't be?

'Or else he's been torpedoed.' Brenda's chest tightened as she imagined the explosion: an ear-splitting boom followed by a fireball then hot metal flying through the air; a hole blasted in the ship's hull, seawater rushing in, men who had survived the blast flung overboard without life jackets, swimming for their lives.

Joyce put a comforting hand on Brenda's shoulder. 'Not having any definite news is hard,' she acknowledged. 'All we can do is wait and see.'

Brenda took a deep breath. 'What's your secret, Joyce? How do you get through your days so calmly?'

'I don't. I'm like the proverbial duck gliding along smoothly with its feet paddling like fury under the surface.' There wasn't an hour when she didn't think of Edgar at the controls of his Lancaster, flying through the darkness, hands gripping the joystick, the blackout-defying, filigree lights of Dresden spread out below. Not a moment when she could relax until he came home for good and they could live without fear.

Yet all around them, civilian life went on as normal. Evelyn worked behind the bar with Fred Williams while Laurence sat alone on a stool with his pint. Then Bernard and Cliff Huby walked in out of the cold, followed by Geoff Dawson, who acknowledged Joyce with a wave then sauntered across, glass in hand.

'How's that cow of Laurence's doing?' he enquired. 'And the ulcer on Flint's foot? Or is it too soon to tell?'

'Too soon,' Joyce confirmed. 'I'll carry on with the disinfectant and the ointment and hope they do the trick.'

Geoff gave Brenda a friendly nod then introduced himself. 'Do you mind if I pull up a chair?'

'Make yourself at home.' Brenda made room for him and soon they were deep in conversation about the best breed of goat for milking and the growing trend of keeping rabbits in hutches for their meat.

'How about it, Mr Huby?' Brenda asked her employer who stood nearby with his son. The old man was in his work clothes, while Cliff was spruced up in checked shirt, green tie and his tweed jacket. 'Shall we build a hutch and keep rabbits? One buck and two or three females to start with. Once they pop out a few babies, we'll have meat for the pot without the bother of taking a gun on to the moor and waiting for them to stick their heads out of their burrows.'

'But then we'd have to feed them,' the farmer pointed out.

'Not for long, though. Geoff here says the baby bunnies can be butchered at three to four months.'

'Poor little blighters.' Cliff's contribution came with a wink. 'There again, rearing pheasants is my job. They end up in a pie, just like the bunnies.'

'Quite!' Brenda crowed. 'Baby pheasants, baby rabbits – what's the difference?'

Deciding to make a fourth at their table, Cliff positioned himself next to Brenda and pointedly ignored Joyce and Geoff. 'I saw your bike parked outside,' he told her. 'You've polished her up nicely. Does she run smoothly for you?'

'Sweet as a nut.' Ever eager to plunge into a conversation about motorcycle maintenance, Brenda caught Joyce's watchful eye and decided to change tack. 'I've just written to my fiancé saying how nice it was to have Old Sloper back. I've been lost without her this week.'

'Were you, now?' As Cliff tilted his head and reassessed Brenda's situation, there was a flicker of disappointment in his hazel eyes. 'What did he say, this fiancé of yours?'

Her gaze was fixed steadily on the gamekeeper's handsome features. 'I wasn't able to tell Les face to face, worse luck. He's in the Royal Navy so that's why I had to write it in a letter. He'll be pleased for me, I'm sure.'

Cliff eased back in his chair to include the others. 'How about you, Joyce? I'll bet a week's wages that some lucky chap has already snared you?'

Joyce stiffened then replied quietly. 'Yes, I'm engaged, if that's what you mean.'

'You hear that, Geoffrey? Here we were, looking

forward to giving a warm welcome to these two lovely new lasses and showing them all the local sights, but it looks as if we're out of luck as usual.'

Lasses? Local sights? Both Joyce and Brenda had to bite their tongues at the none too subtle innuendo.

Geoff had the grace to blush as, with a wink and a rueful grin, Cliff stood up and rejoined his father. 'I'm sorry about that,' Geoff said.

'No need to apologize.' Brenda shook her head. 'It happens all the time: a certain type of man expecting us to swoon and fall at their feet. Perhaps we would have done, once upon a time, but not any more. Things are different now.'

'And long may it continue.' Geoff glanced at Joyce, who nodded. 'Maybe I should warn Cliff that he's going about things the wrong way.'

'Don't bother,' Joyce advised. 'I doubt it would make a scrap of difference.'

Brenda and Joyce both believed they had the young gamekeeper's measure: good-looking and happy-go-lucky but with a vain, shallow streak reminiscent of his sister Dorothy.

'I agree,' Brenda said. 'A leopard can't change its spots.'

'Unless he gets his comeuppance. Then he might have to alter his ways,' Joyce added.

'Blimey.' Geoff puffed out his cheeks and rolled his eyes. 'Why do I suddenly feel like Daniel entering the lions' den?'

Brenda gave a loud laugh. 'We're Land Girls, that's why. You men had better watch out!'

'At which point I'll love you and leave you.' Joyce was ready for bed after her afternoon hike. She put on her coat and said cheerio to Brenda and Geoff then to Laurence and Evelyn as she left. 'Ta again for the guided tour of the castle earlier,' she told her.

'Any time!' Evelyn's transformation from lumberjill to barmaid was spectacular. Gone were the dungarees and gumboots and in their place was a tight-fitting green dress with a black velour collar, a pearl brooch gleaming at her throat. Her glorious hair was swept up and held in place by a mother-of-pearl comb. Her lips were vivid red.

'And ta for the tea,' Joyce added, stepping out into the cold, black night. She was all set to take out her torch and begin the walk home when she noticed that Cliff had followed to offer her a lift.

'I'll behave myself,' he promised. 'You being engaged to be married and all.'

'You'd better,' she teased back.

'Yes, miss.' He walked her to his car and held open the door. 'We don't want you getting lost on the moor, do we now?'

'Evelyn showed me round the castle grounds earlier today.' Joyce made easy conversation as Cliff set off along the rough, narrow road. 'She pointed out your billet.'

'I'm sorry I missed you. I didn't get back until teatime. Did you see the old man?'

'Colonel Weatherall? No, I didn't.'

'He'd see you, though. And you can bet he gave Evelyn some stick about it afterwards.'

'What for?' Joyce steadied herself by grasping the door handle as the car swayed round a bend then jolted over potholes.

'For letting a stranger set foot on his land. His

bark is as bad as old man Bradley's who you're lumbered with. And his bite is ten times worse.'

'Ta, I'll remember that.' Joyce decided that the gossipy streak certainly ran in the Huby family.

Cliff swung the car round another bend, dim headlights glimmering across the bare hillside and back tyres throwing up mud. 'On the subject of your Laurence Bradley, though, he's forty-five if he's a day and he doesn't have a good word to say about anybody, especially since Lily ran off and left him to drag up their lad as best he could.'

'Lily?'

'His first wife; the one before the one he's got now. What I'm trying to say is, how does a brute like Laurence manage to snag himself two wives on the trot? Mind you, he had to go out of the dale to find them both. I'm not sure where Lily was from but she wasn't local.'

'And Alma?'

'From Shawcross originally, before she went to live with an aunt in Northgate. You know the story?'

'Yes.' A screech of brakes and the sound of dogs barking told Joyce that they'd arrived at Black Crag Farm. She stayed in her seat while Cliff made an expert three-point turn in the yard. 'Geoff mentioned the fire,' she said quietly.

'Poor kid. She lost everyone: mum, dad, a sister and a brother. The coppers put it down to a paraffin or an oil lamp knocked over in a downstairs room while the family was in bed. They reckoned it was an accident.'

'But you're not convinced?' A sense of unease crept over Joyce as she listened to Flint and Patch's din and made out a dim light through the kitchen window, meaning that she would probably have to face Alma when she went inside.

'Who knocked the lamp over if everyone was asleep? That's the question that never got answered.' After manoeuvring the car to face the gate, Cliff got out to open Joyce's door. 'Never say I'm not a gentleman,' he quipped.

'I wouldn't dream of it.' She got out of the car to renewed barks and whines. 'Thanks very much.'

He raised his eyebrows and smiled broadly. 'Now you owe me a favour, Miss Cutler.'

'Goodnight, Cliff.' Joyce gathered her dignity and was halfway across the yard when he called her back.

'You forgot something.' He wound down the window and passed her handbag to her.

She took it with a quick, flustered thank-you, certain that his eyes were still on her and that he was laughing at her as she opened the door and went inside.

CHAPTER EIGHT

For the whole evening Alma had had the house to herself.

She'd moved easily from room to room, knowing that no one was watching her, taking her time to run a finger over surfaces to check that they were dust free, fetching the dustpan and brush to sweep under the dresser in the kitchen then going upstairs, sweeping each riser as she went. In the two bedrooms she took up the rugs and shook them out of the landing window, lips pressed tightly together for fear of breathing in the dirt. Tomorrow was Sunday; if the weather allowed, she would spend the day washing curtains and cleaning windows.

She paused on the landing and glanced at the steps leading to the attic. Hopefully the Land Girl had high standards as far as keeping her room tidy was concerned. Curiosity almost overcame Alma and she had a foot on the bottom step when she heard the dogs bark and a car drive into the yard. She ran along the landing and down the stairs, expecting to see Laurence but instead finding Joyce in the kitchen.

'It's freezing out there,' Joyce said as she hung

up her coat. 'I wouldn't be surprised if we got snow tonight.'

Alma busied herself at the sink.

'What happens if it does?' Remembering that Laurence was still at the Cross Keys, Joyce made the most of the opportunity to draw Alma out. 'Do we bring the pregnant ewes into the field barns or do we leave them out in the snow?'

A shrug was all the answer she got.

'Swaledales are a hardy breed, I suppose. I don't envy them, though; up there by the crag with a wind whistling in from the west.'

Alma took a tea towel from the rail and methodically wiped dishes. Her expression was blank.

'Let me put them away for you.' Joyce carried a stack of plates to the dresser. 'Do I arrange them any old way, or do you have a system?'

Alma put down the towel to show Joyce which order she preferred. As usual, she kept her face turned away.

She's young, Joyce thought, not for the first time. Her figure was almost that of a child, her fair hair soft and falling in wisps across her face. The high-necked jumper and long pleated skirt disguised rather than emphasized her slenderness. *Young and angry.*

'I see,' she murmured as she watched Alma arrange the plates. 'I'll try to remember that's the way you like them. By the way, I spotted a spare paraffin lamp in one of the outhouses. Would you mind if I gave it a clean and took it up to the attic? That way I wouldn't have to ask you for new candles.'

Alma's fingers fumbled over the last plate then

she froze, still gripping it with both hands. Her face turned pale.

'Here, give me that.' Joyce quickly put the plate away before leading Alma to a chair. 'Are you feeling dizzy? Come and sit down. Take a few deep breaths.'

Alma tilted her head back with a look of out-and-out panic. Her breathing was broken by dry catches in her throat, her cheeks were deathly white.

'Do you keep spirits in the house?' Joyce ran to the cupboard beneath the dresser. 'In here? Brandy or whisky; something of that sort to revive you?'

Making an attempt to stand, Alma collapsed forward against the table so that Joyce had to give up her search and run to steady her.

'Sit,' she pleaded. 'Let's forget about the whisky, just concentrate on taking deep breaths. There, that's better.'

Gradually Alma was able to draw oxygen into her lungs and her colour returned. The look of fear subsided.

'How are you feeling now? Better?'

'Yes.' Alma's first word came out as a faint whisper. 'I'm sorry.'

'Don't be silly, there's nothing to be sorry about.' Joyce drew up another chair and waited. Alma had broken her silence at last.

'The lamp,' she whispered with a shake of her head.

'You don't want it in the house?'

'No. Please.'

Joyce remembered with a shudder what Cliff had told her about the start of the house fire that had robbed Alma of her family and left her permanently scarred. 'I should have realized. I'm sorry.'

It felt impossible to put into words what it had been like to live under a pall of grief and shame, where for years silence had been the only refuge. Alma shook her head again. 'The smell,' she tried to explain. 'The smoke.'

'I understand.'

'No whisky. Laurence doesn't allow it.'

'Not even for medicinal purposes?' Joyce tried to ease the conversation forward, half expecting Alma to cut it short as soon as she felt strong enough to stand.

'Not a drop. He says it's what ruined Lily.'

Joyce decided to let this lie. 'Shall I make us a pot of tea instead?'

'No thank you. Laurence will be back any minute.'

'Water, then?' Without waiting for a reply she went back to the cupboard for a glass. Though Alma was talking at long last, her sentences were stilted and she kept a hand to her neck to partly cover her scars. 'Everything has its place, I see.' Cups and saucers on a top shelf, glasses on the shelf beneath. 'I wish I was half as tidy as you.'

'Thank you.' Alma accepted the glass. 'I keep things the way he likes them. It's easier that way.'

Joyce sat down again. 'I'm glad we're having this chat,' she admitted. 'I'd started to think we never would.'

'I'm sorry . . .'

'Don't be! I appreciate how hard it must be, having to put up with a lodger. We all like our own space and here I am, barging into your new home, leaving my mucky boots in your porch, letting my coat drip on to your nice clean floor.'

'I don't mind.'

'Well, that's a relief.'

'You're ten times better than Gordon.' Alma's speech gathered pace. 'He left his things anywhere he liked: dirty shirts, socks, you name it. I was sick and tired of tidying up after him.'

Joyce glanced at her in surprise and saw that her cheeks had grown flushed, resentment replacing fear in her eyes.

'It would've been a waste of breath me complaining to his father, though. As far as Laurence is concerned, Gordon can't put a foot wrong.'

'Two against one?'

'Yes and Gordon opposed the marriage. He and Aunty Muriel both refused to come to the wedding . . .' Alma's voice trailed off and she ran her finger around the rim of her glass.

'Was that the aunt you lived with?'

'Yes. She didn't approve of Laurence when he began to show an interest in me. She said you had to wonder why he did, given the way I am.'

Joyce drew a sharp breath. 'That wasn't very nice of her.'

'No, but it was true. No boys of my own age ever came calling.'

Before Joyce had time to respond, the dogs barked a warning that another car was approaching.

'Laurence!' With this single word, a startled Alma swept the glass from the table and took it to the sink. She'd washed and dried it, put it back in its cupboard and disappeared upstairs before the Land-Rover had turned into the yard.

Joyce was alone in the kitchen when Laurence came in.

'You left the pub early,' he commented as he kicked off his boots.

'Yes, I was tired.'

'But you're still up, I see.'

Excuses popped into her head – jobs to do, a letter to write – but Joyce preferred the truth. 'Alma and I broke the ice,' she said calmly as she headed for the stairs. 'We had a good, long talk.'

Brenda found that a light covering of overnight snow had transformed the landscape as she set out on Sloper for Acklam Castle. It lent the hills a pure, smooth beauty that made her heart soar. Distant ridges sparkled against a light blue sky, while to either side of the lane the mossy tops of the stone walls were coated with a thin white layer like sugar-frosting on a cake.

Riding Sloper was tricky in these conditions so she paid attention to the road ahead, meeting the challenge by changing down the gears as she approached a bend, feeling the back wheel slide a little as it kicked up loose snow. She went steadily on and before she knew it she had crested the highest hill and was looking down on the Acklam estate, complete with woodland and ruined castle.

It was only then that it occurred to Brenda that she should perhaps have checked with Evelyn that she would be happy to receive a visit this early on a Sunday morning. *What if she's having a lie-in?* she wondered. Still, having come this far, Brenda decided to go on. She eased slowly down the hill and entered the silent woods, an enchanted world of frost-spangled branches that met overhead and formed a fairy-tale tunnel. Eventually she reached the grey ruins set back from the lane on a rocky promontory overlooking the river.

Brenda killed the engine at the gate and sat astride her bike, taking in the ivy-clad walls and narrow, arched windows. There was no sign of life.

The total stillness of her surroundings forced a rethink; perhaps it would be best to turn back after all. There were plenty of other sights to see on a sunny Sunday: the waterfall behind Black Crag that Joyce had told her about, for a start. Yes; it was best not to disturb Evelyn. Brenda dismounted to turn the bike around in the narrow lane and was about to hop back on when a loud shout accompanied by the sound of gunshot startled her.

An old man stepped wide of the ruins, shotgun raised. He kept it aimed at Brenda as he descended the snowy slope; dressed in plus fours and a tweed jacket, with a deerstalker hat pulled well down over his skull-like face.

'You there!' he bellowed. 'You're on private property.'

Instinctively Brenda leaned her bike against the wall and raised her hands in surrender. Caught between making a run for it and staying put, she watched warily.

'Who are you? What do you want?' Weatherall shouted at the top of his voice.

'My name's Brenda Appleby. I'm Evelyn's friend.' Good Lord, what did this stooping, ancient relic of a bygone age think he was up to, taking a potshot at a perfectly innocent visitor? His hands trembled and his aim was unsteady, alerting Brenda to the possibility that the gun might go off again without him even intending it.

'Can't hear you!' he yelled, tottering towards her. 'You've no right to be here, whoever you are.' He reached the five-bar gate with the gun still raised, feet wide apart, eyes narrowed, and a thin, dark slash of toothless mouth scowling at her.

Brenda kept her hands in the air and stared down the barrel of the gun. Despite the ridiculousness of the situation, she knew that she could be in real danger. 'Colonel Weatherall,' she began in a conciliatory tone, 'I'm here to see Evelyn Newbold, your forestry girl.'

'Save your breath; he's deaf as a post.' Cliff Huby ran nimbly down the hill to save her. As the old man kept on pointing his gun, the gamekeeper came up from behind, clearly amused by his employer's erratic behaviour. 'It's all right, sir,' he yelled in the old man's ear. 'I know who this is!'

'You what?'

'I know her!' Placing an insistent hand on the barrel of the gun, Cliff tilted it towards the ground. 'There, that's better.'

'Tell her to bugger off!' Spittle dropped from Weatherall's mouth and he jutted out his under-lip. 'No trespassers. Go on; tell her!'

Cliff took the old man's arm and gave Brenda an apologetic shrug as he turned him back the way they'd come. 'Bad luck; you were spotted,' he said over his shoulder.

'He scared the living daylights out of me.' Slowly she lowered her hands.

'Have you sent her packing?' Weatherall let the gun dangle from his gnarled hand. He went on grumbling viciously as he allowed Cliff to guide him back towards the castle.

'Yes, sir; she won't bother you any more,' he bellowed at close quarters. Then he turned and spoke quietly to Brenda. 'I'll let Evelyn know you called.'

'Ta.' Gathering her wits, she grabbed Sloper's handlebars and slung her leg over the saddle.

'Next time you'd better give us advance warning,' Cliff advised. 'I'll lock away his gun and keep him occupied while you two girls have a natter.'

A new week started and December crept in with unexpected meekness after the brief weekend freeze. Joyce grew used to the routine of rising early for milking, glad of a more friendly welcome from Alma when she returned to the kitchen for a breakfast of porridge followed by toast and jam. The meal was usually cut short by Laurence who would stand up from the table and set Joyce a series of back-breaking, blister-producing tasks that would keep her busy until late in the afternoon. For three days in a row she hiked across country with hammers and chisels jangling in her haversack. Her job was to mend sections of broken wall in the lambing field adjoining Mary's Fall, taking with her a primus stove, small kettle, tin mug and a screw of brown paper containing tea leaves. At midday she would down tools and fill the kettle at the waterfall, set it to boil and take out her fish paste sandwiches. On the third day she took Patch with her for company. Otherwise she spent the time alone.

Brenda's week was less solitary and her routine

kept her closer to home. For a start there was Nancy the goat to milk and the Rhode Island Red hens to feed with what Bernard called a croudie mix of water and meal – a task that she took over from Dorothy who had been poorly with a cold all week. Then, on the Friday she set about building a rabbit hutch, cobbling it together from old planks and topping it with a roof of corrugated iron.

'Whose idea was that?' Dorothy asked as Brenda covered the front of the hutch with chicken wire. She watched from the doorstep, swaddled in a heavy coat, scarf and woollen hat.

'Your dad's. We talked him round in the pub last weekend, remember? Oh, you weren't in on it – it was me talking to Geoff Dawson and your brother. I think your father liked the idea of having rabbit stew whenever he felt like it.' Brenda was pleased that she hadn't borne a grudge against Dorothy for failing to pass on Donald's message about Les's cancelled leave. After all, they had to rub along together for the foreseeable future.

Dorothy turned up her nose. 'I don't like the taste of rabbit.'

'No, but beggars can't be choosers these days.' Brenda wished that Dorothy would mind her own business. The hutch was taking shape nicely and once it was finished, she had half a dozen other things to get on with, including scrubbing out the hen hut then digging up an area of heather and scrubland behind the farm buildings. She looked forward to making a bonfire of the uprooted shrubs and feeling its warm glow ease her aching joints.

Dorothy showed no sign of shifting. 'I hear you

have my brother to thank for not getting your brains blown out last Sunday.'

Brenda stood back to admire her effort. At this rate the blinking rabbits would have a better billet than her, with an open area to run in and a water-tight hutch lined with straw and shredded newspaper for sleeping on. 'Is that what Cliff said, that he saved my bacon?'

'Yes. Old Weatherall is a liability with his shotgun – mad as a hatter and stone deaf with it.'

'Ta, I'll remember that next time he tries to shoot me.'

'I don't like rabbit stew and I'm not fussed about mutton either.' Dorothy's thoughts were running off at a tangent again. 'Pork's my favourite, but it's hard to come by. Oh, by the way, a letter arrived in this morning's post.'

'For me?' Brenda dropped her hammer with a sudden clang. 'Where?'

'On the window sill in the kitchen.' Dorothy hurried inside to fetch it and returned bearing it aloft. 'Sealed with a loving kiss!' she exclaimed. 'Here, on the back of the envelope: three whole kisses for Miss Brenda Appleby, care of Dale End Farm, Attercliffe, Yorkshire. They've sent it on here.'

Sunday came round again in a flash. In the Cross Keys on the Saturday night, there had been much talk about events leading up to Christmas. Joyce had said yes to a request from the vicar for volunteer carol singers, but no to Emma Waterhouse for a contribution for the New Year bring-and-buy sale. Then Dorothy had come up with the bright idea that they all get together in the church hall on the Saturday evening before Christmas.

'What the devil for?' Cliff had demanded, well into his third pint.

'For a dance, of course.'

'Isn't it a bit late? I'm guessing Glenn Miller and his band are already booked.'

Dorothy had stared at her brother as if he were a simpleton. 'No, silly, not with a real live band. We'll make do with a gramophone and some up-to-date dance records.'

'Cliff might have a point, though,' Evelyn had pointed out. 'It's a lot to organize in the space of a fortnight.'

'Where there's a will there's a way,' Dorothy had insisted with a hint of petulance.

'Who will we get to come?' Joyce had been able to envisage no more than a handful of people under thirty who would be interested in a village hop.

'Everyone. Leave it to me.' Dorothy had spoken and her word was law.

At least Brenda had been in a good mood, Joyce recalled as she worked alone in the dairy next morning, wrapped up in scarf and overcoat, with her hair concealed beneath a grey and red checked headscarf. Brenda had been buoyed up by the delayed letter from Les that had been written on the eve of learning that his leave had been cancelled and forwarded to her by Donald or Arnold, assuring her that he was safe and was missing her dreadfully.

'Wasn't I right?' Joyce had squeezed her hand. 'Didn't I say he was still head over heels?'

Brenda had let her read the precious letter. 'He doesn't mention where he is, of course. But do you see the part where he says that he might be allowed home for Christmas?'

'Yes, right here.' In amongst the protestations of eternal love was the information about Les's re-arranged leave. He'd closed the letter with a carefully drawn heart pierced by an arrow decorated with the initials 'LW' and 'BA'.

'Wouldn't that be a dream come true?'

'Marvellous,' Joyce had agreed.

Now she placed milk pails into the sterilizing apparatus and heard the hiss of steam. Knowing that it was safe to leave the machine to do its job, she judged she just had time to nip over to the house for breakfast.

She was halfway across the yard when she heard voices through the open kitchen door.

'It's not what I hoped for.' Laurence sounded strained. 'You hear me, Alma? This isn't right.'

Alma's reply was calm and firm. 'I'm sorry. It can't be helped.'

'I've been patient.'

'And I've done all you asked.'

'Not all.'

'I made it clear from the beginning.'

The altercation stopped Joyce in her tracks. The snatched phrases were hard to make full sense of but this was the first time that she'd heard Alma stand up to Laurence and she feared the worst. What if he were to lose his temper and lash out?

'How do you expect us to go on living like this?'

Alma continued. 'You watching me like a hawk, me afraid to put a foot wrong. If I'd have known what I was letting myself in for . . .'

He gave a short bark of mocking laughter but there was no follow-on.

'I mean it, Laurence. I wouldn't have said yes. I would have listened to Aunty Muriel.'

Joyce had heard enough. She turned tail and was about to retreat into the dairy when she got the shock of her life in the shape of Edgar's car driving into the yard. Edgar himself sat at the wheel dressed in RAF uniform, leaning his head out of the window and calling her name.

She stood rooted to the spot. It couldn't be him; it simply wasn't possible.

'Joyce!' He stopped the car, stepped out and slammed the door.

It was a mirage. She would blink and he would vanish.

'Joyce, it's me.'

He was walking towards her, holding his arms wide, inviting her into the embrace that she dreamed of day and night. He was laughing.

'Oh!' she breathed as she took a small step forward.

'They gave me twenty-four hours' leave. I wanted to surprise you.'

Edgar! Her Edgar; tall, too thin by far, his face pale and smiling. Oh and the smart air-force-blue uniform, the upright stance of a man who was proud to wear it, opening his arms and hugging her as she stumbled forwards. She had to feel those arms wrapped around her before she could believe that he was really here.

'Don't cry,' he murmured as he tilted her chin back and kissed her wet cheeks. 'I thought you'd be happy.'

'I am,' she managed to whisper, eyes closed, clinging to him. 'Does Grace know?'

'Not yet. I drove straight here.'

His voice, deep and slow, the smell of carbolic soap on his skin.

'Can you have the rest of the day off?'

She nodded then opened her eyes. 'I'll be five minutes. Wait here while I get changed.'

She left him standing in the yard, no longer caring about the interruption to Laurence and Alma's disagreement. She ran into the kitchen and flew across the room, up the stairs and up again to the attic where she tore off her clothes and changed into her light brown woollen dress, nylon stockings and tan-coloured shoes. She didn't even run a comb through her hair; she simply dashed downstairs again with a few words of explanation – 'My fiancé. Home on leave' – for the two astonished onlookers.

Miracle of miracles: Edgar was still there in the flesh. It had not been a dream.

They drove away from Black Crag Farm in thrilled silence, hearts pounding, snatching rapid glances at each other. She reached out to touch his arm.

'Where to?' he asked.

'Anywhere. I don't care. Somewhere quiet.'

They sped between walls, around bends, by the river and over hills into the next dale.

'They're sending me to join a new squadron,' he explained.

'Where?'

'Down south, to Biggin Hill to fly a Spitfire.'

'You've lost weight.'

'Yes. More than a stone. This time last week I was in Malta. The *Luftwaffe* are bombing hell out of the place, trying to wipe us out. Messerschmitts come at you from the sun – that way they blind you and gain the advantage. There are no supplies coming in so we were on ship's biscuits for four weeks solid. The bloody things damned near break your teeth if you're not careful.'

He talked as if being bombed and coming close to starvation was nothing. She sat and held her breath.

'If Malta falls, then so does North Africa, the Suez Canal, the Middle East – the whole bang lot. Starving or not, we were still scrambling four times a day.'

'Why Biggin Hill?' she asked quietly.

Edgar looked straight ahead. 'We lost all the men in our squadron bar two: me and my gunner, Mike Kirk. The two of us limped back on one engine after the last scramble. I'll be better off in a Spitfire – they're lighter and faster than a Lancaster.'

He talked and she listened, not shying away from the gravity of war and the risks he took. Words spilled from his mouth as if at any moment they would run out of time to say what must be said to seal their love.

'Just last week Jerry saw me and Mike run out of ammunition as we flew over one of their reservoirs. He was after us in a flash. In the end all I could do to get away was spiral down, hoping and praying that I could level out at the last second.'

'And?' Joyce almost felt the impact of Edgar's plane hitting the water.

'Luckily Jerry ran low on fuel and had to turn for home.'

She thought how different he'd become; how much going back to war after his convalescence had changed him. A year ago, when she'd first met Edgar, he had been in despair, badly wounded and drinking heavily; a brooding, isolated figure brought low by the loss of his co-pilot in a crash over Brittany. What had crushed him the most was the feeling that he hadn't deserved to come out alive. He ought to have died alongside his pal, Billy. Eventually, just before Christmas of the previous year, he'd emerged from his bouts of drinking and bitter silences, restored by Joyce's patient tenderness and the knowledge that he could both love and be loved in spite of all that had occurred. In the New Year an RAF doctor had examined him and declared him mentally fit for combat.

Now here he was, dicing with death again, talking of ship's biscuits.

'You're quiet,' he said as they drove along the wide-open sweep of Swinsty Edge.

'Yes. It's a lot to take in.' His sudden appearance, his change of squadron . . . new dangers to be faced. 'Where are we going?'

'To Burnside. I thought we ought to drop in on Grace, to see how she is. After that we can do whatever you want.'

'It's nice to be back on our old stomping ground.' Joyce had missed the familiar landmarks. 'And it'll be good to see Grace again.'

'Let's see if she's in.' Edgar drove into the village and stopped the car outside Grace and Bill's terraced house. He and Joyce went together to knock on the door and wait.

No one came so Edgar nipped across the road to the Blacksmith's Arms to speak to his father.

'Dad says she's driven into town with Edith Mostyn,' he reported back. 'There's a key under the plant pot. He said to go in and make ourselves at home.'

Joyce looked up and down the street. Strains of organ music came from the church next door, a reedy rendering of 'O Little Town of Bethlehem', but other than that the village was deserted.

'Ought we to?'

'Why not?' Edgar found the key and opened the door. He stood aside to let Joyce step in first. She went down the narrow corridor into Grace's spick-and-span kitchen. There was a crimson chenille cloth on the table and the net curtains at the window were freshly washed and starched. A set of watercolour paints, brushes and a sketchpad on a shelf near the window reminded them of Grace's artistic streak.

'Sit down. I'll make us a pot of tea.' Edgar drew out a chair from under the table.

'Are you sure Grace won't mind?' It felt odd to be in someone's home without their knowledge,

'Of course she won't mind.' He got busy with kettle and tea caddy.

'She'll be sorry she's missed you.'

'But it means I have you all to myself.' He presented her with tea in one of Grace's best cups. 'This beats keeping in touch by letter, eh?'

'It does.' She looked at his face as he sat down

beside her: in need of a shave but still irresistibly attractive, his eyes clear and alert, a smile playing on his lips. She reached out a hand to hold his. His fingers were warm. One touch was worth a thousand words.

'I can't wait until all this is over,' he confessed with a toss of his head towards the window and the grey sky beyond. 'Though I don't suppose it'll be any time soon. Jerry left Stalingrad in a rotten state, by all accounts.'

'Yes, I heard Mr Churchill's broadcast last week. And they're not letting up in London either.'

'It's Italy for us next; Turin or Naples.'

'Shouldn't that be top secret?'

Edgar shrugged. 'It's common knowledge. Do you know what will get me through this? It'll be you, Joyce.' He unbuttoned his top pocket and took out a small, creased black-and-white photograph of her. 'This comes with me on every mission. You see this smile? This is what keeps me going, and the sound of your voice inside my head, telling me that you love me.'

She grasped his fingers more tightly.

'One day it *will* be over. No more raids, no more dogfights. Just blue skies and summer days, back here in Burnside with you.'

'No more digging ditches for me,' she murmured. 'Or getting up at the crack of dawn to mend Laurence Bradley's stone walls.' She told Edgar a little about her situation at Black Crag Farm. 'I expect to have to work hard but it's his manner that sticks in my craw. Never a smile, never a thank-you. And his poor wife.' She shook her head and sighed.

'Joyce?'

His questioning look penetrated deep under her skin and squeezed her heart. He took her by both hands and they stood up to embrace, his arms wrapped around her waist, hers around his neck. They kissed softly, drifting towards a space where time and place didn't exist.

Gently he released her and she took him by the hand and led him upstairs to the small bedroom at the back of the house.

'Are you sure?' he asked.

'Totally.'

It was natural and inevitable, a completion. To kiss and touch and kiss again, to gaze and give, not to think.

He felt the soft warmth of her dress against his hands. She raised it over her head, her face disappearing under its folds before she cast it aside and lay down on the bed. She watched him as he took off his clothes. Then they lay quietly together, not hurrying, absorbing every loving moment. Her hair against her neck, curling into the hollow created by the angle of her collar bone. The scar across his chest. The strength of their arms as they clung to each other.

And when it was over, the quiet, pure joy.

CHAPTER NINE

Les's long-awaited letter carried Brenda happily through the early part of Sunday morning. What did it matter that the cockerel woke her before dawn and she had to break the ice in the barrel in order to carry water into her primitive billet? Cold water was good for the complexion, she told herself as she splashed it on to her face. Soap would have helped, but that, like everything else, was in short supply.

She looked round the goods wagon that she now called home. Colourful pictures from magazines adorned the grey walls; fashion plates and photographs of the film star Ingrid Bergman who was a recent favourite of Brenda's. There was a pale blue eiderdown on her bed, donated by Dorothy once she'd learned how cold Brenda was at night, and a failed attempt at basket weaving lay cast aside in one corner.

'I'll come clean with Mrs Waterhouse at church,' she announced when she went into the house to discover that Dorothy had developed another cold and had stayed in bed. 'She won't be getting a contribution from me for the bring-and-buy sale after all.'

Dorothy's eyes were red and swollen, her voice

thick with catarrh. 'Remind Geoff Dawson that he's promised to lend us his gramophone on the nineteenth. Don't let him forget.'

'If I see him,' Brenda promised. It irked her that Dorothy took to her bed so readily and that she didn't lift a finger to help her father run the farm. She'd begun to suspect that she played on her so-called delicate constitution in order to get her own way. Her babyish, round face, with its small, curved lips and wide-apart brown eyes fell naturally into a pouting, petulant expression that did little to counter this impression.

'And tell Evelyn from me that I'm cross with her.'

'Why's that?' Brenda regretted popping her head around Dorothy's door to see if there was anything she needed before she went to church. The room was stuffy and the bed cluttered with magazines, hair curlers, vanity mirror and hairbrush.

'She promised to bring us a fresh load of logs – when was it? Anyway, ages ago.'

'I'll remind her.'

'Tell her we're still waiting. Cliff would do it but he's far too busy.'

'All right.' Brenda closed the door on Dorothy's complaints. When she went downstairs, she found Bernard hovering anxiously in the kitchen.

'Well, how is she?'

'Full of cold, but otherwise not too bad.'

'Has she got a temperature?'

'She didn't say.'

'Did you bank up the fire for her?'

Brenda shook her head. 'It's half past ten. We'll be late for church.'

'You go ahead. I'll fettle Dorothy's fire.'

Brenda heard the old farmer mount the stairs, his joints stiff with arthritis. *Each to his own,* she thought as she donned hat, scarf and gloves. *But I wouldn't pander to Dorothy in that way, even if she is under the weather.*

She emerged on to the yard and sent Rhode Island Reds clucking in all directions. The black goat brayed and strained at her tether. Later that day Brenda would have to remember to check the humane traps she'd set in the rabbit burrow behind the farmhouse. Until now the wily little blighters had evaded capture and the deluxe new hutch still awaited its first occupants. But before that there was the morning service: the social highlight of her week.

The ancient church had stood at the centre of village life for seven hundred years, through feast, famine and civil unrest. Damage to the medieval stone carvings behind the altar was said to have been caused by Oliver Cromwell's men, intent on destroying popish symbols. A Plantagenet king had been decapitated, the wooden rood screen depicting saints torn down. The rest of the interior was intact, complete with an eighteenth-century marble plaque to a Sir Thomas Weatherall and his wife, Jayne, and a recent stained-glass window dedicated to the men of Shawcross who had fallen in the Great War of 1914 to 1918. The pulpit from which Walter Rigg spouted his sermon was Victorian – a monstrosity in Brenda's eyes as she stared with a glazed expression at its elaborate carved eagle during the vicar's rambling explanation of the meaning of Advent.

There was no Joyce at this morning's service, Brenda noticed, though there were some faces in the congregation that she didn't recognize: old farmer types with their weather-beaten faces and stooping shoulders, their wives in cloche hats and coats with fox-fur collars, twenty years behind the times. She noticed hardly anyone of her own age, other than Evelyn, Cliff and Geoff Dawson. Alan Evans was in the front pew, presumably where the vicar could keep an eye on him. The boy clutched his hymn book so hard that his knuckles turned white. He stood to attention to mouth the words of the hymns then knelt down to pray before sitting and staring straight ahead while Rigg droned on. At the end of the service, Emma Waterhouse ushered the boy out into the graveyard and stood him next to the dreaded white angel to wait for the vicar.

'Don't move,' she instructed as she went to round up more support for the bring-and-buy.

'Who'd be an evacuee?' Brenda collared Evelyn on her way out of church. She pointed to the lonely, sad figure hunched beneath the imposing statue.

'Not me.' Evelyn was in Sunday best, which consisted of a fitted light brown coat, belted at the back, with a matching trilby-style hat perched at a jaunty angle with a cockade of pheasant feathers pinned to the hatband. 'I'll give him one more week at most.'

'What then?' Brenda scanned other members of the congregation gathered outside the porch, intending to waylay Geoff and remind him about the gramophone.

'Alan will plead with Mama to let him come home,'

Evelyn predicted. 'She'll relent and he'll go back to the bombs and doodlebugs.'

'Is that what's happened in the past?' Brenda's attention turned to Walter Rigg who was shaking hands with each departing parishioner. His white surplice billowed in the wind, his bare, bald head shone.

'Yes. Why, does it bother you?' Evelyn queried.

'No, it's none of my business.' Brenda paused then thought better of this cool response. 'I mean, it can't be much fun . . .'

'It's not, believe me.'

'Meaning?'

'Meaning, I've seen a few things that I wish I hadn't.' Evelyn led Brenda towards the church gate where no one could hear them. 'The truth is, Walter Rigg isn't all sweetness and light, especially when he thinks no one's looking.'

Brenda felt a flutter in her stomach as she went on watching the smiling, ruddy-cheeked churchman. 'What does he do?'

'He keeps a ruler tucked into his waistband for a start.'

'For hitting?'

Evelyn nodded. 'Across the palm mostly, but once across a boy's backside. I've seen that with my own eyes.'

'But is that allowed?'

'In school, yes. We've all had the ruler at one time or another. I don't know about the rights and wrongs of it in the vicar's situation, though.'

Brenda shook her head. 'What else?'

'There was a boy here in September who didn't

last long. He wrote to his mother to say that he'd been flogged with a cane; six of the best with his trousers round his ankles. The mother kicked up a right fuss, I can tell you. She reported the vicar to his bishop but it seems nothing was done.'

Brenda had more questions lined up but they were interrupted by Cliff who whisked Evelyn away without ceremony. 'Shift your stumps if you want a lift home,' he told her. 'I've to see a man about a dog.'

Brenda noticed the way he took ownership of Evelyn, catching her by the elbow and marching her away. She was surprised that Evelyn didn't object.

'Hello, Brenda.' Geoff distracted her with a genial greeting. 'How's old man Huby treating you up at Garthside?'

She smiled back at him. Here was someone she didn't mind passing the time of day with, both outside the church and in the evenings at the Cross Keys. She agreed with Joyce that Geoff was an affable sort, knowledgeable about all aspects of veterinary medicine and animal husbandry and not in the least stand-offish, despite his apparently wealthy background. This interested Brenda, as did the question of why he lived as a bachelor in his large house.

'He treats me pretty well,' she replied, turning up her coat collar and pulling on her knitted gloves. She glanced up at gathering rain clouds and regretted her decision to walk down from the farm instead of bringing Old Sloper. 'He's been converted to the idea of keeping rabbits. The only trouble is, we haven't managed to catch any yet.'

'And where's fair Dorothy this morning?'

'In bed, poorly.'

'Again?' Geoff pursed his lips. 'Give her my regards. Tell her I hope she gets better soon.'

'Oh yes; she asked me to remind you—'

'About the gramophone? It's all right, I wouldn't dare forget. I've even sorted out some dance records for her: foxtrot, quickstep and a couple of jazz numbers thrown in for good measure.'

'Ta, it'll buck her up to hear that.'

As they hovered by the gate, feeling the chill of the winter wind and the first icy drops of rain on their cheeks, they too were interrupted, this time by the sight of a grey Rover pulling up in the village green.

'Excuse me,' Brenda said swiftly as she hurried towards it. 'That's my fiancé's brother's car. I wasn't expecting him.'

It could only be bad news, she told herself, breaking into a run.

Donald stepped out into the rain. His mac hung open and he wore a checked blue and grey scarf with a pale grey trilby. His grey eyes were serious as he greeted her. 'Don't worry; it's not about Les,' he said quickly, allaying her worst fears. 'It's Hettie. She's asking to see you.'

Brenda's heart skipped wildly then resumed an even beat. 'Is she worse?'

He nodded. 'I tell her she has to eat but she can't keep anything down. She's fading away in front of our eyes.'

'I'll come,' Brenda said.

It was at this precise moment that Alan Evans decided to escape from his stone nemesis by fleeing across the graveyard and vaulting the low, mossy wall. He glanced over his shoulder to see if he'd been spotted and cannoned into the back of Donald who caught him by the scruff of the neck then hoisted him into the air where he wriggled and squirmed.

'It's all right – you can put him down.' Brenda saw that the boy was crying and there was a look of abject terror on his face. 'There, there; calm down. No one's going to hurt you.'

Donald eased him down to the ground then took out a silver cigarette case, intending to light up. This was evidently going to take time to sort out.

'Angel!' Alan said between sobs. 'Staring at me. Flapped its wings.'

'No, sonny, it didn't.' With a flash of inspiration, Brenda saw how to kill two birds with one stone: a way to ensure that Donald didn't overstep the mark on the journey to Dale End and at the same time offer a rare treat to one unhappy little boy. 'Does Hettie still have the same girl to help her?' she asked Donald, who nodded. 'Very good. Look after Alan while I have a word with the vicar.'

She hurried back to the church porch where Walter Rigg was saying goodbye to the last of his congregation. Brenda quickly explained that she had the chance to take Alan to Dale End in Attercliffe to see his sister. They would get a lift in a car and be back in time for tea. She said she knew that the vicar would have no objection, thanked him breathlessly and ran back before Rigg had time to frame a response.

'You're coming with us,' she told Alan, getting out a hankie to wipe away his tears then bundling him into the back of Donald's car. 'You'd like to see

Judith, wouldn't you? So let's go and give that sister of yours a nice big surprise.'

'You know what they say about parting?' Edgar walked with Joyce in the wood behind the Blacksmith's Arms. A wind blew up fallen birch leaves from under their feet and whisked them like dark confetti through the air. 'That it's a sweet sorrow.'

She stuck a sprig of mistletoe through his buttonhole and kissed his lips. 'Hush,' she whispered. 'I don't want to think about it.'

A different sweetness was still with her – that of their lovemaking, even though they'd got dressed in good time for Grace and Edith's return and they'd gone on to talk of everyday things: the bootees that Edith proposed to knit for the baby, the two new recruits at Fieldhead and the general goings-on in Shawcross.

Grace had invited her father to join them for a make-do-and-mend dinner of beef stew and dumplings and there'd been a pleasant family atmosphere in spite of Bill's empty chair. No one had spoken of the fact that his battalion was at that moment making its way to the Far East, to Burma to fight the Japanese.

'The days are short and getting shorter,' Cliff Kershaw had remarked to his son as Joyce and Edgar had prepared to set off on their late-afternoon ramble. The old publican and blacksmith had taken to walking with a stick, plagued by rheumatism after a lifetime of shoeing horses and hammering hot metal. 'It'll be Christmas before we know it.'

He'd patted Edgar's shoulder. 'Goodbye, son. Look after yourself.'

'Goodbye, Dad.'

The simple words had been weighted with strong emotion as Edgar and Joyce walked on into the woods.

'Will you be home again for Christmas?' she asked through the whirl of gusting leaves, though she knew it was a question without a definite answer.

'It all depends,' he said. 'I won't find out until the last minute. But I'll write to you as soon as Mike Kirk and I get settled in our new quarters; you can rely on that.'

'Yes. Tell me all about it, every last detail: what they give you for breakfast, dinner and tea; who you share a bunk with; whether or not he snores.'

'All the life-and-death stuff.' Edgar kissed her cheek, put his arm around her waist and insisted that they swayed their hips and stepped out in unison, left-right, left-right.

The sky darkened and dusk fell over the silent trees. Foxes stayed in their dens, badgers in their setts. Winter had driven squirrels into deep hibernation. Edgar and Joyce walked on without speaking, wishing that the soft trance of walking through the wood would last for ever, knowing that it could not.

'Donald would far rather I stayed in bed,' Hettie told Brenda from her settee in the sitting room at Dale End. Today her shawl was pinned at her scrawny throat by a cameo brooch, her straight, dark hair flattened against her scalp. The shawl covered a long-sleeved nightgown that couldn't disguise the fact that Hettie's once-strong figure was now skeletal. 'I prefer to be carried downstairs where I can look out at the garden.'

Brenda glanced out through the French windows at empty flower beds and lifeless winter lawns. There was a path leading to a fish pond with a fountain and beyond that a vegetable plot and then a yard with several large stone barns. 'Donald is worried about you. He says you won't eat.'

'*Can't* eat.' Illness had robbed Hettie of her physical strength but it hadn't knocked the edges off her sharp manner. 'I can take a little milky tea, that's all.'

Brenda hardly knew what to say. There'd been a marked deterioration since she'd last seen Hettie and, in spite of her sharpness, she gave off an air of resignation to her fate. 'Has Donald or your father written to Les yet?'

'No, and I don't want them to. I haven't changed my mind about that.' She looked suspiciously at Brenda. 'You've kept your promise not to?'

Brenda nodded. 'But if you let him know how poorly you are, he could apply for compassionate leave; you do realize that?'

'I don't want him to. It would only add to his troubles to see me like this.'

'But have you thought how Les might feel?'

'Once he knows he's been kept in the dark?' Hettie tackled Brenda's point head-on. 'Look, when I'm gone I won't have any further say in the matter. Father will no doubt bring Les home for the funeral if the Navy can spare him. And then will be the time for Les to grieve; not before.'

'Honestly, Hettie, I'm not sure how I'd feel in your position.' Drawing her chair closer, Brenda spoke earnestly and directly. 'But part of you must want to see him, surely?'

'Of course.' Hettie fingered the brooch at her throat. 'I've acted as a mother to Les for a long time, and to Donald too. I've looked after those boys and done my best to keep them on the right track, worrying about them and having high hopes for them in equal measure. From the start I felt Donald could fend for himself but Les was the one I fretted over. It came of him being the youngest and more sensitive, I suppose.'

'You two are very close.'

'It's true, we are. I want to shield him from this, Brenda. You do understand?' She placed her hand on Brenda's arm and there was a strong, urgent appeal in her large, dark eyes.

'I do,' Brenda murmured.

'Good. Then, while my mind is still clear and I have my wits about me, I want you to make me one last promise.'

'Anything.' With a sore heart Brenda covered Hettie's cold hand with her warm one.

'Carry on looking after Les for me.'

'Of course I will.'

'You won't do it in the same way as me because you and I are not alike.'

'Chalk and cheese,' Brenda acknowledged.

'Quite. Our worlds are different. I'm stuck in the past. You stride into the future. That's one of the reasons why Les fell in love with you.'

'It works both ways. I love him because of the good, old-fashioned values you taught him. Les is true and honest, one of the few men I know I can rely on. That doesn't sound very romantic, does it? But for me it's the main thing.'

'This war is hard for us women.' Hettie withdrew her hand and sank back into the soft cushions supporting her. 'Mothers, daughters, sisters, lovers; it doesn't matter. Our duty is to support the men, whatever it costs.'

'And I will,' Brenda vowed.

As the time came for her to leave, she felt a surge of tenderness and her eyes pricked with tears. She stooped to kiss Hettie's cheek. 'Les won't ever forget his big sister; I'll make sure of that.'

At the sound of the sitting-room door clicking shut, Arnold White came out of his study, cable-knit cardigan hanging open and reading glasses perched on the top of his head.

'Good of you to come,' he told Brenda without looking at her, instead glancing up towards the landing. 'Donald, are you there?'

Donald leaned over the banister to reply. He was silhouetted against an arched window so it was impossible to see his face. 'What is it?'

'Brenda's ready for her lift home.'

'Whenever you are,' she added obligingly.

'Give me five minutes,' he said, disappearing into his room.

Brenda smiled awkwardly at Arnold. She was relieved when she heard children's voices coming from outside the house. 'That must be Alan and Judith,' she said to excuse herself before opening the front door.

Sure enough, the brother and sister sat shoulder to shoulder on the top step, hands clasped around their knees, staring out towards the road and the steep hill beyond. Brenda decided to sit down next to them.

'This is nice,' she said cheerily. 'I bet you two have had lots to talk about.'

Judith flipped her plaits over her shoulders then tucked her pinafore skirt more firmly under her thighs. She screwed up her mouth and didn't answer.

'What have you been gossiping about?' Brenda asked Alan.

'Nothing.' His tremulous voice gave away the fact that he was close to tears.

'Has Judith had time to show you her room?'

'Yes.'

'Did you like it?'

'Yes, thank you.'

'And did she offer you a drink and a biscuit?'

He shook his head.

'We could go to the kitchen now, if you like. Shall we?'

'No, thank you.'

Brenda's well-meaning questions bounced off the barrier that the brother and sister had erected. Judith's nails were bitten to the quick, she noticed. 'It's nearly time for us to leave,' she warned. 'Shall I arrange another time for us to visit?'

'We're not allowed.' Judith spoke in a slow, low voice then hugged her knees more tightly.

'Who says?' Hearing Donald's footsteps cross the hall, Brenda stood up to challenge the ruling. 'Alan is allowed to come here again, isn't he, Donald? I can bring him over on my day off.'

'It's not up to me,' Donald said with a shrug.

'Who, then? Your father?'

'No. The vicar – what's his name?'

'Walter Rigg?'

'That's the one. Dad had a telephone call from him saying the boy left without permission and we weren't to let it happen a second time.'

Brenda's response was quick and strong. 'That's a load of rubbish. I asked him myself. They're brother and sister. Who does the Reverend Rigg think he is, trying to stop them from seeing each other?'

'Don't ask me.' Donald strolled on towards his car while Brenda turned to Judith and Alan. 'I'll sort this out, don't you worry,' she tried to reassure them. 'We'll be back in a week or two.'

Hearing the car engine start, Alan suddenly jumped up and took flight around the side of the house. He hadn't got far when Brenda caught up with him and took him by the arm.

'Steady on,' she insisted. 'What's the matter? Whatever it is, running away isn't the answer.'

By now the boy was sobbing in earnest and tugging to free himself, pulling his trapped arm out of the coat sleeve then twisting free and setting off again. Brenda caught him once more. This time she wrapped both arms around him and hugged him until the sobs subsided.

'I don't want to go back.'

With his face pressed against her, it was difficult to make out the words. 'You don't want to . . . ?'

'Go back to the vicar's house!' he cried, shaking from head to foot. 'Please don't make me!'

She prised him away, held him at arm's length and tried to speak calmly. 'Listen, Alan, tell me why not. Is that nasty statue still giving you the heebie-jeebies?'

'Yes!' he yelped, turning his face away.

'And is there anything else?'

When he finally looked up at her, his face was a picture of misery. 'No,' he said faintly.

'Then let me have a word with Mr Rigg to explain the problem and see if he can put you in a different room.'

With one abject nod of his head, Alan agreed to let Brenda do what he'd prevented Joyce from doing. He let himself be walked back towards his sister, who hovered on the top step. Judith, too, was on the verge of tears.

'I'll keep an eye on him,' Brenda promised. 'And I'll put things right with Mr Rigg. I'll tell him it was my fault we left in such a hurry, so not to take it out on Alan.'

Judith nodded then adopted a grown-up voice. 'Don't be a cry-baby, Alan. Mummy and Daddy wouldn't like it.'

He choked back fresh tears.

'I mean it. We have to be brave.'

He gave a whimper and recoiled as if his sister had delivered a physical blow. Then he broke free from Brenda and walked to the car with his head bowed.

'Good show.' Brenda gave Judith's shoulder a reassuring pat then said goodbye. Seconds later, she joined Donald and Alan in the car.

'It doesn't seem fair,' Donald muttered with a glance in his overhead mirror at the boy's tear-stained face. 'If it wasn't for Hettie being so poorly, I'd offer to keep the lad here at Dale End.'

Brenda shot him a look of surprise. 'My, my, Donald; I didn't have you down as the caring type.'

He smiled as he revved the engine for the steep climb ahead. 'Never judge a book by its cover, Miss Appleby. That's Rule Number One in life, don't you know?'

CHAPTER TEN

On the Thursday morning following Edgar's twenty-four-hour leave, a letter arrived for Joyce by special delivery in the shape of Edith Mostyn, who had driven to Shawcross to check on both Joyce and Brenda.

'Edgar posted it on Monday to Grace's address, asking for it to be forwarded to you as soon as possible.'

Joyce's hand shook as she took the letter and slid it into her coat pocket. That was Edgar for you: thinking ahead and knowing how poor the postal service was out here. 'Thank you, Mrs Mostyn; it's good of you to bring it.'

'It's no bother, since I was coming anyway.' Edith was glad to have caught Joyce before the Land Girl set off to repair more gaps in the walls beyond Mary's Fall. She took in details of Laurence Bradley's tidy farmyard, including the well-stocked feed store, the two dogs watching warily from their kennel by the gate and the neat row of boots lined up in the house porch. 'Is all well?' she asked Joyce, notebook in hand. 'You have no complaints?'

'None,' Joyce confirmed.

'The meals are nourishing? Your quarters are adequate?'

'Perfectly, thank you.'

'And the hours Mr Bradley expects you to work – they're within the rules?'

'Yes, Mr Bradley is very fair in that respect.'

'What work does he ask you to do?'

'It varies. I milk the cows first thing then do the dairy work with Mrs Bradley. After that, it could be taking feed out to the sheep or penning them to deal with any foot-rot and to check the condition of the pregnant ewes. Some of the walls on the fell side are in a poor state, so mending them takes up a fair amount of my time.'

'Very good.' Edith made rapid notes on all Joyce said then broached a subject that had been on her mind in the run-up to her visit. 'Now this may interest you: I've received a request from my colleague in the Yorkshire branch of the Women's Timber Corps. They're looking for a part-time assistant for their worker on the Acklam estate, for tree felling and coppicing duties. Apparently there's too much work for one girl to manage. How would you feel about that?'

'That would be perfectly fine with me.' Joyce said a quick yes to working alongside Evelyn. Apart from anything else, it would add variety to her routine. 'Provided Mr Bradley can spare me.'

'Naturally.' Edith glanced round the deserted yard. 'Where is he now?'

'Out in his tractor, taking beet to the ewes.'

'I'll leave him a note then inform you of his answer. You'd still be billeted here at Black Crag

Farm, of course.' Edith tucked her notebook into her handbag then asked to see Joyce's living and sleeping quarters, which took her into the kitchen and up the stairs to the rickety flight leading to the loft. 'Up here?' she queried uncertainly.

Joyce nodded and led the way. There'd been no sign of Alma in the kitchen, which must mean that she'd retreated into her bedroom.

After a quick look around, Edith recorded Joyce's accommodation arrangements as primitive but satisfactory. 'Plenty of head room,' she noted. 'And sufficient daylight. Is there a bathroom and a WC in the house?'

'No. We use an earth closet outside. I have an all-over wash here in my room, in water warmed in the kitchen copper.'

'Electric lighting?' Edith saw only candlesticks – one at Joyce's bedside and one on an improvised dressing table made out of an old washstand with a mottled mirror propped against the wall.

'Not in the attic; only downstairs on the ground floor and out in the dairy,' Joyce reported.

'A paraffin lamp at least?'

'No, just candles.'

'Hmm. I should mention that to Mr Bradley . . .'

Mindful of Alma's strong aversion, Joyce stepped in quickly. 'There's no need. I'm fine as I am, thanks.'

Edith frowned before making a mental note to record Joyce as a particularly good type of girl who had adapted well to her reduced circumstances. Then she led the way downstairs and they shook hands in the porch before Edith drove on to Garthside to see Brenda.

*

Dear Joyce,

Edgar's letter began with a low-key endearment. No darlings or dearests. Joyce held her breath as she began to read.

I'm back in my billet and spending my last night here before being transferred. Mike is snoring away in the bunk below while I burn the midnight oil.

There are things I want to tell you that I didn't have the time or the courage to say while we were together. They come from the bottom of my heart and must be kept between us two and never shared with a living soul.

Joyce laid the letter flat on the washstand, glancing in the mirror at her own dim reflection and telling herself to be strong. Whatever Edgar had to say must be faced honestly; there could be no shying away.

When I fly my plane over enemy lines I am not a brave man. I believe few of us are. There; it's out in the open. We're simply obeying orders without any thought of the consequences. That's the opposite of bravery when you stop to think. We kill the enemy because we're told to, and to save our own skins.

I wish I could swear, hand on heart, that I'm driven on by a conviction that our cause is the right one, that Hitler must be stopped. I believe it, of course. But at what cost? That's the question keeping me awake at night.

And here's the crux of the matter: every single one of us has lost a pal who we loved and respected – men who we knew better than our own family sometimes. Gone in a flash, in a hail of bullets. My pal Billy was among the best. You know that I tried to reach him in his cockpit as our plane went down but it was no use. I'll spare you the details. You also know that our plane found a soft landing in amongst trees. We hung suspended in their branches, flames all around. I scrambled clear and left Billy behind. The plain fact is: I ran away.

Joyce paused, her heart too full to carry on reading. She understood that Edgar would bear this burden for the rest of his life. She also knew that he might lock it away and never talk of it again, so she steeled herself to read on.

And what was I left with after that, besides the physical scars? I scraped through with your help but with the certain knowledge that war brings out the worst in us as well as the best. Kill or be killed.

It's not much of a motto to live by when it comes down to it; not one that I would want to pass on to my . . . to *our* children if we're lucky enough to have them, something I wish for with all my heart. My hope, my heartfelt wish, is that they grow up in a better world than the one we have now and that they follow in your footsteps, not mine, so that they are able to give to others and will always be kind, not fearful.

She turned the letter over and stroked her fingertips over the last few closely written paragraphs.

> What luck that I found you, Joyce, or rather you found me. More than luck; we were led by God's grace or the Buddha's, or Mohammed's – whatever guiding spirit we choose to put our faith in. God is good enough for me.
>
> My dearest Joyce, I've reached the end of what I wanted to share with you and find there's a peace of mind that comes with getting this off my chest. I needed to be honest with you while I have the chance. I hope that you won't think less of me and trust that my feelings for you come through some of the nonsense I've been spouting. To me, nothing else matters.

Joyce touched his name, 'Edgar', sighed and closed her eyes, then rested a while in the deep, clear pool of his love.

When Joyce came down from the attic, she met Alma emerging from the bedroom at the back of the house. Through the open door she caught sight of a single bed with a jade-green eiderdown and three or four dresses hanging from a rack in an alcove. There were tapestry pictures of roses and lilies on the wall above the bed.

With a look of defiance Alma closed the door and went downstairs.

Joyce paused on the landing to think back over the morning routine in Black Crag Farm, registering that it was the sound of Laurence emerging from his room that woke her: the click of a door, his footsteps treading along the floorboards. He slept in the front bedroom, she realized with a slight shock. Alma's room, it turned out, was at the rear.

The realization helped Joyce make sense of the snatched phrases she'd heard from the argument just prior to Edgar's unexpected visit. 'Not what I hoped for', 'I've done all you asked', 'Not all'. Laurence's stern voice had been set against Alma's light, girlish one, as she stood up to him in a surprisingly resolute way.

They sleep in separate rooms, Joyce decided. *Laurence doesn't want to. It's Alma's idea.*

What kind of a marriage was one without love-making and all the closeness that went with it? Instead of settling on an answer to the question, Joyce cleared her throat, knotted her headscarf more firmly under her chin and went downstairs.

'You saw,' Alma said defiantly as soon as Joyce set foot in the kitchen. Instead of carrying out her usual chores, she sat at the table and looked out of the window with an unfocused stare. 'Don't pretend you didn't.'

'Saw what?' Joyce buttoned her coat as if to go straight outside, making it plain that Laurence and Alma's sleeping arrangements were none of her concern.

'My room. It came as a surprise.'

Joyce shook her head. 'I'm sorry. It's none of my business.'

'I thought you might have put two and two together before now.' Alma skimmed over Joyce's apology, sounding distant but determined. 'This is not a marriage in the normal way of things. I don't mind you knowing.'

'Oh dear.' Unable to walk away, Joyce sat at the table. 'You don't have to explain, unless you want to.'

'I do.' Alma redirected her gaze at Joyce. 'I'd like you to understand.'

Joyce took a deep breath. She had a sense of trespassing and was acutely aware of how furious Laurence would be if he found out about this conversation.

'There's nothing normal about it.' Alma made a slight, hopeless gesture towards her damaged neck and cheek. 'How could there be?'

'Your face is not so bad—' Joyce began but Alma cut her off.

'You wouldn't say so if it had happened to you. I was in hospital for three months after the fire. I've had four operations since. It's the first thing that people notice about me, what they always, without fail, talk about behind my back.'

'I'm sorry.'

The anger that was always close to the surface, pitiful fruit of her grief and disfigurement, broke through. 'For goodness' sake, Joyce, why are you always saying sorry? You're not doing anything wrong. And anyway, I don't want you to feel sorry for me; I only want you to know the truth. It was pity that drove Laurence to ask me to marry him in the first place – that and the fact that he was in need of a housekeeper.'

Joyce's grimace made it plain that this was a conversation she would rather not have. She stood up suddenly, scraping back her chair. 'I ought to get on . . .'

Alma caught her by the wrist and held it in a firm grip. 'It's true. *He* felt sorry for me. Does that surprise you?'

Joyce nodded. Mixed in with the fury that still flared in Alma's eyes, she thought she detected sadness and fear too.

'He caught me off guard. I remembered Laurence from the time when I lived in Shawcross with my family. I was only a child but I was aware of his reputation even then. He was a man that people were afraid to cross. Early this year, we met again in Northgate, through my aunt, who was friends with his first wife, Lily. I hadn't seen him in years. Aunty Muriel bumped into him by accident and I happened to be with her, shopping for blackout blinds. It was obvious from the way she acted that she blamed Laurence for what had happened to Lily. His first wife drank herself to death; did I mention that? And it was the simple fact that Aunty Muriel bore a grudge against Laurence that swayed me in his favour when he first showed an interest in me. Make of that what you will.'

'I really must go.' Joyce wrenched her wrist free. 'I'm sorry, Alma.'

'Sorry again!' Alma mocked. Then she reined in her irritation and was contrite. 'It's me; I'm the one who should apologize. I spend far too much time brooding over how I came to end up here. I have no one to talk to, you see.'

'You're unhappy. Anyone can see that.' *And who wouldn't be, after such tragedy?*

'Yes, but now I've put you in an awkward position. I didn't mean to.'

'It'll go no further.' Joyce's promise brought the conversation to an end and she made good her escape. But as she went out into the porch to put on her boots, she glanced back.

Alma still sat at the table, twisting a corner of the tea towel that lay on her lap, the corners of her mouth turned down and her gaze directed straight ahead. Her stiff posture was intended to fight off any remnant of sympathy that Joyce might feel. *Don't pity me,* she seemed to say. *I made my choice and now I must live with it.*

It's true, Joyce thought, as with a heavy heart she picked up her haversack and went out on to the fell.

'What do you think of this?' Dorothy held aloft a note that had been dropped off by Cliff earlier in the day. 'The RAF has accepted my invitation to our Christmas hop.'

Brenda paused, duster in hand, her fingers blackened by silver polish that she'd applied to the set of dull tankards and some sporting trophies that Bernard displayed on his kitchen mantelpiece. She'd covered the table with newspaper then set out the tarnished items and started polishing, observed by Dorothy who sat in her fireside chair. 'How long is it since you cleaned these?'

'Brenda, never mind the dratted tankards; listen to me.' Dorothy wafted the paper to and fro. 'I wrote to the base outside Rixley, hardly daring to hope that they'd say yes. But look: they snatched my hand off!'

'Good for you.'

'You could try to sound more pleased. They're

sending over an RAF truck with a dozen trainee pilots. It means we'll have our pick of dance partners.'

'I mean it: well done.'

'And I've had another brainwave.' Dorothy's excitement drew her to her feet and to the table where she demanded that Brenda put down her duster. 'Why not invite your friends from your old hostel to the dance?'

'Really?'

'Yes, why not?'

Brenda pointed out the pitfalls. 'First off, I'm not sure how they'd get here. Second, what if the weather's too bad for anyone to travel? They've forecast more snow for next week.'

Dorothy would hear none of it. 'Pooh, what a killjoy! A few measly inches of snow won't stop those Land Girls, not if they know there's a dozen strapping RAF boys waiting for them. And doesn't the hostel have a truck that the girls could use?'

'There's a van.' Slowly Brenda came round to the idea. It would be a good chance to catch up with Una, Elsie, Kathleen and the other girls in the run-up to Christmas, so why not? 'I suppose I could ask. Ma Craven would have to agree to doling out late passes, though.'

'Do it now!' Dorothy pointed gleefully to the telephone on the window sill.

'Hold your horses; let me wash my hands first.' Brenda went to the sink and ran the tap while Dorothy prattled on.

'This is turning out to be even more fun than I thought. We can decorate a tree, make paper chains and blow up balloons to brighten up the hall. We'll need plenty of holly and mistletoe, of course. I'd better talk to Geoff again about his selection of gramophone records; we'll need some slow Viennese waltzes as well as modern ballroom. I just hope he doesn't mind.'

'About what?' Failing to find a towel, Brenda dried her hands on the bib of her dungarees.

'About the Rixley contingent. They're bound to be stiff competition for our local boys.'

'Geoff doesn't strike me as the sort to be put out by that.'

'No, but Cliff will be in a bad mood over it. In fact, I doubt that he'd have played messenger boy if he'd realized.'

'You know your brother better than me.' Brenda paid little attention to Dorothy's rapid prattle.

'Not that he has any reason to complain,' she rattled on. 'Evelyn will be there, in any case.'

Brenda's hand hovered over the telephone. 'Evelyn and Cliff . . . ?'

'Oops!' Dorothy put her hand to her mouth and her face turned bright red. 'There; that's torn it.'

Hiding her surprise, Brenda lifted the receiver to dial the operator.

'I was sworn to secrecy. Not a word to anyone; do you promise?'

Of course, it was obvious when Brenda thought about it. Evelyn and Cliff worked on the Acklam estate together. Both were young, single and fancy-free. What was there to stop a romance developing? 'But why do they want to keep it a secret?'

'Don't ask me!' Dorothy's dismay evaporated and her tongue ran on. 'If it was me, I'd be so thrilled that I'd shout it from the rooftops. I'd be talking to the vicar about the service, booking the church hall, sending out invitations, planning my wedding day down to the last detail.'

'It's that serious?'

'Oh yes; Cupid's arrow has well and truly hit its mark. There's an engagement ring and everything.' She put a forefinger to her lips. 'But hush, not a word. I promised Evelyn. As for Cliff, he doesn't even know that I know.'

'My lips are sealed,' Brenda promised as the operator asked which number she required and she turned her back on Dorothy. After all, people were entitled to keep their private lives to themselves. It was up to Evelyn and Cliff to announce their engagement as and when they chose.

Friday arrived in a snow flurry, but that didn't prevent Laurence from ordering Joyce and the dogs to go with him to Mary's Fall. The aim was to round up half a dozen sheep in the far field and bring them down past the crag to the lambing field on lower ground where they would stay through the rest of December and into January.

'I don't want to have to dig them out of snowdrifts if I can help it,' he grumbled as Flint and Patch got to work. The dogs crouched low to the ground, watching the sheep and waiting for instructions. 'I had enough of that last year, when Gordon was still here to lend a hand. We lost two ewes up here and three by the crag.'

'Let's hope we can do better this year.' Joyce was optimistic that her repairs to the walls would pay off.

She cast a critical eye on Flint as he responded to Laurence's whistle by darting forward to drive the sheep around the side of the waterfall. 'He still has his limp,' she noted with a frown.

Laurence brushed aside her concern. 'As long as he can do his job.'

'Even so.' Despite the dismissal, Joyce decided to take another look at the dog's foot later that evening. 'If the ulcers haven't cleared up, maybe we should give Geoff a call.'

'Yes, so long as you're willing to dig into your own pocket.' Laurence's whistle brought the knot of bedraggled sheep down the slope towards them.

Joyce bit her tongue and ran to open a gate that would allow the dogs to work the sheep in the direction of the farmhouse. There was a mile to cover and limited daylight in which to achieve their goal.

'And while we're at it, I've a bone to pick with you.'

What bone? Set on edge by his hostile tone, she let the dogs harry the ewes through the gate then closed it briskly. Flint's limp definitely couldn't be ignored, whatever Laurence said.

'The money, I mean.' In between whistles, he threw disjointed remarks in Joyce's direction, his face hidden by the peak of his cap, small muscles in his cheek twitching as he talked. 'If you go and work part time on the Acklam estate, I'll be obliged to cut your wages.'

'You've read the note from Mrs Mostyn?'

He nodded. 'I'll still deduct sixteen shillings for board and lodging and I'll only pay you for the hours you work. Understood?'

'Yes. Does that mean you agree?'

'Does it make any difference what I think?'

Another whistle pierced the air and a thick flurry of snowflakes swept down the hillside. Joyce was chilled to the bone and heartily sick of Laurence's churlish ways. *I'm not surprised Alma refuses to share a bed with him,* she thought. Luckily, she was wise enough to keep this to herself.

'There's less for me to do here now that the walls are mended,' she pointed out. 'I'll keep to my milking routine and lend Alma a hand in the dairy. Then I'll walk over to Acklam and put in four or five hours with Evelyn.'

'How many days a week?'

'Two or three? Whichever you prefer.'

He grunted then concentrated on getting the sheep through the next gate.

'About Flint's foot,' Joyce said once her gate-closing duty was done. 'I am willing to fork out for the vet.'

'Fair enough. It's your own money you're wasting,' he muttered, watching two ewes veer off to the left and whistling to the dogs to fetch them back. Flint lagged behind Patch then took the weight off his foot by lying on the snowy ground.

'So it's settled.' She meant both the visit to the vet and the part-time work at Acklam. Her frustration didn't ease until they got the sheep into the lambing field and she and Laurence arrived back in the farmyard where she rubbed snow off the dogs' backs with a piece of sacking. It was caked on their bellies and legs. Flint whimpered when she wiped the affected paw. 'I'll get it seen to tomorrow,' she promised as she led him to his kennel.

When she went into the house and took off her

hat and coat, the bad atmosphere continued. Alma peeled potatoes at the sink and ignored Joyce as Laurence rattled coal from the scuttle on to the fire. It grated against the metal and fell with dull thuds on to the glowing embers, sending a shower of sparks up the chimney.

'Who left this dampener open?' Laurence demanded, seizing the poker and knocking the baffle sideways. 'Was it you, Alma?'

Joyce saw her stiffen and stop peeling.

'Do you think we have money to burn? Coal burns twice as fast this way. How many times do I have to tell you?'

Joyce watched Alma turn with the knife, seemingly fighting an urge to use it as a weapon or to rip and slash and destroy the perfect order she'd imposed – to fling crockery on to the floor, smash glasses and scatter burning coals. Instead, she slowly and deliberately put down the knife and raised her apron over her head. She folded it and placed it neatly over the back of the nearest chair. Then she took her coat and scarf from the hook. She opened the door and put on her gumboots. Outside the snowstorm continued.

Joyce stared at Laurence, who hadn't said a word. 'Aren't you going to stop her?' she demanded. 'The snow's set to get worse later on.'

Refusing to meet her eye, he thrust the empty coal scuttle at her. 'Fill this up,' he snapped before striding to the sink and lifting out the bowl of half-peeled potatoes. Water slopped on to the floor as he set about washing his hands.

To fetch coal Joyce had to put on her own coat and

go outside to the shed next to the WC. Meanwhile, Alma had set off across the yard.

Joyce ran after her. 'Where are you going in this weather?'

Alma pulled the woollen scarf over her chin so that only her eyes were showing. Delicate white flakes settled on her bare head. 'Anywhere.'

'But where exactly?'

'I don't care.'

Joyce made a spur-of-the-moment decision and put down the coal scuttle. 'I'm coming with you,' she told Alma. 'We'll walk together. Wherever you're going, I'm coming too.'

'When you think about it, she had nowhere to go.' Joyce leaned on her broom as she came to the end of telling Brenda about her previous night's wintry expedition with Alma. The two Land Girls had got together in the church meeting room, armed with brushes, mops and dusters to make the small hall ready for the Christmas dance due to take place in a week's time. 'It was dark and snowing like billy-o. So we walked as far as Mary's Fall then had to turn round and retrace our steps as best we could. By the time we got back to the farm, the snow was six inches deep.'

'What did his lordship say?' Brenda made no effort to conceal her low opinion of Laurence Bradley.

'Not a word. He didn't even look up from his newspaper.'

Brenda climbed on a chair to use a soft brush to sweep cobwebs from the picture rail and cornice, doubting that they'd get rid of the musty smell that pervaded the hall. She heard Evelyn and Dorothy talking and laughing in a small side room where refreshments were prepared for the local cricket and football teams. In a week's time it would be used to serve sandwiches and tea to the dancers at the Christmas hop. 'And you say it was over an argument about coal?'

'It was and it wasn't,' Joyce replied. 'Really, the coal was just an excuse for Mr Bradley to find fault. And I know for a fact that Alma is unhappy with her lot.' Reminding herself that it was best to say no more on this score, she went on to describe Mary's Fall in deep snow. 'There was ice on the pond and icicles as thick as your wrist hanging from ledges. Everywhere was pure white.'

'You can't beat a good snow scene,' Brenda agreed. 'Until it all gets trampled on and spoiled.' The laughter next door grew louder so she jumped down from the chair and flung open the door to find Dorothy and Evelyn studying pictures in a magazine. 'Aren't you two supposed to be counting cups and saucers, and so on?'

Dorothy whipped the magazine out of sight. 'We are!' she claimed, while Evelyn opened a cupboard door and began the task.

With an exaggerated school-ma'am frown, Brenda returned to her cobwebs. 'I've had a phone call from Una, by the way,' she told Joyce.

'Saying what?'

'Saying that they can only fit six in the van. They'll have to draw straws.'

Joyce went on sweeping. 'But Ma Craven has issued late passes?'

'Yes, provided the weather is decent. Did I tell you that I finally managed to have a word with the vicar?'

'No. Was it about Alan?'

Threads from a cobweb drifted across Brenda's cheek and she brushed them away. 'Yes. Mr Rigg agreed to let him change bedrooms but I could tell he wasn't best pleased.' She recalled the sour-lemon look on the clergyman's face as he'd listened to her reasoning behind the boy's request and the homily he'd delivered to Alan about guardian angels being forces for good, not evil. 'I only hope he doesn't take it out on the boy with that ruler of his when there's no one looking.'

'For doing what?'

Brenda shrugged. 'For having the nerve to complain.'

'But he didn't. He daren't.'

'We know that. But Mr Rigg doesn't seem to. Put up and shut up is his philosophy. And he made it clear that Alan mustn't expect to trot off and visit his sister whenever he feels like it. That's how he put it. Oh, and he's decided that it's not worth him starting school in Thwaite until the new term starts in January, so Alan's stuck in the vicarage, day in, day out.'

Brenda and Joyce worked on to the background sounds of crockery and cutlery being checked until Dorothy decided that it was high time they all stopped for a cup of tea.

'You know what they say about all work and no play,' she said with a wink as she ordered everyone to congregate in a corner of the hall.

'Yes, counting saucers is slave labour.' Brenda's

dry remark brought about a fresh peal of laughter as they arranged chairs so that they could put their feet on the radiator pipe running at floor level around the room. They sat back, cups in hand and gazed up at the high rafters festooned with yet more cobwebs – four young women dressed in slacks and dungarees, with sleeves rolled up and headscarves worn like turbans.

'We'll need the ladder to hang the paper chains,' Joyce observed. 'And does anyone know where we'll get a decent Christmas tree at short notice?'

Evelyn pointed theatrically at her own chest. 'Look no further!'

'Of course, silly me.' Joyce realized that Evelyn must have dozens of fir trees growing in amongst the oaks and chestnuts on the Acklam estate.

'You can help me choose one on your first day; when is it to be?'

'Tuesday.' Joyce took a sip of strong, sweet tea. 'I can't wait.'

'Anything to escape from Farmer Misery Guts, eh?'

Brenda's comment was swiftly followed by a 'Miaow!' from Dorothy.

'What do you mean? I'm not jealous.'

Dorothy raised an eyebrow.

'All right, then; just a tiny bit.' Brenda had to admit she fancied having a go with chainsaw and axe.

'So Joyce and I have the tree situation in hand,' Evelyn went on. 'And we'll bring holly and mistletoe. Dorothy, can you organize the decorations? You'll be a dab hand at that.'

'Tinsel, baubles, a fairy on the top,' Dorothy promised eagerly. 'Don't worry, I'll see to it.'

'Gramophone and dance records?' Evelyn ticked tasks off on her fingers. 'When are they due to arrive?'

'That'll be Geoff's job.' Dorothy told them that she'd reminded him twice already. 'I promised I'd go to New Hall and help him choose the records.'

'That's more of a threat than a promise, if you ask me.' Brenda made sure to return the teasing taunts. 'I'm only kidding,' she said before Dorothy could retaliate, then she stood up to collect the empty cups. She took them into the annexe and was about to rinse them when she noticed the magazine that Evelyn and Dorothy had been looking at. It lay on the window sill, open at a page displaying the latest style of wedding dress: a silky, frothy confection photographed on a sleek fashion model posing with a bouquet of pink carnations. Brenda picked it up and leafed through pages of more brides and bridesmaids standing in church porches and beside wedding cars. She didn't notice that Evelyn had crept up on her until the magazine was snatched from her grasp.

'This isn't mine.' Evelyn's hasty explanation came with an embarrassed frown.

'I didn't think it was,' Brenda said carefully.

'It belongs to Dorothy.'

'Yes. She loves her magazines.'

Brenda's bland responses roused Evelyn's suspicions and she grew more defensive still. Her cheeks flared red as she spoke. 'We were wondering how many clothing coupons it takes to make a wedding dress; idle curiosity, that's all.'

'Dozens,' Brenda guessed.

Evelyn stared angrily at her. 'What has Dorothy said?'

'Nothing, I swear.'

The colour vanished from Evelyn's face as quickly as it had appeared, leaving her cheeks white and her grey-green eyes flashing. 'I don't believe you.' Instead of waiting for a response, she rolled up the magazine like a baton and rushed into the hall. 'Dorothy Huby, you're a blithering idiot!' Her voice echoed round the empty room.

'Steady on.' Joyce put down the broom that she'd just picked up and stepped between Evelyn and Dorothy, who had retreated into a corner.

Beside herself, Evelyn flung the magazine on to the floor where it fell open again at the wedding pages. 'You promised hand on heart that you wouldn't say a word!'

'I didn't, I swear.' Tears sprang into Dorothy's eyes and her face crumpled into an expression that was half defiant, half helpless.

'You're a rotten liar,' Evelyn fumed, ignoring Joyce and turning to Brenda who had followed her into the hall. 'She told you about me and Cliff, didn't she?'

Brenda nodded without saying anything.

'Dorothy, I could wring your neck!'

'Evelyn, calm down.' As always, Joyce tried to smooth things over. 'You're upsetting her.'

'It slipped out; I didn't mean to.' Dorothy changed her story between sobs.

It made no difference to Evelyn, who was carried on a wave of emotion that crashed over Dorothy's bent head. 'And now the whole of Shawcross will find out. Cliff will blow a gasket. Colonel Weatherall will sack us both.'

'Wait a minute.' It was Brenda's turn to intervene. 'Are you saying that the reason behind all this secrecy is because your jobs are at stake?'

'Yes!' The admission robbed Evelyn of all her strength and she was forced to sit on the nearest chair and hold her head in her hands. 'Yes, yes. It's against the old man's rules. Cliff and I are not allowed to spoon. That's the word he uses. We're to stick to our own quarters: me in the stable block, Cliff in his cottage.'

'But you fell for each other regardless and now you're engaged?' Brenda sat beside her until she gathered her thoughts.

'Is that true?' Joyce's whispered question was directed at Dorothy who nodded miserably.

Evelyn took a deep breath and sat up straight. 'It's not me I'm worried about. If and when the old man kicks me out, I can easily be sent on to a new billet and carry on doing my tree felling and cross-cutting work and what have you. But it's different for Cliff. Gamekeeping jobs are few and far between. He might have to go all the way up to Scotland to find a new one.' The last sentence trailed away and she lowered her head into her hands once more.

'Yes, I can see that might be a problem,' Brenda acknowledged.

'The point is, it's best for Cliff to stay in Shawcross. Apart from anything else, it takes some of the weight off his dad's shoulders.'

'She means me,' Dorothy groaned. 'I'm the weight; I have to be looked after and driven everywhere.'

Evelyn didn't argue or offer any further explanation. She simply raised her head again and looked from Brenda to Joyce in silent appeal.

They spoke over each other, eager to reassure.

'No one needs to know.'

'Don't worry, we won't say a word.'

With two jobs on the line, there was no doubt in their minds that they would keep Evelyn's secret.

'Are you sure?' Evelyn whispered.

Joyce stooped to pick up the magazine and hand it to her with a firm nod. Brenda smiled. 'We're happy for you,' she assured Evelyn. 'We enjoy a good love story as much as anyone, don't we, Joyce?'

'Oh, I love Cliff more than anything.' Evelyn spoke with new energy that brought a shine to her features and seemed to light up the neglected hall. 'And he loves me. We're to be married just as soon as he manages to find a new job in Yorkshire; somewhere nice and close to home.'

CHAPTER ELEVEN

Evelyn's confession had brought the girls together and they worked on with a will. They swept and dusted, mopped and scrubbed until every surface in the church hall shone and they were sure that the Rixley RAF boys and the Fieldhead Land Girls would find no fault with their preparations. It was two o'clock by the time they'd finished and Dorothy had sloped off somewhere, leaving Brenda, Joyce and Evelyn to finish washing the windows inside and out.

Joyce was up a stepladder, wiping the window above the main entrance with a soft chamois leather when Emma hurried up the path.

'You haven't clapped eyes on Alan, by any chance?' she boomed in her foghorn voice.

Joyce came down the ladder. 'No. Why?'

'He's given the vicar the slip, that's why.' The old woman didn't seem unduly worried; in fact, she folded her arms and took a step back to critique the finish on Joyce's newly washed windows. 'I'd give that one more going-over with the chamois if I were you,' she commented.

'I'm afraid I haven't seen Alan, but let's check with the others.' Joyce led the way into the hall.

'The vicar's on the warpath.' Emma barged in front of Joyce to make her announcement. 'His latest lad has gone AWOL. Has anybody seen him?'

'Not since I arrived here first thing this morning.' Evelyn was pacing out the length of the hall to estimate how many yards of paper-chain decoration they would need to make. 'I spotted him standing on the bridge by New Hall.'

'What time was that?' Emma asked.

'Around half eight. It was hardly light so I was surprised to see him out and about so early. Then I came inside and forgot all about it.'

'Have you tried Geoff's house?' To Brenda it seemed the obvious line of enquiry.

'Yes, the vicar's looked everywhere: New Hall, the pub, the riverside footpath, the lanes leading to all the farms. No one's seen hide nor hair of him.'

Brenda frowned at Joyce and Evelyn. 'You don't suppose he'd try to reach Attercliffe on foot, do you?'

'Why would he do that?' Evelyn asked.

'Because his sister is living at the Whites' place and Donald drove Alan and me there last Sunday. Alan's got a bad case of homesickness. I thought a visit to see Judith might help.'

'But it could actually have made him pine all the more,' Joyce suggested. 'What if he's taken it into his head to walk all the way to Attercliffe?' She imagined the boy lost on Swinsty Moor with darkness falling and with it the threat of more snow.

'Let's hope he stuck closer to home.' Evelyn decided

it was worth conducting a thorough search of the church hall. She went outside and quickly looked inside the lean-to building at the back where the mops, buckets and brooms were stored then came back in and opened every cupboard in the kitchen. 'Where would I try to hide if I ran away from the vicarage?' she wondered out loud. 'Maybe a barn or a shed; somewhere I could keep warm.'

'That would make sense,' Brenda agreed. 'But maybe Alan wasn't thinking straight. The truth is, he could be anywhere.'

Evelyn, Joyce and Brenda shook their heads while Emma ran her fingers over the surfaces that they'd cleaned. 'I told the vicar not to fret; the lad will find his own way back when his stomach starts to rumble. They always do.'

Concerned nevertheless, Joyce told the others that she would run and check again at New Hall. No sooner said than she grabbed her coat and hurried down the track next to the churchyard, crossing over the bridge and running up the drive to Geoff Dawson's house. She raised the knocker and rapped loudly on the main door.

Geoff opened it with a welcoming smile. 'Joyce, it's nice to see you. And before you ask, it's all in hand. I've arranged with Dorothy to bring the gramophone tomorrow after church.'

'It's not that,' she said breathlessly. 'Little Alan Evans has disappeared. We wondered if you'd seen him.'

Geoff invited her to step inside out of the cold. 'I've only just got back from my morning calls. Let's take a look around the back, shall we?'

She followed him into the kitchen and out of a door leading to the garden where they called the boy's name and began to search sheds containing gardening tools and lawnmowers. They disturbed a black cat, which jumped out from under an upturned wheelbarrow and fled across the orchard.

'Is that supposed to be lucky or unlucky, I can never remember?' Geoff asked with a tight smile. 'There's no sign of the lad, I'm afraid.'

Joyce stood, hands on hips, surveying the veg patch and watching the cat disappear into a cart shed beyond. She was about to thank Geoff and report back to Emma when a movement in the shed's dark interior caught her eye. She stiffened and looked again as the cat re-emerged into the daylight. Its back was arched and it stalked off towards the orchard. 'Wait a second,' she murmured.

She approached the cart shed warily and stopped a few yards short of the entrance. Her view of the interior was obscured by a length of hessian curtain screening off the contents of the shed. 'Alan?' she called softly.

There was no reply, only a strong sense that some-one or something had taken refuge inside.

Joyce persevered. 'Alan, are you there? Come out if you are. You're not in any trouble.' She waited again and saw the hessian screen shift. The runaway emerged, his face grey and peaky, his body shaking with cold. She crouched down to his level and waited for him to approach while Geoff took the wise decision to hang back out of sight.

Alan stepped forward, eyes darting this way and that.

'Are you hungry?' she asked.

He nodded.

'Then come into the house. Let's see what we can find for you to eat.' She took his hand and led him across the lawn into the warm kitchen where Geoff waited. 'Look who I've found!' she said as brightly as she could. 'A little stowaway in need of ship's biscuits and a big helping of grog!'

'Biscuits and grog coming up,' Geoff said with a wink. He opened a tin containing cream crackers then produced a glass of blackcurrant juice. 'Now knock it back,' he urged, having made sure that the boy could grasp the glass between his frozen fingers.

Alan ate ravenously, cramming crackers into his mouth and ignoring the crumbs that fell down the front of his mac. Occasionally he paused to swig down some of the sugary drink.

'Mr Rigg has been looking for you,' Joyce said in an even tone.

Alan let the biscuit drop on to the table. His whole body deflated like a pricked balloon; his head dropped and his shoulders hunched and he let out a long sigh.

'He was worried that you'd got lost,' she explained. 'The thing is, Alan, you have to tell Mr Rigg where you're going instead of just wandering off. You see that, don't you?'

Still hunched forward, he refused to respond.

Joyce glanced at Geoff. 'I suppose I'd better tell everyone the good news.'

'No, let me. You two stay where you are.' Before Joyce could argue, Geoff went off to find Walter Rigg.

'I'm sorry, Alan.' Resisting the urge to hug him, she watched him stare unseeingly at the half-eaten cracker. 'Mr Rigg has to be told.'

The boy remained silent but the look of panic in his eyes said it all.

'I know you're not keen to be sent back to the vicarage, but we don't have any choice.'

Shaking his head, he backed away into a corner. 'He'll give me the cane,' he whimpered, scarcely audible. 'It hurts.'

'Let's hope not.' After a while Joyce heard footsteps approaching round the side of the house and saw through the window that Geoff was returning with the clergyman, whose face was mottled and unsmiling. With a flash of insight she saw how big, cold, unfriendly and terrifying the world must seem to a child completely cut off from family and familiar surroundings, and she determined to have a strong exchange of words with Walter Rigg if necessary. She put an arm around Alan's shoulder and steeled herself as the men came in.

'There you are!' The vicar's bland comment gave nothing away. He put on a fixed smile and nodded at Joyce and Geoff. 'I'm very sorry that Alan has been such a nuisance. Rest assured that I'll do everything in my power to make sure that it doesn't happen again.'

'No trouble,' Geoff assured him. His Adam's apple moved up and down repeatedly as he swallowed back what he was tempted to say and looked intently at Joyce.

'No trouble at all,' she echoed, her intention to confront the vicar wilting under his blank, brick-wall gaze. 'In fact, I'd like Alan to help us decorate the hall after church tomorrow if that's all right with you.'

Wrong-footed, Rigg gave a startled blink then made a hasty excuse. 'No, the boy would only get in the way.'

'Not at all. And it would do him good to join in with events in the village in the run-up to Christmas. We can help Alan to get in the festive mood by letting him hang paper chains and so on.'

'I disagree.' A glint of resentment at Joyce's interference appeared in Walter Rigg's eyes. 'Treats have to be earned through good behaviour and I'm afraid Alan has still to learn that lesson.'

Joyce's reply was slow and deliberate. 'On the contrary, I find him very polite and well behaved, if a little shy. In my opinion he should be encouraged out of his shell by joining in with whatever is going on.'

Rigg jutted out his bottom lip and stood his ground. 'No, not tomorrow.'

She judged her next move then spoke even more firmly. 'That's a pity because I hear that Alan isn't due to start school in Thwaite until after Christmas and that means he has no chance to make friends of his own age. That certainly wouldn't be what his mother and father had in mind when they sent him here. I'm sure they thought that he would be carrying on with his schooling straight away.'

The colour deepened in Rigg's face, prompting Geoff to clear his throat and take a step forward. 'I'll tell you what, why don't we make a decision tomorrow morning when things have cooled down?'

A curt nod from Rigg brought the conversation to a close. 'Come with me, Alan.'

The boy cringed as the vicar held out his hand.

Rigg took a firm hold of his wrist and marched him towards the door. 'And when we get home I will expect you to give a full account of what you've been up to since eight o'clock this morning. No fibs, no excuses.'

Joyce swallowed hard. 'I'll walk part of the way with you,' she volunteered.

'And I'll see everyone at church tomorrow morning,' Geoff promised as he held open the front door. He smiled ruefully at Joyce as she walked down the drive with Rigg and Alan in miserable silence.

They went over the bridge and up the lane towards the church, to be met by a relieved Brenda and Evelyn. Emma had already disappeared into her cottage and Dorothy was hurrying across the green to rejoin the group.

'Good; all's well that ends well!' Brenda declared when she saw Alan with the vicar.

Walter Rigg hurried the boy on towards the vicarage without saying a word.

'Oh dear,' Evelyn commented as she fetched her bike from the church hall porch.

'Yes; oh dear.' Joyce was forced to accept that her latest attempts to help could well have backfired. Her only hope was that Rigg wouldn't be too harsh on Alan now that he knew that she and Geoff were keeping a close eye on him. *Whatever happened to the spirit of good will?* she wondered. She was about to set off on the long walk to Black Crag Farm when Dorothy joined them.

'Brenda, you have to get on your motor bike and ride like the wind to Attercliffe,' she said, her face flushed with excitement. 'Now, right this minute!'

Brenda's heart thudded against her ribs. 'Why? What's happened?' But she knew without being told. 'It's Hettie, isn't it?'

'I don't know. They – he – didn't say.' Dorothy's words came out in a rush. 'There was a telephone call. It was a man's voice. He said please could you go straight away, without any delay. There; that's all I can remember.'

Brenda's heart went on knocking against her ribs and her mouth was dry but she forced herself into action. She set off across the green at a run, through the gate and up the lane to Garthside, dragging air into her lungs, afraid that her legs would give out before she reached the farmyard. She arrived at last and ran inside for her jacket and goggles, was out again and kicking Sloper into action almost without knowing it. Then she set off for Attercliffe, weighed down by the prospect of what lay ahead.

Donald waited at the door of Dale End, his face drained of colour. There was no greeting for Brenda, only a gesture that said she should hurry inside.

With mounting dread she went in to find Arnold hovering at the entrance to his study, his face similarly grim, his stance uncertain.

'She's upstairs in bed.' He rolled his eyes towards the wide staircase, indicating that Brenda should go up.

She hesitated and glanced at Donald. 'Will you show me which room it is?'

He nodded then took her upstairs and along the landing, opening a door into his sister's room before backing up against the banister overlooking the hall below.

Brenda stepped inside, leaving the door open and waiting for her eyes to adjust to the gloom. The blackout blinds were down and the four-poster bed was draped with scarlet brocade curtains whose swirling pattern caught the yellow light of a table lamp next to the bed. Its sheen held Brenda's attention as she went closer. Then she forced herself to look at the bed's occupant.

Hettie lay with her eyes open and her hands free of the white sheets. They rested on the counterpane and her dark hair was loose on the pillow. Only her eyes moved as Brenda approached then sat on the edge of the carved oak chair at the side of the bed. 'What are you doing here? I didn't ask for you to come,' she said with infinite weariness.

'I think it was Donald's idea. Shall I go away again?'

Hettie's eyes closed briefly. When she opened them, tears formed and trickled down her deathly pale cheeks. 'He told Les to come too. I didn't want him to.'

Brenda reached out to touch the gleaming red bed cover. 'Will the Navy let him?'

'I don't know,' was the agonized response. 'Brenda, you understand that I don't want Les to see me like this.' One skeletal hand moved to clasp her visitor's.

'I do,' Brenda whispered back. She cradled the bony hand. 'But dear Hettie, Les loves you. He won't mind how you look. And Donald loves you, too – very much. He's done what he thinks is best.'

The dying woman's sunken eyes were fixed on Brenda's face and her breath came in shallow, uneven bursts. 'I didn't let them see Mother in this state. Was that wrong of me?'

'No, they were very young then. You wanted to shield them. But they're grown men now and they love you.' She repeated this idea, hoping that it would break down the last barrier that Hettie would ever build so that the family could say their good-byes to this dignified, imperious, handsome woman. Brenda thought of what Hettie had sacrificed in her life – independence, marriage, the chance of having children of her own – all through unquestioning devotion to her father and brothers. 'And I've always looked up to you, Hettie. I was scared of you at first, I don't mind admitting. I called you the dragon-sister.'

'Yes, Les told me.' Hettie's fingers closed softly around Brenda's hand.

'The first time we met, you lent me a pair of your slacks, do you remember?'

Hettie nodded. 'You were riding your motor bike. Donald forced you off the road in Les's sports car. Your trousers were ruined.'

'It was Fate,' Brenda told her. 'If I hadn't had the accident, I'd never have met the man I'm going to marry.'

Outside the room, Arnold had joined Donald. Their low voices attracted Hettie's attention and frown lines creased her forehead.

'Shall I close the door?' Brenda asked.

'Yes, please.'

So she trod softly across the room. 'You don't

mind?' she checked with the two men as she made as if to shut the door.

Arnold put out his hand to stop her. 'Is Hettie awake?'

'Yes, but she's very tired.'

'Les is here.' Paralysed by a sense of impending loss, Hettie's father and brother looked to Brenda to tell them what to do. Nothing remained of Arnold's clipped, military manner or of Donald's devil-may-care gregariousness. Grief had stripped them bare.

'Tell him to come up,' Brenda whispered. 'Or rather, wait a second.' She retraced her steps to Hettie's bedside. 'Will you see Les after all?' she asked as she stroked her hand.

A faint nod gave Brenda the permission she needed so she withdrew again and hurried straight downstairs to find Les waiting in the tiled hall, Royal Navy cap in hand, the gold braid on his dark blue jacket denoting his rank of chief petty officer. He was the same but different; his fair hair was shorter, his face more tanned, but he was still slight and had kept the edge of vulnerability that his smart uniform couldn't completely disguise. Her heart almost burst to see him.

'I came as quick as I could,' he stammered.

She took a deep, shuddering breath to keep control of herself.

'I'm not too late?'

Brenda shook her head and took his hand. They went upstairs together. On the landing Les exchanged looks with his father and brother but didn't speak to them as he went on alone into his sister's room.

'Thank you,' Brenda whispered to Donald as Les closed the door behind him.

The light faded quickly in a sky that had been leaden all day. Les was with Hettie when she breathed her last, stroking her forehead and leaning in to touch her cheek with his lips. Then he sat with her in the deepest of all silences, watching the change in Hettie's physical being as life departed; an absence where there had been a presence, an absolute stillness.

After a quarter of an hour he went to the door. He held it open to let his father and brother see and understand.

Downstairs he found Brenda in the sitting room, turning towards him with quiet certainty in her dark brown eyes.

'She's gone,' he confirmed.

Brenda held his hands. She felt the weight of them and sensed his acceptance, knowing that the sharp stabs of loss had not yet set in. Then they sat together on Hettie's favourite sofa, looking out on to her garden. Her bed of yellow roses was pruned and bare; it would be many months before new flower buds formed.

'They gave me twenty-four hours,' Les said quietly. 'I've to be back in Portsmouth by midday tomorrow.'

'You were here when it happened. That's what matters.'

Upstairs there was the click of a door closing followed by the tread of two sets of footsteps along the landing. Then silence again.

'I don't know how Dad will manage without her.'

'He will, though. He still has Donald and you.

And a farm and a business to run.' But Brenda acknowledged that there was a particular type of savage sorrow when a child died; an upsetting of the natural order that made it all the harder to bear. It would take a long time for Arnold to get over this, or to live with it at least.

'I'll apply for funeral leave, once we know when it is. Before Christmas, let's hope.'

Christmas! Brenda's thoughts flew back to the time in the Cross Keys where Dorothy had encouraged them all to share light-hearted seasonal wishes, when it had been Joyce who had introduced the sober note and fervently wished for the safety of loved ones during the war-torn times. *Trust Joyce to hit the nail on the head.* 'Will you still be in Portsmouth?' she asked.

Les shook his head. 'We're due to sail up to the west coast of Scotland on Monday. That's as much as I can tell you.'

The snippet reassured her a little. 'That has to be better than the Med?'

He was tight-lipped as he stood up and walked to the French windows. 'I'll write,' he promised. 'But there's no guarantee that my letters will get through.'

'No. We'll have to take each day as it comes.'

They talked quietly in the presence of death, careful not to open a Pandora's box of ragged emotions: their endless, unfulfilled longings to hold each other through day and night; her fears for his safety in the face of stealthy torpedoes and whining, roaring Messerschmitts; his image of her as a wild spirit who could at any moment escape from the cage of their engagement and fly free.

'I love you,' they whispered to each other before Donald opened the door and entered the room, his cheeks wet with tears. He came to stand between them and stare out of the window at the bare, frozen earth.

At church next morning, Brenda stood next to Joyce with her hymn book open, unable to sing the words. Events of the day before and a sleepless night had left her feeling that she existed inside a strange bubble, unable to experience what was going on around her.

'Hello there, Brenda, you look shocking!' Dorothy had exclaimed in the church porch as they'd filed in behind the Hubys and in front of Geoff, who stayed at the back of the church to discuss a course of treatment for mastitis with one of his dairy farmer friends.

'Ta for that,' Brenda had replied with none of her usual verve.

Joyce had frowned at Dorothy who had taken the hint then immediately caught up with Evelyn and ostentatiously linked arms with her and made sure that they sat together in a pew wedged between Bernard and Cliff.

The vicar had glided out of the vestry in his white sail of a surplice and led his flock in prayer, filling the church with loud, unctuous certainty while his unhappy evacuee sat cowed and alone in the front pew. Joyce had occasionally caught sight of the boy's back view between taller members of the congregation: the bristles of his closely cropped hair, the red ears that stuck out, the scrawny neck. She'd remembered Alan's dread of the cane and tried not to imagine what had gone on the day before, once the vicar had closed his front door on the world.

At the close of the hymns, prayers and seemingly endless sermon, Joyce leaned in towards Brenda. 'Dorothy was right: you do look as if you've been through the mill.'

A heavy sigh showed that Brenda was too tired to deny it.

'Don't you think it would be best to put off decorating the hall until later this week?'

Brenda nodded weakly.

'Good, that's settled. Leave it to me; I'll fix a new time with Evelyn and Dorothy while you take yourself off home.'

At the church gate they went their separate ways: Brenda back to bed in her goods wagon, Joyce to Black Crag Farm on her bike. The air was bitterly cold and she was glad of the thick woollen scarf pulled over the lower part of her face and of her Land Girl hat pulled well down over her forehead. Still, she arrived at the farm with pinched cheeks and frozen fingertips and was stamping her feet on the flagstones to restore circulation when a smart Ford car followed her into the yard with a woman she had never seen before sitting at the wheel. By the time Joyce had taken her bike into the shed, the slim, well-dressed woman had stepped out of the car and was knocking impatiently on the farmhouse door.

Laurence opened it and waited for the visitor to speak first.

'Well?' Her voice was low and matter-of-fact, as if

continuing a conversation rather than greeting someone afresh. She wore a camel-hair coat with a lustrous fur collar and a matching hat with a fashionable, narrow brim. Her heeled shoes were unsuitable for the countryside: thin-soled with a pointed toe and a slender T-strap.

Laurence didn't stand aside to let her in. Instead, he beckoned for Joyce to join them. 'A ewe's got out of low field,' he told her. 'We'll need to fetch her back.'

'Right you are.' Joyce was willing to set off immediately.

'Not now. Later will do.'

The visitor studied Joyce with undisguised curiosity. 'Who is this, pray?' she said as she pushed past Laurence and entered the kitchen.

'None of your business.' With another quick nod of the head, Laurence gestured for Joyce to follow them in. 'Now then, Muriel, to what do we owe the honour?'

'I've come to see Alma; what else?' The visitor scanned the tidy room as she set her crocodile-skin handbag down on the table then gave a small, satisfied grunt. 'At least her housekeeping's still up to scratch.'

Laurence glared at her then turned to Joyce. 'This is Alma's aunt, Muriel Woodthorpe.'

'And you are?' Muriel ignored Joyce's tentative offer to shake hands.

'Joyce Cutler. I help Mr Bradley with the sheep.'

'I see.' She scrutinized Joyce through narrowed eyes, taking in her best woollen dress and trim figure as she hung up her coat and hat. 'Is this what a

Land Girl looks like? I'd expected corduroy breeches and gaiters.'

'Most people do.' Joyce returned the stare. 'But Sunday is my day off.' Despite Muriel's careful attention to her appearance and a small, even-featured face, Joyce thought she'd rarely come across anyone as immediately off-putting as Alma's aunt.

There was an awkward silence as Muriel took off her own coat and gloves. She left her hat on, patting the sides of her grey, permed hair into place as she sat down at the table. 'I presume Alma would have heard my car arrive?'

'She did.' Laurence didn't budge from his position by the door.

'So where is she?'

'Upstairs.'

Muriel tapped her forefinger on the table. 'Do I have to go up and fetch her or will you bring her down?'

He tilted his head to one side. 'What if she doesn't want to see you? Has that crossed your mind?'

'Tell her I've got all day if necessary.' Equally immovable, Muriel went on tapping, only stopping when they heard slow footsteps descend the stairs.

Alma came into the room, head down and hands clasped in front of her. Her hair was loose, held clear of her face by a pale blue Alice band that matched her blouse. She wore the same long pleated skirt as usual.

'Hello, stranger.' Muriel's disdainful voice cut through the silence and she patted the seat of a chair next to her. 'Come and sit down. I'm eager to hear how married life suits you.'

'Hello, Aunty Muriel.' Alma sat reluctantly, every nerve straining to stay as far away from her aunt as possible.

Muriel turned to Joyce. 'Since you're here, why not make yourself useful?' she suggested with a glance in the direction of the kettle on the hob.

Joyce busied herself at the tap, suspecting that at this rate the atmosphere in the room was set to reach boiling point long before the water in the kettle did.

'Well?' Muriel said in the same way as before.

'It suits me perfectly, thank you.'

'That's just as well, since there's no going back once the vows are exchanged, eh, Laurence?'

With a face like thunder he joined Alma and Muriel at the table. 'Why are you bothering us?' he demanded. 'You've left Alma alone all these months, so why turn up now?'

'Because!' Muriel's airy reply was accompanied by a waft of the hand. 'Why not? It's coming up to Christmas, the season of good will. Besides, Alma is my niece, my dead sister's girl. I brought her up as if she was my own.'

'It's all right, Laurence.' Alma spoke with quiet resignation. 'You and Joyce should go after that ewe while Aunty Muriel and I have a chat.'

Ready to take her advice, Joyce produced cups, saucers and a milk jug from the cupboard. 'There are two scoops of tea leaves in the pot,' she told Alma. 'All you have to do is pour in the hot water.'

But Laurence stayed where he was. 'Whatever you have to say to Alma, say it in front of me. Go on, Muriel, ask her how I've been treating her. Ask her if

I'm as bad as they say. Am I driving Alma to drink the way I did Lily?'

Joyce took a sharp breath and shot a look of alarm at Alma, whose right hand flew automatically to her face.

Muriel's lip curled. 'Ever the gentleman, eh, Laurence?'

His fist thumped the table and he knocked his chair over as he stood up. He stooped to set it right, looking for a moment as if he might use it as a weapon against the visitor.

Alma reached across the table to put a restraining hand on his arm while looking directly at her aunt. 'It's no good, Aunty Muriel; if you can't be civil, I'll have to ask you to leave.'

The older woman's tongue tutted rapidly against her teeth. 'Did you hear that?' she appealed to Joyce. 'My own niece is turning me away!'

'You can stay so long as you behave yourself.' Alma's voice grew clearer and her chin was up. 'It's not on, Aunty Muriel.'

Surprise flickered across the older woman's features: a blink, a twitch of the mouth. 'What's got into you?' she muttered, once she'd recovered her composure. 'Back in the old days, you knew not to give me any cheek.'

'If she stays, I'm off.' Laurence didn't wait to hear more. Instead, he jammed his chair back under the table. 'Hurry up and get changed, Joyce. I'll wait for you outside.'

He slammed the door behind him and Muriel tutted again. Tap-tap-tap went the manicured finger. 'Honestly, Alma, you can't say I didn't warn you.'

Joyce flicked her hair back as if swatting a fly. The woman was a nightmare and she wondered how her niece had managed to survive under her roof for so long. Instead of changing her dress, she grabbed her Land Girl overcoat and jammed her feet into her wellington boots. In less than a minute she'd joined Laurence in the yard.

He ordered her to follow him. 'The ewe that got out has a bad case of sheep scab. We have to find her and treat it before it spreads to the rest of the flock.'

'I know the one you mean,' Joyce said, running to keep up.

'Bloody woman,' was all he said about Muriel Woodthorpe as a blast of icy wind buffeted them sideways. 'I could wring her sodding neck.'

CHAPTER TWELVE

Joyce imagined that this would be Laurence's last word on the subject of Alma's aunt. She expected them to work together in silence, rounding up the escaped ewe and bringing her back to the yard where they would break the ice in the sheep dip, add a fungicide powder to the water then fully submerge the animal. This would deal with the mites that had caused the scabs on her back and shoulders.

They achieved the first part of the job without difficulty; the pregnant ewe hadn't strayed far and offered little resistance to being rounded up by Patch. She was in a sorry state, with strips of matted fleece hanging from bare, scabbed flesh that had become red and infected from her rubbing against stone walls and rough tree bark.

Laurence looked concerned. 'Let's hope we can cure this before she drops her lamb.'

Joyce watched the dog drive the sheep along the lane then ran ahead to open the gate into the farm-yard. 'What fungicide do you use?'

'Cooper's Dip; old fashioned but it does the trick. You'll find it on a high shelf in the feed shed.'

Skirting wide of Muriel's parked car, Joyce hurried

to fetch the powder, keeping her fingers crossed that they could finish the job and be out of the way before the visitor emerged from the house. She rejoined Laurence in a corner of the yard, beside a concrete tank that had been sunk into the ground. He stood astride the sick ewe while Patch lay obediently to heel.

'Use that mattock to break the ice.' He pointed to some heavy tools resting against a nearby wall.

Joyce picked one up, lifted it over her head and brought it down hard. The thick ice shattered under the first blow. Now the shards had to be lifted out and the powder poured into the tank.

'Be careful,' Laurence warned. 'It's got a fair bit of arsenic in it.'

Their backs were turned to the house and they were too busy to notice when Muriel stepped out into the yard. Alma looked on uncertainly from the doorway.

Joyce used a spade to mix the contents of the tank, making the murky water swirl and the powder dissolve. 'You won't like this,' she warned the sheep, whose ears had gone back and whose eyes had started to roll. 'But it's for your own good.' Her sheep-rearing background told her that the ewe must stay underwater, head included, for at least sixty seconds. 'Ready?' she asked Laurence.

'Yes. I'll deal with the back end. You take her by the horns. One, two, three . . . lift!'

Together they raised the pregnant sheep and swung her over the dip. Then they plunged her in and knelt to hold her firmly under the water. They felt her squirm and kick then go limp. At the end of one minute they heaved her out and set her back on her feet.

She gave a long, pathetic bleat then put her head down and charged blindly across the yard, straight towards the parked car. Spying the danger to her vehicle, Muriel raised her fist and yelled. Joyce heard Laurence give a loud guffaw; it was the first genuine laugh she'd heard from him in all her time at the farm.

'Shoo! Get away!' The irate town dweller used the only weapon she had. She ran forward and swung her handbag at the drenched ewe, which skittered sideways at the last second, causing Muriel to over-balance, totter forwards then go crashing down on to her knees.

Alma ventured slowly out of the porch to offer a hand. 'Here, Aunty Muriel; let me take a look.'

'My knees!' Allowing herself to be helped on to her feet, she looked down in dismay at her ruined nylon stockings and grazed legs. Blood had already begun to trickle from the wounds.

Alma quickly decided she couldn't allow her aunt to drive away in this state. 'Come back inside. Let me clean you up,' she offered.

Meanwhile, Laurence and Joyce set about the task of recapturing the ewe. Together with Patch, they drove the panicky, dripping creature out of the yard and along the lane, back towards the lambing field.

'I wouldn't have helped her,' Laurence growled as they went. 'I'd have left her to pick herself up off the ground after all she's done.'

'To Alma?'

'Yes. My wife doesn't owe that woman any favours. Muriel reckoned to look after her when she was growing up but what she did was turn her into an unpaid skivvy – never bought her any nice clothes or said anything kind, never let her go out by herself.'

The outburst took Joyce aback. She'd always imagined that it was Laurence himself who had set up the strict regime for Alma once she'd arrived at Black Crag Farm. Now it seemed it had been established a long time before their marriage.

'Worse than that,' he went on as Joyce opened the field gate and he and Patch drove the ewe in, 'she wouldn't ever let Alma forget about the scars on her face, kept on telling her not to think about having what she called "a normal life".'

'That's shocking,' Joyce said firmly. It fitted in with what Alma had told her and did nothing to improve her opinion of the visitor.

'But nothing compared with what she said after Alma and I started courting.' He watched the ewe join the others bunched together under a stand of hawthorn trees.

'I can imagine.'

Laurence closed the gate with a firm click and turned up the lane. 'No, you can't,' he contradicted without looking back. 'You're a good-hearted lass, Joyce. Muriel Woodthorpe is a nasty piece of work. Never in a month of Sundays could you understand what goes on in the mind of a woman like that.'

'At this rate I'll be seeing paper chains in my sleep!' Evelyn stood on a stepladder in the church hall, holding the coloured decorations that she and

Dorothy had been making over the previous few days. Some were already hung between the beams but as yet there was no sign of a Christmas tree, holly or mistletoe to complete the decorative effect. 'How many days have we got before the dance?'

Dorothy counted them off on her fingers. 'Today's Monday. Tuesday, Wednesday, Thursday, Friday, Saturday – that's five days for us to get everything ready.'

Evelyn separated one of the chains from the bundle and handed an end to Joyce. 'Hold on to that while I sort myself out.' She came down the ladder then stretched the chain towards a corner of the hall. 'By the way, where's Brenda when we need her?'

It was Dorothy who leaped in with the answer. 'Her fiancé's sister has passed away. Brenda's lying low in her room for a bit.'

'I see.' Evelyn climbed the ladder again. 'That's poor timing, just coming up to Christmas. How old was the sister?'

'In her early thirties.' Joyce stood patiently holding her end of the chain while Evelyn secured the other with a drawing pin. She'd hardly finished her sentence when Cliff breezed in.

'Look what the cat dragged in,' Dorothy remarked. She and her brother were still at loggerheads over her letting slip the news about his and Evelyn's engagement. That was the thing about Cliff; he always knew when Dorothy had done something wrong, just by the look on her face. So he'd wormed a confession out of her then lost his temper and demanded to know exactly who she'd told. She'd retorted that it wasn't her fault if he and Evelyn chose to keep the whole thing a secret. It was bound to come out sooner or later.

'Where's Geoff?' Cliff ignored both his sister and Evelyn and instead made a beeline towards Joyce. 'He was meant to bring his gramophone.'

'That was yesterday, silly,' Dorothy interrupted. She pointed to a smart walnut cabinet set in a corner of the hall. 'What do you think that is?'

'Geoff says the plug's faulty. I promised to take a look at it.' Pulling a screwdriver out of his jacket pocket, Cliff got to work.

Up her ladder, Evelyn's movements grew stiff and awkward and she fumbled with her box of drawing pins.

The chilly atmosphere was only broken when Walter Rigg appeared unexpectedly with Alan at his side. 'Good evening, all.' His sonorous voice carried around the high-ceilinged room. 'Look who I've brought to lend a helping hand.'

The announcement astonished Joyce, who had been convinced that Alan would still be in solitary confinement after his ill-judged bid for freedom.

The vicar evidently had a point to prove. 'He can fetch and carry for you, can't you, Alan? After all, he's learned his lesson.'

The last phrase made Joyce wince but she determined that it was best to gloss over the clergyman's zeal for corporal punishment. 'Well, that's grand,' she said with a forced smile as she gave the boy her end of the paper chain.

Alan's hand shook as he took it and his face had the haunted look that Joyce recognized: eyes wide and dark, brow furrowed, mouth slightly open. He stood stock still in the middle of the hall, awaiting his next order.

'Alan can stay for an hour,' Walter Rigg announced with a tap of his wrist watch. 'I'll come and collect him at eight on the dot.'

Joyce assured him there was no need; she would bring the boy back to the vicarage herself.

'Very well; I'm much obliged.' He beamed up at Evelyn and said a pleasant goodbye to Dorothy and Cliff, crossing paths with Geoff on his way out of the building.

'Good evening, all. I can't stop.' Geoff had dropped by with more dance records. He had on a casual dark grey jerkin that fastened with a zip and a dark red cravat with a paisley pattern. His wayward lick of hair was combed and smoothed down with Brylcreem. 'Have a listen to these, Dorothy. There's a Victor Silvester and a Glenn Miller in amongst that lot.'

Dorothy sorted through the records with a broad smile until a sudden thought struck her. 'There's one thing I haven't taken into account,' she admitted. 'Who's going to stand by on Saturday night, ready to change the records when they finish?'

'Me; I'm your man,' Geoff assured her. 'It'll save the embarrassment of asking some poor soul to dance if you put me in charge of the music.'

'Your dancing can't be that bad, surely?' Joyce pictured Geoff cutting a fine figure on the dance floor. After all, he was tall and trim and went about his daily business with an understated grace.

'Two left feet,' he assured her. 'Ask Evelyn – she has the bruises to prove it.'

Evelyn descended her stepladder, one wary eye on Cliff who was still busy with the electrical plug. 'It's true. For a man who likes his music, Geoff's sense of rhythm goes AWOL when it comes to the Circassian Circle and Strip the Willow.'

He blushed then laughed. 'My brain refuses to tell my feet what to do. Evelyn and Dorothy found it out to their cost at the Whitsuntide barn dance, which was the last do we put on here.'

Dorothy smiled coquettishly as she took the pile of records to the gramophone and selected the top one. 'Hurry up with the plug, Cliff.'

He'd removed the back and inserted a new fuse. Now he was searching on the floor for a dropped screw. 'What's the hurry? Just put the bloody things down and come back when I'm finished.'

'I'll be off, then.' Geoff made a point of smiling at Alan, who still hadn't moved from the spot. 'Do we know what Father Christmas is bringing us this year?'

Alan frowned and shook his head.

'What would you like him to bring?'

'Nothing.'

'That can't be true, surely? What about a toy train or an Airfix kit? A sailing boat, perhaps?'

'Nothing,' he whispered again. 'Father Christmas is like fairies: he isn't real.'

'Who says so?' Evelyn asked as she disentangled a second length of paper chain.

'Mr Rigg.'

'He does, does he?'

'Yes. He says only God is real, and angels. Angels stand guard when you go to Heaven. They know when you've told a lie and then they won't let you in.'

Evelyn puffed out her cheeks then let out a light, popping breath. 'That's me done for,' she said with a wink.

'And ninety-nine per cent of the rest of us.' This time Geoff really did make his exit. 'Take care not to overdo it,' he warned Dorothy on his way out.

'Not much chance of that.' Cliff's dark mood continued to cast a shadow over proceedings. He went on ignoring Evelyn and finding fault with Dorothy until at last he'd mended the plug, tested the gramophone to make sure that it worked then carried his black cloud away with him to the Cross Keys and a pint of Fred Williams' best bitter.

Before long it was time for Joyce to take Alan back to the vicarage. 'Thank you, you've been a big help,' she told him as she knocked at the door.

After an hour of happy activity, the short walk home had seen him retreat into his shell. By the time Walter Rigg answered the door, the boy's shoulders were hunched and his face pale with anxiety. 'I hope to see you both at the dance on Saturday,' Joyce said to ease the moment. 'There'll be sandwiches and cake. Everyone's welcome.'

The vicar's earlier show of bonhomie had vanished without trace. He simply glared at Joyce while Alan stepped into the hallway with the look of a boy approaching the gallows, then the vicar silently closed the door. By the time she got back to the hall, Cliff had already taken Dorothy home and Evelyn was about to set off on her bike for Acklam.

'Will you be all right cycling that rough road by yourself?' Joyce asked as Evelyn put on her beret and scarf.

'Yes, ta; I've done it dozens of times before.'

'Couldn't Cliff have given you a lift?'

Evelyn fiddled with the faulty dynamo light fixed to the front of her bike. 'He's not talking to me,' she confessed in a croaky voice.

'I did notice that.' Joyce took up her own bike and flicked on the dynamo switch ready for action. 'That's not fair, though; it wasn't you who gave away the secret.'

'Yes, I know. But Dorothy never gets the blame for anything.'

'I've noticed that too.' Seeing that Evelyn hadn't managed to mend the light, Joyce offered to walk part of the way with her. 'What exactly is the matter with Dorothy that makes everyone mollycoddle her?'

Evelyn wheeled her bike across the green with Joyce beside her. The moon was bright so their eyes soon adjusted and they had little trouble seeing the way ahead. 'The doctors say she has a weak heart, like her mother. It means she mustn't over-exert herself on any account.'

'So it runs in the family.' Joyce considered this new nugget of information. 'I'm sorry to hear that.'

'Of course, Dorothy milks the situation like billy-o. You've seen how her father runs around after her.'

'Yes, but I understand that better now.'

'And Cliff, too; except when he's in a bad mood.' As they walked their bikes over the packhorse bridge leading out of the village towards Black Crag Farm and the Acklam estate beyond, Evelyn edged the conversation in the direction of her recent quarrel with her fiancé. 'Even then, he lets her off lightly. I'm the one who takes the brunt.'

'I'm surprised you let him get away with that.' From the beginning Joyce had viewed Evelyn as the confident, independent type, always ready to stand up for herself. Now she was seeing a different side that was more hesitant and unsure.

'The trouble is, I can see his point of view,' she said with a sigh. 'If Colonel Weatherall gets wind of our engagement then bang goes Cliff's job.'

'Still.'

'Don't worry, it'll blow over,' Evelyn said without conviction.

'Fingers crossed.' They slowed down as they approached the fork in the road where they must part ways.

'It's not the first time it's happened,' Evelyn admitted. 'As a rule we go along happily guarding our precious secret then we have a tiff over nothing and Cliff goes cold on me. It can be over the smallest thing; if I'm running five minutes late, for instance. I say sorry but he storms off anyway. Then I get the silent treatment until suddenly he's all right again.'

Though surprised that Evelyn was willing to put up with this, Joyce was wise enough to recognize that she didn't know all the ins and outs. Nothing was ever as simple as it seemed. 'Perhaps when he finds a new job . . .' she began quietly.

'Yes, you're right.' Setting off along the lane to the castle, Evelyn adopted a more determined air. 'That will solve all our problems: a new job, no more secrets and plain sailing from there on in.'

The next morning, after Joyce had finished her milking duties then checked a new dressing on Flint's paw, she set out for her first day as a lumberjill, eager to learn what tasks Evelyn had in mind. It was a dank, dark day and she cycled under heavy grey clouds through a swirling mist that hid familiar landmarks until Acklam Castle loomed up, seemingly out of nowhere. It stood on its knoll overlooking the river, gloomier than ever; a desolate place at the best of times. On this bleak Tuesday in mid-December it sent a shiver down Joyce's spine.

She leaned her bicycle against the padlocked gate, uncertain what to do next. Should she holler to announce her arrival? Or should she climb the gate and risk an encounter with the mad old estate owner?

Her dilemma was resolved by the appearance of Cliff Huby, dressed for the weather in a waxed jacket, waterproof gaiters and flat cap. He carried a shotgun under his arm and still didn't seem to be in the best of moods.

'Can I help you?' he called as he strode towards Joyce, sounding as if giving assistance was the last thing he had in mind.

'I've come to do forestry work,' Joyce explained. 'Didn't Evelyn tell you?'

'No; nobody saw fit to mention it. Lucky for you I spotted you before the old man did.' He braced his free arm against the top bar of the gate, making no move to unlock the padlock and let her in.

She looked straight at him, noting the belligerent light in his hazel eyes and the defiant set of his jaw. 'Will you let Evelyn know I'm here?'

'No need!' a voice called and Evelyn herself strode out of the wood bordering the castle grounds. She wore dungarees under her overcoat and her hair was hidden beneath her green Timber Corps beret.

Cliff turned on his heel and walked swiftly back to the castle.

'Things are no better, then?' Joyce asked as Evelyn unlocked the padlock to let her in.

Evelyn shook her head. 'No; I expect it'll take a couple more days. Anyway, follow me. Let me show you our job for today.'

Joyce fell in behind Evelyn, who took her up a track a few hundred yards into the wood. As they walked quick march between stark, bare trees, Joyce noticed uprooted beeches and oaks that had toppled to the soft, leaf-strewn ground. Their black roots clawed at the air and their rotting trunks were covered in vivid green moss and lichen; the only patches of colour in this greyest of days. Unruly saplings grew in amongst mature specimens and everywhere there were brambles and thick bracken barring easy access to the inner depths of the wood.

'You see what a mess we're in?' Evelyn gestured to left and right before coming to a halt in a small clearing where there were tools – axes, spades and saws – stacked in a wheelbarrow.

'Yes, but somehow I like it.' The peacefulness of their surroundings was almost tangible. It fell like a cloak of silence around Joyce's head and shoulders. Even the smell of damp decay seemed fitting for the time of year.

'Tell me that at the end of a long, hard day of snedding.' Evelyn handed her a billhook from the barrow and explained, 'That's where we take away the lower branches of these young ash trees over here. We've to get them ready for cropping in early spring.'

Joyce looked down at the heavy, curved-steel blade. The handle was six inches long and fitted snugly into the palm of her hand. 'Where do we stack the waste?'

'Here in the middle of the clearing until the weather improves. As soon as we get a decent day, I'll be able to drive the tractor and trailer out to fetch it.'

'Then do what with it?'

'We leave it to dry out in one of the old stables then chop it up so the Colonel can use it for kindling.' Evelyn took up her own billhook to demonstrate how the job should be done. 'Strip the side branch back as close to the trunk as possible. Stand to one side, like so, while you're doing it; we don't want you slicing your own leg off. And wear gloves, otherwise you'll end up with blisters.'

Having watched carefully, Joyce got to work. The sharp billhook blade took off the slender limbs with one clean stroke and she let them fall to the ground with a light swish. Once she had an armful, she gathered them and carried them to the stack that Evelyn had already begun. She had more questions, mostly about felling and cross-cutting, to which Evelyn gave brief answers.

'Anyway, no more time for jaw-jaw,' she chided, taking up her billhook once more. 'Besides working on the ash, there are brambles to hack through so we can cut a pathway to a young fir I've had my eye on.'

'For the Christmas tree for the church hall?' Joyce had almost forgotten this part of the plan but the notion put a fresh spring in her step as Evelyn forced her way through a tangle of blackberry bushes and blackthorns to show her the tree.

'It's over here by the stream. This is about the right size, don't you think?'

'Perfect,' Joyce agreed. The tree was six feet tall, with well-spaced, evenly balanced branches. 'But hold on a second; how will we get it down to Shawcross?'

Evelyn knotted her brow. 'I hadn't thought that far ahead. Normally I'd ask Cliff if we could borrow his car and the estate trailer.'

'But right now you don't want to run the risk of getting your head bitten off. And we have to do it sooner rather than later.' After a few moments of consideration, Joyce came up with an alternative. 'Why don't we use the wheelbarrow? We can balance the tree sideways across it and tie it down so it doesn't fall off. Then we'll wheel it across country as far as Black Crag Farm and all the way down to the village if necessary.'

'Yes, but when? Today's Tuesday. We promised Dorothy we'd deliver it to the church hall by the end of this afternoon.'

'Dorothy will have to wait until tomorrow,' Joyce decided. 'I'll rope Brenda in. Between the three of us we should be able to pull it off.'

The idea of the gung-ho trio carting a Christmas tree across the wild hillsides was a challenge that both Evelyn and Joyce relished. So Joyce hurried to fetch an axe and within fifteen minutes the fir tree had been neatly felled and carried back to the clearing. After this, there were two or three hours of daylight left and more snedding to be done. But first Evelyn delved into a canvas satchel stored in the wheelbarrow and produced a flask of tea and a parcel of beef-dripping sandwiches. They had just opened up the greaseproof paper and sat down on a fallen tree trunk when shotgun pellets ripped through the clearing.

'Duck, Joyce; duck!' Evelyn spat out her first bite of sandwich and dragged her friend flat on the ground. 'Don't budge!'

There was more firing then feet tramping through the wood towards them, followed by a cry of triumph as a game bird fell dead beside them. Then the shooting stopped and a black spaniel raced into view, ignoring Joyce and Evelyn and seizing the pheasant by the neck.

From ground level Joyce eyed the dog and the dead bird. She saw Colonel Weatherall enter the clearing with Cliff, who was the first to spot Evelyn and Joyce lying face down in a litter of dried leaves and mud.

He shouted into his boss's ear. 'Hold your fire!'

Reluctantly the doddery landowner lowered his gun while Cliff stooped to take the limp pheasant from the dog. Blood dripped from its head on to his boots as he strode with it towards the women.

Joyce sprang to her feet, a protest on her lips. 'What the bloody hell do you two think you're doing? You could have killed someone!'

'You try stopping the trigger-happy blighter.' Cliff tilted his head in the direction of the old man. 'The colonel reckons he can do what he likes when he likes on his own land.'

Evelyn was slower to get up and when she did, she pressed a hand against the base of her spine and groaned.

Meanwhile, the landowner had stomped off towards the castle with his dog.

'What's up?' Cliff demanded. 'The old bastard didn't shoot you, did he?'

'No. It's a bad crick, that's all.' She made light of it and tried to dust herself down. 'Ouch!' she muttered twice while Joyce picked up the scattered sandwiches then put the top on the flask of tea.

Cliff observed Evelyn closely. 'You can't go on working in that state,' he decided. His tone was brisk but he was clearly concerned about her and he put out an arm to support her. 'Let me walk you back to the house.'

'No, I'll be all right. It'll soon wear off.' Despite being in pain, she managed a quick smile.

'Cliff's right,' Joyce agreed. 'You ought to go home and rest.'

'And let the old devil see Cliff and me together?' Evelyn shook her head fiercely.

'Then I'll walk you back,' Joyce insisted. 'Once I've seen you safely home, I'll come back and finish off our afternoon's work. How does that sound?'

Cliff backed Joyce up. 'Go on, Evelyn; do as Joyce says. I'll keep Weatherall out of your hair. He need never know that you've taken the afternoon off.'

It was agreed: Evelyn should go home with Joyce and rest. The two women walked slowly through the wood while Cliff ran on ahead.

'At least we're back on speaking terms.' Evelyn's face was pale, her movements stiff, as she leaned on Joyce's arm and they made slow progress towards the house.

'I should hope so.' Joyce remembered Cliff's face

when he'd appeared on the scene. There'd been a second or two of genuine fear that Evelyn had been shot and then relief.

'Oh, Joyce!' Evelyn groaned as, with each step, pain shot through her back and down her legs. 'The sooner Cliff and I are free of this place, the better.'

For Brenda, the parting with Les on the previous Saturday had been the hardest yet. There had been tears on all sides: from Arnold, who had lost his only daughter, and from Donald as they'd stood looking out over Hettie's garden.

'I was hoping that she was strong enough to beat it,' he'd admitted to Les. 'Until yesterday, when I finally telephoned you. That's when I knew.'

'I had no idea,' Les had said when he and Brenda had walked together, away from the house, across the fields and up the hill overlooking Attercliffe. The wind had been bitter. 'I still can't believe it.'

'Hettie made us all promise not to tell you.' Brenda had let her hand rest in his, treasuring every precious moment that they had to themselves. 'She said you had enough on your plate.'

'That's typical of her,' he'd said under his breath. 'It's strange; when I was growing up, I thought all women were like Hettie: strong and stern, not to be trifled with. My dragon-sister.'

'And now you know we're not.'

'No. But what I'd give to hear her roar, just one more time.'

They'd walked up on to the ridge and looked down on Dale End.

'Is this where we'll live after we're married?'

Brenda had expected him to say yes. After all, there was Arnold to think about and the family business of renting out farm machinery.

His answer had surprised her. 'I'd rather not. If all goes to plan, Donald can carry on running things here. We'll find a house of our own – not too far away. Somewhere to call our own.'

She had felt a surge of hope. She and Les would marry and live together, perhaps in a terraced cottage like Grace and Bill. There would be a dog and some children – if all went to plan, as Les had put it. 'I'd like to carry on working,' she'd said as they'd walked on.

'What at?'

'I'm not sure. At something where I can use the knowledge I've picked up from my Land Army work. I'm young and strong and I enjoy being outdoors.'

Les had listened and nodded. He'd said it was right that Brenda should go out to work. He wouldn't dream of clipping her wings.

They'd sheltered for a while under a rocky overhang, dreaming of their future.

'How much do you think about me when I'm not here?' he'd asked when it grew close to the time for him to leave.

'Every hour of every day.' She'd insisted it wasn't true what people said about absence making the heart grow fonder. Now that she could actually see Les and touch him, her heart almost burst with love. There simply wasn't room inside her for this much pent-up emotion. She ached with it and wanted to weep it all out, to be hugged and held.

'Likewise,' he'd murmured. He'd kept from her

how, three weeks earlier, his ship had gone down off Gibraltar, how he'd leaped from the upturned hull into the water, how the sea was alight with blazing oil from the sinking ship and he'd had to dive down and swim underwater until his lungs had run out of air and he'd surfaced a hundred yards away. He'd been one of only three sailors to make it ashore. What was the point of sharing with Brenda how narrow his escape had been?

They'd walked hand in hand down to the farm and theirs had been a sad, sad kiss of farewell and longing. Les hadn't been able to promise that he would make it back for Hettie's funeral and Brenda had vowed in return that nothing would stop her from taking his place in the cortège.

They had shared one last, long kiss before Donald had driven Les to the railway station in Rixley, the car disappearing over the brow of the hill. And then there was only silence inside the big house.

On Sunday Brenda had spent the rest of the day alone, walking the hills above Shawcross and the evening hunkered down inside her goods wagon. On the Monday she'd worked with Bernard digging out a channel for rainwater to run more freely out of the field where they would bring in the sheep for lambing and won praises from him for putting her back into the heavy work. In her billet that night she'd written the first instalment of a long letter to Les that she intended to post on the coming Friday. Perhaps by then she would have received firm news from Dale End about Hettie's funeral. Now, late on the Tuesday afternoon, after more ditch digging, she fed the chickens and Nancy the goat then set off once more to investigate the traps that she'd set for the rabbits.

This time she was in luck. She found three captives cowering in the first trap and two in the second, but the business of transferring the rabbits into the sack that she carried with her was trickier than expected. One of the three gave her a sharp nip with its teeth as she reached in and when she jerked her hand away, two of them – the biter and another – made good their escape. She put the third more docile one in the sack and pacified it with a handful of dried oats. At the second trap, she donned gloves before reaching inside and this time successfully added two wide-eyed prisoners to the sack. She returned hotfoot to Garthside to install the three rabbits in their luxurious new quarters.

The light had almost faded when Dorothy came out of the house with a message. 'Dad ran into your Land Army pal out by Black Crag,' she reported.

Brenda took satisfaction in watching the rabbits hop along the run she'd built for them. 'So?' she prompted.

'Joyce asked him to tell you that they'll be bringing the tree over from Acklam tomorrow morning, all being well – if they can take time off from snedding, that is. It depends on old man Weatherall being kept in the dark.'

Brenda was slow to tune into Dorothy's garbled message. 'Tree?' she repeated.

Dorothy sighed. 'The Christmas tree, silly. Evelyn has let me down, worse luck. She was supposed to bring it to the church hall today but now it has to be tomorrow. At this rate I'll have all on to get it decorated in time. You will go and help them, won't you,

Brenda? You're the only one I can rely on to get things done around here. Don't worry, I'll tell Dad to give you time off to go over to Acklam. He never says no if I ask him nicely.'

'That's fine by me.' Brenda welcomed the chance to catch up with Joyce. She stared ruefully at her calloused palms. 'It beats digging ditches, at any rate.'

'And tomorrow night you can help me hang the glass baubles and tinsel on the tree.' Dorothy offered this to Brenda as a reward. 'We can play a few records while we're at it. I'll let you choose your favourite; how about that?'

CHAPTER THIRTEEN

An image of a carved plaque in the village church, memorial to a long-dead Weatherall, stuck in Brenda's mind the following afternoon as she hiked across country towards Acklam. It was odd that she couldn't dislodge the vision of worn lettering engraved in stone, given how little she'd had to do with the current landowner since she'd arrived in Shawcross and how much she disliked the whole business of country squires lording it over the little people who farmed their land and rented their cottages.

Families like that are stuck in the past, she thought as she entered the wood leading to the castle, leaving behind bright sunlight and buttoning up her coat against the cold. *Like flies in aspic. It's not right for them to carry on ordering everyone around in this day and age: do this, do that or I'll aim a gun at your head? It's flipping medieval, if you ask me.*

No one did ask Brenda as she tramped on through the dark, deserted wood, catching glimpses of blue sky through the branches and avoiding drifts left over from the snowfall of a few days earlier. Snow lingered a long time in these shaded spots and remained on the high ridges as a reminder that winter could tighten its grip at any moment.

'Ah, here you are!' Evelyn called from the castle yard, as, still lost in thought, Brenda emerged from the wood and approached the gate.

Almost recovered from the trapped nerve in her back, with only the odd twinge to remind her to take things easy, Evelyn stood with Joyce, wheelbarrow at the ready. At the sound of her raised voice, her dark bay cob stuck his head over his stable door and gave it a hopeful kick.

'Not today, Captain,' Evelyn said with an apologetic shake of her head. She went to fetch a length of rope from the tack room next door, careful to stay out of sight of Weatherall's first-floor bedroom window in the dilapidated, ivy-covered manor house.

Meanwhile, Joyce greeted Brenda with a warm smile. 'Hello, stranger. It's good to see you out and about again.'

Brenda was warm from the exertion of hiking across country. She took off her coat and flung it across the empty wheelbarrow. 'I'm sorry, Joyce – I've been a bit of a hermit. But that brisk walk has done me no end of good.'

Joyce outlined the task ahead. 'I hope you're ready to wheel this tree all the way to Shawcross. Apparently there are no volunteers to lend a hand with transport.'

Brenda spat into the palms of her hands and rubbed them together. 'Ready and willing,' she said with a wink and something of her usual eagerness.

Evelyn dropped the coil of rope on top of Brenda's

discarded coat. 'Many hands make light work, eh, Brenda?'

'So they say. So where is this precious tree?'

'Not too far away.' Evelyn made sure they had everything they needed before tapping the haversack strapped to Joyce's back. 'There's a flask of tea in there and some rich tea biscuits.'

'Thanks to Alma.' Joyce too was looking forward to the expedition. 'When I explained what we were up to, she filled the flask of her own accord and made sure we had three cups to drink out of. It was all done behind Mr Bradley's back, of course.'

'The old misery guts,' Evelyn added. 'It would serve him right if Alma upped sticks and went back to live in her aunty's house.'

The comment caught Brenda's interest. 'Why, what have you heard?'

Evelyn dipped eagerly into the gossip that surrounded Alma and Laurence's unlikely marriage. 'That Bradley keeps her cooped up in the house and won't let her out. According to Emma Waterhouse, who, as we all know, is the fount of all knowledge in these parts, he dishes out the orders and Alma doesn't dare answer back. Otherwise why doesn't she come to village events?'

Brenda turned to Joyce for confirmation.

'It might look that way from the outside, but I'm not so sure.' Joyce was the first to take up the wheelbarrow and set it in motion, putting an end to the small flurry of speculation.

They were almost at the gate when Cliff rushed out of the main house and called Evelyn's name.

'Oh, drat, the old man's spotted us,' she said through gritted teeth without turning round.

'Evelyn!' Cliff shouted a second time, striding towards them. 'Are you deaf?'

'What is it, Cliff?' Making up her mind that Joyce and Brenda should go ahead without her if necessary, Evelyn drew a deep breath and waited for the axe to fall.

'Don't worry; it's not what you think.' His expression softened as he surveyed their three disappointed faces. 'His lordship didn't have his spyglass out. As a matter of fact, he's taken to his bed.'

'Is he poorly?' Evelyn wouldn't be surprised by this; the colonel was shakier on his feet each time she saw him and his memory was getting worse and worse.

Cliff nodded cheerfully. 'Bingo! He says it's a bad cold, that's all. He doesn't want the doctor. I offered to fetch one but he said no.'

'No, because he'd have to shell out for a visit, that's why.' Evelyn's dislike of her miserly boss kept sympathy at bay and she was eager to set off on her Christmas mission. She opened the gate to let Brenda and Joyce through.

As Evelyn was about to follow them, Cliff stepped ahead of her and spoke in a low murmur. 'Wait a sec; don't you want to hear my own thoughts on the matter?'

Whenever Cliff gave Evelyn what she called 'that look', she felt her willpower crumble. It was never what he said but the mesmerizing way he had of looking into her eyes as if they were the only two people in the world, as if a camera and bright lights were trained on them and a spellbinding drama was being played out in which he was the handsome hero and she was cast as the innocent heroine captivated by his charms. And, idiot that she was, she fell for the cinematic cliché every time.

'Do you or don't you?' His mouth curved upwards in a smile meant only for her.

'Tell me,' she said as curtly as she could, aware that Brenda and Joyce stood close by.

Cliff kept his voice down, deliberately excluding the two Land Girls from the conversation. 'If you ask me, it's more than a bad cold. I don't like the sound of the rattle in the old man's chest. He needs to see a doctor right away.'

'Is that so?' Evelyn's heart rate quickened, partly because Cliff stood so close and partly because the old man's well-being seemed really to be at risk.

'Yes. It could turn to pneumonia if it's not seen to. He's eighty-five years old, for God's sake.'

'Then go over his head and fetch the doctor,' she advised quickly. 'We can't risk him taking a turn for the worse.'

'Right you are.' Cliff nodded then lowered his gaze. The spell was broken.

'What was that about?' Brenda asked as she, Evelyn and Joyce set off for the clearing to collect the fir tree.

'Cliff's worried in case the old man shuffles off this mortal coil,' Evelyn informed them with incongruous cheerfulness. 'There's no telephone here so he'll have to drive down to Shawcross to call for Dr Brownlee to come to the house with his bag of tricks.'

'And what about you; would it bother you if it turns

out to be serious?' Brenda couldn't work out Evelyn's attitude. On the surface she seemed not to care whether or not the old man got better; on the other hand there was a definite air of anxiety about her.

'In a way, yes.' Evelyn overtook Joyce and Brenda, hurrying to the spot where their fir tree stood propped against the broad trunk of an ancient oak. 'If Colonel Weatherall needs to be carted off to hospital, it might bring the relatives flapping around the place like a bunch of crows.'

'That dry old stick has a family?' Brenda didn't hide her surprise.

'One widowed sister who has a son and a daughter, but no wife or offspring of his own.'

'Blimey.' Brenda was lost for words.

'Once the relatives start sticking their noses in, signing bits of paper on Weatherall's behalf, there's no telling what might happen,' Evelyn concluded. 'Before you know it, they could have the old man locked up in a loony bin and throw away the key. Then where would Cliff and I be?'

'Yes, blimey,' Joyce agreed with Brenda.

There was nothing else to say. But now they understood why Cliff and Evelyn had talked so earnestly by the gate and why a doctor ought to be called, for there was a lot more at stake than a simple bad cold keeping the old man in bed.

Progress with the wheelbarrow was slow through Acklam wood but once Brenda, Joyce and Evelyn reached open countryside with their pretty little fir tree, they found they got on more quickly.

'Steep dip ahead!' Brenda warned from the front

as Evelyn pushed the wheelbarrow and Joyce brought up the rear. 'Steer to your left, mind this bump, now full steam ahead!'

With the tree firmly tied down and with Brenda as her guide, Evelyn avoided a boulder then trundled on at high speed across rough heathland. 'Sir Malcolm Campbell, watch out – we're hot on the heels of your world record!'

Joyce closed her eyes and held her breath. At this rate they'd never deliver the tree to the church hall in one piece.

Brenda gave a shriek of laughter as the barrow tilted to one side and then the other. Then, in an act of derring-do, Evelyn let go and allowed it to roll down the hill without her, only springing forward and grabbing hold again when it threatened to crash into another large rock. She was quickly pushed aside by Joyce who took control and steered it towards the landmark of Black Crag, standing out on the horizon against a backdrop of heavy grey clouds that had sailed across the wintry sun. 'Let's hope we get to Shawcross before it starts to snow,' she remarked, one wary eye on the bank of clouds.

The threat of a storm didn't prevent them from stopping for their picnic tea, however. Brenda chose a spot that was sheltered from the strong west wind, shooing away half a dozen sheep marked with Black Crag blue dye. She dusted a sprinkling of snow from a flat rock that would serve as an ideal seat. Then Joyce took off her haversack and pulled out Alma's flask, her fingers numb with cold, she poured the tea.

'No sugar, I'm afraid,' she said as she handed the first cup to Evelyn.

'We're sweet enough without,' Brenda and Evelyn said in unison.

Evelyn sipped her tea, watching Joyce pour out the last drops from the flask. 'Have you left enough for yourself?'

'Yes, plenty.' Joyce raised her cup to her lips and felt the warm liquid trickle down her throat. 'By Jove, that tastes good.'

They sat in contented silence, basking in the wild beauty of their surroundings, until a rapid movement on the slope below attracted their attention. Gradually they were able to make out the dark shape of a sheepdog heading their way.

'Goodness gracious!' Recognizing Flint, Joyce strode a few yards down the hill to meet him. 'Hello, boy; what are you doing here?'

The dog ran up to her, wagging his tail and pushing his nose against her hand.

'Yes, I'm happy to see you too. That paw of yours must be feeling better.'

'He must have smelt the biscuits.' Evelyn took the carefully wrapped rich teas out of the haversack and offered them to Brenda and Joyce.

They took two each. Joyce gave a morsel to Flint then there was silence again except for the crunch of biscuits and the rush of wind in their ears.

'Ah, the simple things in life!' Brenda said as she picked the last crumbs from the front of her jersey, dabbing at them with her moist fingertips then lifting them to her lips.

Joyce took a good look around at the dramatic slab of fissured rock that formed Black Crag and the steep hillside rolling away towards Mary's Fall then on again into the valley below; a mixture of grey limestone, brown heather and white hollows where snow still lingered. 'It feels as if we're on top of the world.'

Evelyn too felt her recent worries drift away. She sat on the rock, shoulder to shoulder with Brenda and Joyce, with Flint resting at their feet, drinking in the scenery. 'Shall we just stay here?' she asked dreamily.

'For ever?' Joyce chuckled.

'We'd freeze to death.' Brenda pointed to the first large snowflakes drifting down from the leaden skies.

Evelyn sighed. 'There's endless space here. Who would ever know there was so much going wrong in the world?'

Hitler, Rommel, Churchill, Stalin – in this moment the world leaders were mere names on the radio, faces on Pathé News. Armies marched to military tunes that couldn't be heard in the Yorkshire Dales, submarines crawled along the beds of distant oceans. Spitfires soared, tilted and rolled beyond the clouds over Dresden and Eindhoven, as far from Shawcross as it was possible to imagine.

'No, not for ever,' Evelyn said in reply to Joyce's question. She tilted her head to feel the soft flakes land on her forehead and cheeks then opened her mouth to let them melt on her tongue. 'Just until the war ends.'

Brenda was the first to land back in reality. 'Not even for five more minutes,' she said briskly as she hauled the others to their feet and Flint jumped up, ready for action. 'We've only got an hour or so of daylight and at least a mile still to go.'

'Slave driver,' Joyce complained, even though she knew Brenda was right. She packed up the flask and cups while Evelyn tightened the knots that held their tree in place.

Brenda took hold of the barrow and forged ahead.

'Mind the sheep!' Evelyn called as a ewe blundered across Brenda's path. Flint crouched low to the ground, awaiting an instruction that didn't come. 'Steer to your right, make a beeline for Black Crag. There's a public footpath from there to the village. It's by far the quickest way.'

This proved good advice and, as the group approached the landmark, the tall figure of Laurence Bradley strode towards them. He whistled to his dog then acknowledged Joyce with a brief wave before turning back and heading towards Mary's Fall.

'Bye-bye, Flint!' Brenda was sad to see him go.

'Did you see that, though?' Evelyn picked up on Laurence's greeting. 'The man of steel is human after all.'

They went on, minus their four-footed friend, aware of the failing light and the thickening snow. By the time they reached the village, the flakes were falling fast and already lay two or three inches deep on the ground.

'All our effort could come to nothing,' Evelyn predicted as she wheeled the barrow across the pristine layer of snow covering the green. 'At this rate, we'll be well and truly snowed in by the time Saturday comes.'

'Not if Dorothy has anything to do with it.' Brenda spotted her in the church-hall doorway, eagerly awaiting their arrival. 'Mark my words; she's not one to let a few inches of snow get in her way.'

Swathed in a thick red scarf, with her round face almost invisible beneath her father's oilskin, Dorothy clapped her hands. 'Well done, you three! Come along, carry the tree inside. Will it fit through the door? Be careful! Oh yes, that's a very decent specimen!' Brenda and Joyce shook the snow from the tree's branches then carried it into the hall.

'I'll love you and leave you,' Evelyn called from the porch. 'It's high time for me to head back to Acklam before the snow gets any worse.'

She was gone before Dorothy could protest. 'You two will stay and help me decorate, won't you?' she wheedled.

'For a little while,' Joyce agreed. She too needed to keep an eye on the weather but she took off her coat and helped Brenda to stand the tree upright in a bucket that had been filled with sand from government-issue sandbags stacked behind the hall in case of emergency.

Dorothy opened up a cardboard box filled to the brim with shiny glass baubles. 'The tree's leaning to the left,' she advised. 'That's better. Now turn the whole thing around – let me work out its best angle. Round a bit more. Stop!'

'Aye, aye, Captain!' Brenda stood back while Joyce checked her watch.

'Right, I'm off.' Employing Evelyn's rapid-exit method, Joyce departed, crossing paths with Emma and Alan outside the door. She brushed snowflakes from the boy's mop of dark hair. 'Cheer up, Christmas will be here before you know it,' she said with an encouraging smile.

The boy sat down on a bench in the porch and

Emma warned him not to stray. 'I promised I'd keep a close eye on you,' she reminded him. 'I don't want you wandering off again, especially not in this weather.'

He hung his head and watched snowflakes melt on his bare hands and knees.

'I might as well talk to myself,' the old housekeeper muttered before shedding an outer layer and preparing to make her mark on proceedings inside the hall. 'That tree won't last five minutes if you leave it there,' she told Dorothy and Brenda, who had tied the first shiny decorations to its branches. 'It'll get knocked over in no time. Why not put it in the corner next to the gramophone?'

A long argument began over the best place for the tree, with Brenda on the sidelines. 'Come inside and get warm,' she said to Alan when she spotted him. 'Help us with these baubles.'

He shook his head.

She went to join him. 'I can't say I blame you. It's definitely a case of too many cooks in there. But you will come to the dance on Saturday?'

Another shake of the head was all the answer he gave.

'Why not? Won't Mr Rigg let you?'

'I haven't asked him.'

'Do you think he'd say no?'

'Don't know. Don't care.' He stared at the flagged floor.

As always, Brenda's heart went out to the lonely youngster. *It's not fair*, she thought. *Anyone can see that the vicarage is not the right place for him to be. He should be with kids of his own age, playing games, having fun.*

'Would you like me to ask him for you?' she asked gently.

'No.' The answer came quickly. He gripped the front of the bench until his knuckles turned white. 'I don't want you to.'

'All right, then, I won't.'

'He changed his mind about letting me have a different room and he read my last letter,' Alan went on in sudden anguish. He hadn't meant to tell tales, but Brenda seemed kind and the words burst out of him.

'To your mum and dad?'

'Yes. He said there was too many spelling mistakes. He tore it up and threw it in the fire.'

'What did your letter say?'

'I said it was all right living here except I hadn't made any friends and I didn't like the graveyard.'

Brenda took a deep breath. *Spelling mistakes, my backside!* She leaned in and spoke in a whisper, choosing her words carefully. 'Why not write another letter?' she suggested. 'Only this time, bring it to me instead of to Mr Rigg and let me check it for mistakes. I've got a spare stamp so I could put it in the postbox for you.'

His eyes widened in astonishment and there was a long pause. Then he nodded.

'Good, let's shake on it.' She offered Alan her hand as Emma left the hall with her tail between her legs.

'A person knows when she's not wanted,' she grumbled to Brenda as she put on her coat.

'I know, but Dorothy's put herself in charge of the Christmas hop so it's best to let her get on with it.'

'As per usual,' Emma muttered. 'If you ask me, Bernard Huby has a lot to answer for.'

'What do you mean?' Brenda prompted.

'That girl is a prime example of spare the rod and spoil the child. The same goes for her brother. Weak heart or not, there wasn't enough discipline in that house when they were growing up.'

With a shrug of her shoulders, Brenda stood up. 'I don't know about that, Mrs Waterhouse. But you'll have to excuse me; I'm starving and I've still got yards and yards of tinsel to hang before I'm allowed to go home and tuck into my stew and dumplings.'

Cliff stood at his window watching out for Evelyn's return. He felt weary after what had turned out to be a long, hard day of running around after his decrepit, ailing boss that had ended with a drive into Shawcross to use the telephone at the Cross Keys. He'd called Dr Brownlee's surgery in Thwaite and explained the old man's symptoms, only to hear that the doctor's road was already blocked and there would be no further house calls until the snow plough had been through.

'Keep the patient warm and make sure he has plenty to drink,' Brownlee had advised. 'No need to call me again unless he develops a high temperature or his breathing gets worse. But for now just keep an eye on him.'

All that for nothing. Cliff had driven back to the castle in a foul mood. He'd arrived to find the old bastard lying in a pool of piss on his bedroom floor.

'What the heck do you think you're doing?' he'd demanded angrily.

The silly fool had got up to use the toilet but his legs had given way and he'd been curled up on the bare boards for over an hour, catching his death. When Cliff had picked him up off the floor to put him back to bed, he'd been shocked by how little he weighed. And the smell! He'd been forced to strip the old devil down and find some clean pyjamas then fetch a tot of rum to see if it revived him. Weatherall had downed the rum in one go and demanded more. *If it makes him sleep through the night, where's the harm?* Cliff had thought.

He'd watched and breathed a sigh of relief when the old man finally closed his eyes. 'Night-night,' he'd muttered as he'd closed the door and trodden along the creaking landing, running his hand along the banister that was riddled with woodworm, down the stairs, across the hall and out into a Christmas-card scene of untrodden snow.

That had been half an hour earlier; enough time for Cliff to return to his keeper's cottage and change his clothes, ready for Evelyn to come home after her escapade with the fir tree.

He saw her torch beam in the dark lane. Nothing fazed her, he realized. No shrinking violet, she would tackle fire and flood or any other disaster that came her way. His bad mood lifted and he went out to meet her.

She was through the gate before she raised her head and saw him framed in the doorway. He was smiling at her, standing without a coat.

'What kept you?' he asked as she drew near.

'A blooming Christmas tree, that's what.' Her spirits were still high after the afternoon's adventure and they rose again when Cliff put his arms around her waist and kissed her. 'Don't!' Glancing at the upper-storey windows of the big house, she broke free.

But he simply laughed and kissed her again, this time lifting her clean off her feet. 'Weatherall's dead to the world.'

Evelyn freed herself a second time. 'You don't mean to say . . .'

'Oh no, not *dead* dead! He's asleep, that's all.' Giving a quick account of the old man's fall but leaving out his own liquid remedy, he led her towards his cottage.

When they reached the threshold she resisted. 'What if he wakes up?'

'He won't.'

'But what if he does?'

Cliff laid his right hand on his heart. 'Believe me, Evie, he won't. Come in, take your coat off. Sit by the fire.'

'The look' and the pet name he used to woo her with turned Evelyn to putty, as they always did. Her first love, Jim, had been a steady, straightforward sort, so when she ran up against Cliff on her arrival at Acklam, his brazen flirting had knocked her for six and now she had as little power to say no as an ant has when a man's foot is about to step on it. Instead, she sat and let him stoop to take off her boots, noticing nothing except his broad shoulders and the strong curve of his back. She ran her fingers through his thick, dark hair and wriggled her toes in the warmth of the fire.

'Has the doctor been?' she thought to ask as he straightened up and she glanced around the room.

Cliff's gun rested as usual to one side of the stone fireplace, next to a basket of logs and a wire-mesh fireguard. There were two pewter tankards on the mantelpiece beneath a big, black-and-white engraving of the famous *Monarch of the Glen* painting. Light from the fire flickered across the low ceiling.

'No, the snow was too bad.'

A small frown creased Evelyn's forehead.

'Not to worry. Brownlee said to keep an eye on him, that's all.' Cliff pulled her to her feet and stroked her forehead then wound a lock of her hair around his finger. 'What if I told you that you were more beautiful than ever?'

Her heart skipped. 'Looking like this?' She glanced down at her dungarees and bare feet. 'I'd say you were a rotten liar.'

'Well, you are.' Unwinding the strand of hair, he watched it curl on to her shoulder. 'You always look good, no matter what.' It was the copper-coloured hair that did it, and the pale skin flecked with freckles, her eyes that were green in some lights and grey in others. And the rest of her; it was almost too much.

Evelyn's body relaxed into his. There was no doubt in her mind about what would happen next.

He held her tight and kissed her on the lips. Her arms were around his neck as he guided her towards the door. There was one room upstairs with a bed and red curtains, a faded Turkish rug on the floor. Cliff's jackets and shirts hung from a peg behind the door. There was one small chest of drawers. A plain room with lime-washed walls.

'It's all right,' he murmured at the bottom of the narrow staircase.

She felt his breath on her ear.

'We have plenty of time.'

She closed her eyes and let him lead her upstairs. The bedroom had his smell – of bracken, peat and heather brought indoors, of Palmolive soap and the oil he used for cleaning his gun. When she opened her eyes, he was taking off his shirt.

Her chest tightened, her heart beat fast. There was no doubt that they would make love and the pleasure of it would sweep her into a different world where all rules could be broken and she would give herself up to sensation. The shirt was cast aside. She touched the hollow at the base of his throat then ran her fingers along the ridge of his collar bone. He was waiting for her to unhook the straps of her dungarees and step out of them, leaving them crumpled on the floor as she crossed her arms to pull her shirt over her head. He liked to look at Evelyn like this, dressed only in her underwear, the flicker of uncertainty in her eyes.

'I'll look after you,' he assured her. 'Tell me what you would like.'

She was too shy to say the words. Instead, she lay down on the bed, spreading her hair across the pillow and opening her arms to him, feeling his weight press her down. Her hand touched the nape of his neck. There was no need to tell him; he would know what to do.

CHAPTER FOURTEEN

The work in the dairy was Joyce's favourite part of the day at Black Crag Farm. For a start it was indoors, out of the constant, biting wind that chilled her to the bone; and, what's more, the bulky bodies of the three Friesian cows gave off steaming heat in the enclosed space of the milking shed. Secondly, the work brought her into contact with Alma.

'What's going to happen with the weather today?' Joyce asked her when she carried two pails of milk into the dairy on the day after the Christmas tree adventure.

Alma stood waiting, dressed in gumboots and heavy overcoat, a brown scarf tied around her head. 'Laurence says there'll be no more snow.'

'Let's hope he's right.' Joyce placed the pails on the stone table. 'Those are the last two. We're not back to a full yield yet, but we're on the right track.'

'Good. The disinfectant has done the trick.'

Work talk was interspersed with easy silences as the two women carried on with their tasks.

'Are the cows still next door?' Alma listened out for movement.

'No. I took them back to the barn and gave them

their silage. I haven't mucked out the milking shed yet, though.'

'There's no rush. By the way, Laurence told me that he saw you up on the fell yesterday. He asked me who you were with. I said I hadn't the foggiest.'

Joyce grinned. 'I was with Evelyn and Brenda. We were carting the blessed Christmas tree to the church hall. That was high jinks, I can tell you. Mr Bradley had the dogs with him. Flint saw fit to pay us a visit.'

'They were bringing sheep off the high fell but the snow got too bad. He says you and he will have to go back for them later today.' Alma pressed the switch to operate the sterilizing and bottling machine. Glass chinked as the conveyor belt started to move. When she spoke again, she stood back from the machine and looked directly at Joyce. 'Laurence said something interesting just now.'

'What was that?'

'He said he hoped you weren't thinking of making a permanent move.'

'To Acklam?'

'Yes. He admitted he would miss you if you did.'

Joyce shot her a look of surprise. 'Tell him not to worry. Two days a week doing forestry work suits me for the time being.'

'And likewise,' Alma went on, her cheeks reddening, 'I would miss you too.'

Choosing her response carefully, as she would if she approached a deer in the wood, Joyce spoke softly. 'Ta, that's very nice of you.'

'I mean it. Since you came to live here things have been much easier for me. I've had someone to talk to.'

'Yes, I enjoy our little chats.'

'Do you really?' Alma shook her head in disbelief. 'You're not just saying that?'

'No. I mean it.'

'Even after the way I acted?'

'I didn't blame you for wanting to keep your distance. After everything that has happened to you in your life, it must take quite a while to trust a stranger in your midst. Anyway, that's in the past.'

'And we're friends now?' The word sounded strange on Alma's lips.

To the background hum and clink of the machine, Joyce assured her that they were.

'And you don't notice . . . ?' Alma raised her hand to her scars.

Joyce shook her head.

'You're sure?'

'Quite sure.'

'Thank you.' She let out a loud sigh. Fourteen years of withdrawal from the world had built a high wall that must be chipped away at, stone by stone. But this, at least, was a beginning.

'I'm glad life isn't such a battle for you any more.'

Alma risked a smile. 'That's exactly how it felt when I was growing up. Every day was a fight to survive, partly because of what had happened in the fire but it was because of Aunty Muriel too. She wanted me to do as I was told but I couldn't always; not if I thought she was in the wrong.'

'Good for you.' Convinced that this was the first time Alma had talked about this, Joyce said little but listened attentively.

'She did her best, but . . . She owns a milliner's shop on Kitchener Street in Northgate. Aunty Muriel minds about how people look; that's just the way she is. But she took me on after . . .'

In the pause that followed Joyce remembered her own life as a child, growing up with her mother, father and sister in their farm close to Stratford-upon-Avon, surrounded by love and the wondrous cycle of the seasons; how it had all been snatched away by her mother's death and her father's heavy drinking. Her sister had left home and the farm had failed. All that remained of that happy time were her precious memories.

'Aunty Muriel didn't believe the fire was an accident, even though the police decided there was no foul play,' Alma went on. 'She wanted someone to feel angry with and there was no one except me because I was the only one left alive. There was a little workroom at the back of the shop, with a curtain across so she could hear the bell ring when a customer came in. She made a strict rule: I was to stay behind the curtain while she talked about bows and feathers, silk flowers, ribbons and silver buckles in case I put people off by the way I looked.'

'Did she use those words?'

'Oh yes, many a time. There were hat-blocks made of wood sitting on the shelf behind me, big pairs of scissors on the bench. I knew off by heart every type of decoration you can put on a hat. I can still hear Aunty Muriel's voice going on and on about what was the very latest fashion.'

The door of the dairy room was open and a shaft of early-morning sunlight fell across the flags. Laurence had been standing in the doorway for a while before Joyce and Alma noticed his long shadow.

Their conversation broke off and Alma's expression shut down as if at the flick of a switch.

'Get on with your work,' Laurence told Joyce, who nodded and went next door to hose down the milking shed.

'It wasn't her fault, it was mine,' Alma told him.

He rested one hand on the doorpost, blocking the light so that he was in silhouette against a sparkling snow-covered backdrop and the expression on his sharp-featured face was impossible to make out. He'd heard voices in the dairy and jumped to the conclusion that the two women were gossiping about him behind his back.

'It was me who held Joyce back from her work,' Alma insisted with a hint of stubborn defiance.

'So I gathered.'

She rinsed her hands under the tap then dried them on her apron. Then she took a mop and bucket and started to swab down the floor. Laurence stayed in the doorway observing her. 'If you want to blame anyone, blame me.'

He went on watching then spoke at last. 'Bernard Huby has half a dozen spare eggs he says we can have. Tomorrow's baking day. Why not borrow Joyce's bike and ride over to Garthside to fetch them?'

Evelyn worked alone in the stable yard at Acklam. She'd woken late to find the space in the bed next to her already empty and Cliff nowhere to be seen. She'd pulled on her clothes and gone downstairs.

'Here, lazybones; drink this,' he'd said, handing her a cup of tea. His gun lay on the table, taken apart ready for cleaning. His boots stood in the hearth next to a newly built fire.

It had been the first time they'd spent the whole night together, after Cliff had convinced her that there was no chance of old man Weatherall waking up and catching them. 'Anyway, what if he did? He'd have forgotten it ever happened by this time tomorrow.'

So Evelyn had stayed in the warmth of Cliff's bed and they'd slept on their sides, his body curled against hers, his arm resting over her stomach, his breath on the back of her neck.

She would remember for ever the wondrous strangeness of waking up in his room, the warm indent of his body in the mattress, of his head on the pillow; a foretaste, she hoped, of their future life together. There would come a day when she took such a thing for granted, but this first morning when light had crept in to the eastern sky and she'd heard his footsteps in the kitchen below, she'd treasured every moment.

Soon enough the tea had been drunk and toast eaten.

'I'd best nip over and check on the old man,' he'd told her. He'd been gone less than five minutes before returning for his car keys. 'He's no better – worse, if anything. He keeps on trying to get out of bed. I think we need the doc sooner rather than later.'

And before Evelyn had had a chance to comment, a worried Cliff had set off for Shawcross. 'Check in on him every now and then,' he'd told her as he'd driven out of the yard.

This kept Evelyn tied to jobs close to home. She began by tethering Captain to an iron ring by his stable door then mucking out and laying a fresh bed of straw. Then she filled a hay-net and left the horse tethered as she went into the big house, climbed the stairs and knocked on Weatherall's door. There was no answer so she knocked again. This time she heard a volley of curses followed by a fit of violent coughing. Gingerly she opened the door.

'Who's there?' The old man sat propped up by pillows with, of all things, a rusty old sabre laid across his chest. He tried to seize it by the handle and swipe it towards Evelyn but he didn't have the strength to lift it. His pyjama top was unbuttoned, revealing yellow, wrinkled skin. Veins bulged in his forehead and incoherent threats emerged from the cavern of his toothless mouth. 'Damn it, I'll have you court-martialled if you come any nearer, whoever you are. I'll have you shot at dawn!'

'It's me, Evelyn.' At this rate he'd fall out of bed and knock himself out and she didn't want to have to answer for that. 'Evelyn Newbold, your forester.'

He tried again with the sabre and failed a second time. 'Don't come any closer; I'm warning you!'

Poor old beggar. Pity overtook her sense of the ridiculous as she approached the bed. 'Is there anything you need, Colonel Weatherall? Can I bring you a glass of water?'

'Who is it you say you are?' He peered at her through almost sightless eyes. 'Are you Winifred? No, that damned sister of mine hasn't been near me for years. You're not her.'

'I'm Evelyn,' she repeated. God, he looked to be at

death's door; the flesh on his face and neck was shrunken away, the skin papery, his hands like claws. She noticed that the glass at his bedside was empty and steeled herself to reach over and refill it from the ewer close by.

Insults poured from his mouth: old army words mixed with biblical oaths. He waved his fists at her as she lifted the glass, picking up the smell of a strong spirit, most likely rum, as she filled it with water. Avoiding his flailing fists, she offered him the glass. The rim touched his lips and instinct told him to swallow.

'That's better,' she said quietly.

His eyes rolled towards her.

'Another?'

He drank again then sank his head back against the pillow.

'There now, let me take this away from you.' She lifted the old sword and put it out of reach. 'We don't want you to hurt yourself.'

He closed his eyes, flicked them open then closed them again.

'Cliff's gone for the doctor.' Evelyn wasn't sure whether or not he could hear her. 'The snow's eased off so Dr Brownlee should be able to get through today.'

There was no response but the old man was breathing normally, which must mean that he was asleep. She would come back in an hour, she decided.

Then she went downstairs out into the yard, running a hand down Captain's smooth, warm neck and giving him a fond pat before leading him back into his stable. 'I've made a nice clean bed for you,' she murmured.

His big, feathered feet shuffled through the straw and he gave a satisfied snort as she closed the door on him. 'I'll be out here chopping logs. You can watch me if you like.'

Call me old fashioned, but give me a horse over a tractor any day, she thought as she got to work with her axe, standing each log upright on the chopping block and bringing the blade down with a swift action that split the log clean down the middle. Place in position, strike and cleave; the repetitive routine had the effect of soothing her after her upsetting encounter with the sick old man. She smelt the resin of the pine logs and watched the firewood tumble to the ground. When she judged that she had chopped enough, she filled a barrow and wheeled it into the lean-to log store close to the house.

When she came out again, she saw an unfamiliar Humber Hillman car at the gate and strode across. There was a portly man in a trilby hat in the driving seat. His passenger was a youngish woman dressed in a nurse's cap and cape.

'Dr Brownlee?' she enquired.

The man nodded and asked her to open the gate, which she did. He drove slowly into the yard. 'That lane gets worse,' he complained. 'It's full of potholes. The snow and ice doesn't help either.'

'Did Cliff telephone you just now?' Evelyn was surprised that the doctor had got here so quickly.

Dr Brownlee buttoned up his overcoat. He took a brown portmanteau from the back seat of his car. 'Not this morning; why?'

The woman stepped out and quickly shook Evelyn's hand. She was neat from head to foot in starched collar, apron and cuffs, with clipped, clean finger-nails and short brown hair held in place by a net. 'I'm Gillian Vernon. Samuel Weatherall is my uncle.'

'Good heavens!' Evelyn couldn't hide her surprise.

'You weren't expecting me, I know. I work at St Luke's Hospital in Millwood. Dr Brownlee is under strict instructions from my mother to telephone me in the event of my uncle falling ill.'

'The family is entitled to be kept informed in a situation such as this.' The doctor offered Evelyn a rapid justification as they entered the house. 'I mean, when the patient is not of sound mind.'

'I received the call last night.' Gillian Vernon followed Brownlee up the stairs. 'I promised Mother I'd see to things. How is my uncle this morning?'

'He's sleeping at the moment.' Well aware that this turn of events wasn't what Cliff had hoped for, Evelyn nevertheless was impressed by the niece's no-nonsense manner. 'Cliff and I have kept an eye on him like you said, Doctor. The trouble is, the moment he wakes up, he tries to get out of bed. I don't think he knows where he is.'

By this time they'd entered the sick man's room and one quick listen with his stethoscope told Brownlee that they needed to move quickly. 'Do you hear that, Samuel?' He spoke loudly and plainly. 'You're a sick man. We need to get you to hospital.'

'Hospital, be damned! You're a quack, Brownlee. May you rot in hell!'

'He knows me, at least,' the doctor muttered to Gillian as he felt Weatherall's pulse. 'But he's in a bad way.'

'Uncle Samuel, listen to me.' She took his ancient,

mottled hand and squeezed it with a professional mixture of compassion and briskness.

'Winifred?' the colonel wheezed, turning his head towards her.

'No, Mother is at home. She asked me to come. I'm your niece, Gillian. Do you remember me?'

He snatched away his claw-like hand. 'Clear off, leave me alone! Who's that?' he screeched, pointing at Evelyn. 'Is that Winifred?'

'Hmm.' Brownlee decided to take charge. 'The difficulty lies in persuading him to come with us. Can he walk or will we have to carry him?' he asked Evelyn.

'Carry,' she replied.

'Wait, let me see what I can do.' Buttoning up her uncle's pyjama jacket, Gillian searched for slippers under his bed. 'Come along now; let's get you out of bed into a nice warm dressing-gown. We can bring the car right up to the front door. Do you hear me? We're going to look after you.'

'Winifred?' he asked again, his chest heaving as he struggled for breath.

Gillian cast a resigned look at the doctor. 'Yes, that's right. Now Dr Brownlee is here too; you remember him? He wants to take you to hospital. Are you strong enough to stand up and walk?'

'Walk? Walk? Of course I can walk!' He tried to swing his legs over the edge of the bed but collapsed forward in a bout of fresh wheezing and swearing.

'What if we sit him in the cane chair and carry him down in that?' Evelyn pointed out the chair by the window.

The others nodded. 'Do it quickly,' Dr Brownlee

told them. 'With luck we can get him in the car before he has time to realize what's happening.'

'Ready?' Gillian and Evelyn managed to transfer the patient from bed to chair then carry him along the landing and down the stairs. Brownlee hurried on ahead in order to back his car up to the front door.

'Poor Uncle Samuel, you're skin and bone,' Gillian murmured as she cast a last, lingering look around a house that she'd played in happily as a child, in the days when her uncle and mother had got on well and she'd stayed here during school holidays, building dens in the woods and scaling the crumbling castle walls. She'd never known what had happened to make the grown-ups argue; only that the visits had stopped abruptly and her uncle had become more and more of a recluse. Her mother had refused to explain the rift. It wasn't talked about; frankness was not the family way.

Dr Brownlee held open the car door while Evelyn and Gillian carried Samuel Weatherall out of the house for what everyone knew could be the final time.

'Hold on a second; where are you taking him?' Cliff had driven up unnoticed and jumped out of his Morris at the moment that Evelyn and Gillian brought the old man out into the yard. He left Weatherall's spaniel whining in the car and strode towards them.

Brownlee looked irritated by the interruption. 'Stand back, Cliff. Samuel needs to go straight to hospital.'

At first he stood his ground. 'And who's she?' He pointed at Gillian.

Evelyn intervened. 'Cliff, this is Colonel Weatherall's niece.'

The old man made out Cliff's outline and waved an imaginary sword at him. 'Take that!' He was back again in his sabre-wielding cavalry days, leading men and their mounts to their deaths in the Transvaal. He heard the rattle of gunfire, saw his soldiers fall.

'Quickly, Cliff; we need to get him on to the back seat of the doctor's car,' Evelyn said.

Cliff grunted then stepped to one side to let the two women complete their task. Then, before they could drive away, he ran to his car and picked up the dog. He carried it back and thrust it at Gillian. 'Here – take this with you.'

The spaniel wriggled and whined in her arms. 'What's its name?'

'It doesn't have one, as far as I know. Anyway, it's not part of my job to look after it.'

The niece turned to Brownlee for advice.

'Bring it,' he said. 'I'll find it a good home if need be.'

Gillian put the spaniel into the car then shook Evelyn's hand and thanked her before sliding on to the back seat beside her uncle.

'Well done; you were right to telephone me and I'm sorry I couldn't get here yesterday.' Brownlee failed to register the exasperation on Cliff's face. 'Now move your car out of my way and let me out through the gate – there's a good chap.'

Dorothy always enjoyed her visits to Geoff Dawson at New Hall and today, two days before the big event, was no exception. She'd turned up at the house uninvited, armed with a list of refreshments for Saturday. Geoff was about to set off for Northgate to attend an evening lecture given by a man from the Ministry of Information on grants available to farmers: useful knowledge that he could then pass on to his neighbours during his veterinary rounds. There was sixty-four pounds per year up for grabs – a sum not to be sniffed at.

'Guess who!' she trilled as he came to the door. 'It's me, Dorothy! Put the kettle on, Geoff. I want to talk to you about Saturday night.'

He stood in his coat and hat, car keys in hand. 'Does it have to be right now?'

'Yes; there's still such a lot to organize.' She bustled past him and made her way to the kitchen where she sat down at the table and unfolded her list. 'Emma is happy to make two plates of sandwiches – one fish paste and one cheese and pickle, but I still haven't found anyone to do scones and biscuits or sausage rolls and pork pies.'

'And you'd like to enlist me as chief scone maker?' With a sigh of resignation Geoff took off his hat and sat down. The Ministry of Information was no match for Dorothy Huby on a mission so the drive to Northgate might have to be postponed.

'Oh no, you're much too busy; I wouldn't dream of asking you to do that.' She settled into her spacious surroundings, so different from the cramped, dark kitchen at Garthside. The New Hall set-up had lovely glass-fronted cabinets containing fine china and a grandfather clock ticking away in the background. She especially liked the crimson, jade-green and cream Turkish rug on the polished wooden floor and the two big ornaments on the mantelpiece: white cockatoos with curved beaks and chrome-yellow crests that were so lifelike she swore they would flap their wings and fly off if you went too near.

'So if it's not scones you want from me, can I provide the biscuits?'

'Yes, please.' Taking a pencil out of her handbag, she licked the lead and ticked them off her list. 'Not home-made, of course. I'm not expecting that. They can be rich tea or ginger nuts; whatever you can spare.'

'Consider it done,' he said with a smile.

'What about Mr Rigg?' she wondered, chewing delicately at the blunt end of her pencil. 'Should I ask him to make a contribution?'

'Yes, why not?'

'Yes; after all, we are using his church hall. He is the vicar.' She thought, as she always did, how nice it would be to live in a place like New Hall; to have Emma Waterhouse coming in to do the cleaning a couple of times a week, to have green lawns and an orchard to look out on in the summer months. Lady of the manor. 'And who else? Can you think of anyone?'

'To help with refreshments?' Geoff thought for a while then had a brainwave. 'I've got it. Why not get in touch with the girls from Burnside to see what they can bring?'

'Of course; the Land Army! Why didn't I think of that?' Dorothy felt that her refreshment problems were solved in one fell swoop. 'I can ask Brenda to contact the warden at the hostel. She'll be able to bake the scones. She might even have some spare butter and jam that she can send.'

'Or ask Joyce. She's more reliable.'

'But Brenda lives with us. It'll be easier to ask her.' For the first time Dorothy noticed that Geoff was wearing his coat. 'Oh dear, am I stopping you from going out?'

'Yes, I was hoping to get into town to listen to a lecture.' A glance at his watch told him that he might still make it. 'I've arranged to meet a friend afterwards.'

'Oh, and who's the lucky lady, may I ask?'

Geoff gave a low laugh. Dorothy was nothing if not predictable. 'Someone I met through veterinary college. No one you know.'

'A mystery,' she murmured, her imagination running on along a well-worn track. She pictured a studious girl with glasses, wearing a white blouse with a Peter Pan collar, a pleated skirt and flat shoes; the type who ignored fashion and whose head was stuck in books containing diagrams of cows' insides. 'Well, if that's the case, I'd better be off.'

He watched her fold the list and put it in her bag. 'I'm glad I could help,' he told her as he led her to the door.

'Oh yes!' she enthused. Truth to tell, the décor at New Hall was a bit old fashioned; it could do with new wallpaper and a lick of paint. But a man living alone didn't notice these things. 'You've been a big help, Geoff. I can't thank you enough.'

Cliff had moved his car for Brownlee then stood next to Evelyn to watch him pull out of the yard.

'That's torn it,' he'd said viciously.

He'd locked up the house, taken his gun from his cottage and disappeared into the woods without another word. Evelyn had gone back to chopping logs, though she was convinced that it was now a waste of time, given that the old man might never return and the fires in the big house would never again glow with warm life. The sound of her axe falling seemed to signal an end to her present situation and sent her mind splintering off in different directions. Would the house be shut up and left to crumble? Would the estate with its acres of badly managed forest be sold off? What if the Timber Corps sent her to work miles from here? And what of Cliff? He would lose his cottage along with his job.

Eventually she put down her axe and fetched Captain's saddle and bridle from the tack room. Cliff had been gone for three hours; she felt she should ride out and find him. They needed to talk and work everything out. If the worst were to happen and Samuel Weatherall stayed in hospital until he died, she and Cliff would have to rethink their plans.

She led the horse out of his stable and hoisted the saddle on to his broad back, buckled the girth tightly around his belly then took the bridle and slid the bit into his mouth. Using the stone mounting block to step into the saddle, she noticed details about the house that usually passed her by: signs of neglect such as a broken upstairs window and a fallen chimney pot lying shattered on the stone flags, the moss and weeds that had taken over what had once been a flower garden. Why hadn't the family stepped in before now? she wondered. Gillian Vernon had seemed a decent, practical type and a nurse to boot. She must have known what a bad state of health her uncle was in.

'It's beyond me,' she said out loud as she rode Captain out of the yard into the wood.

They followed the track leading to the nearest clearing. Evelyn ducked under low branches and glanced up towards a clear sky, trying not to dwell on the uncertainties of her life. *Look on the bright side. Change is in the air and it could be a good thing if it gives me and Cliff a fresh start.* Captain's feet fell softly on the snow-covered ground and his tail swished against the undergrowth. The rhythm of his walk and the slow sway of his body from side to side calmed her and allowed shafts of bright hope to enter her mind.

Why must everything depend on Cliff? she thought as Captain walked quietly on. *Why not step in and tell him what you want to happen? If I'm sent to work in a different part of Yorkshire or even further afield than that, what's to stop us from both going to the same place and starting a new life together? The only tie he has here is to Dorothy and his dad but the truth is that Bernard is still fit enough to run Garthside without Cliff's help. This truly could be the time for us to start afresh.*

On she rode, trying to plan ahead, unaware that dusk was falling.

Shock had hit Cliff like a sledgehammer when he saw the old man being carried out of the house. *No, this is not meant to happen. There must be medicine that Brownlee can give Weatherall to bring his temperature down, pills to calm him and clear up the cough.*

But then he'd spotted the woman in nurse's uniform helping Evelyn to put the patient into the doctor's car. How had she got here and why had Brownlee jumped the gun? It didn't add up.

Then he'd placed the nurse-niece as the mousy girl who'd called on the old man one Sunday in the spring, driving up in the same model of Morris as the one he owned, only newer and smarter. He'd watched from his cottage as she'd knocked on the door and got no answer. After five minutes she'd given up and gone away, then he'd slipped across with a key and picked up a note she'd put through the letter box: 'Dear Uncle Samuel, I'm sorry I missed you, blah-blah.' Signed 'Gillian', followed by two kisses. Without any qualms he'd torn up the note then burnt it. There was a precarious apple cart that mustn't be upset and he, Cliff, would do everything he could to make sure that it wasn't.

But now the return of the niece and them carting the old man off to hospital had ruined everything. Cliff had been forced to stand by in silent fury. Evelyn had watched on tenterhooks as the car drove away.

'That's really torn it,' he'd said before storming off. He needed a few hours to himself, time to think.

So he walked the boundaries of the estate, checking stretches of weakened or broken wall and the winter holding pens for the pheasants, catching long-distance views of the castle through the trees, striding on again to walk off his frustration before he returned.

Evelyn's ride through Acklam wood had done the trick. Though she'd seen no sign of Cliff, she returned to the castle with a strong hope that they could work their way through the present uncertainties. She'd groomed Captain with brush and curry comb and was giving him a bucket of feed when she looked out into the yard and spotted Cliff smoking a cigarette at the door of his cottage. He was leaning against the doorpost, one ankle crossed over the other, blowing a plume of blue smoke high in the air.

He came over to greet her with a peck on the cheek. 'Hello, Evie, have you had a nice ride?' he asked.

'I went out looking for you.'

'Did you? Sorry if I put you out.' With an arm around her waist he walked her into the cottage. 'It was a shock to see them cart the old man away. I needed to clear my head.'

Evelyn accepted the explanation. 'The niece was nicer than I expected. She'll see that he's properly looked after.'

'That's not the point, though.' Cliff stubbed out his cigarette in the grate then flicked it into the fire. 'I mean, is it?'

'No,' she admitted with a sigh. 'This leaves us well and truly in the lurch, but I couldn't have stopped them taking him away even if I'd wanted to.'

'Did you try?' He picked at a shred of tobacco left on the tip of his tongue. 'Did you explain that we were willing to carry on looking after him? No, don't answer that. I already know you didn't.'

'It wouldn't have made a scrap of difference.'

'It might of.'

'Might *have*!' she snapped back meanly. 'Look, Cliff, calling Dr Brownlee was your idea in the first place. I don't see why you're trying to blame me.'

'Because you don't seem to grasp what this means.' He turned his back to kick off his boots then he took off his jacket and threw it on to the table, knocking a packet of cigarettes to the floor.

Evelyn still stood close to the door. She lifted the latch to leave but he rushed across and stopped her by taking hold of her arm.

'I'm sorry, all right? It wasn't your fault. It wasn't anybody's.'

'Let go of me,' she warned.

'I'm sorry, I'm sorry.' He backed off with his hands raised in surrender.

'I'm sorry too.' She took a deep breath. 'But you're wrong, Cliff; I do understand what it means. Colonel Weatherall is gone, probably for good. The house is shut up. We have no idea what the relatives will decide.'

Cliff rubbed his temples wearily as he stepped back towards the fire. 'So what do we do now?'

'We wait,' she answered. 'I carry on with my forestry work and you look after the pheasants until we hear any different. It's Christmas in just over a week. I don't suppose they'll make any decisions before then.'

'You're right,' he conceded.

'So that gives us a bit of time. I won't get in touch with the Timber Corps rep until we find out for certain whether or not the old man is coming back.'

'What about my wages?' Cliff's mind began to clear. 'Who's going to pay me?'

'Good point.' Evelyn paced around the table. 'Have you got any money put by that you can live off until that gets sorted out?'

'No, but I suppose I could ask Dad to tide me over.'

'In the meantime, what's to stop you from looking for a new job – a better one than this? Or would it make more sense to wait until I learn what they intend to do with me? Then we can make sure we don't end up working at opposite ends of the country.'

He stopped to pick up the cigarettes then took one from the pack. 'There's something you haven't taken into account,' he began hesitantly as he struck a match and lit up. 'Something that makes a big difference.'

'What is it?' She braced herself by resting both hands on the back of the nearest chair.

Breathing smoke deep into his lungs, he tilted his head back and looked at her through hooded eyes. 'Do I have to remind you why I'm not out there in Egypt or Burma, doing my bit for King and country?'

'No, of course not. I've known all along that it was because they wouldn't pass you as fit to fight.' She remembered word for word what he'd said soon after they'd got together: 'According to the Army doctor, my ticker isn't quite right. Don't worry, it's nothing serious.'

It had taken her aback but he'd played it down and she'd taken him at his word. They'd even joked about it because he said it kept him off the front line and in the Home Guard instead. 'There's sod all for Dad's Army to do around here,' he'd said with a wink. 'How many bombs do you see dropping on Acklam Castle? One look from Jerry and he knows it'll fall down without any help from him.'

Now, though, she was forced to reconsider. 'Are you saying the heart problem is worse than you let on?'

'Yes, in a nutshell. The quack did say not to worry; I wasn't likely to kick the bucket before I reached thirty, but that it was no-go on the conscription front and it would be on my record for all to see – ventricular cardio . . . something or other.'

Evelyn felt a band of pressure around her chest that made it hard to take a deep breath. 'Ventricular . . . ?'

'Cardiomyopathy. They recommended a job that wasn't too strenuous; clerking or working in a shop. I didn't fancy either of those. That's why I came back to Shawcross. Dad helped me get the job of gamekeeper for Weatherall. The old man wasn't the type to check my medical record, was he? But you see why finding another job won't be plain sailing. Most bosses ask questions about a bloke of my age who hasn't been called up.'

'And you didn't think to explain it to me properly before now?' She felt the world shift under her feet; Cliff, who looked the picture of health, with his lithe limbs and broad shoulders, his smooth olive skin, bright hazel eyes and unlined brow, was in real danger, like his sister, of dying of a heart attack as their mother had before them.

'What for? You'd only have worried about me.' The second cigarette stub landed in the fire. 'I don't want your pity, Evie.'

'But I love you, in sickness and in health. That's what we'll promise if and when we get that far, and that's how I feel.' The world tilted and pushed her into a frank declaration. 'I want to be your wife, Cliff – more than anything in this world.'

He leaned against her and let her encircle him with her strong arms. 'I know you do.'

His arms were around her waist. He gave her the smouldering Valentino look that she could never resist.

'And we'll tell everyone we're engaged,' she declared as their lips came together and she closed her eyes. 'There's nothing to stop us now.'

CHAPTER FIFTEEN

After milking duties, Joyce's task for Friday morning was ditch digging in the low lambing field. Given the choice, she preferred mending walls because the job required a certain amount of skill and there was more satisfaction at the end of it. Still, she was content enough, cutting back brambles and bracken before digging through a crust of frozen snow into a deep layer of oozing mud, heaving it to waist height then dumping it on the banks to either side.

Every now and then she would rest on her spade to gather her breath and look up to see rooks and pigeons fly overhead. The black rooks soared highest against grey banks of clouds. Then they would dip and wheel on air currents that carried them towards the farmhouse where they landed on chimney pots and calmly surveyed their domain: the dark, furrowed clods of sloping fields below acres of brown heather patched with white snowdrifts and limestone outcrops stretching as far as the eye could see.

Joyce was contemplating the jagged outline of Black Crag when Laurence appeared in the lane connecting Mary's Fall to the farmhouse. His two clever dogs needed few commands as they worked a dozen sheep towards the field where she worked and, observing where they were headed, she climbed out of the ditch and ran to open the gate before blocking the lane so that they were forced to turn sharply into the field, jostling and shoving as Patch and Flint snapped at their heels.

Laurence closed the gate behind his ewes; a job well done. 'Time for a tea break,' he decided.

So she walked with him and the dogs, discussing the weather – no snow was forecast for today but possibly tomorrow – and the latest war news – the Americans were still bombarding mainland Italy, and the British navy fought to keep open supply routes into the Med.

'What about you?' he asked her as they crossed the farmyard. 'Am I right in supposing you have someone out there, doing his bit?'

It was the first time he'd shown an interest in Joyce's personal life. 'I do,' she replied briefly. 'His name is Edgar Kershaw. We're engaged.'

Laurence entered the porch. 'He's a Navy man?'

'No; RAF.'

'Good chap.' He directed a quick, questioning glance at her. 'Come on in,' he told her. 'We'll ask Alma to make us a nice, strong cup of tea.'

A smell of baking filled the kitchen. Rows of scones were set to cool on a wire rack and a dirty bowl, jug and spoons sat on the draining board by the sink.

'The tap needs a new washer,' Alma told Laurence matter-of-factly. Hearing him and Joyce talking in the porch as they took off their boots, she had already put the kettle on to boil and set out cups and saucers in her methodical, neat way.

'I'll see to it later.' He pulled out a chair for Joyce to sit down.

'And one of the stair rods has worked loose. I noticed it when I came down first thing this morning.'

Laurence promised to add the job to his list.

Alma filled the teapot and brought it to the table. 'Oh, and don't be surprised if Aunty Muriel decides to pay us another visit.'

This went down less well. Laurence rocked back in his chair and shook his head vigorously. 'Not if I have any say in the matter! I don't want that woman anywhere near this house.'

Alma brought a small jug of milk to the table. 'I didn't say she would definitely come again, but I have a feeling she might.'

'What makes you say that?' His expression was sulky as he took his first sip of tea.

'I think she wants to make amends. That's not such a bad thing, is it?' Alma looked to Joyce for support.

'I really couldn't say.' Joyce sat determinedly on the fence.

'Well, I can't stomach her.' Gulping down the rest of his tea, Laurence made it clear that he wouldn't discuss the matter further. He was up on his feet and heading for the door when he seemed to have second thoughts. 'I don't want Muriel Woodthorpe here at Black Crag,' he insisted. 'But there's nothing to stop you from visiting her on Kitchener Street if you want.'

Alma's face didn't show any reaction as she picked up his used cup and saucer. 'And how am I to get there, pray?'

'On the bus.'

'It only comes twice a week.' The peevish excuse

only drew attention to Alma's real reason for wanting to avoid public transport. People would stare. They might not comment out loud but she would recognize that covert look of surprise followed by inevitable distaste. She would know exactly what they were thinking. So she pursed her lips and turned her back on Joyce and Laurence. If this was his last word on the matter, then so be it.

But he came up with another suggestion. 'Or you could learn to drive,' he said from the porch as he slid his feet into his boots.

Alma let out a gasp of astonishment. 'How?'

'I could teach you,' he replied.

'When?'

'We could start on Sunday in the Land-Rover. Learning to use the clutch is the tricky part, but you'll soon get the hang of it.'

Out in the yard Laurence whistled for his dogs. In the kitchen Alma and Joyce stared, open mouthed.

'Did you hear that?' Alma said breathlessly. 'Did Laurence just say he would teach me to drive?'

'He did.' Joyce took her cup to the sink. 'You weren't imagining it.'

'Good Lord!' Alma shook her head over and over at this sudden possibility. 'I would be able to go anywhere I wanted, wouldn't I?'

'You certainly would.' A smile spread over Joyce's face as she tackled the washing-up.

'I wouldn't have to rely on anyone.' The penny dropped slowly but surely. 'My whole life would change.' Alma imagined driving the Land-Rover into Shawcross and on through picture-perfect Burnside towards smoky Millwood with its woollen mills and canals and on to fashionable Northgate. Or she could head off in the opposite direction towards Rixley and the North York Moors. Beyond that lay the seaside: Scarborough, Robin Hood's Bay, Whitby, where she'd once been taken on a day trip by her mother and father to see the abbey and the fishing boats in the harbour. Learning to drive would mean she was as free as a bird.

When Joyce turned from the sink she saw that Alma was crying. Tears ran down her cheeks and she didn't try to hide them. 'Say yes before he changes his mind,' she advised.

'Yes!' There was no time to lose. Alma ran out into the yard without her coat and caught Laurence as he was about to set out again with Flint and Patch. 'Yes!' she called. She took hold of his hand and let him see her tear-stained face. 'Yes, please! I'd like that very much.'

A busy Friday night at the Cross Keys was the norm but this was the run-up to Christmas and when Evelyn arrived at the pub she found that many of the usual customers had stayed away and her services behind the bar were not required.

'I wish Fred had given me advance warning,' she complained to Brenda as they took up residence in a cosy corner, both wearing dresses that did little to keep out the cold. Brenda's was made of a bright blue jersey material with a pork-pie frill around the hem and neckline, while Evelyn wore a red shirt-waister with a gathered skirt. 'If I'd known, I wouldn't have cycled all this way for nothing.'

'Then you wouldn't have had the pleasure of my

company.' Glad to find Evelyn at a loose end, Brenda settled in for a chat. 'Have you seen our Christmas tree since it was decorated? Dorothy never does things by halves, does she? It's got more baubles and tinsels than, well, any Christmas tree you've ever seen!'

Evelyn nodded. 'I popped into the hall on my way here. Honestly, though; I would have stayed at home if I'd known Fred didn't need me.'

'Why, what's up?' Evelyn didn't seem her usual buoyant self. 'Do I detect a lovers' tiff with you-know-who?'

'Hush!' She put her finger to her lips. 'No, if you really want to know, they've had to cart old man Weatherall off to hospital. It's a long story.'

'He's not dead, is he?'

'Who knows? He's definitely not tip-top.' There had been no news from Dr Brownlee or Gillian Vernon since they'd left and Evelyn couldn't decide if this was a good or a bad thing.

Brenda sympathized. 'So everything's up in the air?'

'Everything.' Evelyn held back a strong urge to share all the details.

'No, now is not the time to announce our engagement,' Cliff had said late last night as they lay in his bed and she'd pressed him to make firm wedding plans. 'Let's hang fire until after I've told Dad.'

'When will that be?' The fact that Cliff was still dragging his heels had niggled at Evelyn through a long, sleepless night. After all, it made her sound needy, like orphan Oliver begging for more.

'Soon,' he'd assured her, his lips against her forehead.

'Before Christmas?'

'Soon,' he'd repeated before turning away. He'd got out of bed to switch off the light then come back and gone straight to sleep without a final goodnight kiss.

And this was really what had put her in a bad mood all day.

'How about a game of gin rummy?' Brenda suggested, glancing around the sparsely populated room. 'Or dominoes? Oh no; wait a second. Look what the wind's blown in!'

The door opened and Grace entered with Una.

Brenda jumped up and ran to greet them with enthusiastic hugs. Both were wrapped up in winter coats and hats, attracting plenty of attention from the few drinkers at the bar.

'I've brought a letter for Joyce.' Grace took the pin out of her hat then removed it and ran a hand through her fair curls.

'From Edgar?' Brenda drew her old friends across the room and made mock-formal introductions. 'Mrs Mostyn, Miss Sharpe, meet Miss Evelyn Newbold of the Women's Timber Corps.' She drew up two more chairs and sat them down to form a close circle. 'Joyce should be along to join us any minute.'

'Good; I hoped she would.' Grace didn't mind driving in the dark but having to dim her headlights according to wartime regulations made her wary of the back roads. 'I didn't fancy driving all the way out to her farm. I hear it's not easy to find.'

'You can say that again. Anyway, Mrs Mostyn, it's good to see you. Let me buy you a glass of sparkling lemonade. And Una, what'll it be?'

Taking their orders, she went to the bar where Fred Williams served her more slowly than she would have thought possible, fiddling with bottle tops and fumbling with glasses so that by the time she returned with the drinks Joyce had joined their group.

'A letter!' Joyce's face lit up as she took the longed-for envelope from Grace. She'd only just sat down but she sprang up again and retreated to the quietest corner to read its contents.

'Lucky her,' Brenda murmured. 'I'm still waiting.'

'For one from Les?' Una wasn't up to date with events at Dale End and hadn't heard about Hettie. While Brenda told her, she listened quietly, head to one side. 'That's terrible news,' she whispered. 'I'm very sorry.'

'It just shows: you never know what's round the corner.' Grace took in her surroundings. The Snug at the Cross Keys was small and badly lit, with rows of horse brasses glinting to each side of the fireplace and scenes of fox hunting decorating the walls. Everything could do with a good spruce-up, she decided.

'You can say that again.' Brenda had waited almost a week for a message about the funeral. Every time she'd heard the faint ring of the telephone from inside her billet, she'd hoped it would be Les but it had only ever been a call for Dorothy, worse luck. 'Anyway, you're looking well,' she told Grace.

'I am well, ta,' Grace confirmed while Brenda explained to Evelyn about the baby. She sat quietly sipping her lemonade, one eye on Joyce.

'No offence, Grace, but she has the look, don't you think?' Brenda asked.

Una was puzzled. 'What look?'

'The one all women get when they're having a baby. They have an air, as if they belong to a club that the rest of us can't join. Do you know what I mean?'

'Perhaps.' Una hadn't thought of it before, but now that Brenda mentioned it, Grace's look over the past few months had softened yet grown more distant and secretive at the same time. 'It doesn't seem five minutes since we were bridesmaids.' Time stretched and contracted like elastic. Grace's husband was in Burma; her Angelo had been moved again – this time from the seaside sanatorium to a POW camp in Lincolnshire, where he'd been given a job in the canteen, cooking for his fellow prisoners. The letters came every week, no less loving, and yet . . . Well, he was so far away.

'Have you heard from Bill?' Brenda wanted to know all of Grace's news.

'Not for a while. I write to him twice a week, though.' Burnside happenings: rehearsals for a Christmas carol concert, the ups and downs of Bill's tractor repair business now that Maurice Baxendale was in charge, changes for the worse at Brigg Farm since young Neville Thomson had died. 'Fingers crossed my letters reach him.'

Evelyn listened with a distracted air to stories about people she didn't know. She learned that Grace and Una, as well as Joyce and Brenda, had something in common. Each woman at the table, like so many others in the country, lived with an aching lack of certainty about the fate of their loved ones. They laid their heads on their pillows at the end of each day and closed their eyes without knowing if their nearest and dearest lived to fight another day or were wounded, imprisoned, tortured or dead. Staving off the hammer blow to their hearts, shrinking away from the sword over their heads – nothing could describe the agonized feeling of long-distance, war-torn love.

Then the door opened and Cliff came in with Dorothy and it was back to the here and now, back to Christmas trimmings and gay talk.

*

Dearest Joyce,

Well, here I am in sunny Biggin Hill, a long, long way from deepest, darkest Yorkshire. As you know, I was flung straight into the thick of things; no time for settling in and getting to know the chaps in my new squadron. Mike Kirk and I flew out to Eindhoven on the second night we were here; a short hop over the Channel, and we came back safe and sound, thank goodness.

I'm not complaining, though. I like the set-up here – it's clean and efficiently run under Squadron Leader Mason, who seems a decent chap. You know the type – clipped moustache with an accent to match. He's seen more action than most, with a bigger tally for direct hits than any of us serving under him. On my third day here he gave me a guided tour of my new Spitfire PR Mark V. You'll be pleased to know that this little beauty has a higher victory-to-loss ratio than either the Hurricane or the Lancaster so she's set to become the backbone of Fighter Command. The squadron leader himself took me up on a test flight, full throttle at 2,850 rpm. We flew her into a flick-roll at 460 mph and got two and a half rolls out of her.

Joyce read slowly, relishing the confidence that Edgar placed in his new plane. She smiled at his attention to technical details.

So, it's been a whirlwind of activity since I arrived and this is only my second chance to sit down and write a letter to the girl I love – that's you, Joyce Cutler, in case you were wondering. I hope you didn't take too much to heart the guff I spouted in my last letter. I'm feeling more cheerful now and more hopeful that I'll soon be back with you for good. How are you, my darling? Do you still miss me as much as I miss you? These are strange times that we live in – using our brains and brawn to meet the challenges war sets us while at the same time our hearts are elsewhere. Mine is with you and always will be, for ever and ever, amen.

Are you still happy to hear this, or has it grown old and stale? You're so far away, Joyce. All I want is for us to be close.

This was more like it – Edgar laying his heart bare, trusting her, holding nothing back. *My absent, far-away love!*

The murmur of background talk grew louder with the arrival of Dorothy and Cliff but Joyce didn't look up from Edgar's letter.

And now, dearest, I have some important news that I hope will please you. Squadron Leader Mason has put me on photo reconnaissance duties. This takes me away from our nightly raids over Germany, so less midnight scrambling and dicing for me, for a while at least.

Joyce felt her heart leap and her hands shook as she reread this last paragraph. Less dicing with death, less fear of bullets tearing through flimsy fuselage, the seizing up of propellers, the plunge to earth.

It'll be mainly daytime flying for me from now on, with a photographer on board to gather the information we need on enemy aerodromes, factories, dams and such like, with maybe the odd dogfight thrown in if we're unlucky enough to be spotted. But don't worry; this new Spitfire of mine will keep me out of trouble.

There – how about that? Reconnaissance is my bag from now on. I was pleased as punch, as I hope you will be.

Joyce's eyes skimmed the rest to focus on Edgar's signature at the bottom. Written boldly, ending in an upward flourish, followed by three crosses – kiss, kiss, kiss. She would read it properly later, again and again by the light of her candle.

Cliff entered the Snug and rapidly took in the situation. He looked for Evelyn behind the bar then scanned the room to see her sitting with her new Land Army pals, gossiping like a bunch of old washerwomen. He bridled and went to order himself a drink, leaving Dorothy to join their group.

'So, you two, we're expecting to see you tomorrow at our village hop,' Brenda said to Una and Grace.

'Am I invited?' Grace reminded Dorothy that she was no longer a Land Girl. 'Anyway, you'll have to count me out. My mother-in-law has invited me to supper.'

'Oh, what joy!' Brenda recalled some of the differences of opinion she'd had with Edith Mostyn over petty rules and regulations. 'Rather you than me. How about you, Una – will you be putting on your glad rags for the Rixley contingent?'

'I wish I could,' she said with a sigh. This was only half true, since Una was devoted to Angelo and no RAF boy would ever get a look-in. Besides, she was perfectly happy to spend the Saturday before Christmas in her room writing cards and wrapping presents. 'We all put our names in a hat, and I wasn't one of the lucky ones.'

'So who was?' Joyce rejoined the group with a spring in her step, smiling at Grace as she sat down next to her. 'Ta for this,' she said, patting the letter in her skirt pocket.

'Kathleen and Elsie will be coming, all being well. Then there's our new recruits, Pat Holden and Joan Quinn—'

'Girls!' Dorothy interrupted. Energy and excitement sparked off her like electricity. 'Can we concentrate on who's doing what tomorrow night? Joyce, will you take hats and coats as people come in? Not so fast,' she remonstrated with Evelyn who had stood up hastily to go to the bar. 'I'm putting you in charge of serving the half-time refreshments. Brenda, I hope you remembered to telephone the hostel about sending over a big batch of scones and some sausage rolls?'

'Oh, drat,' Brenda muttered. 'No, sorry – it completely slipped my mind.'

'Don't worry, I'll ask Ma Craven for you,' Una offered before Dorothy had time to go off the deep end. 'It's very short notice but I trust she'll manage it somehow. Scones, sausage rolls and what else? Shall I ask her to send over some slices of pork pie?'

At the bar Evelyn squeezed in next to Cliff, who was still waiting for his beer. 'How does your dad stand it all day long?' She jerked her thumb towards Dorothy, who was busily orchestrating the final preparations for the dance. 'In my opinion, a little goes a long way as far as your sister is concerned.'

His smile was thin and he was on edge, hoping that Evelyn wasn't about to renew the pressure she'd put him under the night before. 'Dotty isn't like this all the time,' he replied defensively. 'Actually, this is her on a good day. You wouldn't want to see her on a bad one: flat out in bed, moaning and groaning.'

'Well, your dad's a saint to put up with it. Half a pint of shandy, please, Fred.'

Cliff was about to move away with his own drink when Evelyn put her hand on his arm. 'Hang on; I'm not infectious, you know.'

He flinched but stayed where he was. 'Sorry.'

'I haven't said anything, if that's what you're thinking. No one knows our secret except for Joyce and Brenda – and Dorothy, of course.'

'Fair enough.' He relaxed and took his first sip. 'The thing is, Evelyn, there's been a development.'

She frowned then let him take her by the elbow and steer her away from the bar. 'What kind of development? When?'

Better get this over with. Cliff was wary of women's emotions; he found that they often ran out of control. *Let's hope she doesn't make a scene.* 'This afternoon. I had to drive over to Dr Brownlee's surgery for some new pills for Dorothy.'

Evelyn thought back through the day; she'd spent a morning in the woods cross-cutting followed by an afternoon divided between snedding and stripping bark. When she arrived back at the castle, Cliff's car had been missing. 'So that's where you went. And Dr Brownlee had some news?'

'About the old man. They got him to St Luke's but he was too far gone. He didn't last the night.'

Evelyn drew a deep, shuddering breath, allowing the news to sink in.

'Pneumonia; the old man's friend. There was nothing they could do.'

'Was anyone with him?'

'The niece, for what it was worth.'

Struggling for something to say, Evelyn nevertheless felt glad that Colonel Weatherall hadn't died alone.

'That's him; snuffed out like a candle. That's us; well and truly up the creek.'

'But it's not as if we didn't expect it,' she remonstrated. 'And at least we know where we stand.'

'Yes, in the middle of bloody nowhere!' Why couldn't Evelyn get it into her head that Acklam was the best place for them? Where else would they be able to live rent-free without anyone poking their noses in?

His raised voice attracted the attention of one of the old-timers propping up the bar. 'What's wrong with you, Cliff? Have all your birds flown the coop?'

'No, nothing like that.' He banished the frown and forced a smile. 'So, Evie, now you know the latest,' he went on more calmly. 'Brownlee asked me to keep an eye on things on behalf of the family. I promised I would, as long as my pay was guaranteed.'

Evelyn nodded, though it unnerved her to see how quickly Cliff could switch moods and how he chose only to see what was under his nose. 'What about me? Am I to stay or go?'

'Your name didn't come up. The main thing is, I'm under orders to board up the doors and windows. I'm to put up Keep Out notices.'

'I wasn't even mentioned?'

The smile softened and his voice grew more cajoling. 'No, but that's a good thing, don't you see? It means that with luck no one will think to notify the Timber Corps that your boss has died. For the time being we can chug along as before.'

Dorothy freely admitted that she loved being in charge of the hop. 'I'm the only person with enough spare time to get things organized,' she confided to Una, who looked much younger than she said she was, which was twenty-one. It was because she didn't wear any make-up, Dorothy decided. Plus the fact that she was so small and slight. *Hardly any bosoms. She should invest in a better brassiere.* 'Besides, someone has to take charge. Otherwise Christmas would consist only of roast turkey and Yorkshire pud.'

'I agree.' Una wondered what to make of Dorothy Huby. She was like a splash of glorious Technicolor in a black-and-white film: out of place but impossible to overlook. 'And I'm sure your dance will be a big success.'

'Bigger than anyone realizes,' she proclaimed.

Grace, Brenda and Joyce broke off from their conversation. They looked expectantly at Dorothy.

'It's a secret,' she added coyly.

'Ooh, let's guess.' Brenda played along. She rubbed her hands together. 'You've baked us a surprise Christmas cake? No? Then it must be an early visit from Father Christmas, complete with Rudolph the Red-nosed Reindeer?'

Dorothy held on to her surprise for as long as she could. 'Any more guesses?'

'You're going to teach us all a new dance?' Joyce suggested.

'Wrong! Try again.' She knew they would never get it.

'You've saved up your clothing coupons and bought yourself a brand-new party dress. Cinderella, you shall go to the ball!' This was Evelyn's contribution as she split off from Cliff and came to join them.

'Wrong, wrong, wrong!' Dorothy almost burst with glee. 'Shall I tell you?'

'Yes, go on!' they chorused.

'And this had better be good.'

'It is.' She managed to hold her breath and hang on for fully five more seconds before she finally popped.

'I've had another telephone call from the officer in charge at Rixley – a very nice man, as it turns out. His name is Squadron Leader Oates. The RAF lorry will bring twenty men, not twelve. And . . .'

'Get on with it, Dorothy,' Evelyn chided. She felt out of tune with the mood at the table, mistrustful of any fresh plans that Cliff's sister might have arranged.

There was another pause for effect, brown eyes twinkling, dimples appearing in rosy cheeks. 'The squadron leader will send us a four-piece band! Two fiddles, a saxophone and an upright piano. Forget Geoff's old gramophone; now we shall have real live music to dance to.'

CHAPTER SIXTEEN

'It's sod's law.' Brenda stood with Dorothy outside the church hall waiting for the vicar to arrive. She gazed up at the clouds that had dumped three more inches of snow on Shawcross overnight. Light flakes still drifted down on to the scene spread out before them: the row of cottages where Emma Waterhouse lived, the village green with its stone cross, the Cross Keys and the churchyard, vicarage and church itself were all magically transformed by the pure white covering.

'What about the roads over from Burnside and Rixley?' Dorothy fretted. 'I'll bet the fell tops are far worse than this.' Her face was pinched by the cold, her mouth turned down at the corners. 'Oh, Brenda, what if we have to call the whole thing off?'

'It's early yet; try not to worry.' Brenda used the boot scraper to kick lumps of snow from her wellingtons. They had to wait for Walter Rigg to bring the key before she could carry a bag of fairy lights into the hall. They'd been a last-minute suggestion from Geoff, who'd said he had plenty of spare ones and would leave them in the porch for Dorothy and

Brenda to arrange. 'Come on, Vicar, what's keeping you?' she muttered, stamping her feet to encourage her circulation.

'I'll drop them off first thing tomorrow, before I start my rounds,' Geoff had promised in the pub the night before.

True to his word, the bag of coloured lights had been waiting for them. Now all they needed was a key to get into the hall.

Dorothy poked the snow on the path with the toe of her fur-lined boot. 'But what if it carries on all day? Before we know it everything will grind to a halt. The roads will be blocked; there'll be drifts six feet deep.'

'Best not to think the worst.' Brenda glanced at Dorothy's woebegone expression. 'Like I say, it's only nine o'clock and the snow already seems to be easing off. Two or three measly, powdery inches won't be enough to stop people coming to the dance of the decade!'

'But all this build-up will be for nothing!' Determined to turn the weather into a major villain in the drama of the Christmas hop, Dorothy ignored Brenda's advice. 'It's all right for you; you haven't put as much effort into it as I have.'

'Hold on a minute! Who dragged the blessed tree all the way from Acklam?'

'Yes, but what if we do have to cancel at the last minute? All that food will go to waste. Your Land Army pals will blame me.'

'No, they won't.' *Get a move on with that key, Vicar!* Brenda thought. *Put me out of the misery of having to listen to this moaning Minnie.*

'It'll all have been for nothing. We'll be snowed in like Eskimos.'

At last! Brenda saw Walter Rigg emerge from the vicarage with young Alan in tow. They came down the path together, the boy trailing a step behind the vicar, who was full of bluster and skin-deep bonhomie.

'Good morning, girls! Or, in fact not so good as far as the weather is concerned. The mercury in my thermometer tells me that it's three degrees below freezing. That's the reason why we're late; I made Alan put on an extra jumper. And then the silly boy found that he'd mislaid his gloves. They should have been on the hall table, but where did we find them?'

Alan shrank under Rigg's inquisitorial stare. 'In the kitchen,' he mumbled.

'And where in the kitchen, pray?'

'On the table, hidden under your newspaper.'

'Where you'd left them by mistake. The *kitchen* table rather than the hall table, you see, ladies?' He took a heavy iron key from his coat pocket. 'I'll do the honours, shall I?' he asked as he unlocked the door then stepped inside.

'Ta, Mr Rigg.' Brenda shoved Dorothy ahead of her. 'Don't let us keep you, though. I'm sure you have plenty to do.'

'We're in no rush,' he assured her as he stood in Dorothy and Brenda's way, his bulk and pompous pronouncements making him impossible to ignore. 'Well done, girls; the hall is looking suitably festive. That's a splendid tree. Where did it come from? No, don't tell me. Least said, soonest mended, eh?'

This reference to the bending of an official ruling

forbidding the felling of fir trees during wartime was a deliberate dig at Brenda in particular. Rigg considered her to be a bad influence on Dorothy, who was a harmless enough creature, if a little vain and silly. Brenda, on the other hand, was a born rule breaker; he could tell this by her bold, boyish way of dressing and styling her hair and by the fact that she rode a motor bike, of all things. He turned to Dorothy. 'Remind me; what time is the dance due to start?'

'At half past seven.' She made a beeline for the Christmas tree. 'Oh dear, the angel on the top is crooked.'

'Half past seven, weather permitting.' Rigg made a mental note that the boiler to heat the radiators should be fired up as soon as he got hold of Cliff Huby who acted as general handyman for church property in return for the odd shilling or two slipped his way.

Weather permitting! If anyone else mentioned the dratted snow, Brenda swore to herself that she would down tools and go on permanent strike. She heaved a sigh of relief as Walter Rigg rounded up his young charge then headed for the door.

'Come along, Alan. It's time to start clearing snow from the church path. We must keep on top of it, ready for tomorrow's morning service.'

They were gone; Alan to shovel snow under Walter Rigg's eagle eye, no doubt. Brenda sighed on the boy's behalf as she lifted a tangle of fairy lights from the bag that Geoff had left. 'Here, take this end,' she told Dorothy, 'and don't be such a gloom merchant. Look on the bright side; tell yourself that a flurry of snow won't beat us. This dance will go ahead regardless!'

'Knock, knock; is anyone there?'

From the top of her stepladder, Brenda heard a man's cheerful voice call from the porch. 'Go and see who that is,' she told Dorothy, who promptly dropped her end of the flimsy fairy lights and dashed to the door. It stood ajar so she peered through the narrow gap.

'It's the RAF!' she gasped as she made out two figures in uniform and a smart air-force-blue van parked nearby. Flinging the door open, she invited the men in without ceremony. 'Have you made it through from Rixley? How bad were the roads? Why have you come so early?'

'Whoa, Neddy!' The first visitor mimed a hard tug on a runaway horse's reins. 'My name's Ernie – Ernie Black – and this here is my mate, Malcolm Dawes.'

'Dorothy Huby; pleased to meet you, I'm sure.' She shook both men by the hand. 'That's Brenda up the ladder. What's in the back of the van? Is it something for tonight's dance?'

'Piano,' Ernie confirmed. He came across as cocky but likeable, with a Jimmy Cagney grin, light brown, curly hair and a cheeky glint in his blue eyes. 'Squadron Leader Oates ordered us to bring it over in good time.'

Brenda draped the last of the lights across the ladder and came down to ground level. 'How will you get it in?' she wanted to know.

'Good question.' Malcolm Dawes surveyed the room. He was beefier and paler than Ernie, with dark brows and lashes and a broad face adorned with the pencil-thin moustache that so many young pilots had adopted. 'There's a ramp at the back of the van to wheel her out.' So far, so good, but there was an awkward step up into the hall and he said he doubted that he and Ernie could manhandle the Edwardian joanna into the room unaided. 'Marie Lloyd's bloody heavy,' he warned, scratching his head.

'Marie Lloyd?' Dorothy echoed.

'Alias our old pi-anner.' Malcom put on a broad cockney accent.

Brenda said she was more than willing to lend a hand. She went outside with them, relieved to see that the snow had eased off completely. Though she noticed Alan still hard at it with his snow shovel while Walter Rigg supervised, she quickly discounted the notion of asking the vicar for help. 'We need a flat board or a couple of planks to make a temporary ramp,' she decided. 'That way we could wheel your Marie Lloyd up the step and in through the door.'

'As luck would have it, I might have the very thing in the van.' Ernie winked at Malcolm then let Brenda in on the joke as he strode to their vehicle. 'Mal likes to pull the wool over a pretty girl's eyes. But we always follow the Boy Scouts' motto: "Be prepared"!' Lifting out two stout planks of the sort that Brenda had suggested, he handed them to his Oliver Hardy pal who pretended to stagger under their weight.

Within five minutes they had the piano out of the van and in place in the corner of the hall.

'Further to your right, please.' Dorothy stage-managed its final position. 'We want people to be able to see the tree properly.'

Malcolm and Ernie put their shoulders to the piano and shoved, grunting theatrically. 'There; how's that?'

'Champion. How many chairs will you need? One for the pianist, naturally.'

'Thank you, ma'am – that'd be me.' Ernie tipped her a mock salute.

Dorothy dipped him a curtsey and smiled back sweetly. 'But what about the others; will they want to sit or stand?'

'Stand.' Malcolm sawed in the air and tapped his foot on the floor as if playing the violin. He stopped when he noticed three girls armed with piles of table linen and cardboard boxes full of crockery enter the hall. 'Aye, aye, here comes the cavalry!' he joked.

Evelyn led the way, ahead of Alma and Joyce.

'Have you and Alma got time to lend a hand at the church hall?' Evelyn had asked Joyce when she'd called in at Black Crag Farm soon after nine. She'd explained how the fresh snowfall had held her up. Everything took longer – from mucking out Captain's stable to sorting out his hay-net then breaking the ice in the stone trough to fetch his water. 'Cliff took Dorothy home after the pub last night,' she'd explained. 'Afterwards he must have decided not to battle through the snow and stayed over at Garthside instead.'

'How about it, Alma?' Joyce had asked, as if it were an everyday thing for her to drop what she was doing and come down to the village.

'I'm not sure.' Fear of facing people flew out of its dark cave at the forefront of Alma's mind. It hovered and flitted overhead. 'What would it involve exactly?'

'Picking up boxes of crockery and so on from Geoff's house and delivering them to the hall.' Evelyn too had made it sound like the most straightforward thing on earth. 'But don't worry if you don't have time.'

'No – I do!' Alma had taken off her apron. *Back into your cave you go!* 'I'll come,' she'd decided with a quick glance at Joyce for reassurance. She would write a note for Laurence, telling him where she'd gone.

And this was how she found herself face to face with two strangers in RAF uniform.

'Where do you want these?' Evelyn rattled her box of crockery at Dorothy as Malcom and Ernie lit up two Woodbines and took a breather after the strenuous work with the piano.

Alma felt her chest tighten. She stopped to let Joyce overtake her.

'You can put them down on the floor for now.' Dorothy hadn't yet got round to asking her two new RAF pals to set up trestle tables for refreshments in the kitchen annexe. She didn't hide her surprise at seeing Alma. 'Hello, stranger!' she called out across the room. 'You're the last person I expected to see.'

Malcolm and Ernie stepped in like gentlemen. They stubbed out their cigarettes and rushed to take the boxes.

'Here, give me that,' Ernie told Alma as he flashed her one of his lopsided smiles.

She waited for the click of repulsion; a split second's hesitation followed by the inevitable pulling back.

It didn't happen. 'Blimey, love; this weighs a ton. How far have you had to carry it?'

'Not too far.' Her face was burning and she kept her eyes on the floor, which seemed to spin uncontrollably under her feet. She wished that it would open up and swallow her. In a second he would notice. The grin would vanish.

'I'm Ernie, by the way. This other layabout is Malcolm.'

'Alma,' she breathed.

'We're part of tonight's band.'

How had he not noticed? Alma flashed him a startled glance and found that he was looking straight at her, still smiling.

'I take it that you three young ladies will be getting your glad rags on?' He looked from Alma to Brenda and then to Joyce.

'Oh yes, sirree!' Brenda replied.

'I wouldn't miss it for the world,' Joyce agreed.

To everyone's relief, as the snow clouds cleared and the sun rose in the sky, a rapid thaw set in. By eleven o'clock, snow slid from the roof of the church hall and landed with a thud on the ground, narrowly missing Evelyn, Joyce and Alma as they carried in more supplies. Brenda, meanwhile, had stayed inside with Dorothy to blow up balloons and put the final touches to the decorations.

'Shall we move Geoff's gramophone out of the way?' Brenda asked the commander-in-chief.

'No, don't bother. Cliff will do that when he comes to light the boiler.' Dorothy looked at her watch. 'He's due here any minute.'

Alma placed two boxes of biscuits on one of the tables set up by Malcolm and Ernie before they left. 'It's time I was going,' she announced. 'Laurence is a stickler for routine. He likes to eat at twelve on the dot.'

'Surely he won't mind getting his own dinner for once.' Brenda ignored Dorothy's instruction to leave the gramophone where it was. 'Here; give me a hand with this. Let's stow it in the annexe.'

'All right, I'll stay a while longer,' Alma agreed. Brenda was right: Laurence could fend for himself.

'Let me go backwards.' Brenda waited for Alma to take her share of the weight of the heavy cabinet. 'Easy does it. So anyway, Alma, I'm trying to decide what to wear tonight. I'm torn between two choices: my blue jersey knit or the pale lavender I wore when I was a bridesmaid at Grace's wedding. What do you think?'

'The pale lavender sounds nice.' Alma steered Brenda through the door.

'I wouldn't be over-dressed?' Brenda checked with Evelyn.

'I don't know without seeing it. It's up to you.'

'Hum-ha!' Brenda made a great show of indecision. 'What about you, Alma? What are you planning to wear?'

Alma frowned as they shuffled the gramophone into an out-of-the-way corner. 'Me? I won't be coming,' she said in a quiet but firm voice.

Brenda felt sorry but not surprised. 'Fair enough.

Come to think of it, I can't see Mr Bradley being the type to trip the light fantastic.'

'It's my choice,' Alma said.

'Right, but if you change your mind—'

'I won't.'

'Rightio.' Satisfied that Geoff's gramophone was stowed in a safe place, Brenda was the first to react to a loud squeal from Dorothy from inside the main hall. 'Oh Lord, what now?'

'Let's find out.' Alma rushed ahead of Brenda to find Evelyn, Joyce and Dorothy staring in dismay at the Christmas tree.

'We turned the fairy lights on to test them and bang – we blew the main fuse,' Evelyn explained as she flicked a panel of light switches on and off. 'There was a loud pop then nothing. See – no lights anywhere in the building.'

'Oh, blimey.' Brenda foresaw fresh disaster. 'We can hardly go ahead without lights.'

'Where's the main fuse box?' Ignoring Dorothy's wails, Alma's practical streak came to the fore. 'It should be easy enough to fix a fuse.'

So they tracked down the box to the front porch and immediately saw the cause of the problem. The sudden thaw had caused a downpipe to burst and water had seeped in and was dripping on to the wiring that led to the fuse box.

'Oh, no wonder,' Alma muttered. She looked apologetically at the others. 'This isn't so simple after all.'

'Oh!' Dorothy sat down with a bump on a nearby bench. 'Everything's ruined! What are we going to do?'

'Not panic; that's what.' Brenda went outside to

check the source of the leak. 'First off, we have to fix this pipe. I'll fetch the stepladder.'

'And nobody touch the wiring.' Evelyn added a timely warning. 'It could give you a nasty shock.'

'I'll get a mop.' Joyce ran to the annexe.

'How will we let everyone know in time?' Convinced once more that the end of the world had come, Dorothy sagged forward, head in hands. 'People will have started to get ready, washing their hair and so on. The food from Fieldhead will already be on its way.'

Brenda rushed back with the ladder. 'Let the dog see the rabbit,' she muttered as she carried it outside and set it down in the melting snow. A closer inspection told her that the cast-iron pipe had split at the junction with the guttering. 'This will be tricky to mend,' she reported glumly.

Evelyn, who had observed quietly until now, came up with a suggestion. 'Cliff's very handy; I'm certain he could mend both the downpipe and the fuse box if only we can dry it out in time.'

Dorothy saw a ray of hope. 'Yes; fetch Cliff!' she cried, springing up from the bench. Her brother was the one to turn to in any emergency.

Evelyn nodded. 'Shall I run up to Garthside and get him?'

'What for? He's not there.' Dorothy sagged and sat down again.

Evelyn's stomach lurched. 'Not at Garthside?'

'No. Isn't he on his way over from Acklam? Yes, he must be. He's probably been held up. Someone – Brenda, hop on your motor bike and find him. Tell him we need him here, right this minute.'

'No,' Evelyn insisted. Her stomach had clenched tight and she began to feel light headed. 'I knocked on his door earlier; he definitely wasn't there.'

Joyce came back and set her bucket down with a clang. She asked everyone to stand back while she mopped up the puddle on the floor, failing to pick up the sudden tension between Evelyn and Dorothy.

'Didn't you say that Cliff was due here anyway?' Brenda reminded Dorothy, whose spirits zoomed up and down like a yo-yo. From the top of her ladder, she spied Walter Rigg coming down the vicarage path and then noticed Cliff's Morris pull up by the gate. 'Panic over,' she reported as the two men engaged in conversation. 'The wanderer returns.'

Up at Black Crag Farm, Laurence wished that the weather would make up its mind. Snow followed by a quick thaw brought hill farmers a set of problems they could do without during these short winter days: namely overflowing streams and flooded fields that led to lone sheep getting cut off from the flock. So he tramped the fell with his dogs, herding the stragglers to safer ground and unblocking streams and ditches. He found two ewes marooned behind the crag and three more stuck on a ledge beyond Mary's Fall, so it was almost midday by the time he'd brought them all down to the lambing field. From there he made his way back to the farmhouse, expecting to find his dinner on the table. Instead, he saw Muriel Woodthorpe's car parked in the yard.

Laurence halted in the lane. For two pins he would have turned back the way he'd come, but Patch and Flint gave him away by running ahead to investigate. They entered the yard and sniffed at the wheels of the Ford while Muriel sat nervously behind the wheel, waiting for him to call them to heel.

He entered the yard intent on having as little to do with Alma's aunt as possible.

She wound down her window. 'There you are!' she said archly.

'Here I am,' he grunted.

Muriel gave several tuts at his glowering expression and surly reply. She would never understand what Alma had seen in this uncouth individual; he was old enough to be her father for a start and Muriel had done her best to warn Alma about how he had driven Lily to drink. 'Typical farmer,' people said about him. 'Tight-fisted and ill-mannered. And if he doesn't get his own way, there's merry hell to pay.'

'I've been sitting here for a full hour,' she complained.

He shrugged. 'Have you tried knocking on the door?'

'Of course I have.' *Silly question; again, just like him to be so disobliging.*

'Then she must be out.' He strode to the door and opened it to check. 'Alma, are you there?' Spying her note on the table and quickly scanning its contents, he came back again to where Muriel sat. 'Yes, she's out.'

'I can see that. When will she be back?'

'Search me.' *Don't you know when you're not wanted?* he thought.

Muriel pointed to the large, colourfully wrapped

parcel perched on the passenger seat beside her. 'I've brought her a Christmas present.'

He glared but said nothing. *Bloody woman with your fur collar and daft hat. Who do you think you are?*

'Do you know where she is?'

'No idea.'

'How long will she be?' *Two can play at this game. I'll carry on asking the questions, you carry on batting them away; let's see who gives in first.*

'I haven't the faintest idea. Why not leave the present with me and I'll give it to her?'

Muriel gave a short sniff. 'No, thank you. I've driven a long way to hand it over in person.'

'Please yourself.' Faced with a choice, his frown deepened. Should he run the risk of Muriel barging her way into the house uninvited or should he send her on her way to find Alma? He chose the latter. 'If you must know, she went to the village hall with her Land Army pals. You'll find her there if you shift yourself.'

At last! 'Thank you, Laurence,' she said with queenly politeness, before turning on her engine and executing a three-point turn. 'I'm much obliged.'

A Christmas present! A peace offering, more like; for all the wrong you've done to Alma over the years – the browbeating and snobbish put-downs, the deadly blows you've dealt to her self-confidence. Laurence turned his back and went into the house. *Good riddance to bad rubbish.*

Muriel felt a simmering resentment as she drove to Shawcross, splashing through muddy puddles that had formed at the sides of the road. This was why she'd sworn never to visit Alma at Black Crag Farm.

The man's boorish behaviour was beyond the pale. He was everything that his first wife Lily had described and worse: sullen, silent, uneducated, with a shaky hold on his temper that could and did explode into anger at the least provocation.

He'd been handsome in his youth; Lily had been prepared to concede. His hair had been dark and thick and there'd been no lines etched into his face. In those days Lily had interpreted his silences as thoughtfulness or shyness until she'd found out different – the hard way.

The fact was, Muriel had done everything she could to stop her niece from tying the knot with Laurence Bradley. She'd pointed out the everyday hardships of living as a hill farmer's wife – the shortage of home comforts, the scarcity of buses into town to visit the shops and cinema, not to mention the duties of a wife that could only be hinted at. Muriel herself had never married or even been curious about what that aspect of marriage might involve. In fact, a romantic embrace viewed on the cinema screen tended to embarrass, even repel, this prudish spinster so she had no information to impart to Alma on that score, even if she'd wanted to.

And how right I was, she thought now as she drove over the packhorse bridge and spotted a gathering outside the church hall at the far side of the village green. Alma's life at Black Crag Farm was obviously every bit as bad as she, Muriel, had warned her it would be and she regarded the Christmas present as a first step towards rescuing her niece from her fate. Gradually Alma would admit that she ought to have listened to her aunt's advice. There would be a reconciliation, and who knew where that might lead? A return to Northgate, to the hat shop on Kitchener Street and a job as Muriel's assistant, perhaps.

Cliff shook his head at the water dripping into the porch. 'It's no good, Dorothy; you'll have to call it off.' He'd gone outside for a closer look at the burst pipe then delivered his brutal verdict.

'Can't you mend it?' she cried.

Walter Rigg stepped in to have his say. 'Cliff is right. Without electricity the dance can't go ahead.'

'Even if I had time to replace the pipe, the fuse box would still be sopping wet,' Cliff pointed out. 'That's that, I'm afraid.'

Evelyn, Alma, Brenda and Joyce took the news more calmly than Dorothy, who wept loud, bitter tears.

'We could postpone it until after Christmas,' Joyce suggested. 'I'm sure it wouldn't be too hard to rearrange.'

'But how will we let everyone know?'

'Easy,' Brenda assured her. 'All we have to do is pick up the phone.'

'But not everyone has a telephone. And who's to say that the RAF boys will get another chance to come? After Christmas, it might all be different.'

Still brooding over the question of where Cliff might have spent the night, Evelyn did her best to concentrate on the problem that stared them all in the face. 'Do we actually need to get the electricity back on? Couldn't we carry on and do it the old-fashioned way with oil lamps?'

Joyce noticed Alma's sharp intake of breath and

sudden exit from the porch. She followed her quickly on to the green to ask her if she was all right.

'Yes, don't worry about me.' She swallowed hard. 'It really is time for me to get back to Black Crag.'

Joyce gave her a reassuring smile then watched her fetch her bicycle from the railings in front of the vicarage. For a moment she thought that the black Ford driving slowly towards them belonged to Cliff, but then realized that he was sorting out the fuse box fiasco inside the porch.

Alma was astride her bike when she looked up and recognized the driver. 'Aunty Muriel!'

Muriel stopped and pulled on the handbrake. She stepped out of the car with a large, bright parcel. 'Alma, there you are!' The habitual phrase with its underlying implication that Muriel had somehow been inconvenienced slipped out of her mouth. Why couldn't Alma make more of herself? she wondered. Must she always wear that dowdy blue skirt and brown coat? 'I've brought you a Christmas present.' Without more ado and with a self-satisfied smile she thrust the parcel at her.

'For me?' Alma's pale cheeks coloured up.

'Of course it's for you.' Aware of the group of girls standing outside the hall, observing the scene of Christmas cheer taking place at the gate, Muriel tapped the top of the parcel. 'Open it, why don't you?'

'Shouldn't I wait until the twenty-fifth?'

'No; open it and see if it fits.' Muriel was adamant.

So Alma took off the paper wrapping to reveal a large, round cardboard box. She removed the lid and saw a pale blue felt hat with a curved brim, trimmed with dark blue ribbon and a sprig of seed pearls. 'A hat,' she whispered. She took a sharp breath; the second in so many minutes.

Her aunt sailed blithely on. 'Do you like it? I made it especially for you. Why not try it on for size?'

'Not now, Aunty Muriel,' Alma pleaded. Everyone was staring. Cliff and Mr Rigg emerged from the porch. 'I'd rather do it later.'

Muriel glanced round at their growing audience of three women and two men – the older one wearing a dog collar, the younger of the pair dressed in shirtsleeves and corduroy breeches. He was tall, bare-headed, with an olive complexion that gave him a distinctly Italian look. She blinked twice and when she opened her eyes her manner had stiffened. 'Very well; if the hat doesn't fit, please let me know.' She backed away towards her car. 'Happy Christmas, Alma.'

'I will, I promise.' Alma felt the tension ease as her aunt hurried to her car. 'Thank you, Aunty Muriel. And a Happy Christmas to you too.'

CHAPTER SEVENTEEN

It was decided: oil lamps would light the hall for the Christmas hop.

'It'll be more romantic,' Dorothy had consoled herself after Cliff had at last persuaded her that the electricity supply could not be mended in time. 'Dim lighting is more flattering for a girl's complexion, don't you know? The main drawback is that we won't be able to use the fairy lights.'

The cup-half-empty afterthought, so typical of Dorothy, had brought a wry smile to Brenda's face. 'Never mind about that. Why don't I whiz around the farms on Old Sloper to scrounge some spare lamps? How many will we need?'

'Twenty should do it.' Scatterbrain Dorothy was sharp as a tack when she needed to be. 'A dozen for the hall and the rest for the annexe. Luckily we've got bottled gas to boil kettles for the tea and Cliff has fired up the boiler for the radiators. Try the Cross Keys for oil lamps. I know for a fact that Fred didn't chuck out his old ones when he had electricity put in.'

So, while Joyce and Evelyn had cycled off to Black Crag and Acklam to get changed for a half-seven start, Brenda had set herself the task of buzzing around the village and local farms on her motor bike and Dorothy had headed home to beautify herself by putting rollers in her hair, cold cream on her face and pearly pink polish on her fingernails.

'I want them all back in good working order,' the pub landlord growled at Brenda as he handed over eight dusty lamps from a damp storeroom next to the beer cellar. 'And tell everyone I'm open for business as usual tonight.'

'I will, Mr Williams.' Brenda stowed the borrowed lamps in a cardboard box strapped to her pillion seat. 'I'd stand by behind the bar if I were you; dancing is thirsty work.'

On she went, fetching more lamps and riding back with them to the as yet deserted hall. She dusted them down, filled them with oil and primed the wicks then placed them on window sills down the length of the hall.

'Hello, Brenda. It's six o'clock; shouldn't you be getting ready?' Geoff asked when he dropped by to pick up his gramophone. He was surprised to find her still in Land Girl dungarees and sweater.

'Oodles of time,' she replied airily. 'It doesn't take me long to spruce myself up. Anyway, I'd far rather keep busy.'

'And stay out of Major General Dorothy's way?' he guessed correctly.

'Would you like a hand with that?' she asked as he eased the gramophone out of the corner.

'No ta – I've brought a pal along. Giles, come in and meet Brenda.'

Brenda wiped her palms on her trousers, ready to shake hands with Geoff's friend.

'Giles Pickering, this is Brenda Appleby.'

'Pleased to meet you.' She immediately liked the look of Giles who, at six feet and a bit, towered over her. He had a warm smile and a firm handshake, a mop of straw-coloured hair and pale freckled skin.

'Giles and I were at veterinary school together,' Geoff explained. 'I hope you don't mind; I've invited him along to the hop.'

'Mind? Of course not; the more the merrier.' Brenda stood to one side to let the men get on with the task of taking away the now-redundant gramophone. She followed them from the annexe into the porch where water from the melting snow still trickled down on to the fuse box. 'On condition that you two promise not to tuck yourselves away in a corner and reminisce the night away. Dancing is obligatory, I'll have you know.'

'Scouts' honour,' Giles promised with his easy smile.

'Steady; try not to tilt it,' Geoff warned as they eased the cabinet down the path and into his Land-Rover. 'We'll see you in a couple of hours,' he called to Brenda as he drove away.

'How do I look?' Dorothy made her grand entrance into the kitchen at Garthside Farm. As she twirled on the spot for her father and brother, her gored skirt flared to reveal a pink silk petticoat trimmed with lace.

'Like the bee's knees.' Bernard decided not to voice his opinion that the skirt might be a little too short. After all, this was Dorothy's big night; something that she'd been looking forward to for weeks.

'Is that what they're wearing these days?' Peering over the top of his father's *Yorkshire Post*, Cliff took in the off-the-shoulder pale blue satin dress set off by a corsage made of darker blue silk flowers strategically placed to draw attention to Dorothy's cleavage.

She fluffed up the curls piled on top of her head. 'Yes; I made it with a pattern from the latest Butterick catalogue,' she confirmed. 'Do you like it or not?'

'You look very nice,' he conceded.

'What about you? Isn't it time for you to dash home and get changed?'

Cliff shrugged. 'What's wrong with what I'm wearing?' He lowered the newspaper to reveal his open-necked checked shirt and corduroy trousers.

'Cliff!' He needed to put on a decent jacket and a collar and tie at the very least.

'I'm kidding,' he said with a grin as he made for the door. 'I brought my smart gear with me. It's laid out on the bed in my old room.'

'Well, hurry up then.' Her reflection in the shaving mirror above the sink showed the care she'd taken; her eyebrows were plucked to perfection and a touch of rouge gave her cheeks a rosy glow. The mirror was in line with the door and she saw a reflection of Brenda entering the room in her royal blue dress with the frilled neckline and hem, dressed up with a marcasite brooch and matching earrings. She carried her leather jacket over one arm.

'What happened to the bridesmaid's dress?' she asked without turning round.

'I changed my mind.' At the last minute, in the

privacy of her billet, Brenda had gone for the warmer, less showy option. 'Oughtn't we to get a move on?'

'Why, what time is it?'

'Half six. The Rixley boys said they'd be here early, to allow time for the band to get set up.'

'Oh, Lord!' Dorothy dashed to the foot of the stairs. 'Cliff, Brenda and I are going to be late. You'll have to give us a lift!'

He came down in shirtsleeves, carrying his shoes in one hand and hitching his braces over his shoulders with the other. His tie hung loose around his neck. 'Don't rush me,' he muttered. 'I'm going as quick as I can.'

But Dorothy pestered and chivvied until he was ready to go. 'I knew you ought not to have left it until the last minute. Why do you always cut it so fine? Honestly, Cliff; you're the limit!'

'Have a nice time,' Bernard called after them as Dorothy succeeded at last in getting Cliff out of the house and Brenda closed the door with a firm click. The dress was decidedly too short and the neckline left nothing to the imagination but it needed a mother to advise on that score, Bernard thought. Anyway, Dorothy wasn't a child any more. He sighed as he took up his newspaper and looked ahead to a rare evening of peace and quiet.

It was the uniform that did it; or rather the material it was made of. The RAF kitted out their boys in smooth, air-force-blue worsted, not the rough khaki cloth that the army used. The jackets were tailored to be nipped in at the waist, with epaulettes that squared the shoulders. It created the perfect, manly shape, Dorothy thought admiringly, when she saw twenty pilots step out of their lorry with musicians Ernie and Malcolm in the vanguard.

She beamed as they approached the hall.

'Brrr – someone will catch their death,' Malcolm remarked when he saw her standing in the doorway in her short, sleeveless dress. The goosebumps on her plump, pale arms proved his point. 'Come inside and show the lads where to set up their instruments.'

'This way; follow me.' The tree looked glorious, even without its fairy lights, and the paper chains were now set off with multicoloured balloons – a last-minute touch, courtesy of Emma Waterhouse. Sprigs of holly lined the window sills.

Brenda had been waiting inside for the RAF to arrive. She pointed out the lamps to Ernie and explained the reason. 'Will there be enough light for you to read your music by?'

'Plenty,' he assured her as he set his sheets on the piano stand then played a couple of scales. 'Anyway, we know most of it off by heart.'

As the hall filled up with eager trainees, their faces boyish, their hair trimmed into regulation short back and sides, Brenda felt herself relax. She reminded herself that it was coming up to Christmas and, despite recent events at Dale End, this was a night to be enjoyed. Hettie's death had weighed heavily this past week, with Brenda expecting to hear news about the funeral, only to be disappointed. It seemed now that it might not happen until after the twenty-fifth; perhaps even into the New Year.

Am I being disloyal to Hettie's memory? she'd wondered as she'd chosen what to wear for the dance. *Ought I to stay away?* But the temptation to meet up with her old Fieldhead friends had proved too strong. And now here she was, greeting the Royal Air Force, showing them where to bring their hampers of sandwiches, explaining again about the lack of electricity, smiling and laughing as she told them that the Land Army was due any time now and they'd better hang on to their hats because, make no mistake, the girls were a force to be reckoned with.

'In what way?' One of the trainees who had brought in the food hampers looked apprehensively towards the door as if expecting to be steamrollered by a gang of girls.

Brenda winked at two of the others. 'Let's just say that the door will be locked after the music starts and the key will be well hidden.'

The man closest to the entrance glanced outside at the sound of a vehicle arriving. 'Crikey!' he said as half a dozen Fieldhead girls piled out of the van, sporting frills and high heels and bursting with excited chatter. They surged towards the porch. 'I see what you mean.'

'Elsie, you forgot the pork pie!' Kathleen's voice rose above the rest.

'Where is it?' came the reply.

'Where you left it; in a Jacob's Cream Cracker tin under the back seat.'

Brenda laughed out loud at the flash of alarm in many of the young trainees' eyes. 'It can't be worse than facing Jerry's Messerschmitts, surely to goodness?'

'Ten times worse!' one insisted as the women burst through the door.

'Colin – Douglas – Albert – Joe.'

'Kathleen – Elsie – Pat – Joan.'

Names were exchanged and immediately forgotten amidst a hubbub of coat-taking, the tuning of instruments and setting out of refreshments. The tree was admired; a bunch of mistletoe was hung in a prominent position inside the porch.

Malcolm, the thickset violinist, collared Brenda as she passed by. 'Tell Mae West over there that we're ready to start whenever she is.'

'You mean Dorothy?' Brenda grinned at the cheeky reference to the busty blonde film star. 'She insists on waiting until half past on the dot.'

'Right you are.' Malcolm went on tuning his violin while speaking to his fellow band members about the order of play. 'Let's kick off with "Kalamazoo" followed by "Chattanooga Choo-Choo".'

Meanwhile, new girls Joan and Pat admired the decorations while Elsie and Kathleen, dressed up to the nines in purple and scarlet, set out food on the tables in the annexe. Colin or Douglas fell over himself to help. Joe or Albert took over from Brenda in the coat-collecting department.

'Where's Cliff?' Dorothy bleated when she found out from a pilot named Mouse that only half of the radiators were turned on.

'We just saw him going into the Cross Keys,' Joyce reported as she and Evelyn entered the hurly-burly.

'Trust him.' Dorothy turned helplessly to the nearest raw recruit. 'Mouse, what's your real name?'

'Erasmus, after my great-granddad, Erasmus Jackson.' It was a burden the poor bloke had carried for nineteen years. 'But I generally go by Mouse. Will you dance the first dance with me?'

Albert shouldered him aside. 'Sorry, pal; I beat you to it.'

'The second dance then?' Mouse called after her.

Dorothy was too busy to answer. 'Vicar!' She raised her voice above the busy hum. 'What's happened to the radiators? Half of them are cold.'

Walter Rigg had popped in to supervise the start of proceedings. He had Emma with him but there was no Alan, who, for some undisclosed reason, had been sent to bed in disgrace. The two village elders stuck out like sore thumbs among the uniformed youths and brilliantly decked girls – round-bellied Rigg with his dark suit and dog collar and stick-thin Emma whose heyday, if she'd ever had one, had been back in the 1890s when hems had touched the ground and leg-of-mutton sleeves were all the rage.

The vicar placed a hand on the nearest radiator. 'Stone cold,' he muttered with a displeased frown before sending Emma to find Cliff.

'He's in the Cross Keys.' It was Evelyn's turn to report his whereabouts. She stood aside from the hubbub, trying to hold her nerve for the night ahead. What if Cliff snubbed her in public as he had been doing ever since Colonel Weatherall had been taken off to hospital? Should she react by giving her fiancé a taste of his own medicine, cold-shouldering him in return and making a great show of dancing the quickstep and tango with an array of RAF boys?

At present men outnumbered girls by almost two to one so there would be no shortage of partners.

'Can I have the first dance with you?' Mouse sidled up to prove her point, attracted by her free-flowing auburn locks. She wore an eye-catching halter-neck dress made of shimmering silver-grey satin that showed off her smooth shoulders, slim hips and long limbs to their best advantage. 'You don't mind me asking?'

'Of course I don't mind.' Evelyn accepted the invitation with a smile.

'No Alma, I see?' Brenda took Joyce aside.

'No, I couldn't persuade her.' Joyce shook her head. 'She's still getting over the shock of a second visit from her aunty. Anyway, even though she's missing out tonight, I really think she's slowly coming out of her shell—'

'Thanks to you,' Brenda put in quickly.

'No,' Joyce corrected. 'Alma is doing this all by herself. But coming to the dance was definitely a step too far.'

'Maybe next time,' Brenda murmured as they watched the hall fill up. They saw Emma return with Cliff, who listened to what the vicar told him about the radiators then went around adjusting knobs on the defective ones. He stopped to say hello to Joyce and Brenda then, as the band struck up with 'Kalamazoo', he moved on to where Evelyn stood by herself.

'Blimey, Evelyn, you could have made a bit more effort,' he said with a wink that acknowledged how stunning she looked. Her hair was pinned back on one side but cascaded loosely to her shoulder on the other. He was about to slip his hand around her waist and lead her on to the dance floor when an over-eager, gangly RAF lad stepped in.

'Ready?' Mouse held out his hand and Evelyn took it.

'I've got a gal in Kalamazoo . . .'

Cliff turned away abruptly and felt in his jacket pocket for his cigarettes. But before he could light up, Dorothy whirled by with her partner, Joe. She whipped the packet away and pointed in wallflower Elsie's direction. 'Dance with her!' she ordered. 'Don't leave the poor girl standing there!'

Cliff did as he was told. After all, two could play at Evelyn's game.

The jaunty tune put smiles on everyone's faces and energy into their steps.

'Zoo zoo zoo zoo zoo . . .'

Spare men stood at the side of the room discussing their favourite tipple or football team, eyeing the girl they would move in on for the next dance. All the Land Girls twirled and turned under patriotic clusters of red, white and blue balloons.

So far, so good. Walter Rigg was satisfied that, for the time being, decorum would not be breached. He would call back in an hour. On his way out with Emma, he made sure to pile a plate high with sandwiches and sausage rolls and take them to the vicarage for his supper.

'Good evening, Geoffrey,' he said as the vet and a man he didn't recognize arrived. They stood aside to allow his exit. 'Everything is in full swing, as you can hear.'

Geoff and his companion smiled and nodded.

'"Once more into the breach",' Giles quoted with a grin as they entered the hall.

It wasn't until the fifth number of the evening that Cliff finally managed to corner Evelyn. He'd already danced with Elsie and Kathleen, then Joyce and Brenda, while she had been snapped up by a variety of RAF boys, all eager to impress with their waltzes and foxtrots. One had launched into a modern jitterbug number with her, clearing a space in the centre of the floor and teaching her the moves as they went along. They'd bounced along on the balls of their feet to a rhythm set by the saxophone, holding hands and dipping their shoulders then leaning right in, with him using his weight to send her backwards, arms extended before swinging her around.

Dorothy was the first to applaud the exhilarating spectacle. 'How about that! Come along, Geoff; let's give it a go,' she called across the room when she saw the vet standing idly by. Leaving her current partner in the lurch, she ran to seize him by both hands.

Geoff shrugged apologetically at Giles then joined her. 'Are you sure? This is a new one on me.'

'Me too.' She seized his hands and started to imitate Evelyn and her partner. Of course it ended with a totter and a squeal then a collapse in a heap on the floor. Ever gallant, Geoff put her back on her feet and escorted her giggling towards Giles.

The second the number ended, Cliff stepped in to claim Evelyn at last. Her face was flushed after her up-tempo exertions and a wisp of damp hair stuck to her cheek. The words 'making a show of yourself' were on the tip of his tongue but he bit them back.

Instead, he wound an arm around her waist for a slow waltz. 'About time too,' he murmured into her ear.

'It serves you right,' she whispered back.

'What do you mean?'

'That's what comes of keeping secrets. People suppose I'm single and fancy-free. Anyway, where were you last night?'

'I went to bed early – why?'

'Your door was locked. I tried knocking.'

'Sorry, I must have been fast asleep.' He held her closer and put his cheek against hers. They threaded their way between other couples to the sound of soaring violins. 'Anyway – we're here now.'

'Together at last.'

He drew his head away and threw her a quizzical look. 'Are you having a go at me?'

'Yes,' she admitted.

'Trying to teach me a lesson?' His arm tightened around her waist.

'Yes – you deserve it,' she insisted, before giving in to the feel of his body close to hers.

The waltz ended and Cliff kept hold of her hand as he walked her towards Dorothy, Geoff and Giles. The band began a Percy Grainger number while Cliff decided to persuade his sister to sing.

'Oh no, I couldn't!' she protested in a way that meant the opposite. 'No one wants to listen to me.'

'Of course they do.' He slipped his arm around Evelyn's waist. 'Dorothy can hold a tune, can't she, Geoff? At parties we always get her to sing us a song.'

While Geoff added a word of encouragement, Dorothy blushed and smiled then gave in.

'There's no time like the present,' Cliff insisted as the dance ended and the couples on the floor broke up. He crossed the hall for a quick word with Ernie, who listened then nodded.

'Yes is the answer,' Cliff announced when he returned.

It was settled; Dorothy would sing 'Somewhere over the Rainbow' from *The Wizard of Oz*.

The dance floor emptied as Dorothy took her place by the piano and Ernie struck up the first chords. Joyce and Brenda watched from the doorway into the annexe, noticing the difference between this Dorothy with her plunging neckline and the original on-screen Dorothy in her girlish gingham dress and white ankle socks.

'What's in a name, eh?' Brenda said under her breath.

'Yes; coincidence or what?' Joyce murmured.

But they were silenced as Garthside Dorothy tilted her head back, opened her mouth and sang wistfully about a land that she dreamed of,

'*Once in a lullaby*'. Her voice was deep, sweet and pure, full of longing. It transported her listeners from a grey world of rationing and blackouts to a magical place beyond the rainbow where golds, blues and greens dazzled the senses, scarecrows came to life and a girl in sparkling red shoes sang her way along the Yellow Brick Road.

'Blow me down – she's not bad!' Kathleen was among the spellbound.

Elsie came in from the annexe to listen and look. A few couples drifted back on to the floor and held each other close in a slow waltz.

'Shall we?' Cliff asked Evelyn, who nodded.

They joined the dancers. The violinists and saxophonist faded then fell silent, leaving Ernie's piano to accompany Dorothy's silky voice.

Bluebirds flew over the rainbow. Judy Garland in pigtails raised her eyes to the heavens and yearned to follow them.

A young woman walked in through the main door. She was dressed in sober outdoor clothes: a straight grey coat with a black velour hat and black gloves, a dark red silk scarf showing above her collar. Her face was pale and serious.

'*When happy little bluebirds fly . . .*'

Cliff danced cheek to cheek with Evelyn. He turned slowly on the spot until he faced the door.

'Hello, Cliff,' the woman said in a loud, clear voice.

He stopped and let go of Evelyn.

'Hello,' the woman said again, as she strode towards him. 'I knew I'd track you down in the end. It was only a matter of time.'

CHAPTER EIGHTEEN

Dorothy sang on, oblivious. Her eyes were closed, her head tilted back as she reached the final chorus. *'Why, oh why, can't I?'*

The dancers parted to allow the woman in the grey coat through.

Cliff darted forward to intercept her. He seized her by the arm then whirled her round and marched her out of the door, leaving Evelyn stranded in the middle of the floor.

'What's going on?' Dorothy opened her eyes, expecting applause. Instead, there was an uneasy silence. She caught sight of Cliff leaving with a woman she didn't recognize. While the musicians turned the pages of their sheet music, she dashed up to Brenda, demanding answers.

Brenda shook her head. 'Search me.' A woman had arrived out of the blue. Cliff had got the shock of his life – that was as much as she knew.

Determined to find out more, Dorothy brushed against Evelyn as she ran across the room in hot pursuit.

It was almost time for the interval so Ernie smoothed over the awkward interruption by striking up the opening chords to the tune that would round off the first half. Bing Crosby's 'White Christmas' tempted dancers back on to the floor, while Evelyn stood rooted to the spot.

Brenda took her hand and led her gently to the side of the room. 'Sit down,' she told her when Geoff brought her a chair.

'No. I don't need to sit.' She took a deep breath and clenched her fists. 'There's been some sort of misunderstanding.' Perhaps Cliff owed the woman money. There was an outstanding debt and somehow she'd discovered where he lived. By the look of things she was hell-bent on getting her cash. 'Cliff's landed himself in a tight spot over money and the silly idiot will have to get himself out of it,' she told Brenda and Geoff in a strained, defiant voice.

Brenda pressed her lips together. *Why now? Why, at nine o'clock on a Saturday evening a week before Christmas, would a woman come all the way out to Shawcross to collect a debt?*

'I think you should sit down.' Geoff saw Evelyn sway slightly. He was concerned that she might faint. 'Giles, fetch her a glass of water, quick as you can.'

His friend hurried off to the annexe, threading between couples and returning almost straight away with the drink.

'I might have guessed that money problems were behind his bad moods,' Evelyn went on. *Tracked him down; that's what the woman had said; as if Cliff was a fugitive. Only a matter of time until she caught up with him.*

'Are you sure?' Brenda ventured. *No,* she thought; *this has nothing to do with pounds, shillings and pence.*

'Definitely. Cliff is hopeless when it comes to money. All he cares about is keeping his car on the road and having enough left over for the odd night out.'

Less than a minute after Dorothy had run out into the darkness, she reappeared with a dazed expression. Her face was pale under the carefully applied make-up and she seemed breathless.

'Shall I fetch another glass of water?' Giles asked as once again Geoff rushed to the rescue.

Evelyn and Brenda waited for Geoff to bring Dorothy to them. She sank into the chair that Evelyn had refused, one hand on her chest as she tried to catch her breath.

Geoff crouched beside her. 'All right, Dorothy, take it easy. Deep breaths; that's right. Can you explain what's wrong?'

She panted rapidly and let her head sink forward.

'We have to get her out of here,' he decided instantly. He looked at the throng of dancers as he considered the best and quickest way to do this.

'Let me run to the house and fetch the car,' Giles suggested. When Geoff nodded he departed quickly.

Geoff carried on tending to Dorothy. 'Listen to me, whatever has upset you, it's important for you to try to calm down. You should probably take some medicine to help your heart so I'm going to drive you straight home and see that you take it. Giles won't be long fetching the car. Is that all right? Can you hear me?'

'Cliff,' she whimpered as she tried to push her old friend away.

'Never mind about your brother,' Geoff insisted. 'He can look after himself.'

'He's . . . she's . . . Oh, how could he?' Dorothy flapped her hands to ward him off then covered her face and collapsed forward again.

Evelyn took a short, sharp breath. With a panicky glance at Brenda, she started to push her way towards the door.

Ernie crooned the closing words of the song. '*Merry and bright . . . may all your Christmases be white*.' Douglas deftly steered Elsie towards the bunch of mistletoe hanging in the porch. Kathleen let Mouse lead her towards the refreshment tables.

'Ladies and gents, there will now be a short interval,' Ernie announced as he closed the lid of his piano.

Cold air hit Evelyn as she pushed past Elsie and her dance partner locked in an embrace. It was pitch black outside but she could hear two voices arguing loudly.

'You're wasting your time! Do you hear me, Gladys?' Cliff bellowed.

With rising dread Evelyn followed the sound.

'It won't do any good. You can't make me change my mind.'

'No, but I can queer your pitch here in Shawcross!' the woman yelled back.

'So what?'

'So!' she screeched. 'It will serve you right. Everyone will know you for what you are – your sister, your dad; everyone!'

He laughed mirthlessly. 'I always knew you had a nasty streak, Gladys.'

Gradually Evelyn's eyes grew used to the dark and she was drawn towards two figures standing by the stone cross in the middle of the green. She saw the glowing tip of Cliff's cigarette and felt the prickle of its smoke as it entered her nostrils.

'Is that right?' the woman said. 'You might have succeeded in fooling some of the yokels in this God-forsaken place but you don't fool me. Does that sister of yours have a brain inside her head, by the way? Or is she as daft as she looks?'

'Go ahead, say what you like about my family; I don't give a damn.'

'You knew I had a nasty streak yet you married me.' The woman's voice dripped with scorn. 'You trotted me down the aisle regardless.'

Suddenly Evelyn's legs refused to hold her weight and she sank to the cold ground.

'And don't I wish I hadn't. Who in their right mind would want to tie the knot with you?' Cliff flicked his cigarette to the ground and stamped on it.

'You did, though, didn't you?'

'Yes; because . . . !'

'Because what, Cliff?' The strident voice was relentless. 'Don't tell me it was because you wanted to do the decent thing.'

'Yes, and more fool me,' he said bitterly. 'You can't squeeze any more money out of me, by the way.'

'Chance would be a fine thing!' Gladys gave another hollow laugh then out of the corner of her eye she saw Evelyn collapsed on the ground, struggling to stand up again. 'Oh look; who have we here? No, don't tell me – it's Rita Hayworth, no less.'

With a great effort Evelyn raised herself and carried on walking towards them. Cliff backed away while the woman stood her ground.

'Is it true?' Evelyn asked him. Her heart felt as if it had been ripped out of her ribcage and she could scarcely mouth the words.

'Tell her, Cliff,' the woman said.

There was silence except for the hum of chatter from the hall.

'All right; if you won't, I will.' This was Gladys's moment and she was determined to make the most of it, extending her hand towards Evelyn as if pleased to make her acquaintance. 'I'm Gladys Huby. And you are?'

Huby? She is his wife then. Cliff has lied to me from the start. 'Is it true?' Evelyn repeated. She ignored the woman and stared at Cliff. 'Are you already married?'

'Oh, Cliff, what have you done?' As things clicked into place, Gladys lowered her voice and spoke with mock sympathy. 'Has he been leading you on, love? Yes, that would be my husband's style.'

'Is it true?' Evelyn demanded for a third time.

'You're definitely his type, I'll give you that.' Gladys took a cigarette case from her handbag then pushed her face towards Cliff with a cigarette between her lips. 'Do you have a light, by any chance?'

He swore and pushed her to one side, making her stumble against the stone plinth. Then he turned to Evelyn and spoke urgently: 'Go back inside. I'll explain later.'

Gladys tucked her silk scarf back in place then adjusted her collar. 'Did you see that?' she asked coolly.

'No, Cliff; explain now.' Evelyn kept her eyes fixed on his face.

'Yes, all right; I'm married to this . . . this!' Fury robbed him of the word he was searching for. 'But I haven't clapped eyes on her in years.'

'Three, to be exact,' Gladys confirmed. 'December the fifth, nineteen thirty-nine; that's when he left me in the lurch. We'd been married just under three months.'

'And I'll tell you why I agreed to marry her, shall I?' He stabbed his finger towards Gladys without looking at her.

Evelyn's heart shuddered under the fierceness of his gaze. Her stomach cramped and bile rose to her throat.

'Because she was expecting. That's what she told me, at any rate. But it turned out to be a lie.'

'He means I lost the baby at sixteen weeks,' Gladys countered calmly as she delved into her bag and found a lighter for her cigarette.

'So she says! But I found out there never was any baby. It was all a trick.'

'Stop!' Evelyn pleaded. She turned away to be sick, holding her arms across her stomach and retching violently.

'There was a baby and it died,' Gladys maintained as she offered Evelyn a handkerchief from her bag. 'That's when Cliff scarpered and I found out that he was the one who'd been telling me a pack of lies, not the other way around. He'd given me a wrong address for a start. He said his family lived in Sheffield. That particular wild-goose chase kept me busy for quite a while.'

'I don't want to hear,' Evelyn pleaded.

'I didn't give up, though. I was Cliff's wife and I had the papers to prove it.'

'I married you under false pretences!' he raged, like a beast trapped under a net, snarling and lashing out at his captor.

Gladys inhaled smoke then blew it out from the side of her mouth. 'Eventually I went right back to the start of the trail, to the Red Lion in Northgate where I'd first met him, just as the war was starting. Do you remember, Cliff? We listened to Mr Chamberlain on the wireless, telling us it would all be over before Christmas; no more Herr Hitler and his Nazi army marching into Poland willy-nilly. "I'll drink to that!" you said. Everyone was very merry.

'No one in the pub remembered you when I went back, though. The landlord was the same but he didn't recognize you from the description I gave. Tall, dark and handsome were ten a penny round there, he said. "Ask at the baker's on the corner," he told me. "They might know more about your Cliff Huby. Or else at the Lyons tea shop on the corner of Kitchener Street." One thing led to another – the nippies in the tea shop said to try the lady in the hat shop and finally, here I am.'

'Thanks to me.' A fourth person had stepped unobserved from a parked car and was approaching their group. It was Muriel Woodthorpe, picking her way between mounds of melting snow, as prim and proper as ever. 'I was the one who made the connection earlier today. I never forget a face, by the way. That's him, I realized in a flash. Gladys Huby's husband has gone to ground right here in Shawcross!'

*

'Will she be all right?' As Dorothy was carried from the hall into Geoff's waiting car, Kathleen broke away from her dance partner to speak to Joyce.

'Let's hope so.' Joyce kept her fingers firmly crossed. They must trust Geoff to know what he was doing. But Dorothy looked terrible. She was still struggling for breath, her head lolling forward, as Geoff placed her carefully on the back seat then sat beside her and ordered Giles to drive to Garthside Farm as fast as he could.

'What's the matter with her?' Elsie had joined the growing group of Land Girls standing outside the hall.

'It's her heart.' Brenda was caught between staying with the group and setting out after Evelyn. Shocked by the first firm evidence she'd seen of Dorothy's condition, she regretted how easily she'd dismissed it up till now as exaggeration and an excuse for laziness. 'She has special medicine to deal with it,' she told Elsie.

'Would you believe it?' Kathleen shivered and drew her cardigan around her shoulders. 'One minute she's singing her little heart out then the next thing you know, she's at death's door.'

'Don't say that,' Elsie said with a shudder.

'No, don't,' Joyce added quietly, thinking that it must have been the strain of organizing tonight that had brought on this attack. After all, Dorothy had been so determined to make a success of the event that she'd been on the go non-stop for days.

Brenda alone had kept track of Dorothy's actions just prior to her collapse; she'd seen the determined way she'd reacted to her brother's mysterious exit by running out after him, returning soon after in a state of hysterics. Now, though, Brenda slid away from the girls who were wondering whether it would be best to call a halt to the dance and send everyone home early.

'That would be a shame,' Kathleen said. 'We're all having such a good time.'

'But this has put a definite dampener on things.' Elsie was less in favour of carrying on. 'What do you think, Joyce? If you were in Dorothy's shoes, what would you want us to do?'

Brenda ran across the green towards raised voices. She heard Cliff shout and a woman interrupt him but it was too dark to make out exactly where they were. 'Evelyn?' she called. 'It's Brenda. Where are you?'

'Do you hear that?' Gladys nudged Evelyn with her elbow. 'Someone seems keen to get hold of you.'

Recoiling from her touch, Evelyn backed into Muriel.

'Watch what you're doing,' Muriel complained. 'Well?' she demanded of Gladys with a long-suffering sigh. 'You've found him, so what now?'

'Evelyn, are you there?' At last Brenda made out a group of four people gathered by the cross: three women and one man, caught in silhouette in the light from the open doorway of the Cross Keys.

'What next, hubby of mine?' Gladys repeated Muriel's question as a direct challenge to Cliff. 'Are you willing to come home with me and play Happy Families?'

Cliff swore and lunged at her.

'I didn't think so,' Gladys mocked.

Brenda arrived out of breath. 'There you are!' she gasped at Evelyn, who sat down heavily on the stone ledge behind her, holding a handkerchief to her mouth. 'I was worried about you.'

'She's had a shock,' Gladys told her as she continued to glare at Cliff.

Muriel obviously felt that honour was satisfied and that it was time to go. 'Will you look after her?' she asked Brenda who sat down next to Evelyn. 'Make sure she gets home safely.'

'Bugger off, you two!' Cliff exploded. He shoved Muriel out of the way. 'You – whoever you are – mind your own business.' He squared up to Gladys. 'And you; I swear I'll wring your bloody neck!'

Brenda leaped to her feet. 'Steady on.' She shoved Cliff sideways, away from the two women. 'Can someone please tell me what's going on?'

Evelyn stood up more slowly, her hair tumbling forward over her bare shoulders, her hands shaking. 'It's all right, Brenda; I'll explain later.'

'Go on; bugger off out of here!' Cliff cursed again and raised his fists, forcing Gladys to stumble backwards.

Muriel needed no further telling. 'Don't worry, we're leaving.' She hitched her handbag into the crook of her arm then set off towards her car. 'Come along, Gladys.'

Cliff's wife weighed up the new situation. She hadn't bargained on a hysterical sister or a jealous girlfriend when she'd planned this little expedition into the Dales, or on a friend being willing to stick her oar in. And, to judge by a quick glance towards the hall where a large group had gathered, there was every chance that others would join them. 'Rightio,' she decided. 'I'll say ta-ta for now.'

Cliff lunged again but was restrained by Brenda while Gladys caught up with Muriel. He shook himself free then turned to Evelyn and spoke roughly. 'Come on; I'll give you a lift home.'

'Don't!' Brenda warned her not to accept. Cliff's mood was dangerous. Evelyn seemed dazed and confused.

'It's all right,' she insisted. 'I want to have this out with him.'

'Are you sure?'

'Yes.' A dozen questions whirled inside Evelyn's head. They couldn't wait.

'I'll be in the church hall if you need me,' Brenda said warily.

'Ta. I'll come and find you in a while.'

'It doesn't feel right to leave you.'

'I'll be all right. Go back inside.'

So Brenda turned and walked slowly across the green. She'd almost reached the hall when she remembered she hadn't told Cliff about Dorothy. She turned again to retrace her steps but he and Evelyn had already disappeared.

'Why?' Evelyn wanted to know. The shock was subsiding, leaving her with an empty feeling that needed to be filled with answers. 'Why ask me to marry you when you were already married?'

They'd left the green and walked over the packhorse bridge leading to Black Crag. Cliff was ready with his answer. 'Because I love you, that's why.'

She quickened her pace. 'What does that mean: you love me? It's a word, Cliff – that's all.'

'No, it's more than that.' He beat his fist against his chest as if to say that was where the feeling for her was seated. 'It's deep down. It's never happened to me before; you've got to believe me.'

'Still just words.'

He caught at her hand. 'What about when we're in bed together? Is that just words?'

'Let go of me. Don't touch me.'

'Is it, though?' He ran ahead of her and walked backwards as he spoke. 'Think of that, Evie.'

'I don't want to think of that.' His reminder of their lovemaking made her furious. 'I want to know why you lied to me.'

His head drooped and he stopped walking. 'Because I wouldn't have stood a chance if I'd told you the truth,' he said plainly and simply.

'That's right; you wouldn't.' Her mind flew back to the day in summer when she'd arrived at the castle and first set eyes on Cliff as she'd stood with her suitcase in the yard. He and Weatherall had come out of the fresh green wood carrying a shotgun apiece and a brace of pheasants. The contrast between them – the old and the young – had struck her. She'd noticed the way Cliff had of managing his doddery boss by yelling explanations in his ear then leading him by the elbow into the house. He'd come out again and shaken her by the hand. 'I must say, you're a pleasant surprise.' There'd been no attempt to hide his admiration. A searching look had had its intended effect, leaving her flustered and speechless. 'Things are definitely looking up,' he'd said as he'd sauntered into his cottage, leaving her standing there.

No mention that he had a wife or a girlfriend. Everything about his behaviour suggesting the opposite.

'I didn't set out to lie to you,' he muttered miserably above the sound of the stream rushing under the bridge. 'It just happened.'

Her anger rose still higher. 'Lies don't just happen – you *make* them happen!'

'Not on purpose. The subject never came up. And then I was in too deep – it was too late.'

'That's still not good enough. It's a weak thing to say.'

'Weak or not, it's the truth. Anyway, Evie, I couldn't have stayed away from you even if I'd tried. Every morning I looked out of my window, there you were, harnessing the horse or heaping tools into a wheelbarrow, sleeves rolled back, hair lifted up off your neck, showing off your figure in those trousers.'

'I never showed off my figure on purpose.' Exasperation overtook anger. 'The uniform is given to us – two pairs of riding breeches, two pairs of dungarees. We don't get a choice.'

They faced each other in silence for a while. She thought back again to her reasons for coming to Acklam. 'I wanted a fresh start,' she remembered. 'I'd had a hard time at home and was still nursing a broken heart. I was keen to tackle something new. The war gave me that chance. And then I got here and it was a shock – out in the middle of nowhere with Colonel Weatherall breathing down my neck.'

'But no secrets, dark or otherwise, to queer your pitch,' he reminded her. 'That must have been nice and straightforward.'

'I'd never have done what you did,' she retorted. 'I wouldn't have led you on.'

'You don't know that. If it had been the other way around, you could easily have got carried along just like me.'

'Never. For a start, if I'd been married, I wouldn't have run away.'

'Not even from Gladys?' he said. The mean jibe slipped out and he regretted it. 'I'm sorry. She wasn't always the way she is now.'

'No; you made her like this by doing the dirty on her.' Didn't he see this? Was he totally clueless?

Cliff's anger, lurking close to the surface, rose again. 'There never was any baby,' he said savagely, hitting the side of his fist against the trunk of a nearby tree. 'She's the liar here; not me!'

'Oh, for heaven's sake!' She saw him now: hopeless, heartless, dishonest through and through. She turned back towards the bridge. 'The baby is not the point. Anyway, I don't believe you. I don't know a woman in this world who would invent a baby just to get you to marry them.'

He laughed at her naivety. 'Lucky you.'

'Don't laugh at me, Cliff Huby! You're the one who's made a bloody mess of things, not me.'

'Yes, yes.' He ran after her as she strode away. 'And I'm sorry. I'll put it right; I'll get a divorce.'

She gasped incredulously and stopped. 'A divorce?'

'With a proper solicitor. I'll find out how to do it.'

'And then everything will be all right, will it?' She

went on again, with greater purpose in her stride because she wanted to put an end to this stupidity once and for all. 'Don't bother, Cliff. Not on my account.'

He watched her walk away. *What more does she want, for Christ's sake?*

'Don't worry about giving me a lift home,' she flung back over her shoulder as she crested the stone bridge and the water rushed under her feet. 'I'll stay at Brenda's tonight.'

CHAPTER NINETEEN

Earlier that evening Brenda had collected the oil lamp from her billet and taken it down to the hall, so when she and Evelyn arrived at the goods wagon late on Saturday evening she had to light two candles that she set down on the washstand next to her bed. Then she gave Evelyn a blanket to wrap around her shoulders.

'Well?' she prompted when Evelyn sat down on the bed with an exhausted sigh.

'I've had it out with him, told him what I think.'

'Good.'

'He said he'd get a divorce.'

Brenda knew this wasn't the moment to be jumping in with an opinion. She sat down next to Evelyn and kept her thoughts to herself.

Tears began to flow. 'Oh, Brenda – I've been buying linen for my bottom drawer for weeks. I bought a pattern for my wedding dress and I've almost finished saving up enough clothing coupons to buy the material. White brocade with a net underskirt.'

The candles flickered from a draught that crept in under the door. They cast long shadows across the poorly furnished room with its magazine pictures tacked to the walls and Brenda's Land Girl uniform flung carelessly over the back of a chair. Outside in the yard Nancy the goat started to bray.

'Oh, drat! Wait here while I see what that racket is about,' Brenda told Evelyn.

She stepped outside to see Geoff and Giles saying goodbye to Bernard at the door of the farmhouse.

'Dorothy is over the worst,' Geoff told the old farmer as Brenda joined them. 'Her pulse is still racing, but nothing like as bad as it was an hour ago.'

Bernard listened intently. He stood in shirtsleeves and slippers, stooping and grasping the edge of the door, blinking rapidly as he tried to take in what the vet was telling him.

'Keep her in bed for the rest of the weekend. If you're still worried about her tomorrow morning, don't think twice about ringing Doc Brownlee. He'll call the hospital and they'll send an ambulance.'

'Right you are.' Noticing Brenda, Bernard ordered her to quieten the goat. 'Be quick about it; we can't hear ourselves think.'

Giles came with Brenda into the barn and together they gave Nancy an extra bundle of hay.

'I bet you're sorry you came tonight,' she said as she hung the stuffed hay-net in the stall. 'You didn't get much chance to sweep us girls off our feet before it ended in calamity.'

'It doesn't matter to me. To be honest, I'm not the world's best hoofer.' His voice was soft and well educated, lighter than expected. His tweed jacket and shiny brown brogues looked expensive. 'I only came because I have to go away to my family's place in

Leicestershire for Christmas and I was keen to catch up with Geoff before I went.'

As Nancy snatched at the hay and started to chew, Brenda and Giles left the barn and saw that the farmhouse door was already closed so they joined Geoff by his car.

'Keep an eye on Dorothy,' he told her, leaning one arm on the roof. 'She'd almost passed out by the time we arrived here. I only just managed to get the pills down her in time.'

'All right; will do. What do I look out for exactly?'

'If she says she has pains in her chest then that's the time to involve Doc Brownlee, double-quick. Otherwise, make sure she has plenty to drink. And keep her in bed, like I said.'

Brenda stood back to let Giles slide into the passenger seat while Geoff went round to the driver's side. She watched them drive out of the yard, then stood for a moment, taking in deep gulps of cold night air and gazing up at a sky glittering with stars.

Back inside the billet, she found Evelyn still huddled in the blanket, not crying now but staring at the flickering candles with a dazed expression. She didn't look up at Brenda.

'What can I do for you?' Brenda sat down next to her, feeling helpless. 'Are you warm enough? Do you want to borrow one of my jumpers?'

Evelyn shook her head. 'How can I have been so stupid?'

'You weren't. Cliff was.'

'I was, though. I should've known.'

'What; that he was already married? I don't think

so. No woman expects a man to keep quiet about something like that.'

'But when he said we couldn't announce our engagement – I should've put two and two together.' Evelyn raked back through the cold ashes of the excuses she'd heard from Cliff: it was too soon to break the news, it was the danger of Weatherall chucking them out or the difficulty of finding other jobs. 'I should have taken a step back and thought it through.'

'Listen, you didn't do anything wrong. I'll bet he was the one who went down on bended knee.'

'He did. He swore he loved me and wanted to marry me and like a fool I said yes.'

'Because you loved him,' Brenda pointed out. 'No doubt you fell for him hook, line and sinker. Whereas, me and my fiancé . . .'

Evelyn glanced up at her for the first time.

'Never mind.' Brenda quickly changed tack. 'It can't have been easy for you, not being able to tell anyone. Joyce and I would never have found out if it hadn't been for that silly goose Dorothy letting the cat out of the bag.'

'The thing is, I believed in Cliff. Let's face it, I *wanted* to believe in him, more fool me! And it turns out he was right about one important thing: other estate managers would have been bound to ask awkward questions about Cliff's state of health. So if Colonel Weatherall had kicked us out of Acklam for getting engaged, Cliff might well have been on the scrap heap, with no money and no job.'

'Yes, I see.' It didn't excuse the rest of it, though. Or quite why Evelyn had put up with watching him flirt with other girls, including Brenda herself, and generally behaving as if he was single and fancy-free. 'He's a good-looking chap; I can understand why you'd fall for him in a big way.'

'It was his eyes,' Evelyn tried to explain. 'How can a girl fall in love with someone just because of the way he looks at her?'

'Because!' That was the way it worked.

'It was just like it happens in books and films: love at first sight. Me standing in the yard with my suitcase, him walking out of the wood; Cliff didn't even have to open his mouth.'

Brenda felt a twinge of envy. 'It *was* different with me and Les,' she admitted reluctantly. 'It took quite a while to decide that I loved him. I thought he was a pleasant enough chap, with a nice twinkle in his eye. But we went out quite a few times, to the pub and for drives in his car, before it got more serious. Les is a quiet type and I was – well, let's just say that I'd had my fingers burned more than once.'

'I wish I'd taken things more slowly,' Evelyn admitted. 'The trouble is, I didn't hold back.' She felt her face grow warm as she remembered her first time in bed with Cliff: waiting for Weatherall's light to go off, creeping across the yard to the cottage for a pre-arranged tryst, and then, almost before she knew it, lying in bed beside him and feeling like it was the most natural thing in the world.

Brenda understood exactly what she meant. 'War changes things. We rush in because we know we only live once. After all, who's to say when a bomb will drop and blow us all to smithereens?' Les was this minute on his Royal Navy patrol up the west coast of

Scotland, dodging U-boats, protecting his country's fleet of battleships. Grace's Bill was currently sweating it out in Burma, while Joyce's Edgar was safer now, not dicing nightly but flying reconnaissance missions instead. Still, safety was relative. Edgar might actually be up there in the starry sky as they spoke, flying his Spitfire into a hail of bullets.

'We forget what our mothers taught us,' Evelyn agreed. 'According to Mum, in her day, everyone behaved themselves until they got married. They kept one foot on the ground, like in love scenes in the cinema; she said they had to if they didn't want to get a bad name. Perhaps it was better that way.'

'I'm really not sure. In any case, there's no going back for either of us.'

'Are you sorry?'

Brenda thought long and hard. 'Not really. On the whole, I think it's better to know what you're letting yourself in for in that regard. In the old days you could marry a man and then the physical side of things would turn out to be a big disappointment that you'd be stuck with for the rest of your life.'

Evelyn managed a weak smile. 'You don't mince your words; I'll say that.'

'It's true, though. If you do it beforehand, you have a pretty clear idea of how much you enjoy it.'

'Or how little.'

'Exactly. That's what I'm getting at.' Brenda got up to block the draught blowing in under the door with a rolled-up towel, allowing the candles to burn more steadily. 'For me it made all the difference; it made my feelings for Les stronger. I knew that he was the man for me, even though his brother carried on being a pest and Hettie took a long time to come round to the idea that Les and I were engaged.'

'I'd say the same about my first time with Cliff. I'd never done it with Jim, my first beau – we were too young and we never had much time to ourselves, what with Mum always lurking round the corner. But with Cliff it all fell into place and it felt marvellous, exciting and frightening all at once, like being bowled over by a big wave and having it swirl and crash over your head. There was no way of getting back on my feet, or if I did, Cliff would be there and we'd do it again and my legs would be swept from under me time after time.'

'You were happy for it to happen?'

'I was and I wasn't. Cliff isn't one for talking, either in or out of bed. There was never time to discuss what was happening between us, and anyway I doubt if I could have found the right words. "I love you" was all we ever said. He thinks that's enough.'

'Whereas you would have liked a bit more – the whys and wherefores?'

Evelyn nodded. 'We women give up a lot to be with a man. Or I did. All of a sudden it was as though I wasn't my own person any more. I was always waiting for the next time I saw Cliff, holding my breath and wondering if a kiss would lead to the next thing and the next, or if he would give me the cold shoulder and take out one of his bad moods on me and pretend in public that there was nothing between us.'

'You're right; we lose a lot of our freedom,' Brenda observed. 'Why on earth do we do it?'

'Because we love them!' they said together then laughed quietly.

'It's what you call a vicious circle. And now all we can do is sit here and talk about it.' Brenda pulled a clean pair of pyjamas from a drawer and tossed them to Evelyn. 'You don't mind topping and tailing with me?'

'No.' She was thankful and completely drained. She said she would be able to sleep on a bed of nails.

'Good. I'll turn my back while you get changed.' Brenda stood, arms folded, staring at a picture on the wall that showed Merle Oberon on the film set of *Wuthering Heights*: wasp-waisted, with her crinoline skirt billowing in the wind. 'Do you feel better now you've got it off your chest?'

Evelyn took off her silvery grey dance dress then put on Brenda's pyjamas. 'Better?' she mused. 'Not so much as if I've been steamrollered. I'm bruised and battered – yes, but still standing. So I suppose I do.'

'And tomorrow?'

She buttoned up the jacket then slid into bed. 'Tomorrow is a new day. Let's wait and see what it brings.'

Next morning Evelyn woke with a start. Early dawn light crept in under the door and a strong wind blew through the gap beneath Brenda's wagon, making it rock from side to side. *Captain!* Evelyn realized she must cycle over to Acklam right away to give her horse fresh water and hay.

So she slid quietly from the bed, doing her best not to disturb Brenda.

'Where are you sneaking off to at this hour?' a sleepy voice asked.

'Sorry to wake you. I have to shoot off home to see to Captain.'

Brenda's face emerged from under the blankets and she saw Evelyn zipping up her dance dress. 'You'll catch your death. Why not borrow a pair of my dungarees?'

'Right you are.' This made sense and soon Evelyn was sensibly dressed and ready to leave.

'Will you be back in time for church?' Brenda asked as she turned towards the wall, intending to get more shut-eye.

'I'm not sure. You go ahead; don't wait for me.'

'All right. You know where to find me if you need me.'

Evelyn opened the door to a blast of chilly air. She closed it firmly then tiptoed past the barn where Nancy was housed, past the hen hut full of clucking Rhode Island Reds then around the new rabbit hutch whose occupants slept in their nests of straw and shredded newspaper. The puddles in the yard were frozen solid.

From an upstairs window Cliff watched her depart.

It was no good; Brenda couldn't get back to sleep. The wind shook the wagon and rattled at the barn doors. It lifted a metal dustbin lid and sent it clattering across the flags. The goat woke up and brayed. The cockerel crowed. The farmhouse door opened then banged shut.

So she crept out of bed and into the warmest clothes she could find: dungarees over pyjama bottoms, two jerseys and two pairs of socks. Putting on her fleece-lined pilot's jacket and jamming her feet into her gumboots, she opened the door and braced herself for the onslaught of wind and cold.

Her first job of the morning was to go into the barn and milk the blessed goat. Straight after that she would go into the house and ask about Dorothy.

It sounded straightforward until it turned out that Nancy wasn't prepared to cooperate.

'Stand still, there's a good girl.' Brenda set down her stool and metal pail inside the black goat's stall.

Nancy flattened her ears and bared her teeth. She kicked out with her back legs then bucked high in the air, knocking over the empty bucket with a loud clatter.

'Steady on. The sooner we get this over with the better.'

The goat stared balefully at Brenda then lowered her head and prepared to charge. Brenda picked up her pail and hurriedly backed out of the stall. She was in the nick of time – Nancy butted her horns against the closing door with a dull thud.

'Please yourself.' Brenda decided to come back later and emerged from the barn just as Cliff drove his car around the side of the house where it had been parked out of sight. She grimaced when she saw him behind the wheel: unshaven, with his jacket collar turned up, glaring at her as she crossed the yard.

Funnily enough, she hadn't given a thought to where he might have gone after last night's scene on the green; if not back to Acklam then perhaps to the Cross Keys to drown his sorrows, or even into town in hot pursuit of Gladys and Muriel. So it came as a surprise to realize that he'd spent the night in his father's house, only a few yards from where she and Evelyn had slept.

Cliff put his foot on the brake, making the back wheels slew sideways across a patch of black ice. He came to a halt and wound down his window. 'Why didn't you tell me what had happened to Dorothy?'

'Why didn't you ask?' she shot back.

He scowled at her. 'How was I to know that she was having one of her dos?'

Brenda shivered in spite of the layers of clothes. It was already clear that Cliff Huby was the sort who never took responsibility for his actions; even so it was a shock to hear him talk so unfeelingly about his own sister. 'How is she this morning?' she asked pointedly.

'Still fast asleep, as far as I know.'

'Is your father up?'

He nodded once, sniffed as if at a bad smell then wound up his window and drove on without a word.

Inside the house Brenda found Bernard setting out a tray with a cup of tea and a plate of toast and marmalade. His clothes looked as if they'd been slept in and his hair was uncombed. His hand shook as he poured the tea.

'How is she?' Brenda kicked off her boots.

'She looks like death warmed up,' he reported, unscrewing the top off a bottle of white pills and carefully tipping two into his palm. His hands were calloused, the nails split and dirty. 'She said she didn't want any breakfast but I've made this toast anyway. And Geoff said to be sure she took her pills.' He tilted them from his hand on to the tray.

'Shall I take it up and sit with her for a while?'

He nodded. 'You've already been a big help, but yes, please.'

Brenda studied Bernard's careworn features as he put on his worn overcoat; the lines seemed deeper, his pallor more grey. 'It's Sunday; you ought to take it easy.'

'I will after I've moved half a dozen ewes down from the moor top. I don't want to risk them being stranded up there if we get more snow.'

It struck her how hard Bernard's life had been, grinding on from day to day, year after year, without any help, yet how little he complained. And he doted on Dorothy, pandering to her every whim. 'Wait there; I'll come with you,' she volunteered, one foot on the bottom step of the stairs.

'No – I'll manage. You stay here with her.'

So she went upstairs with the tray and knocked on Dorothy's door.

'Is that you, Dad?' a faint voice said.

'No, it's me.' Balancing the tray with one hand, Brenda opened the door to find Dorothy curled up on her side underneath a mound of blankets, with only the top of her head visible. Brenda ventured forwards and set the tray down on the floor by the side of the bed. Every surface was cluttered with magazines, make-up, hairbrushes, talcum powder and bottles of scent. 'Can you manage a cup of tea?'

'No,' Dorothy whimpered, curling into a tighter ball.

'Will you at least try?'

'No.'

Brenda cleared magazines from the wicker chair in the corner then set it down by the bed. She sat down and leaned forward to pat the mound of bedclothes. 'Your dad put three sugars in for you.'

Dorothy's head slowly emerged. Her curls lay flat against her head, her pupils were large, her eyes dull. 'Three, you say?'

'Yes, here; let me plump up those pillows. Sit up and lean forward – how's that?'

'Better. 'Where's Dad now?'

'Up on the fell.'

'And where's my precious brother?' Dorothy took the cup from Brenda then obediently opened her mouth for the pills.

'Gone – I don't know where.'

Dorothy sipped then swallowed and handed back the cup. 'Do you know what he's done?'

'I do,' Brenda said cautiously. It was obviously not a good idea for Dorothy to get upset again.

'He only got married without telling me.' Dorothy sounded like a child whose doll had been taken from her. Her bottom lip quivered. 'How could he?'

'You're talking to the wrong person. You'll have to ask him.'

'He didn't even let on to me and I'm his sister!' she repeated. 'Honestly; Cliff and his secrets!'

'Maybe he knew you'd be upset if he told you,' Brenda suggested. 'It seems to have been done on the spur of the moment.'

'Why; what did he say?' Dorothy made her sudden, characteristic transition from soft, sighing helplessness to needle-sharp focus, looking directly at Brenda and waiting impatiently for her reply.

'Not much. Anyway, I only heard bits of the story from Evelyn.'

'But what did he say?'

Brenda knew she was in too deep to pull back now. 'Evelyn says there was an argument about Gladys being pregnant. Gladys said she was, he said she wasn't. Evelyn didn't know who to believe and to be honest, neither do I.'

'A baby?' Dorothy sank back against her pillow.

'Yes, I expect he intended to tell you but then everything went wrong between him and Gladys so he decided to keep schtum.'

'When?'

'A few years back – at the start of the war.'

Dorothy slotted this into place. 'That must have been after he'd fallen out with Dad over Cliff not doing his fair share of farm work. Cliff upped sticks and went to live in Northgate to work as a joiner. But then he and Dad patched things up and Dad got him the gamekeeper's job at the castle.' She shook her head in disbelief. 'It's three years ago and never a word.'

'Drink some more tea.' Brenda wanted to steer away from the subject of Cliff and Evelyn. At this rate she would find herself sticking up for her friend and telling Dorothy exactly what she thought of her cheating, dishonest brother.

'Did Evelyn know he was married?' Dorothy asked sharply, making Brenda feel even more uncomfortable.

'Of course not! She's got her bottom drawer ready and a pattern for her wedding dress – everything. Last night came as a terrible shock.'

Dorothy closed her eyes and groaned. 'What will she do now?'

'I don't think she's decided.'

A silence developed, broken by a door banging in the yard.

'Poor Evelyn,' Dorothy said after a long pause. 'I could kill Cliff; honestly I could.'

Nancy was milked at last and food put down for the hens and rabbits. Bernard was still out on the fell when Geoff and Giles dropped by before the morning service.

'Well?' Geoff asked Brenda who was heading to her wagon to smarten herself up for church. 'How's the patient?'

'Better,' she reported.

'Is she awake or asleep?'

'Sleeping.' Brenda had watched Dorothy nod off after their talk then taken the tray downstairs. She'd washed up and tidied around the kitchen, found some cold beef in the larder that Bernard could have for lunch and made sandwiches for him. A quick check upstairs had told her that the patient was sleeping peacefully.

'Good; that's what she needs. Will we see you at church?'

'You will,' she assured him as they drove away.

She'd gone inside and chosen her white blouse and black slacks when there was a knock on the door and Joyce stood there in her Sunday best, looking fresh and rested. Her cheeks were rosy and she wore a cream silk headscarf over her dark brown hair. The Land-Rover from Black Crag Farm was parked outside the gate.

'Come in!' Brenda whisked her inside.

'I thought you might appreciate a lift down,' Joyce told her.

'Yes, please; I won't be a tick.' She ran a brush through her hair and perched a black velvet beret on top of her sleek bob.

'I didn't drive here,' Joyce said with a hint of mystery.

'So who did?' As far as Brenda knew, Laurence Bradley was not a regular Sunday worshipper.

'Alma.' Joyce's face broke into a smile. 'With a little help from me. She was up early this morning to take her first driving lesson from Laurence, learning how to steer and change gear. It turns out she's a natural.'

'And he let her drive along the lane?' Brenda peered out through the window, expecting to see Alma in the Land-Rover. 'Did she stall the engine?'

'Once or twice. Otherwise she did well.' In fact, Joyce had kept a steadying hand on the steering wheel for most of the way.

The car was empty. 'So where is she now?'

'In the house.'

'Whatever for?'

'She brought Bernard a pot of stew and a pan of soup.'

Brenda stared at Joyce as if the answer had been that Alma had flown to the moon.

'Don't look at me like that.' Joyce went on beaming. 'It's good of Alma, don't you think?'

Brenda popped her lips. 'Good? If you ask me, it's bloody marvellous!'

Alma knocked on the farmhouse door and when there was no reply she screwed up the courage to step inside. She decided to leave the food she'd prepared on the kitchen table with a scribbled note to Dorothy and Bernard saying that she would call back for the pans in a few days' time.

The kitchen was empty as she'd expected. Partly relieved that she didn't have to talk to anyone face to face, she wrote the note and was almost finished when Dorothy appeared in her dressing-gown at the foot of the stairs.

'What are you up to?' she asked indignantly, supporting herself by leaning one hand against the doorpost.

Alma dropped the pencil with a startled gasp. 'I heard you were poorly.' The colour rose in her cheeks and her hand flew up to hide her scars. 'I've brought you and your father something to eat.'

'Good Lord!' Dorothy advanced slowly, clutching the neck of her dressing-gown. She circled Alma in amazement. 'I can't believe . . . I mean, it's very good of you but . . . well, you of all people!'

Alma said nothing but her cheeks went on burning as she pulled out a chair for Dorothy to sit down.

'By the way, I've been meaning to tell you . . . your face is nowhere near as bad . . . well, I expected it to be much worse.' Pleased to have tackled the subject head on, Dorothy smiled encouragingly at her visitor.

Alma stared back at her without flinching. 'Same here. I expected to find you at death's door.'

'But here I am, large as life!' Dorothy plonked herself down with a breathless thank-you. 'We're a pair of frauds, you and I. Now, Alma, you have to stay and tell me all your gossip. We have years and years to catch up on.'

'Fourteen,' Alma reminded her. 'But I don't have any gossip. When I was eight I went to live with my Aunty Muriel; The End.'

'It was as bad as that?'

'Worse,' Alma said. 'Unless you want to hear all about how to measure customers' heads and make hats.' *Or what it had been like to live with a face that no one wanted to look at, to do as I was told and not make a fuss, to be neither seen nor heard.*

'But not as bad as being cooped up here with a weak heart.' Dorothy held a trump card that even Alma couldn't beat. 'At least you must have had a cinema on your doorstep.'

'I did,' Alma conceded. 'I enjoyed going to watch films when Aunty Muriel let me. It meant I could sit in the dark without anyone staring.'

'You see!' Dorothy crowed, turning to Joyce and Brenda who had just sidled in. 'You hear that? This lucky thing has been to see all the Hollywood films in glorious Technicolor. Who's your favourite film star, everyone? Mine is Ginger Rogers.'

'How about Greta Garbo?' Joyce suggested.

'She's too glum,' Brenda argued. 'If you ask me, no one can beat Vivien Leigh in *Gone with the Wind*.'

CHAPTER TWENTY

Brenda and Joyce drove down the hill to church, leaving Dorothy and Alma to carry on chatting.

'Don't say a word,' Joyce warned as they came to the end of the lane and stepped out on to the green. She glanced back up the hill and held up two sets of crossed fingers.

'About Alma coming out of her shell?'

'Yes, and Dorothy being on the mend. We don't want to put a jinx on it.'

Brenda gave a hop and a skip of celebration then adopted a more sober expression. 'I had a heart-to-heart with Evelyn last night.'

'How is she?' Joyce noticed a gathering in the church porch and saw that the door was still locked.

'Heartbroken.' Brenda too spotted the cluster of parishioners outside the church. 'It'll take her a long time to get over Cliff's shenanigans.'

As they drew nearer they made out Geoff and Giles talking with Dr Brownlee and his wife. Fred Williams and Emma Waterhouse stood in the centre of the group, surrounded by other church regulars. Faces were puzzled, voices raised.

'What's going on here?' Brenda opened the gate and marched up the path.

'We don't have anyone to take the service.' Emma, in her Sunday hat of brown felt, with a fox fur stole around her neck, had appointed herself official spokesperson. 'No one has a key to let us in.'

'Why? What's happened to Mr Rigg?' Joyce glanced across the graveyard towards the vicarage and saw that the curtains were still drawn. The tall, narrow house looked bleak in the grey winter light and its ivy-clad walls gave off an air of neglect.

'We think he must be poorly.'

'Has anyone knocked on his door?'

'Of course; what do you take me for?' Emma tutted and fussed. 'I've knocked twice. I've even been round the back and tried the tradesmen's entrance. No joy there either.'

Fred voiced what many people were thinking. 'If the vicar doesn't turn up soon, I'm off. It's too cold to hang around much longer.'

'Even if he's poorly, surely he would have sent word,' Brenda pointed out. 'And what about little Alan? Who's looking after him?'

No one knew. The church was locked, the vicarage closed up and silent. At the click of the gate latch they all turned and watched an unfamiliar, flustered figure hurry up the path.

'I'm sorry, everyone. It took me longer than expected to get here.' The newcomer was an angular young man with a narrow face, dressed in a grey overcoat, trilby hat and a dog collar. He pushed his way through the crowd and inserted a large iron key in the lock. 'I'm afraid you'll have to make do with me this morning. My name's Charles Nicholls; I'm the curate from St Margaret's in Rixley.'

There was a flurry of gasps and low mutterings. What's going on? Where's our proper vicar? Why weren't we told?

'I'm afraid Mr Rigg is indisposed.' Nicholls turned the key, removed his hat then led the way into the church. He moved jerkily towards the vestry as if not quite in control of his long limbs. 'They've asked me to stand in for him.'

Emma scuttled ahead to show the curate where the surplices hung on a hook behind the vestry door. 'There's a Bible on the pulpit,' she informed him. 'It's open at St Matthew's gospel, chapter two, verse one. The vicar's hymn book is on that table over there, next to the wedding register.'

'Thank you, thank you. I wasn't expecting . . . ice . . . almost skidded off the road. No time to prepare.'

Emma watched Nicholls pull an ill-fitting surplice over his head. 'Mr Rigg is a lot bigger round the middle than you and a good six inches shorter,' she commented. 'Still, it'll have to do.'

He tugged at the hem of the garment then glanced through the vestry door at the sparse congregation. Only the three front pews were filled. 'Should we wait a while longer?'

'No, let's get on with it,' Emma told him in her no-nonsense way. 'And I'd keep the sermon short, if I were you. That's what I tell Mr Rigg every year in the run-up to Christmas; short and sweet is what we like, followed by "Hark the Herald Angels" and a quick closing prayer.'

*

Dorothy took a cup of tea from Alma. 'I always thought you were a strange one,' she commented as Alma sat down opposite her.

'Did you?' How could Dorothy bear to live in this pigsty? she wondered. Nothing was where it should be – there was a pair of her shoes on the table, next to a stack of old newspapers and some of her lacy underwear was spread out to dry over a rusty fireguard.

'Yes, and you still are. You turn up in Shawcross after all these years and we're ready to welcome you with open arms. But what do you do? You hide yourself away at Black Crag. We didn't have a single sighting for months. To be honest with you, everyone suspected that new husband of yours was holding you prisoner, like Bluebeard in his castle!'

Alma gave an embarrassed laugh. 'Who's everyone?'

'Me, for a start. "Alma must be under lock and key" – that's what I thought.'

'No. I'd rather keep myself to myself, that's all.' There was a pile of library books on the window sill, threatening to topple on to the floor, and a trail of dried mud from door to hearth. Alma's fingers itched to pick up a dustpan and brush.

Dorothy shook her head and sighed. 'That's what I mean; you'd rather be stuck out there in the back of beyond. Whereas me, I'd be at my wits' end. I don't know why I'm surprised, come to think of it. I remember you at school, always in the corner of the playground with your head stuck in a book. I think that was you. Or was it your sister Connie?'

'It was Connie,' Alma said quietly. *Three years older, the studious one.*

Dorothy frowned at the gaffe she'd made. Sometimes her tongue ran away with her. 'Sorry; I didn't mean to—'

'It's all right.' *Connie with her head in Grimm's Fairy Tales – 'Rumpelstiltskin', 'The Red Shoes'. Edward who ran everywhere full tilt and climbed trees by Mary's Fall. Their mother with her hands covered in white flour, her round face flushed from the oven.* Memories flooded back.

'Sorry; I'm an idiot.'

'No need to apologize. Connie taught me to read. I'd forgotten that.'

'Still . . .'

'Really, it's all right.' Alma decided she would take a book out to the waterfall when summer came. She would sit on a rock and read, letting the written words and splashing water fill her head. 'Shall I say what sticks in my mind about you, Dorothy? You were never allowed to play out at playtime. You had to sit inside, even when it was sunny.'

Dorothy gave a sad little laugh. 'Strictly no running about for me – just sitting, twiddling my thumbs.' *The teacher watching me like a hawk. Me in my yellow summer dress and white ankle socks, not daring to get out of breath.*

'Now I'm the one that should say sorry.'

Heart hammering at the least exertion, struggling to squeeze enough blood through its chambers and out into the arteries. Sit still as a statue in the dress with the zigzag trimming or the one with the bows around the hem, wait for it to stop thumping. Do not move. 'You got married. How's that been?'

'How do you mean?' The sudden switch took Alma by surprise.

'Being married – you know!'

'Oh, that.' Alma took the pair of shoes and placed them firmly on the floor. 'I'd rather not go into it.'

'Of course I've had one or two boyfriends.' Dorothy ploughed on. 'But we've never – you know.'

'Would you have liked to?' Alma's heart fluttered as she pictured her closed bedroom door at Black Crag, her single bed.

Dorothy gave her a wide-eyed stare. *A man's arms around you, his lips on yours and whatever follows, which is something I might never know.* 'Of course I would – wouldn't everyone?'

Night silence was broken by terrifying noises: scratching and rustling, screeches and hoots. The whispering darkness was so thick Alan could reach out and touch it.

He hadn't slept, scarcely even moved. He was cold as a block of ice and every time he'd closed his eyes another sound had invaded his black world. A hedgehog, disturbed by his low whimpering, had crawled out from its winter nest of twigs and leaves and snuffled at his face. Something – bats? – had flapped and squeaked above his head, tree branches had creaked all night long in the high wind.

He lay motionless, longing to be safe at home with his mother and father but desperate that they'd think he'd let them down. *We have to be brave. Don't be a cry-baby . . . Mummy and Daddy wouldn't like it* – these were the messages that ran ceaselessly through his head; in his mother's voice and in Judith's too. But he would never go back to the vicarage. He would stay outside and freeze rather than be dragged back there.

Alan had seized his chance when the house was empty. Mr Rigg had gone to the church hall at the start of the Christmas dance. Alan had watched him from his bedroom window.

'Don't move from that bed,' his tormentor had warned before he left.

The backs of Alan's thighs and his backside stung from where the cane had landed. Six whips through the air – one, two, three stinging strokes because Mr Rigg had caught him hiding his leftover crusts in his trouser pocket. God saw it too – he punished ungrateful boys. Mr Rigg's face had turned red as he'd told him this. He'd shouted and pushed him face-down on to his bed. Four, five, six whistling lashes on Alan's bare legs and bottom, then straight into his pyjamas and to bed without even being allowed to go to the toilet or brush his teeth.

'That's what happens to children who waste perfectly good food,' Mr Rigg had shouted from the doorway. Spit had come out of his mouth and dribbled down his chin. 'They go to bed without supper and stay in their room until I tell them they can come out.'

The door had slammed shut. Alan had lain motionless until the footsteps had faded.

Then he'd sprung out of bed and run to the window; still the one that overlooked the graveyard because the vicar had ignored the kind Land Girl's plea for him to be moved to a different room. He'd seen Mr Rigg walk down the vicarage path then got dressed as quick as he could – short trousers, long socks, shirt and jumper. Dry mouth, heart jumping up into his throat, panting. *Quick, quick,* before he comes back. Along the landing, down the stairs. His coat and scarf from the hook in the hallway, feet into boots. *Quick, quick!*

Outside, a strong gust of cold wind had almost lifted him off his feet. Quick through the graveyard; never mind the rows of humped bodies lying under the frozen ground or the half-melted snowdrifts, the crooked gravestones and the white angel staring at him as he fled.

The wind had buffeted him and the beech trees overhanging the river had creaked and groaned. There'd been happy music coming from inside the church hall – ignore that too and stumble on down the rough riverbank. Pray not to be caught and taken back.

Then there'd been a night so cold that Alan's fingers went stiff and he couldn't feel his toes. An endless night of shivering, scratches and rustles, animals creeping through dead leaves, insects crawling over his skin. He'd found a shed and used rough sacking for a blanket. To the sound of the river whirling and lapping at its banks, he'd curled into a ball and smelt the damp, cold earth, breathed coal dust into his lungs and prayed to an angry God to strike Mr Rigg stone cold dead.

Captain was waiting impatiently at his stable door when Evelyn arrived at the castle.

'I know I'm late; I'm sorry,' she muttered as she leaned her bike against the wall then took off her gloves and immediately got to work. 'First things first.' She took the empty water bucket from the horse's stable and filled it at the yard tap. Then she climbed the ladder into the hay loft and filled his net.

The horse kicked at his door to be let out.

'Steady on; I'm going as fast as I can.' She led him into the yard and tied him up within reach of both water and feed. Then she went across the yard to fetch a barrow for mucking out. On the way back she noticed that the door to her room was ajar.

'That's odd; I'm sure I locked it when I left,' she said out loud. Not that there was anything valuable in there – just clothes and a few personal belongings that no self-respecting burglar would look twice at.

Evelyn wondered briefly if Colonel Weatherall's niece had called by with her own set of keys to check that the house and yard were secure. But no; there were no tyre marks and no other sign of her car having been here. So maybe Evelyn hadn't locked the door after all and it had blown open in last night's wind.

'I'd better go and shut it, eh, Captain?'

The horse tugged hay from his net and chewed noisily.

'Hello, Evie.' Cliff appeared in her doorway. He stood with his hands in his pockets, head to one side.

'Cliff! What are you doing in my room?'

'Waiting for you.'

'Have you been here all night?'

'No. I was at Garthside. I saw you set off on your bike.'

'You've got a damned cheek, barging in like that.' The angry words didn't convey the sick feeling in her stomach as she stared at him tilting his head at her, no doubt having used the spare key she kept hidden in the hay loft to let himself in.

He didn't react. 'I left the car at the far side of the wood and took a short cut. I want to talk to you; it's important.'

'And I don't want to hear it. Get out of my room, Cliff.'

With his hands still in his pockets, he walked slowly towards her. 'Oh, Evie, what are we going to do?'

'"We"?' she echoed. 'There is no "we", Cliff.' She pushed past him and ran inside, slamming then bolting the door behind her. How dare he? What made him think, even for a second, that she would want to hear more lies and excuses? Leaning her back against the door, she tried to catch her breath.

The room was as she'd left it; nothing had been disturbed. Her dresses hung in the alcove next to the fireplace, her shoes stood in a neat row under them. She opened the top drawer of the pine chest in the corner – everything in its place, not touched by him.

He hammered his fist on the door. 'Open up, Evie.'

'Get lost!' She sat on the bed and gripped the iron frame with both hands.

Cliff's face appeared at the window. 'Let me in, please. Give me a chance to explain.'

'Go away. There's nothing you can say that would

make a scrap of difference.' *Lies, more lies and lame excuses.*

He cupped his hands against the glass so that he could see inside. 'Just listen to me,' he pleaded.

Evelyn sprang up from the bed and rushed to the door. She slid the bolt and opened it. She spoke slowly in words of one syllable. 'Get this in to your head, Cliff Huby: I do not want to listen! I will not waste one more second on you and your pathetic excuses. I'm here to see to Captain and as soon as I've done that, I'm off.'

He stepped back under the force of her fury. The scarf had come loose around her neck and there was an angry flush at her throat. All her energy seemed concentrated in her flashing green eyes.

'Where are you going?'

'What's it to you?'

'But where will you go?' he repeated. 'You can't stay another night with Brenda; there isn't room.'

'And I can't very well stay here, either; not with you prowling around, spying on me.'

Cliff was one step ahead. 'I'll stay away, I promise. Once we've had our chat, I'll leave you in peace. You can live here until the Weatheralls decide what they want to do with the place.'

'And you'll move out?'

'If you want me to. I'll stay at Garthside while we sort things out. You can go on working for the Timber Corps.'

'You keep on saying "we", Cliff.' As she shook her head in exasperation, her hair swung forward. She pushed it back then secured it with a comb on top of her head.

'I'll stop,' he promised. God; didn't she realize what effect she had when she was angry? How was he expected to keep his hands to himself when she looked like this? He turned away then back again. 'It was a shock,' he began slowly, referring to Gladys's visit without speaking his wife's name.

'Who for – you or me?'

'Both. It's three years since I saw her and I honestly, hand on heart, never thought about her from one week to the next. Her showing up in Shawcross was the last thing I expected.'

'You don't say.' Sarcasm was lost on him, but she couldn't resist.

'And I meant it, Evie: I can file for a divorce. We can still get married.'

He really thought it was that simple! Evelyn stared at him in stunned silence.

'She did trick me, you know. I was working in town and I came across her in the local pub. She seemed quite happy for it to be a bit of a fling. She was definitely the one who made the first moves. Then before I knew it she was telling me she was having a baby.'

'Stop, Cliff – please!' Evelyn tried to block out what he was saying by striding across the yard into Captain's stable, seizing a fork and lifting soiled straw on to the barrow.

'I didn't even know if it was mine. She said it was and like a fool I believed her. She said we had to get hitched for the sake of the kid. I went along with that, too. You saw her, Evelyn; you could see what she was like.'

Evelyn stopped, leaning forward with her fork

poised over the barrow, and looked him in the eye. 'That's what sticks in my craw, Cliff – the way you automatically blame Gladys as if you were the innocent party. Now I don't know if she deliberately did what she did, but I do know you – your way of treating a woman and making her feel that she's special.'

He took his time to reply, looking directly at her as he carefully took the fork from her, wrapped his fingers around her wrist and led her into the yard. 'All right, and what would you have done?'

She pulled free. 'If I'd been you?'

'Yes. You're me for a minute. You find out a couple of months after you get hitched that there never was any baby and that she – Gladys – has run up debts with the butcher, the baker and candlestick maker; you name it, she owes them money. These men come knocking on your door while she's out gadding somewhere. No baby and bills up to your eyeballs. You look for an escape route, that's what.'

'Maybe. But I wouldn't have kept it all a secret. Why didn't you at least tell your family what had happened?'

He jerked his head backwards. 'What good would that have done? Knowing how old fashioned Dad is, he'd as likely as not have ordered me back to Northgate to "do right" by Gladys. Married is married in his book. And my blabbermouth sister would have had a field day. Without even meaning to, Dotty would have made sure my name was mud up and down the dale. No, ta very much. Anyway, how was I to know that I'd go on and meet someone who would bowl me over the way you did?'

Evelyn put her hands over her ears. She felt her

resistance weaken and began to see new glimmers of understanding. But still, she wasn't ready to forgive him. 'Don't think you can talk your way out of this.'

'I don't. I know I've done wrong.' For the first time Cliff sounded humble. His head went down and he stared at the ground. 'All I'm asking is for you to give me another chance.'

Taking a deep breath, she walked out of the stable and paced the yard, coming to a halt by the gate leading into the lane. Her choice was stark: either she could tell him that he'd hurt her too much and she would never be able to trust him again or she could put her decision on hold. *I shouldn't put it off,* she told herself as she leaned on the gate and gazed out at the grey, leafless trees, rotting stumps and tangle of undergrowth. *I should break free of Cliff Huby right this minute.*

'Evie.' He'd followed her and put his hand on the gate as if to bar her way. 'Please.'

'Don't, Cliff. I need time to think.'

'How much time?' His voice was low and intense.

'A few days. Let's get Christmas over with first.'

He closed his eyes and took a deep breath. 'If that's what you want.'

'Yes, stay at Garthside.' She needed her own space. There would be forestry tasks to occupy her and she would have Joyce working alongside her. Hopefully, after a few days her bruised and battered heart would begin to heal. Her thoughts would settle.

'Right you are.' Cliff gave a small nod then walked back towards his cottage. 'I'll pick up a few things and then I'll be off.'

Evelyn gave a sigh of relief and watched him until

his long, lithe stride took him out of sight. Then she closed her eyes. This kind of love was a trap set to maim but not kill. Her heart quivered, her body shook from head to foot as she pushed through the gate then stumbled blindly into the wood.

Walter Rigg knew that the boy had a sister in Attercliffe. He'd driven there at first light in the hope that they'd made a joint plan to run away; that the sister had found some way of making the journey to Shawcross then assisted Alan in his overnight escape.

Rigg had no idea of exactly when and how it had happened. All he knew was that he'd disciplined the boy after his sly behaviour at tea the night before then gone out to oversee events in the church hall and left him alone in the house. He hadn't looked into his room on his return, simply assuming that Alan was settled for the night. He'd gone to bed himself at ten o'clock and woken eight hours later. It was only then, when he'd gone to wake the boy, he'd discovered that his bed hadn't been slept in. He'd hurried downstairs and found that his coat and boots were missing. Alan had absconded; vanished without a trace.

Fuelled by a sense of outrage at the latest evacuee's ingratitude, Rigg had driven to Attercliffe and at nine o'clock Arnold White had answered the door at Dale End. He'd listened to the red-faced clergyman then, without inviting him to step inside the house, he'd rung the servants' bell and the girl, Judith, had appeared. She'd burst into tears when she heard that her brother was missing.

'I'm afraid we can't help you,' Arnold had said stiffly.

Donald had come down the stairs, still in his dressing-gown. He'd explained tersely about the family's recent loss. 'Now, Mr Rigg, if you don't mind . . .' He'd closed the door in Walter's face.

The sister's sobs had followed Walter to his car.

The journey wasn't necessarily wasted, however. It was a mere thirty-minute drive from Attercliffe into Millwood, to Alan's mother and father's address in Station Street. As he'd parked by the kerb outside their terraced house then mounted five stone steps to the green front door, Walter had prepared himself to be the bearer of bad tidings. He'd squared his shoulders and cleared his throat then knocked long and hard.

'They're not in.' A small, bald man in baggy brown trousers and a collarless white shirt had appeared at the door of number 17. 'Her sister's poorly. They've gone to look after her for a few days. They're not due back until after Christmas.'

Walter had been at a loss. Did the man have the sister's address? No, not a clue. Did he have the wherewithal for him to write the parents a note? The neighbour had grudgingly produced pencil and paper. Walter had written his telephone number followed by the date and time at the top right-hand corner.

Dear Mr and Mrs Evans,

I'm very sorry to have to tell you that Alan has gone missing from the vicarage in Shawcross. Rest assured that I'll do everything in my power to find him. If I don't succeed and Alan hasn't returned by tomorrow morning, I will, of course, inform the billeting officer and he will advise me of the best course of action. Once more, I sincerely apologize and I know that you will join me in praying for your son's safe return.

Yours sincerely,
Walter Rigg.

His duty done, the note had been posted through the letter box and Walter had set off on the long drive home. Luckily, he'd had the foresight to make arrangements with his fellow vicar in Rixley to send a curate to conduct the morning service.

At first the motion of the car and the thrum of the engine had helped Rigg to maintain his calm, but as he left the town and drove along the winding lanes, alarm wormed its way to the front of his brain. What would the parents do when they learned of Alan's disappearance? Would they descend on Shawcross with angry accusations? In which case, he must be ready to defend himself. He would insist that he'd made every effort to instil discipline in the boy. Alan had been given a room all to himself, been well fed within the limits of the food coupons he'd brought with him and plans were in place to send him to school in Thwaite. Even so, he was sure that tongues would wag and fresh rumours might reach the dean or, worse still, the bishop. He signalled right to take the road out of Burnside and looked in his overhead mirror. His reflection showed flabby cheeks drained of colour and a forehead creased with worry.

The boy was gone and, not for the first time, Rigg would have to answer to the authorities. There was ice on the road and his car skidded as he took the corner. Whatever the outcome, he would take in no more evacuees, he decided. The children of today lacked both manners and discipline and he was forced to acknowledge that no amount of correction on his part could bring about the desired result.

CHAPTER TWENTY-ONE

Charles Nicholls had taken Emma's advice and kept the service short and to the point. Even so, there was an air of discontent outside the church as the curate made his way back to his car.

'It's a poor show when your vicar can't be bothered to turn up on the only day of the week when he has a job to do.' Fred Williams collared Emma to air his grumbles. 'Walter Rigg ought to try working the hours I do.'

'It's not like him, though.' The vicar's housekeeper had fretted her way through the hymns and prayers, wondering what on earth could have kept Mr Rigg away.

'My bet is that it's something to do with Alan.' Brenda stood with Joyce by the gate, exchanging theories with Geoff and Giles while other members of the congregation hurried away to their Sunday dinners.

'You're probably right, worse luck.' Joyce went on to explain their worries about the boy to Giles. 'He hasn't settled in with the vicar.'

'That's putting it mildly,' Brenda interrupted. 'And who can blame him? In my opinion, the good reverend is a hard taskmaster and a first-class hypocrite to boot.'

'Alan's run off once already. He was eventually found hiding in the old cart shed at New Hall.'

'Where I keep logs and gardening tools,' Geoff added. 'Are you both thinking what I'm thinking?' he asked Brenda and Joyce.

'That he's scarpered again?' Brenda nodded, aware that Emma had broken away from Fred and was about to join their little huddle. 'When did you last see young Alan?' she asked her.

'Let's see now.' With all heads turned towards her, Emma strung out her few moments in the limelight. 'He helped me with the cleaning on Friday. Alan likes to be given something to do – polishing the silver and such like. It seems to lift his spirits.'

'And he came to the hall with Mr Rigg to help put up decorations,' Joyce too thought back through the week. 'Did anyone see him yesterday evening, though?'

Everyone shook their heads.

'We were all too busy getting ready for the do,' Brenda muttered.

'If we're right and Alan has run away again, that would be a good enough reason for the vicar to miss the service.' Geoff grew convinced that they were on the right track. 'He would be out looking for him.'

'What do you think, Emma?' Joyce turned to her again for advice. 'How did Alan seem on Friday?'

'Quiet,' came the foghorn reply. 'I struggled to get a word out of him. As a matter of fact, I spoke to the vicar about it. I said that I thought something was up, that I'd caught Alan sobbing his heart out more than once.'

'And what did Mr Rigg say?'

'Not a lot. A little while later I did see him pinning Alan up against the wall and telling him not to be a cry-baby. That was a lesson for me – to be careful what I say to the vicar in future.'

'Talking of whom . . .' Geoff had caught sight of Rigg's car coasting towards them after his fruitless morning of trying to locate the runaway. When he pulled up outside the vicarage, they all made a beeline for him.

'Where's the boy?' Brenda demanded the second he stepped out of his car.

Rigg tugged at the lapels of his black overcoat and gave a small, nervous cough. 'I wish I knew. Unfortunately, Alan's bed hasn't been slept in. I can only assume that he's absconded.'

Absconded? The word infuriated Brenda. *What's up – have you swallowed a dictionary?* She glared at Rigg and positioned herself between him and his garden path. *Alan has run for his life, more like*. 'When? Why?'

'I'd be obliged if you'd allow me to pass.' Rigg coughed again as Brenda stood her ground.

'"I'd be obliged!"' she mimicked angrily.

Geoff stepped in and spoke more calmly. 'Tell us: have you any idea where Alan might have gone?'

'And why!' Brenda insisted.

'Dear me.' Rigg was visibly rattled but he managed to maintain his self-control as he stepped sideways. Brenda stepped with him. He was no taller than her, although twice the width. 'Am I to be prevented from entering my own house?'

'Yes, until you tell us everything you know.'

Her adversary took his time to weigh things up. There was a slim chance that his usual bluster and a blast of righteous indignation would see him through but in the end he opted for a more direct response.

'Very well. Not to mince words, Alan has run away. He was not in his room at seven o'clock this morning. I searched everywhere to make sure he wasn't hiding inside the house – from the cellars up to the attics – then I went to the trouble of driving all the way to Attercliffe to see his sister.'

'And?'

'It was a wild-goose chase.'

'So?' Brenda stood, hands on hips, still refusing to budge.

'Really, this is quite unacceptable.' He turned to Emma for back-up. 'Mrs Waterhouse, you know what this boy is like. He lacks backbone – tell them.'

Emma frowned and shook her head. 'I'm not sure about that. But I do know he wasn't happy staying at the vicarage.'

'Precisely.' Rigg was ready to use his weight to push past Brenda. 'If a boy is unable to appreciate his good fortune, what hope is there of him ever coming to anything in later life?'

Geoff had heard enough. 'Come on, Giles; there's a chance that Alan went to ground at New Hall like last time.' He led the way down the pathway leading to the river, breaking into a run as he reached the bridge.

'Good idea.' Joyce went after the two men. 'Let's start in your cart shed,' she suggested to Geoff.

'He wasn't happy and I don't blame him,' Emma

insisted as Brenda continued to block Rigg's path. For once she lowered her voice and she poked her sharp features to within six inches of her employer's face. 'I'm sorry to have to say this, Vicar, but I did warn you. I said you can't expect a little lad of Alan's age to put up with what he had to—'

'Why, what did he do?' Emma's backing strengthened Brenda's resolve and she stood her ground as Rigg attempted to push her to one side. 'Did he beat him to within an inch of his life?' She resisted Rigg's attempt to thrust her to one side by grabbing his arm and pushing him off balance.

'I don't know for sure. But Alan was often in tears and I noticed red marks on his legs and who knows where else on his little body.'

'For heaven's sake!' Brenda's loathing for Rigg boiled over. 'Look at the size of you, compared with him, poor mite! What did you hit him with? Did you use a ruler or was it with your cane?'

Rigg had tottered backwards against the railing. Unable to get past Brenda, he was forced to endure more of Emma's unexpected betrayal.

The village stalwart went on. 'He was scared of his own shadow, that one. I asked you once why he was so nervy and you brushed me off. I went home that afternoon and wondered why you went on taking in evacuees if they were such a nuisance to you. Is it their food coupons, or what?'

'Don't be ridiculous!' Rigg rallied. 'I do it because it's my Christian duty.' He pulled himself upright then straightened his hat.

'And is it your religion that makes you such a bully?' Brenda swore to herself that the hypocrite would be made to pay for what he'd done. 'It gives you the right to throw your weight around and scare that poor little boy out of his wits? I expect you even took it out on him when I brought him back from visiting his sister that time. I'm right, aren't I?'

'As his guardian, it is my right to discipline him . . .' Rigg's voice faltered. ' . . . as I see fit.'

'As you see fit!' Brenda's voice dripped with scorn. 'We'll see what your superiors have to say about that.' At that moment she had no idea who his superiors might be, but she vowed that she would not let the matter rest.

'Brenda!' Joyce called from the bridge but Brenda was so incensed that she failed to hear her.

It was only when Emma tugged at her arm that Brenda turned and saw Joyce. She stepped back reluctantly from the confrontation with Rigg. 'You haven't heard the last of this,' she muttered as she hurried off.

If being left alone to think things through was what Evelyn wanted, that was what she would get.

Cliff strode away from the castle determined to see how she really liked it. He reckoned she wouldn't last long. One or two nights of her own company out there in the mouldering pile should do it then she would come running. Meanwhile, he would keep his head down at Garthside and hope that Gladys would stay out of his hair. On the other hand, if the lying bitch did come back to squeeze some money out of him he would be ready for her. *She won't get a penny,* he said to himself as he reached his car parked at the far side of the wood then drove fast and furiously along the twisting lane. *Sorting out this divorce will cost me a packet as it is. Anyway, I hate the sight of her and that sidekick who put her up to it.*

His mind flew back to Evelyn. Part of him could see why she was annoyed – who wouldn't be? But she'd overdone it last night and again this morning, pushing all the blame on to him and sending him away. It would serve her right if he stayed away for good. After all, though there'd been no word from the Weatherall relatives, the job at Acklam was as good as gone. Perhaps it was time for him to move on – not to Northgate, but to Millwood or another of the mill towns further west, where he could always find light work as a joiner or doing odd jobs that would get him back on his feet.

Let's see if Evelyn comes to her senses, he thought as he reached Shawcross and turned up the lane to his father's farm. *If she does, fair enough. If not, she'll be the loser, not me.*

There was no sign of his dad's tractor in the yard when Cliff arrived. *What does Bradley want?* he wondered, expecting that it would be to do with a lost sheep or a broken boundary wall; definitely not a social visit from their notoriously unfriendly neighbour. So he went inside already on the defensive and was taken aback to see Alma Bradley sitting in the kitchen with Dorothy.

'Why aren't you in bed?' he said to his sister when he flung his cap down on the table.

'Because I'm feeling better. Look – Alma's brought us a hotpot for our dinner.'

'It's mutton stew,' Alma corrected her. After her

long conversation with Dorothy, Cliff's arrival had plunged her back into the familiar knotted self-consciousness that twisted up her stomach and made it hard to breathe properly. 'Look at the time! I'd better be off,' she said as the telephone rang and Dorothy answered it.

Dorothy listened to the operator's voice telling her that she had an Attercliffe number on the line and a Mr Donald White wishing to speak to a Miss Brenda Appleby.

'Brenda's not in,' Dorothy replied, waving at Alma as she picked up her keys then rushed away. 'This is Miss Dorothy Huby. Tell Mr White that I'm happy to pass on a message.'

The operator obliged and Dorothy listened attentively.

'Very well, I'll tell her,' she said and put down the phone. 'You have to go down to the village,' she told Cliff in a no-nonsense voice. 'Find Brenda and tell her that Hettie White's funeral is on Wednesday this week at eleven o'clock.'

'How am I supposed to track her down?'

'She went to church.'

'And can't it wait until she gets back?'

'No, Cliff; it can't. Brenda needs to know now. And tell her that her fiancé has applied for leave to come to the funeral. Can you remember that, or do I need to write it down?'

'Give over, Dorothy.' Opting for the line of least resistance, Cliff took his cap from the table and glanced at his watch. 'Where will she be if the service has finished?'

'How should I know? I'm not a mind reader.' Why

did he always have to make a song and dance? Dorothy lost interest and turned the pages of her latest magazine. 'Just find her, Cliff, and pass on the message. Funeral. On Wednesday. Les White hopes to come. Over and out.'

Once Brenda had learned from Joyce that she, Geoff and Giles had looked in all the outhouses at New Hall but found no trace of the missing boy, they decided to widen their search.

'Put yourself in Alan's shoes,' Brenda said as she stared down into the brown rushing water beneath the bridge. Melting snow had swelled the river until it was almost bursting its banks. 'From what we can make out, it must have been dark when he ran away. I wonder if he had a torch.'

'Let's hope so. Anyway, he'd hear music coming from the church hall and he'd want to avoid that in case someone spotted him.'

'So he'd probably cut across the graveyard then head down towards the river.'

'Or else across the green in the direction of Thwaite.'

'Not so likely,' Brenda pointed out. 'There'd be lots of coming and going on the green: people arriving for the dance or nipping across to the pub for a quick drink. I know Alan would dread going near the stone angel but I don't think he would have had any choice.'

'So let's try to retrace his footsteps.' Without waiting for Brenda's agreement, Joyce headed back to the church and started to search the graveyard. 'If I were Alan and I was running away in the pitch dark,

I'd stick to the path and follow it around the back of the church to the vestry door. I might turn the handle to see if it was locked.' Acting this out, she looked over her shoulder to find that she was alone. 'Come on, Brenda, what's keeping you?'

'Hello there, Miss Appleby!' Cliff had spotted the two women as they entered the deserted churchyard. He had to lean out of his Morris and yell at the top of his voice to attract Brenda's attention.

What now? She waited while he parked then strolled towards her, preparing to tell Cliff Huby exactly what she thought of him. Last night's episode didn't seem to have had a lasting effect, to judge by the cocksure expression on his face.

'Dotty asked me to pass on a message.' A quick glance told him that he was still in Brenda's bad books. 'What?' he cajoled. 'So it turns out I'm not squeaky clean. Who is these days?'

'I never thought you were squeaky clean, Cliff.' She cut him off before he'd finished. 'What's the message?'

'From a fellow in Attercliffe – a Donald something or other.'

Brenda drew a sharp breath and waited for him to go on.

'About a funeral.' Cliff stretched out to the maximum the sudden power his news seemed to have bestowed. 'I take it someone you know has died?'

'Yes. Carry on.'

'It's on Wednesday, apparently.' Should he or shouldn't he tell her the bit about the fiancé? No, leave her in the dark and let her stew for a bit. She would find out soon enough. 'Eleven o'clock, Dotty said. There, I've done my duty. Now I'll head back home for my dinner, if that's all right with you.'

Alan lay under the heavy jute sacks, stiff with cold. He heard voices calling his name and footsteps growing louder and going away again. Then there was only the sound of the river and a chink of daylight creeping under the door.

He tried to pull the sacks further over his head but his fingers wouldn't work. His whole body shook. The air inside the coal house was damp and lumps of coal shifted under him as he tried to ease his position. The grating noise made him hold his breath and close his eyes tight shut. *Don't let them find me. I won't go back. I won't.*

The river roared in his ears.

'Alan!' a woman's voice called.

'Alan!' A man this time.

He shrank further under the sacks. They would find him and drag him out into the open. Mr Rigg would be there with his cane. It hurt when he hit him with it; the swish as he brought it down hard, the sting on his skin before the throbbing ache set in. Even worse, Mr Rigg would snitch on him this time. He'd said he would tell his mum and dad that he'd been naughty and a cry-baby. *Oh, Alan!* He heard his mother's voice, saw the sad look on her face. He wouldn't be her best son any more. He would have let her down.

'Alan?' The voice was close by; a woman's again.

He wished for the darkness to cover him and keep him hidden.

The latch lifted, daylight flooded in.

Emma opened the door to the coal house at the bottom of her small garden. No stone must be left unturned. Brenda had taken charge and knocked at each door in the row of cottages. 'The vicar's boy has gone missing overnight. Please look for him and let us know if you find him.' It hadn't taken long for Emma's neighbours to search their houses and sheds.

Nothing. No sign.

Missing overnight? Freezing cold.

Whose boy? The vicar's.

You don't say.

Emma opened her coal-house door. At first she saw nothing unusual; just a heap of coal, a shovel resting against the wall and a pile of sacks. Then her eyes grew used to the dim light. The sacks had been moved. A living creature breathed underneath them. Gingerly she lifted the corner of the nearest sack and discovered the boy.

Alan covered his face with his hands.

'Oh, lad!' Emma let out a long, heartfelt sigh. Small and black like a little chimney sweep, curled up on his side, shaking, hiding his face. She stepped back out of the stone shed and ran up the path to call across the green with her loud voice. 'Brenda, Joyce; he's here – come as quick as you can!'

'Where's Joyce?' Laurence had spent the morning in the farmhouse, catching up on odd jobs while Alma was out. He was at the sink replacing the washer that had been leaking for a long time when he heard the latch click and he looked round to see her taking off her scarf and coat.

'She's still in the village. I decided to walk back.'

He worked on for a while, finding the right size of spanner to tighten the new washer. She looked different – her head was up and there was colour in her cheeks.

'Did you know that Dorothy Huby was taken ill at the Christmas dance?' Alma asked.

'No, that's news to me.' The job was done so he packed away his tools.

'Well, she was. There was a big panic – she had to be rushed home to take her pills. Cliff gave her a tremendous shock. It turns out he got married without telling anyone.'

Laurence gave a dismissive shrug. What was he to make of this new, talkative Alma?

'That's not all. He tricked a girl into getting engaged even though he was still married.' She watched him wash his hands then offered him a towel. 'Don't you want to know who the girl is and how he was found out?'

'No. It's none of my business.'

Alma snatched the towel back. 'Well, I'll tell you anyway. His new fiancée is Evelyn Newbold, the forestry girl, and it was Aunty Muriel who gave the game away. Yes, now you've pricked up your ears!'

'What had that old witch got to do with it?' Laurence watched Alma keenly.

'The last time Aunty Muriel was here to give me the present, she ran into Cliff outside the church hall and recognized him. She dashed straight back to Northgate and told the wife where to find him.' Lifting the hat box from the window sill she took off the lid then thrust it under his nose. 'Remember; she gave me this hideous thing.'

'How could I forget?' It was hideous all right, with its over-the-top trimmings – not Alma's style at all.

'I don't want it. I'm going to send it back.' She jammed the top on the box and put it back on the sill.

'Please yourself.' He sounded calm but his insides were playing up. He realized that this was about more than a silly hat.

'I am,' she insisted. 'And I'm going to write a note telling her she's not welcome here.'

'Are you sure?' He caught her by the hand to stop her flying around the room.

'Yes.' Alma was adamant that she wouldn't allow her aunt to force her way back in. 'She'll only cause trouble between us.'

He nodded slowly.

'I wouldn't want that. I want us to get on better.'

He felt his heart race. Alma's hand was still in his; small and slim.

'So I've decided to do more work on the farm now that Joyce is going over to Acklam for part of the time. It'll be lambing season before we know it – I can lend a hand with that.'

Laurence grasped her hand more tightly. The moment he'd set eyes on Alma, in a shop buying blackout blinds with her aunt, he'd fallen for her. A single glance had been enough to convince him that she was beautiful, with a rare mixture of quiet simplicity and steadfastness. There was nothing flighty about her. He'd hardly noticed the burn marks but when he did he'd remembered the depth of her loss and his closed heart had opened up.

He'd known that he must bide his time. The farm kept him busy and his trips into town to the hardware shop and the feed suppliers were few and far between. But he'd worked out Alma's routine of running errands for her aunt and put himself in her way until she'd grown used to seeing him. He'd invited her to come with him to the Lyons tea shop on the corner of Kitchener Street and she'd accepted. She'd smiled a bit over tea and scones as she'd remembered going swimming with her sister and brother in the pond below Mary's Fall. She still missed the countryside, she'd said.

It had been a slow, old-fashioned courtship that had taken everyone by surprise. Muriel had been outraged when she'd realized what had been going on behind her back. Laurence's son, Gordon, had been called up and was on the brink of going off to fight. He'd said that his father was a fool for even thinking about Alma in that way.

But they'd gone ahead and got married. Laurence had brought her to Black Crag and waited patiently for her to make herself at home. There was plenty of time. And then there they were a few weeks later, living side by side but not together at night, in the same bed. Alma had cooked and cleaned without complaint. He'd worked with the sheep. She'd hardly spoken, had been keenly conscious of her disfigurement and seemed hardly to know what being married entailed.

And for long enough Laurence had decided not to force her into anything she didn't want. The silences between them had lengthened. Then he'd tried to talk her round to being what he described as a proper wife. She'd shied away and her early steadfastness had turned into stubbornness. She'd refused to explain herself. The arguments had started. Then Joyce had arrived and taken up residence in the attic.

'So you want us to get on better?' he asked in a low voice, her hand still resting in his.

'Would you like us to?'

'Yes.'

'Good.' She stood on tiptoe to kiss him on the lips. One soft touch left him reeling before she broke away. 'Remember that stair rod still needs fixing before you put your tools away.'

He took up his tool bag. 'Which one is it?'

'The fourth one up.' She brushed past him and went up the stairs.

He took out his hammer and knocked in a couple of extra nails. Upstairs on the landing he heard Alma moving quietly back and forth.

Still tingling from the kiss, she took her nightdress and dressing-gown from her room and carried them into his. She laid the nightdress on Laurence's bed, hung the dressing-gown on the door hook then went back for her hairbrush and slippers. She set the hairbrush on the embroidered square of linen on top of the chest of drawers (most likely made by Lily in her early married days) and slid her slippers under the bed. Then she had second thoughts, picking up the embroidered square, folding it neatly and putting it away at the back of a drawer. Tomorrow or the day after, she would arrange for the hat to be sent back to Aunty Muriel. Before Christmas, at any rate; then her past life would be over and done with.

It would soon be 1943 and she and Laurence could look forward to a new beginning.

The old woman had left the coal-shed door open and gone to shout for Brenda and Joyce. Alan took his chance. He threw off the dirty sacks and forced his frozen limbs into action, stumbling over lumps of coal then rushing out to climb a wall that overlooked the riverbank. The ground sloped away steeply towards the fast-running river which slapped against the bank and eddied between rocks. He leaned towards the trunk of a horse chestnut tree and tried to grasp it with his useless fingers. His hand slipped and he slid down the banking towards the roaring brown water.

'Don't move!' A voice yelled at Alan from the opposite bank. It was the vet from the big house, arms raised over his head and waving at him. 'Stay there – I'm on my way!'

Alan's foot had jammed against a rock and stopped his downward slide. Ignoring the vet's instructions, he went on to all fours and tried to crawl towards the bridge, head down, still desperate not to be caught. His shoe came off and fell into the water as he scrambled under the stone arch. He panted for breath, almost toppled backwards but threw himself forward instead. He landed belly-down, his face pressed against slippery, cold rock.

Brenda joined Geoff and leaned over the bridge. She'd answered Emma's call but had arrived too late to stop Alan from escaping. She'd heard Geoff's cry and spotted Alan crawling along the bank. Now she looked down from the bridge at the terrified youngster sprawled across the rock, clinging on for dear life. 'Hang on,' she instructed. 'I'll come and get you.'

He felt himself slide inch by inch towards the water. There was nothing to hold on to – only smooth, wet rock. He cried out as his feet touched the icy water and the current tore off the remaining shoe.

'Hang on, Alan!'

He looked up to see Brenda edging across the rock, holding out her hand for him to grab. She was too far away. He reached out but slid again.

Now Joyce appeared on the bridge with Geoff and they looked helplessly at the scene below. Alan was drenched, spread-eagled on the rock, sliding ever closer towards the water. Brenda found a foothold and then another. She was risking everything to save the boy, reaching a narrow ledge then going down on to her belly and stretching out her hand.

The water roared and tugged at his legs. The stone arch soared above his head. He felt Brenda's fingertips and then her whole hand grasp his. With a groan he let himself be pulled clear of the water and into her arms.

She held him tight and waited for the others.

Geoff came down the bank ahead of Joyce. He handed Brenda his coat and she wrapped it around the shivering boy. Other searchers congregated on the bridge.

'I won't go back,' he whimpered.

'We won't make you,' Brenda promised.

'I won't!' He was too cold to cry, almost too cold to speak, clinging to Brenda and pleading with her as she handed him over to Geoff who took the dripping bundle and carefully carried him up the bank.

'Don't worry – I think I've got the solution,' Geoff said over his shoulder to Brenda, who followed him up the riverbank. Then he called up to Joyce. 'Tell Mr Rigg that Alan is found.'

Rigg's name terrified Alan. He struggled to break free but Geoff held him tight as they reached the path.

'Say I'll look after him,' Geoff insisted. 'And tell Walter Rigg to stay away.'

Brenda, Joyce, Emma and Giles gathered around the rescued boy.

'What else?' Joyce asked before she set off for the vicarage.

'Tell him he's not a fit guardian for this child.' Geoff carried Alan over the bridge towards his house. 'He'll stay at New Hall. The authorities will be informed.'

CHAPTER TWENTY-TWO

'What's the matter?' Brenda asked Dorothy as the eventful day drew to a close. Smoke from Bernard's pipe filled the kitchen and the comforting tap-tapping sound of his small hammer driving nails through the new leather soles of his work boots accompanied their talk.

'Nothing.' Dorothy seemed put out by something but was not willing to explain what that something was.

'Come on; out with it.'

'No, it's nothing.'

'Have you had another row with Cliff?' Brenda had come inside to telephone Dale End and tell Donald that she would arrive at the house in good time for Hettie's funeral on Wednesday. But she'd found Dorothy in a gloomy mood and decided to try to talk her out of it before making the call.

'No. I'm still giving him the cold shoulder, though.' Dorothy huffed and puffed her way through yet another of her magazines, flicking pages then pushing it across the table. She'd sat around all day in her dressing-gown, refusing to go back to bed after Alma's visit despite Bernard's nagging. 'Cliff's moved back in here for a few days, did you know that?'

'Has he now?' Brenda was intrigued. *Good for Evelyn*, she thought.

'Yes. He's threatening to go back to Acklam for his dirty washing and bring it here. I told him not to bother – I won't do it for him.'

'So you have had a row?'

Dorothy shrugged then picked at her fingernails. 'All right, I suppose so. But the point is I've been stuck in the house all day, missing the excitement. It's not fair.'

Bernard finished his boot repairs and put away his tools. 'She means the goings-on at the vicarage,' he explained as he puffed away on his pipe. 'I wouldn't let her go down and watch. The vet gave me strict instructions to keep an eye on her.'

'The vet!' Dorothy echoed scornfully. 'Geoff's not even a proper doctor.'

'Anyway,' Brenda tried to smooth ruffled feathers, 'there wasn't much to see; not once we'd found Alan and taken him to New Hall.'

'What did the vicar have to say about that?'

'Nothing. He wouldn't come to the door when Joyce knocked so she posted a note through the letter box bringing him up to date. In the meantime, Geoff wrapped Alan up in lots of blankets and made him a cup of cocoa. I left him sitting by the fire while Giles read him a story. Giles is Geoff's friend from their college days.'

'I know who he is,' came the huffy reply. 'It's not fair,' she repeated. 'I would have read Alan a story if I'd been there.' It seemed she was destined to sit on the sidelines, never to occupy the centre of the action. 'What is he still doing here anyway?'

'Who – Giles?'

'Yes. Doesn't he have a wife and family to go back to?'

'I have no idea.' It was clear to Brenda that Dorothy's bad mood was set in for the night. 'Is it all right if I use the telephone?' she asked Bernard, who nodded.

So she rang the operator and was soon put through to Arnold. 'I'll be there on Wednesday,' she assured him. 'Please thank Donald for letting me know.'

'Thank you, Brenda. It means a lot.'

'There's no need to thank me. I want to come.'

'We'll have a drink and a bite to eat here after the church service.'

'If there's anything I can do . . .'

Hettie's father sighed heavily. 'Thank you. That's all in hand. Anyway, you and Les will want to spend time together.'

'Les will be there?' Brenda clutched the mouthpiece and rolled her eyes towards the ceiling in silent prayer. She held her breath.

'Yes. They've given him three days – Tuesday to Thursday.'

'Three days!'

'To make up for the leave that was cancelled at the last minute. Didn't Donald tell you?'

Three whole days with Les. A funeral two days before Christmas. Brenda's feelings see-sawed between joy and sorrow. 'No, but that's marvellous news,' she whispered. 'And you're sure there's nothing I can do?'

'No; thanks all the same.' Arnold's voice was scarcely audible.

Brenda pictured him in his study lined with books

from floor to ceiling, sitting at his carved desk with his dogs at his feet, surrounded by the shell of his life. Hettie had been the heart of it and she was gone. 'I'll come over on Tuesday evening,' she promised.

There was another sigh, a click and then the line went dead.

'I take it Cliff didn't tell you the part about your fiancé?' Dorothy said when Brenda put down the receiver. Coils of tobacco smoke drifted up towards the ceiling as Bernard carried his mended boots to the porch. Embers shifted in the grate and sparks shot up the chimney. 'That's Cliff for you: never thinking about others, always putting himself first.'

Joyce's billhook sliced through side branches of some young mountain ashes growing at the edge of a small clearing in Acklam wood. They fell to the ground with pleasing cleanness and the smell of sap filled her nostrils. On she went, from one tree to the next, with Evelyn working beside her – a swish of the blade, a small thud, a rapid slice and then the severed branch would land amongst the bracken.

'Has the Weatherall family been in touch?' Joyce asked as Evelyn stooped to gather an armful of branches, ready to stack them in the centre of the clearing.

'No, not a dicky bird.' Evelyn worked on. 'No news is good news as far as that goes.'

'And what about Cliff?'

'Likewise. It's been a whole twenty-four hours.'

Joyce brought the blade down with another swift slice. 'That's good too, I take it?'

'Yes. I made him promise to stay away until I'd had time to think.'

'And have you decided?'

Evelyn collected more fallen branches. 'No, not yet.' In fact, she'd lain awake most of the night, swayed first this way then that. She would follow a train of thought towards a sensible conclusion, listing all the reasons why she should have no more to do with Cliff – his selfishness, his up-and-down moods, the apparent ease with which he'd lived a lie for three whole years. But then a memory of them in bed together would derail her – skin to skin, the softness of his touch, the light glinting in his hazel eyes. And she would be thrown back into confusion, staring up at the ceiling while outside a strong wind tore through the trees and battered the walls of the deserted, crumbling castle, gusting across the yard and almost rattling doors off their hinges.

'What would you do if you were me?' Evelyn asked Joyce as she set to work with her billhook.

'I really couldn't say.' More branches fell, disturbing a pair of blackbirds in a nearby sycamore. There was a flutter of wings and a flash of yellow beaks as they rose into the dull grey sky. 'It might look like an open-and-shut case from the outside but from where you're standing it's bound to be more complicated.'

'I know what I *ought* to do.' Evelyn missed her aim and the blade cut through the bark deep into the trunk. She worked it free again with a bad-tempered frown. 'I ought to get in touch with my local rep and request a move away from Acklam – it wouldn't matter where to, just so long as Cliff didn't know. I could have done it first thing this morning but I didn't.'

Joyce stopped work. She tightened the knot in her woollen headscarf, which she wore turban-style to keep her hair clear of her face. 'It's up to you, of course. But I will say this: for me the best thing about Edgar is that he's honest as the day. He has his faults, don't get me wrong. He'd be the first to admit it.'

'Such as?' Evelyn was curious. Joyce rarely talked about her fiancé, though it was a wonder to Evelyn how she could bear in silence the razor-sharp slash of fear each time she imagined him setting out on one of his death-defying Spitfire missions.

'He has his dark moods, but don't we all? He can push people away even though they want to help him. Even so, I know he would never lie to me.' Joyce looked directly at Evelyn to measure her response. 'That's the most important thing.'

Evelyn lopped off another branch. 'I envy you.'

'And Edgar cares for me. He would never want to hurt me.' Joyce's voice, always calm and low, grew stronger. 'Deep down he's a kind man.'

'Right.'

'That's it,' Joyce said simply. 'That's what matters to me.'

'And you're right.' Evelyn worked on, slicing through side branches, making room for the saplings to grow straight and tall. 'I know you are.'

And yet, maybe Cliff would change. Now that he had nothing to hide, the mists might lift and there would be a clearer way ahead. After all, he'd said time and again that he loved her.

The work went on. Joyce and Evelyn stopped at noon for tea and sandwiches back at the yard and a general look ahead at what Christmas might hold for each of them – not long now, no turkey this year, Evelyn didn't mind spending it alone at Acklam if it came to it. During the gaps in the conversation Joyce thought of the letter she hoped to write to Edgar that evening. Then, as they brushed away crumbs and drained their cups, Evelyn went back to a topic that Joyce had mentioned earlier.

'You say Geoff has taken little Alan under his wing?'

Joyce smiled as they set off for the clearing. 'That's a nice way of putting it. Yes, he has.'

'And what did Mr Rigg have to say?'

'Nothing so far. He's holed up inside the vicarage, refusing to come out. Brenda and Geoff swear they won't let it drop, though. They've decided to telephone Alan's billeting officer and Mr Rigg's bishop to find out what can be done.'

'Good for them.'

'Alan will stay at New Hall for the time being.' They reached the clearing and Joyce took off her coat, ready for action.

'What do you make of Geoff's friend, Giles?' Evelyn's question hung in the cold, damp air.

'He seems a nice chap. Why?'

'I mean, what do you make of that situation?'

'Oh!' A surprising new thought flew into Joyce's head. It came out of the blue with a force that rooted her to the spot.

'And the blindfold fell from her eyes!' Evelyn said with an affectionate shove.

'I didn't realize.' In her mind's eye Joyce saw Geoff and Giles at the Christmas hop, chatting quietly in a corner, making no moves to join in with the dancing. Their heads were together. Giles was explaining something, Geoff was smiling and nodding. 'Are you quite certain?'

'One hundred per cent.' Evelyn had known for a few months that the two men were more than good friends. The dawning of the light for her had come during Giles's previous visit when she'd been doing gardening work at New Hall and caught sight of him and Geoff in the kitchen in their pyjamas. They sat close together at the table, elbows touching while Geoff spread marmalade on Giles's toast then fed it to him.

'Well, I wish them luck,' Joyce said without hesitation. *Two good, kind men to be respected and left in peace.*

Evelyn nodded. 'Same here.'

No more was said. It was time to get back to work.

*

My darling Edgar,

I realized earlier today how lucky I am to have met you and I wanted to write it down and send this letter to you post haste: I AM SO LUCKY! There is no one in this world who could compare. Every day I miss you more. You're in my head and in my heart and will be for ever. You know that my dearest wish is for the war to end and for us to be together.

I hope by putting this down on paper I can make it come true. Please write back to me as soon as you can.

The words of longing poured out on to the page, a strong current of pure love that would flow between them though war had forced them apart.

Joyce sat for a while in her dimly lit attic room, hearing Alma's footstep on the landing and a short while later Laurence's stronger tread. A door shut and there was silence. The candle flickered. Joyce continued to write.

> The news here is that Hettie White's funeral will take place on Wednesday this week and that Les hopes to be there. Also, there was a great to-do on Sunday over the vicar mistreating his evacuee. Fingers crossed that this will soon be sorted out.

She paused again, pen poised, wondering whether or not to include her latest talk with Evelyn in the letter. It would be hard to do justice to her new friend's heartbreaking situation in two or three short lines so she decided against it.

> I'm enjoying my forestry work at Acklam, learning on the hoof. I hope to move on soon from snedding to cross-cutting and stripping bark then to tree felling and eventually on from there to learning the ropes in a saw mill. That would mean doing a four-week course at the Timber Corps depot near Rixley. I would need approval for a transfer from Mrs Mostyn and I wouldn't want to leave Mr Bradley in the lurch. Luckily, Alma Bradley is now willing to learn how to work with the sheep and so my role here may soon be surplus to requirements. Alma has been through a lot and I'm glad to see that she's happier and more settled than when I first got here.

I had meant to keep this letter short, my dear, but here I am running on. Still, before I close, I want to promise you that my love for you runs deep and will never change. I miss you more than I can say – now, as Christmas draws near and we long more than ever to be with the ones we love. Carry this letter with you, along with the picture you have of me, close to your heart.

Dearest Edgar, I send you all, all, ALL my love,

from Joyce. xxxx

*

'I'm coming with you,' Dorothy insisted as Brenda put on her coat to go down to New Hall. After two whole days cooped up in the house, she was bored to tears so she sprang to her feet and headed to the door.

'Oh no, you don't.' Cliff stood in her way. 'I've had strict instructions not to let you go anywhere.'

'Get out of my road!' Trying to push her way towards the kitchen door, she overbalanced and fell against the table. 'Ouch, that hurt! Cliff, I'm not a baby – I can go where I like.'

'Not if I have anything to do with it. Just sit down and let Brenda go on her own.'

'I won't be long.' Brenda jammed on her hat. I'll take Sloper; I'll be there and back before you know it.'

Dorothy gave a sigh of defeat. 'I want to know everything, do you hear? Who says what – every last word.'

'Right you are.'

Brenda had just come off the phone from speaking to Geoff about Walter Rigg. Dorothy had heard one half of the conversation and managed to fill in some of the gaps but Brenda was refusing to stop and explain, saying she must get down to the village as quickly as possible.

'It's not fair!' Dorothy sighed out her usual refrain and sat down gracelessly.

Cliff stoked the fire against the evening chill.

Brenda slammed the door and was gone.

After his first full day at the big house, Alan had almost stopped being afraid of every mysterious sound and shadow.

'Call me Geoff,' the vet had said at the start of the day as they drove out to farmhouses and cottages to look after people's sick animals. But Alan couldn't call a grown-up by their first name, however nice and kind they were. And Mr Dawson was one of the nicest people in the whole world, handing him humbugs from a bag in his jacket pocket and speaking softly to the sheep whose poor lamb had been born too early and died and to the horse called Captain at Acklam Castle who had gone lame for no reason.

'When did you first notice it?' Mr Dawson had asked the lady with red hair, who'd met Alan when he'd first arrived in Shawcross. The lady had looked worried and told him that the horse had been lame when she'd walked him out of his stable yesterday evening. It had been dark by the time Alan and Mr Dawson had arrived at the ruined castle and the vet had used a torch as he'd felt up and down Captain's leg for swellings. Then he'd lifted up his big hoof and, after a lot of prodding, had found the culprit – a rusty nail that had worked its way into what he called the frog, which hadn't seemed the right word to Alan but the lady had been relieved when Mr Dawson had used a pair of tweezers to pull the nail out.

The lady and Mr Dawson had shaken hands. He'd asked her how she was coping on her own. She'd said, 'Fine, ta!' – a nice, breezy, pretty lady who had ruffled his hair and smiled at him as they'd left the yard.

Now they were back in the big house. Mr Pickering had cooked sausage and mashed potatoes for their tea. When they'd finished eating it, he'd hugged Mr Dawson and said he would see him again in two weeks. They'd wished each other a Happy Christmas and Mr Dawson had looked sad for a moment when Mr Pickering had said goodbye.

It was nearly bedtime and Alan was in the kitchen reading a Rupert Bear story when there was a knock on the front door and the Land Girl who'd stopped him from sliding into the river on Sunday came in without waiting to be asked.

'This is snug!' she sang out as she took off some goggles and a pair of big leather gloves.

Geoff took her jacket and drew her towards the Aga where it was warm. Alan closed his book and waited warily.

'No Giles?' Brenda glanced around the room.

'No; duty calls, worse luck.' Geoff pulled out a seat at the table for her. 'In the shape of a family Christmas in Melton Mowbray. But listen to this – and you too, Alan – I've managed to get hold of someone in the bishop's office in Northgate. The bishop wasn't there but I asked his secretary if there was a way of making a formal complaint against Walter Rigg.'

At the mention of the name, Alan shrank down in his seat but Brenda gave the table a small thump with the side of her fist and said, 'Good for you, Geoff! And then what?'

'There was what you would call a pregnant pause on the other end of the line then the secretary asked what was the nature of the complaint. I told her what had been going on at the vicarage – slowly because she said she was writing it all down.'

'Good again!' Brenda breathed. She smiled and nodded at Alan. 'And what did she say afterwards?'

'That she would inform the bishop but that it would probably be the dean who followed it up. The dean is a chap called Ellis – Nigel Ellis. She said he would call me back as soon as possible – perhaps tomorrow. But then . . .' Geoff paused for effect, raising his eyebrows and planting the palms of his hands on the table close to where Brenda sat. 'Then the secretary lowered her voice and said she was speaking off the record but that this wasn't the first complaint about Rigg that they'd received.'

Brenda thumped the table a second time, making Alan jump. She whispered sorry to him then reached over to stroke his hand.

'The last time it happened, the bishop called Rigg in and warned him to tone down the discipline in future and to remember that all evacuees had the right to be treated well by their guardians.'

'And a fat lot of difference that made.' Brenda pulled a sour face. 'It would've been far better if the bishop hadn't given him a second chance.'

'I agree, but I get the distinct feeling that Rigg won't be given a third.'

'Do you hear that, Alan?' Brenda squeezed his hand. 'It's official – you won't have to go back to the vicarage!'

He let out a long, shuddering breath, slowly letting go of the terror that had gripped him by the throat ever since he'd set eyes on the vicar's thick, plump fingers and the ruler that he kept tucked into the waistband of his trousers.

'And now for my own news!' Brenda beamed at Alan and Geoff. 'I've been toying with an idea since yesterday but I held off from making a move until this evening because I didn't know if it was the right time. Should I or shouldn't I?'

'Do what?' Geoff studied Brenda's face. Her eyes sparkled with excitement, her whole face was aglow.

'Put in a telephone call to Dale End. Alan, do you remember going there with me to visit Judith?'

The boy nodded slowly. Another big house a long way away, his sister wearing her grey pinafore, her hair in plaits. *We have to be brave, Alan. Don't let Mummy and Daddy down.* The tears; that's what he remembered.

'I talked to Les's brother,' Brenda explained to Geoff. 'I asked him if they intended to keep Judith now that Hettie . . . Hettie doesn't need her any more. Donald said yes in his off-hand way; why not? Judith wasn't any trouble. In fact, his father had taken quite a shine to her. They both found that they liked having the girl around. I asked him, did they fancy taking in her brother as well – eight years old and looking for a fresh billet?'

'And he said yes!' Geoff gave a grunt of satisfaction.

'Blow me down, he did!' She stood up and grinned at them both. 'His father was in the study with him. Donald asked his permission while I was on the line. Arnold said yes straight away. It's all settled.'

Alan looked in wonderment from Brenda to Geoff then back again.

'You're going to join your sister,' she explained in plain words that would sink into his fuddled brain. 'For the time being – until the bombing stops and it's safe to go home to your mummy and daddy – you and Judith will live together at Dale End.'

CHAPTER TWENTY-THREE

Bernard grumbled as expected about Brenda's request for leave but she'd banked on being able to sweet-talk him round.

'Three days?' With loud scrapes of his spoon he finished off the last of his porridge then squinted up at her.

'Yes please, Mr Huby. I've already fed the hens and the rabbits and milked the goat this morning. I've left everything shipshape. And when I get back on Thursday I'll put in the extra hours to catch up.'

Cliff was in shirtsleeves, smoking a cigarette and reading the newspaper. Dorothy was still in bed.

'Three days for a funeral?'

'Yes. My fiancé's sister died last week. Les managed to get compassionate leave. He's on an overnight train travelling down from Glasgow as we speak. He has to go back on Christmas Eve.'

'I see.' Bernard shoved his bowl to one side. 'Cliff, if I let my Land Girl go, will you lend a hand instead of sitting around on your backside?'

A dismissive shrug was his answer, followed by a sideways glance at Brenda. On second thoughts, Cliff realized, there was an advantage in having

Evelyn's bolshie ally off the scene for a while. 'Yes, why not?' he mumbled.

'Go on, then.' Bernard gave way with a thin-lipped smile.

Brenda thanked him and ran from the house to pick up a haversack already packed with clothes for the funeral, a nightdress and toiletries. Then she jumped on Sloper and sped down the lane under a sky that was slowly turning from dull grey to soft pink. There were no clouds and hardly any wind.

She found Geoff and Alan waiting for her at the door of New Hall. Geoff was wearing his waxed jacket and flat cap, ready to set off on his rounds. Alan was in his navy blue mac and school cap, holding the shopping bag crammed with his possessions and with his gas mask slung across his chest – just as Brenda and Joyce had first seen him on the bus ride out to Shawcross.

'You see?' Geoff said to him as Brenda hopped off her bike. 'I promised you she wouldn't forget.'

Brenda took the bag and strapped it behind the pillion seat. 'It's a lovely morning,' she said to Geoff as she sat astride Sloper and held the bike steady while Alan climbed aboard.

He nodded. 'But go steady; the roads will be icy,' he reminded her. 'And good luck, Alan.'

Brenda manoeuvred the bike to face the gate. *Thank you,* she mouthed to Geoff above the roar of the engine.

He waved them off then stood in the doorway until the bike had crested the bridge and sailed on past the gloomy vicarage, watching until it disappeared from view.

*

On the journey to Attercliffe the sky turned from pink to blue. The hedges and fields were white with hoar frost, the puddles at the sides of the road frozen solid. Brenda whizzed on between stone walls, past twisted hawthorn trees and grey roadside barns then slowed down to cross a fast-running ford where glittering icicles hung from bushes and Alan clung on tighter as they splashed through the shallow water and pigeons rose from the overhanging oak tree then clattered away.

'Not long now,' Brenda promised as they climbed up the hill towards Kelsey Crag – the landmark that separated the two dales. Once they saw the rooftops of Burnside spread out below them, Brenda felt happy to be back on familiar ground. She knew these lanes and hills like the back of her hand, picturing Una, Elsie and Kathleen as they set out from Fieldhead on their bikes for their day's work, feeling the nostalgic pull of old places and faces.

'Not long,' she said again as they coasted through the village, past St Michael's where Grace and Bill had got married, past the Blacksmith's Arms, the post office and the row of terraced cottages, and out along the moor road towards Attercliffe, finally creeping up a zigzagging single-track road until they came to the top and gazed like two eagles on the valley below.

'You see that spire?' she said over her shoulder.

Alan kept his arms wrapped around her waist as he craned his head sideways.

'That's Attercliffe.' Her heart soared as they made their descent. 'And here we are at Dale End,' she told him. 'Where you'll be staying from now on.'

*

The curtains were drawn, the dark house locked into a period of deep mourning.

'The people who live here are sad,' Brenda warned Alan as they waited at the door. 'Someone they love has died.'

Would Les be here yet? Would it be him greeting her, his arms enclosing her, his mouth murmuring soft words?

The door opened and it was Donald in a dark suit with a black tie, standing stiffly, his face pale and shadowed.

'Les is still on his way,' he told her without her having to ask. 'His train was held up just outside Carlisle. Come in. We're in the sitting room.'

He took Alan's bag and put it down at the bottom of the stairs then led the way across the hall into Hettie's favourite room overlooking the garden. Arnold stood with his back to the French windows, all in black, his grey hair neatly parted and his posture ramrod-straight, as if to give way to grief even for a moment would be to open floodgates that could never be closed. He acknowledged Brenda with the smallest of nods.

Judith stood next to Arnold, her hands clasped nervously in front of her, looking up at him as if waiting for permission.

He nodded for a second time and she ran across the room, pigtails flying. She flung her arms around her brother's neck.

'Give up, you're strangling me,' Alan protested as he pulled away, cheeks red, eyes brimming with tears.

'Welcome to Dale End,' Donald said from the

doorway. He glanced at Brenda as if seeking her approval.

Thank you, she mouthed for the second time that morning.

Alan's tears fell. The gold-framed pictures on the cream walls grew blurred and the sofas and chairs, the tables and footstools crowded in. His sister held his hand tight.

'Go ahead, Judith,' Donald prompted gently. 'Take Alan upstairs and show him to his room.'

Joyce worked with Alma in the pre-dawn calm of the milking shed. The cows were back in their barn and newly filled bottles rattled along the conveyor belt in the dairy next door while the two women mucked out and hosed the stalls.

Outside it was still scarcely light. Half an hour earlier Laurence had set out in the Land-Rover to take feed to the few remaining sheep left on the fell. 'I'll leave them out until after Christmas if I can,' he'd told them. 'Then I'll bring them in for lambing.'

'When's your next driving lesson?' Joyce asked Alma as they worked. It was the first time she'd seen her wearing trousers and noticed how well they showed off her slim hips and waist.

'On Sunday, if Laurence finds time to teach me.'

'You've already taken to it like a duck to water.'

'Thank you. I hope it wasn't beginner's luck.'

The atmosphere was quiet and relaxed, the work almost finished when Joyce broached the topic that had been on her mind. 'How do you think Mr Bradley would feel if I said I'd like to move on?'

'From Black Crag?' Alma used her broom to

swoosh water towards the shallow channel running down the centre of the shed. Her hair fell across her face so she paused to pin it behind her ear.

'Yes. I wouldn't leave until after we've finished lambing; maybe in March or April. And don't get me wrong; it's not because I'm unhappy here – quite the opposite. But I enjoy the work I've started with Evelyn; it would be a fresh challenge for me.'

Alma sighed and leaned on her broom. 'Where would you move to?'

'To Rixley to begin with, to train in forestry methods. I'd have to put in an application first.'

'Laurence wouldn't stand in your way,' Alma decided on his behalf. 'We'd both miss you, though.'

'It won't be for a while,' Joyce said again. 'And you never know, the Timber Corps might turn me down.'

'They won't.'

'They might!'

'No; they'll take one look at you and they'll snap your hand off.'

Joyce smiled. 'So what do you think – will you and Mr Bradley manage?'

Nothing had been said but Alma was certain that Joyce had picked up on the recent big changes at the farm. She'd seen with her own eyes the thaw that had set in between husband and wife soon after Muriel's unwanted visits: the soft, exchanged glances, an occasional touch. She might even have guessed that Alma had moved her things into Laurence's room.

'Yes, if you promise to teach me everything you know about sheep farming before you go,' she replied.

Joyce raised her eyebrows then smiled again. 'I'll do my best.'

'Good. Then leave it with me. I'll mention your idea to Laurence as soon as I get the chance.' Alma picked up the hose and directed more water across the concrete floor.

Joyce took up the broom and swept. The sun had risen. She saw slashes of light fall across the yard, cutting through the dark, cold shadows. *I'll miss this place,* she thought. *But by spring I'll be ready to move on.*

Working all day alone in the wood, Evelyn was cocooned in silence. She was removed from the world, spinning out her thoughts from branch to branch, trying to weave a clear future for herself, not resting until dusk when she gathered her tools and walked slowly back to the castle, still lost in thought, still undecided.

The crumbling ruins stood as they always had; a reminder of past battles. The Weatheralls' locked house would soon be lost to dust and decay.

I won't stay, she said to herself with sudden certainty as she entered the yard. *I'll move away from this place as soon as I can.*

First she must put things in order. Tomorrow she would telephone Dr Brownlee and ask for Gillian Vernon's number. She would discuss with the family what they wanted to do about Captain and suggest that she, Evelyn, should find him a good home on a neighbouring farm. She would tell Gillian that she would stay on until the New Year at the latest.

'Do you hear that?' she said to the old horse as he poked his head over his stable door. 'We're moving on, you and I.'

He whinnied softly and nudged her shoulder, his

breath warm on her cheek. When she turned away, she came face to face with Cliff.

'Hello, Evie.' He spoke as if it was natural for him to be there, pretending not to notice that she had almost jumped out of her skin. 'It's getting dark. What kept you?'

She made an effort to steady herself and act normally. 'Nothing kept me. I've been working. And now, if you don't mind, I have to feed Captain.'

He stepped aside without being asked. 'I dropped by for my dirty washing.'

Evelyn made no comment as she went next door for hay. A sixth sense told her not to challenge Cliff, to let him collect his laundry and be on his way. Still, she felt her hands tremble as she filled Captain's net.

'Here, let me.' Watching every movement, Cliff moved in to hold the net while she stuffed it with hay.

The hairs on her neck prickled. She told herself not to speak or to look at him. Before the net was full, she tugged it free then carried it into the stable.

Cliff followed. He swung the bottom section of the door closed, trapping her inside, then leaned in. 'So what are your thoughts, Evie?'

'That I'm ready for a change.' *Hold steady, don't meet his eye. Avoid that fatal contact.* Her feet rustled through the straw bed as she picked up Captain's water bucket. 'I'm going to ask the Timber Corps to move me on as soon as possible.'

His set expression gave nothing away. 'And what about us?'

We – us! Still singing the old tune. But Evelyn knew

she must hide her feelings, not show how angry she felt. 'Let's wait and see, shall we?'

'Till when?' Half-opening the door to let her out with the empty bucket, he made it impossible for her to pass without brushing against him.

A shiver ran through her. 'Until I'm settled in a new billet and you've heard from the colonel's relatives. Who knows; they might want you to stay on and manage the estate until everything's decided. That could take a while.'

'That doesn't answer my question.' He wrested the bucket from her and set it down. 'I mean: what about you and me? Is there any hope?'

'I told you: I need time.'

'Time for what?'

His questions pinned her down. Without looking at him she felt his gaze cut into her. 'Time to think, Cliff. I haven't got over the shock of Saturday. I have no idea how I'll feel when I do.'

'So you're leaving me up in the air?' He lowered his voice to a murmur, folding his arms across his chest and staring at the ground.

Darkness thickened around them. Night-time sounds of the forest reached them – an owl hooted, branches sighed and creaked.

'How many times do I have to say it, Evie? I love you from the bottom of my heart.'

She drew a sharp breath then looked at him at last. His face was in shadow but she could make out his eyes. She spoke falteringly. 'Do you? Oh, Cliff – I did so want to believe you.'

'It's true. Doesn't that mean anything to you?'

'Perhaps,' she whispered.

Slowly he reached out and stroked his thumb against her cheek. 'You see. That's all that matters – not the rubbish about Gladys. I love you, Evelyn Newbold, and no one else.'

She felt him move in. His arm was around her waist, the other hand cradled the back of her head. His features blurred as his lips touched hers.

'No!' Evelyn pulled away. She twisted out of his grasp and walked quickly across the yard. 'This isn't right, Cliff. I can't breathe – it's not right.'

He ran after her and caught up with her outside the door to his cottage. Seizing her by the shoulders, he pushed her off balance then thrust her inside. She staggered sideways against the table, knocking over a paraffin lamp and sending it crashing to the floor. The glass cover smashed and the light went out, leaving a sharp smell that caught in the back of Evelyn's throat.

'I'm sorry!' He picked up the remains of the lamp then made as if to help her. 'I shouldn't have done that. I didn't want you to walk away; I wanted to carry on talking, that's all.'

'Stay away from me!' Broken glass crunched under her feet as she backed towards the fireplace. Her heels came into contact with the iron fender.

'Evie, calm down.' He stayed by the table to give her time to catch her breath. 'I'm sorry – all right?'

The smell of leaking paraffin made her stomach churn. Behind her a fire burned low in the grate. Cliff had been here a long time; this was no spur-of-the-moment thing. 'You said you'd just called by to collect your clothes.'

'True,' he said cautiously.

'So why light a fire?'

'Why not?' He circled the table with his hands in his pockets then pushed at the fender with his toe-cap. There was a scrape of metal against stone. 'I'm allowed to keep warm, aren't I?'

Her anger flared into the open. 'You had no intention of going away again. You were sure that you'd talk me round then stay the night and take me to bed. I'm right, aren't I?'

'So what's wrong with that?' He'd said that he loved her – why wouldn't she listen? 'This is daft. *You're* being daft.'

Without warning he darted forward and backed her against the wall, using his weight to trap her in a corner, pressing his body against her and trying to kiss her. She fought back, attempting to kick him and bring her hands up against his chest to push him off. But he was stronger. He jammed her against the wall then took hold of her shirt collar, tugged it then tore the shirt open to the waist. She struggled, pummelling him with her fists, hair falling across her face, the flesh of her shoulder and breast exposed.

It had all gone wrong, fallen apart in a moment, and they were fighting instead of kissing – Cliff had no idea why. He would pin her down and let her struggle until she ran out of energy then he would talk sense into her.

Evelyn made out his face in the firelight: his mouth set hard, his eyes cruel as he put a hand across her mouth to stop her yelling out. She bit his finger. He swore then slid the hand over her chin, down her soft neck and on to her breast.

If that's the way she wants it . . . He pressed against her with his whole body. He was much too strong. But she could cry out and keep on kicking. She dislodged the shotgun that he kept propped by the side of the fireplace and heard it fall on to the flags.

Her skin was pale and warm. 'Hush!' He slammed her against the wall again.

She would not give in. He grasped her shirt and attempted to tear it from her, lifting her off her feet and swinging her round towards the table. He threw her down on her back. She gasped and tried to push him off.

'What's wrong with you? Why are you being like this?'

As he climbed on top of her, she drew her knees up then kicked his chest with such force that he let out a gasp and fell backwards. As he bent forward to drag air into his lungs, she rolled off the side of the table then ran for the door.

'Come back, damn you!'

His rough voice followed her into the darkness as she fled.

CHAPTER TWENTY-FOUR

Brenda borrowed Donald's car to drive to Rixley railway station. Les had missed his connection in Carlisle and had telephoned to say that he would need to be picked up at half past six – a full four hours later than expected.

'I'll go,' she'd offered as soon as Arnold had put down the phone. 'Please!' she'd added.

There'd been no argument; Donald had handed over the keys to his Rover and she'd set off from Dale End, through Attercliffe then on to the main road connecting the village with the smart spa town that lay twenty miles away at the edge of the Dales. It was already dark and she drove with regulation dimmed headlights and without the help of sign-posts that had all been removed as a wartime measure so as not to aid foreign spies. Sometimes she had to stop at junctions and guess the way, losing valuable minutes when she took what turned out to be an obvious wrong turning and had to ask at a farmhouse for directions. She made up for it once she was back on the right road, putting her foot down and building up to a speed of forty miles per hour along the final stretch.

It was almost half past when she reached Rixley and drove along empty streets between shuttered shops, past elaborate churches, rows of terraced houses, a school, a large library then a cinema until she reached the Town Hall overlooking a central square with a statue of Queen Victoria, orb of state in hand, surveying her empire. The grandiose council building was flanked on one side by an art gallery and on the other by the train station.

Her fingers trembled as she fumbled with the handbrake before leaping out of the car and running under the wide, arched entrance into the wrought-iron and glass cathedral.

A train pulled away from its platform in a cloud of steam. Passengers muffled in overcoats and scarves hurried towards her and pushed through the squeaking turnstile as she leaned over the barrier, looking for Les. The minute hand of the giant clock jerked forward. Where was he? Had she missed him? The platform emptied, the steam cleared.

'Here I am,' he said. He stepped out from under the clock, the collar of his coat turned up.

For a few seconds Brenda didn't move. She wanted to drink in every detail: the white shirt and dark tie; the double-breasted, belted overcoat; the white Royal Navy cap set forward at an angle; but most of all his dear face with eyes that were somewhere between grey and blue – grey in this light – his fair colouring, the faint beginnings of frown lines between his eyebrows.

Les saw her start then hold her breath as she turned towards him. He'd never be able to tell her how much he'd missed her, how she filled his every waking moment. She inhabited all of his dreams; small, dark and quick, her brown eyes alight with love. Better to hold her tight rather than to try to speak. He reached out and drew her to him.

Brenda sank into the oasis of his embrace.

Evelyn fled from Cliff's cottage towards the wood. Her only thought was to get away, to hide in the darkness and pray for him to give up and go away.

But he didn't; she heard footsteps behind her, trampling the undergrowth and snapping twigs, the sound of him swearing and breathing hard, calling out for her to stop.

These were her trees, this was *her* territory. She was swift footed and sure. He was clumsy. He tripped over roots, crashed down to the ground, picked himself up and followed. *He won't catch me!* she promised herself as she ducked under branches and wove between the trunks of tall birches and elms without making a sound. She reached a clearing then paused to listen.

Cliff would not admit defeat. Evelyn might know these woods better than him but she couldn't make herself disappear – she must be hiding in here somewhere. 'Evie!' he yelled. *Damn her. Damn all women.* Darkness and silence. *Damn her!*

As she listened, the sound of her own breathing roared in her ears. Her throat was dry and she had to drag air into her lungs – in then out, in again with a loud rasping sound. There was no cover in the clearing – he would be able to track her down and attack again. This time she might not have the strength to fight him off.

'Evie!'

His voice was louder, nearer. She had to run again, this time from the clearing into a section of the wood that hadn't been coppiced. The way ahead was thick with saplings, brambles and ferns. Fallen trees blocked her way.

He followed the sounds of her stumbling through undergrowth. She would have to slow down and eventually she would come to a dead end: up against an impassable boulder or trees growing too densely for her to push her way through. All he had to do was bide his time. 'I'm sorry,' he called after her. 'Do you hear me, Evie? I overstepped the mark. I won't do it again. I'm sorry!'

Brenda and Les drove through the quiet night under a clear sky. The moon cast a silvery light over hills and streams.

'How's Dad?' he asked as they approached Dale End; house and barns nestled against the steep, shadowed fell side, close to a stream that wound across the flat valley bottom.

'He's holding up.' She braked to turn into the drive. 'He doesn't say much but you can see in his face what he's going through.'

'Typical Dad.' Upright, stern, often impatient. 'He never tells you what he's thinking.'

'He's taken in Judith's brother – you remember, I wrote to you about the little boy, Alan?'

The news surprised Les. It seemed out of character, but then again perhaps it was his father's attempt to bring more life into the house – to fill a gap that couldn't be filled. He looked ahead at the dark house, listening to the sound of tyres rolling over gravel, dreading tomorrow.

'Come on.' Brenda got out first and opened Les's door. She held out her hand.

It was prim, eager-to-please Judith who opened the door at the sound of their car. Alan hung back at the bottom of the stairs, not daring to let his sister out of his sight.

'Where's Mr White?' Brenda asked her.

'In the sitting room.' Judith took their coats then stepped to one side.

Seeming not to notice the children, Les walked ahead as Brenda hung back.

'Thanks, Judith.' She wanted to say a few more words of encouragement but now Les hesitated uncertainly at the sitting-room door.

Donald came down the stairs and the brothers shook hands. 'Is my car still in one piece?' he asked Brenda with a touch of his usual flippancy. 'It'd better be – I just had the front wing fixed after a run-in with a sheep.'

'Ouch!' She said she was sure that the sheep had come off worst.

Donald turned back to Les. 'How was the journey?'

'Not too bad until we were nearly at Carlisle, then we had a spot of bother with the engine. That's what held us up.'

Death had transformed everything at Dale End yet no one mentioned it. Was this how everyone got through such times? Steeling herself to take a lead from them, Brenda followed Les and Donald into the room where Arnold waited.

'My boy,' he said simply, his voice choked with emotion when he saw Les in his uniform.

'Dad.'

Arnold had fought in the First War; he'd known mud and blood, gas and the deadly rattle of machine-gun fire. But this was the hardest battle of all. 'It's good to see you, son.'

Les shook hands with his father.

Late that night, when Les came to Brenda's room, he lay with her and wept.

The memory of Cliff's cruel face as he'd pushed her down on to the table drove Evelyn on. Hearing him say sorry a thousand times wouldn't erase the fear and disgust she'd felt. Still he pursued her, calling her name, gaining on her again.

She ran clear of the wood and now Cliff had her in his sights – she was running like a rabbit, blind with panic. But there was no rabbit hole for Evie to vanish down and the moon shone brightly so that her outline was easy to make out against the rocky hillside. He paused for a moment to observe the dark silhouette of Black Crag on the horizon. Beneath it there was a glimmer of yellow light.

Evelyn also saw the solitary light and knew that it came from the Bradleys' farm. If she reached it she would be safe – there would be help there from Joyce, Alma and Laurence. Her chest ached and her legs weakened. She stumbled as she ran. Suddenly the ground went from under her and she fell.

Cliff saw her lose her balance and grasp at thin air. He watched her slide on her side down the icy slope and slam against a boulder where she lay motionless. The chase was over. There was no need to hurry now so he slowed his pace and walked steadily towards her.

In the yard at Black Crag Farm the dogs raised their heads and listened to sounds that could not be heard by the human ear. Suddenly alert, Flint and Patch emerged from their kennel and started to bark. Inside the house, where Joyce sat by the fireside with Alma and Laurence scanned the latest news columns about Stalingrad, there was a break in the women's conversation.

'What's set them off?' Laurence glanced up from his newspaper. The dogs never made a noise unless something was up.

The barking grew louder and more insistent.

The racket reached Evelyn where she lay bruised and winded after her fall. Her ribs ached as she tried to raise herself from the ground. She groaned and collapsed forward on to her knees, crying out in pain as Cliff seized her arm and yanked her on to her feet.

'Don't do that!' he warned as she tried to resist. Another couple of minutes and she would have made it as far as the farm. There would have been a lot of explaining for him to do. As it was, he would have all on to get her back to Acklam and calm her down.

'Shall I go out and take a look?' Joyce asked Laurence. Without waiting for an answer she strode out into the yard to find the dogs at the gate, barking out a warning that all was not well.

'What is it?' She opened the gate and let them out into the lane. Flint and Patch quietened for a moment, pricked up their ears then sped off across the hillside.

'You hear that?' Cliff snarled at Evelyn as she struggled to escape. His grip on her arm was tight. 'Now look what you've done!'

The physical pain in her chest as she lashed out with her free arm took her breath away but the mental torment was worse. At last she saw Cliff for what he really was: a brute and a coward who would do anything to get his own way. What lay behind the eyes that once had mesmerized her was nothing but cruelty and selfishness. Making one last effort to free herself, Evelyn called out for help.

The dogs charged up the hillside and Joyce followed. She saw two figures: a man and a woman. The man was trying to drag the woman behind an outcrop of rock but she resisted. Flint and Patch reached the spot and circled them. They crouched low and bared their teeth.

The game was up. Cliff let go of Evelyn's wrist and thrust her in the path of the dogs. She cried out as she fell forward.

Joyce sprinted up the slope. Evelyn crawled towards her, while Flint and Patch drove Cliff against the rock face and kept him at bay.

'You see, Evie!' he yelled as he flung his arm towards Joyce. This was what happened when women ganged together; it was why a man should always look for one who wouldn't answer back.

'Bugger off with your friend. And good riddance to the pair of you!'

Joyce saw that Evelyn's shirt had been ripped. She quickly took off her jersey and wrapped it around her friend's shoulders then crouched down beside her.

'Here, boys!' she called to the dogs as Cliff took to his heels.

He'd gone two paces when Laurence stepped out from behind the rock, shotgun raised.

Cliff saw him and took a step back. He put up his hands in a gesture of surrender.

Evelyn collapsed against Joyce who held her tight.

'We have to get her back to the farm before she freezes to death,' Joyce told Laurence.

'You go first; we're right behind you.' Laurence gestured with the gun for Cliff to follow.

So Joyce led a trembling Evelyn down the hill, step by painful step, trying to make sense of her sobbed, garbled phrases. 'He wouldn't stop . . . I tried . . . he promised, but . . .'

With a gun at his back, Cliff had no choice but to go with them. 'There's no need for this,' he said to Laurence, attempting a man-to-man tone. 'I can tell you what happened without you pointing a damned shotgun at me.'

Laurence said nothing but kept his gun raised. The dogs stayed to heel, tongues lolling, until they reached the lane then they loped ahead towards Alma, who stood waiting by the gate. When she saw Evelyn, she ran to help.

'What can I do?' she asked Joyce.

'We'll need blankets and a hot drink.'

Evelyn clutched at Joyce's jumper to keep herself covered, letting out another sob as they entered the yard. The women went into the house, closing the door behind them and leaving Laurence and Cliff out in the yard.

'Put the gun down,' Cliff said. 'There's been a misunderstanding, that's all.'

Slowly Laurence lowered the weapon, letting it hang at his side.

'That's a good chap.' Cliff watched it warily. 'Like I said, I'm happy to explain.'

As Alma flew upstairs for blankets, Evelyn heard Cliff's muffled voice and clutched at Joyce's arm. Her eyes were dark with fear and she shook uncontrollably.

'It's all right – I won't let him come anywhere near you,' Joyce promised.

'He wouldn't stop . . . I tried . . .' *His face, his mouth, his hands.* She shuddered again.

Alma came down with the blankets and wrapped them around Evelyn. Outside, the men went on talking.

'What was I supposed to think?' Cliff demanded. 'Evelyn's never said no to me before. And let's be honest, sometimes women say no just for the sake of it, when really what they mean is yes.'

'How did her clothes get torn?' Laurence asked in an even tone. The gun swung at his side.

Cliff paused then launched into an explanation. 'You might not realize this, but Evie's got a temper. She flew at me and I had to fight her off – things may have got out of hand for a minute or two. You know what it's like.'

Laurence gave no sign that he did know. 'And how did she end up here?'

Cliff shrugged. 'You'd have to ask her. Who knows what goes on in their heads?'

Laurence's face was like stone as he listened to Cliff's version of events. He'd known of Bernard Huby's son since he was a lad, had occasionally seen him out on the fell snaring rabbits and taking pot-shots at crows. Cliff was a few years older than Gordon so Laurence had never had much contact with him. After all, the Hubys were not a family with whom he had much in common.

'It's a load of fuss about nothing.' *Get rid of the gun, damn you.*

'That didn't look like nothing,' Laurence countered. 'Not from where I was standing.'

Inside the house, Evelyn clutched the blankets around her. The voices in the porch continued at a low mumble. She pushed away the tea that Alma offered and stood up. 'No,' she said as Joyce tried to prevent her. 'I won't let him get away with this.'

'I can't help it if Evie decides to make a big song and dance,' Cliff told Laurence. *No witnesses, Your Honour. No proof.*

Evelyn flung the door open to challenge him. 'You're a cheat and a liar, Cliff Huby. No one believes you.'

In a sudden flash of fury he swore then swung his fist at her. He missed then wrenched Laurence's gun from his grasp. Before anyone could react, he pointed it at Evelyn.

She was beyond all limits, careless of whether she lived or died. She stared him in the eye. 'Go on, Cliff – do it.'

His elbow was out at an angle, his finger hooked around the trigger. One pull was all it took.

Laurence cut through the stifling silence. 'A gun is no good unless you load it first.'

Not loaded? Back at the crag Bradley had cornered him with a trick. *Damn and blast!* Cliff swung out again, this time with the butt of the gun, catching Laurence in the solar plexus. The next moment, Joyce sprang at him from behind. There was a tussle. The gun clattered to the ground.

Cliff felt Joyce's arms around his neck, pressing on his Adam's apple. He broke her grip and threw her to one side then he was off, across the yard, over the wall and into the black shadow of the crag, sprinting for all he was worth.

Ice ran through Evelyn's veins. Let the fool go. Let him run off like the coward he was. She allowed herself to be led back inside by Alma.

Recovering from the blow, Laurence called his dogs to his side then stooped to pick up his gun. He and Joyce set off after Cliff. Soon they too were swallowed up by the looming shadow of Black Crag.

Up ahead, Cliff heard his pursuers. He sensed the dogs hot on his heels so he picked up a handful of stones and launched them one at a time. One of the dogs gave a sharp yelp, telling him that a missile had found its target.

'What are you going to do when you catch me?' he yelled down the hill. Bradley's gun was empty so Cliff wasn't afraid.

But he hadn't reckoned on the dogs. They appeared out of nowhere, leaping the stream with fangs bared, forcing him back against the massive crag. Loose stones rattled down the slope as he kicked out and missed Flint's head. Without noticing Joyce, he saw that Laurence was closing in on him and that he was trapped. It would be one to one in a bare-knuckle scrap.

As Cliff raised his fists ready for the fight, Laurence aimed his gun. A shot rang out.

Joyce stifled a cry of alarm as she realized the gun was loaded after all.

'Bloody liar!' Pellets ricocheted against the rock and Cliff's arm went up to shield his face. He jerked back his head to look up at a sheer fifty-foot climb – in total darkness, with two dogs and a man with a gun after him.

'I wouldn't if I were you,' Laurence called when he saw what Cliff was intending. He reloaded the gun and spoke under his breath to Joyce: 'Take this and one of the dogs – go back across the stream then climb up round the back of the crag. Keep quiet and don't let him see you.'

'You're not me, though.' With Cliff, bravado always won through. He would show the old bastard that he could climb anything and leave him standing. He would reach the top then head off over the moor. In the morning he would be ready with his excuses and lies.

Laurence paused to make sure that Joyce had begun to skirt the crag with Flint then he turned his attention back to Cliff, who was feeling for his first footholds, hauling himself up. He climbed quickly and nimbly, hurling insults as he went.

'Come on, old man – why don't you come after me?' He reached a ledge and paused to look up again. The sky was dense black, pricked with stars. On he climbed with strength in his legs and arms, still confident that he could outwit his opponent. There was an overhang directly above; one that he would have to work around by edging sideways. Cliff's foot slipped on an icy patch; the near miss sent an arrow of fear through him but he had firm hand-holds and he managed to right himself then move on.

Laurence watched silently from below. He kept Patch by his side and waited for Joyce and Flint to appear at the top of the crag.

'Too steep for you, eh?' Cliff yelled as he glanced down.

With the gun at the ready, Joyce edged her way forward. She heard Cliff call down to Laurence. She would aim the gun as soon as he came into view, but would she have the nerve to fire it? Crouching beside her, Flint snarled.

The rock face above Cliff's head narrowed into a fissure that was too tight for him to squeeze through, damn it, and it stank of sheep dung. It would take another sideways move before he could reach the top. He looked down again at Laurence then felt his way along. A rock dislodged, giving him another scare. The fingers of his right hand slipped from their crevice. *Damn it, damn it! Try again.*

Laurence shook his head. The fool would never make it. Joyce hid out of sight and waited.

Cliff edged back towards the foul-smelling chimney of rock. For the first time he saw that he might have bitten off more than he could chew. What would happen if he tried to squeeze up through the fissure after all?

Laurence shook his head again.

Cliff eased himself upwards. He found one small niche for his hand that seemed firm enough. He balanced on his right foot and sought for another foot-hold with the left. He found a ledge but would it take his full weight? Testing it out, in a split second both toe-holds crumbled and gave way. For a full ten seconds he clung on with his hands then lost his grip on the icy surface and slid downwards.

Joyce heard him cry out. She rushed forward and peered over the edge of the cliff to see Cliff's body slide then bounce clear of the rock face. A second later she heard him crash to the ground.

CHAPTER TWENTY-FIVE

'At first I thought the worst had happened.' Joyce sat with Evelyn and Alma in the kitchen of Black Crag Farm as the first grey streaks of dawn light appeared in the sky. She'd heard Cliff's agonized cry and seen him fall. Then silence, darkness; nothing.

Laurence had got to him first and by the time Joyce had scrambled down the slope to join him, he'd been crouched over him, undoing the top button of his shirt. Cliff lay on his back, features contorted into a grimace and his limbs twisted under him.

In the Bradleys' kitchen Evelyn pictured the fall, the loss of control, the flash of fear. She hung her head and sobbed.

Alma put an arm around her shoulder. 'Hush,' she murmured. 'There, there.' Then she turned to Joyce. 'You say that Laurence has driven him to Dr Brownlee's?'

Joyce nodded. 'He asked me to let Bernard and Dorothy know. That's my next job.'

'How bad did it look?' Evelyn asked between sobs. She was swaddled in blankets, still clutching at her torn shirt, remembering Cliff's hands on her body and seeing his cruel eyes. 'Could you tell?'

'He was conscious,' Joyce replied. 'He said he couldn't walk so Mr Bradley and I decided to carry him here, then drive him on to the doctor's house. Dr Brownlee will be able to check the damage and call for an ambulance if necessary.' Her weary muscles felt the effect of Cliff's sagging, broken weight as they'd brought him down the hill.

'I wish . . .' Evelyn drew a deep breath. 'This isn't the way I wanted it to end.'

'We know that. But try not to worry too much. Doctors can work wonders these days.' Without really believing it, Joyce spoke words of comfort, hoping to distance herself from the sound of Cliff's cry as he'd lost his grip and fallen, from the black space, from the fear in his eyes as Laurence loosened his collar. The knowledge that he might never be whole again.

Joyce rode her bike through the half-light along the dirt track towards Shawcross. She reached Garthside Farm as the cock crowed and the goat began to bray. There was a light on in an upstairs window.

From his bedroom Bernard watched Joyce lean her bike against a low wall. He knew something bad had happened and it was to do with Cliff, who had set off for Acklam at around noon yesterday and hadn't returned. Steeling himself, the old farmer got dressed and crept downstairs, careful not to wake Dorothy. He went out without his coat into a world not yet fully light.

Joyce took a deep breath before delivering the bad news.

Bernard approached with certainty in his heart. 'Is it my lad?'

'It is.'

'I knew it.'

'He fell from the top of the crag and hurt himself.'

'Not dead?'

'No, he's alive. Mr Bradley has taken him to Dr Brownlee's.'

Bernard didn't speak but he swayed and had to steady himself against the wall top.

'The doctors; they can work wonders—'

Cliff's father put up his hand to stop her. 'I'll have to tell his sister.'

'The police will be involved.'

A slight nod indicated that he'd heard. 'How did it happen?'

'It started with a fight between him and Evelyn. I don't know much more than that.'

In the heavy silence that followed, the beam from a torch flickered towards them. Dorothy had woken to the sound of her father descending the stairs and had followed him. She'd overheard Joyce say the name 'Evelyn' and drawn her own conclusions. 'What has my silly fool of a brother done now?' she demanded, her voice trembling. 'Come on, Dad; spit it out. Whatever it is, we'll face it together, you and I.'

'And how is Evelyn?' It was Christmas Eve and Brenda sat with Joyce in the Blacksmith's Arms in Burnside. She'd headed there soon after saying goodbye to Les at Rixley station and she'd just learned from Joyce that Cliff Huby was likely to be in hospital for weeks, if not months, and that the doctors were still not sure if he would ever walk again. Meanwhile, in a final act of unparalleled spite, his wife Gladys had announced that she was filing for divorce.

'Evelyn is coming round slowly,' Joyce reported as she looked around for Grace and Una, who were soon to join them. For now, however, the two women enjoyed the warmth of the fire and the comforting hum of conversation at the bar.

Joyce took her time to reflect on the events of the last few days. 'I was there in the sitting room at New Hall when she talked to the police.'

'The poor thing.' Brenda sipped her drink. 'That can't have been easy.'

'Yes, and you know that better than most.' Joyce recalled how Brenda had felt when she'd reported John Mackenzie's attack to Squadron Leader Jim Aldridge.

'You know it wasn't your fault; it was his. But you feel . . .'

'Ashamed?' Joyce prompted.

'Yes. And guilty.' Brenda remembered the way mean-spirited people looked at you afterwards – how they made you partly to blame.

'But you know Evelyn. She's like you – you're both made of stern stuff. She got through the police interview pretty well.' Only stumbling when it came to her account of how Cliff had thrown her down and torn her shirt and exposed her flesh, looking to Joyce for support while the police sergeant had written it down. 'Then she had to sit through me giving my version of what happened to Cliff at Black Crag. Geoff stood by with stiff whiskies all round after the police left. He says Evelyn can spend Christmas with him if she wants.'

'Give that man a medal.'

'I know. What would we have done without him? Anyway, how was Hettie's funeral?'

'Big. The church was full – people came from as far away as Northgate to pay their respects. Les saw to it that there were yellow roses on her coffin.' Brenda had sat with the family in the front pew, sharing her order of service with Arnold, helping him to stand for the hymns, holding his trembling hand as Donald delivered the eulogy. Full-throated organ music had risen to the rafters as the mourners had followed the coffin into the churchyard. Ashes to ashes, dust to dust.

'And afterwards?'

'Tea and sandwiches at Dale End. Old school friends swapped stories about Hettie being the bossiest class monitor in the history of the school, neighbours remembered how she was the backbone of Attercliffe WI, organizing village galas and so on. It ended up quite cheerful.'

'I meant you and Les. How were you?'

Brenda paused then gave Joyce a quiet smile that said it all.

'And now we have to keep our fingers crossed.' That Les would rejoin his ship and stay safe, that Joyce's own Edgar would soar over enemy territory and return unscathed – day after day, night after night until the fight against Herr Hitler was won.

Joyce and Brenda savoured the quiet moment. 'It makes you think,' Joyce continued after a while. 'There we all were in the Cross Keys, not too long ago, making our Christmas wishes.'

'Ah, yes.' The memory brought a smile to Brenda's face. 'Dorothy hankered after going to see *Aladdin*.'

'And Evelyn was all for equal pay with men, and

quite right too.' So much water had flowed under the bridge since then, Joyce realized.

'But you were the one who hit the nail on the head.' Brenda leaned forward to place her hand over Joyce's. 'You wished for all our loved ones to stay safe . . . and so far, so good!'

'Yes, thank heavens.' It was the only wish that truly mattered. 'Let's hope it'll all be over by this time next year.' By Christmas 1943 – surely, surely . . .

The door opened and Grace and Una came in. In the middle stage of her pregnancy Grace lived up to her name. In a flowing dark blue dress with white collar and cuffs, with her fair hair pinned back, she glided serenely towards Joyce and Brenda's table while Una bent to remove her bicycle clips then straighten her blouse.

'Guess who else has just got here,' Grace announced as she sat down next to Joyce.

'Let's see now – Father Christmas?' Brenda suggested.

'Wrong.' Una joined them, the wind still in her hair and roses in her cheeks after her ride from Fieldhead. 'Guess again.'

'We don't know – we give in.'

The door opened a second time and Alma came in ahead of Evelyn. Under scrutiny from the farmers gathered at the bar, she strode towards their group, head up and with a confident swing of her hips. Evelyn followed more quietly but still attracting attention in her tailored grey jacket and a green dress.

'Don't look so surprised,' Alma told Joyce and Brenda as she dangled a car key in front of them.

'You drove all this way?' Joyce opened her eyes wide.

'Only from New Hall, with a little help and advice from me,' Evelyn confirmed. 'After she and Laurence dropped by and she made me come with her. She said it would do me good. It turns out Alma can be quite the bossyboots when she wants to be.'

Chairs were drawn up and Grace went behind the bar to pour glasses of sherry all round – an inch of tawny liquid in six small crystal glasses.

'To celebrate Christmas,' she told them when she returned with the drinks.

Evelyn took her glass and raised it. 'Here's to a better year ahead of us,' she said quietly then added, 'By the way, I thought you'd like to know – Walter Rigg has finally been knocked off his perch.'

Brenda and Joyce gasped. They shot back questions at Evelyn – who, when, why?

'The bishop's office issued an order with immediate effect – no more evacuees, no more Reverend Rigg, thank you very much. The vicarage is locked up and Charles Nicholls from St Margaret's will stand in for tomorrow's Christmas services.'

'Praise be!' Brenda and Joyce both raised their glasses.

'What else is new?' Joyce glanced around the table until her eyes rested on Una.

'Angelo sent me this.' She drew a card from her pocket with a robin redbreast in the centre, surrounded by a filigree pattern of cut paper. The signature inside was surrounded by red hearts. 'Drawn with his own fair hand,' she said softly as she handed it round to murmurs of approval.

'Grace?' Joyce prompted.

'A long letter from Bill with this lock of his hair.' She opened the locket dangling from a chain around her neck. Inside was a curl of jet black hair.

Brenda squeezed her hand. 'Will the baby take after him, I wonder?' She thought of Les heading for his narrow bunk bed, under new orders to set sail on steel-grey waters on board a cargo ship loaded with supplies for forces in the Med – ammunition, bombs, torpedoes and fuel. Then she set her mind back on the here and now. 'Which would you prefer – boy or girl?'

Grace blushed at the attention. 'I don't mind. Either. Maybe one of each.'

There was another gasp and a chorus of 'Never!', 'Good heavens!' and a 'Blimey!', that last from Brenda.

'Is it really twins?' Joyce asked.

The secret was out. 'We think it might be. We hope so.'

Light from the fire reflected in the cut-glass surfaces as Alma and Evelyn raised their glasses for a toast.

Brenda stood up and the others followed. 'We wish you and Bill all the best!'

Glasses chinked. The sherry was sweet on the tongue, hot on the back of the throat.

'And Happy Christmas, everyone.' Joyce spoke quietly as she smiled at Alma and then at Evelyn. The circle of women drank again. A new year beckoned – new jobs, firm friendships, babies to be born and perhaps wedding invitations to be sent – grief for some and joy for others.

'Happy Christmas,' Alma whispered to Joyce who leaned in towards Evelyn and repeated the message.

'Thank you,' Evelyn replied. She drank again. *Look to the future, deal with the past.*

Soon the days would lengthen. Meanwhile, there were warm fires and friendship to light their way.

AUTHOR'S NOTE

My mother, Barbara Holmes, joined the Women's Land Army in 1943, aged 19.

I have two black-and-white photographs of her in uniform that were taken in the back garden of her family home in Beckwithshaw village just outside Harrogate, North Yorkshire. In one she stands bare-headed in shirt and tie, knitted sweater, corduroy breeches, long socks and brogues. The other shows her in a short, belted coat and felt hat, complete with Land Army badge. They capture her in characteristic stance – her head tilting shyly forward, but smiling proudly.

Like Grace in the novel, she continued to live at home to help her father run the village pub, with her two older sisters Connie and Sybil, and twins Joan and Myra. Brother Walter was in the RAF and Ernest had joined the army.

Practical by nature and upbringing, she took to Land Army tasks with determination and gusto, working alongside old school friends for neighbouring farmers whom she'd known all her life; namely, the landowning Williams family who held an almost feudal status in the village (they owned the Smith's

Barbara Holmes in her Women's Land Army uniform.

Arms and most of the houses, built the church, vicarage and village institute) and the Wintersgills' hen farm that was close to the now famous RHS Harlow Carr.

There was a certain glamour attached to being a Land Girl – at least to the image of it if not the reality, which meant ploughing, tractor driving, digging, weeding, trimming and labouring in all weathers. After working all day in the fields, Mum would cycle home to join her sisters behind the bar in the Smith's Arms. It was here that she met my father, Jim Lyne, home on leave from the Royal Navy in 1944. The story goes that Connie looked out to see him and his pals crossing the yard. 'Watch out, here comes the Navy!' she warned. Well, the Navy arrived in Mum's life and never left. There was a whirlwind courtship and an engagement soon after; a ruby and emerald ring and long separations while Dad served in the Mediterranean, only returning home on leave on rare occasions.

Meanwhile, disaster! Mum's precious ring was lost while working in the hen huts. She and her Land Girl pals were down on their knees in a frantic search through beds of straw. Triumph; the ring was found and safely restored to Mum's finger in time for Dad's next shore leave.

Like many women of the time, once the war ended, Mum settled into the more traditional roles of housewife and mother. She rarely looked back to her wartime service, except perhaps to mention that the uniform was hard wearing and well made, especially the coat, or that the life was hard but worthwhile. She never boasted about her contribution to the war effort or softened her experience with fond nostalgia. That was not her style.

But I found among her possessions after her death in 2008 a plain, somewhat scuffed cardboard box. I opened this little treasure carefully and folded back the tissue paper to reveal a small green and red enamelled badge, embellished with a wheat sheaf and a royal crown with three words that sang out Mum's unspoken pride. The badge read 'Women's Land Army'.

If you loved A Christmas Wish for the Land Girls *don't miss . . .*

The Telephone Girls

1936. George Street, West Yorkshire, houses a gleaming, brand-new telephone exchange where a group of capable girls works the complicated electrical switchboards. Among them are Cynthia, Norma and Millicent, who relish the busy, efficient atmosphere and the independence and friendship their jobs have given them.

But when Millicent connects a telephone call for an old friend, and listens in to the conversation – breaking one of the telephonists' main rules – she, and then Norma and Cynthia too, become caught up in a story of scandal, corruption and murder.

Soon, the jobs of all three girls are on the line.

Norma's romance is in ruins.

And Millicent has entered a world of vice . . .

In tough times, the telephone girls will need to call on their friends more than ever.

Available now . . .

Find out more about the Land Girls in . . .

Wedding Bells for Land Girls

Summer, 1942.

Britain is in the depths of war and the Women's Land Army is hard at work looking after the farms while the men are away fighting. While patriotism, duty and a wonderful spirit of camaraderie sustain the Land Girls through tough times, it's no surprise that love is also often on their minds.

For Yorkshire Land Girls and firm friends Grace, Brenda and Una, romance in wartime comes with a host of challenges. There's a wedding to plan, but married bliss is threatened when the time comes for the groom to enlist. With lovers parted, anxious women have no idea whether they'll see their men again. And while single girls dance and flirt, will they be able to find true love among the men who've stayed behind?

With the uncertainty of the times hanging over them and danger ever closer to home – **can love stand the test of war?**

Available now . . .